"A hint of cyberpunk, _____ a sprinkle of techno-magic bake up into an airy genre mashup. Lots of fast-paced action and romantic angst up the ante as Ravirn faces down his formidable foes." —*Publishers Weekly*

"One long adrenaline rush, with a few small pauses for Ravirn to heal from his near-fatal brushes with the movers and shakers of the universe, all while trying to figure out how to survive the next inevitable encounter." —*SFRevu*

"Imaginative, fascinating, with a lot of adventure thrown in . . . Mr. McCullough has followed his first two books with a worthy sequel. *CodeSpell* will keep the reader on edge." —*Fresh Fiction*

"This third book featuring hacker extraordinaire Ravirn is every bit [as much] of a fast-paced, energetic page-turner as its predecessors. Ravirn continues to be a fascinating protagonist, and the chaotic twists of the plot carry the reader through to the end." —*Romantic Times*

Cybermancy

"McCullough has true world-building skills, a great sense of Greek mythology, and the eye of a thriller writer. The blend of technology and magic is absolutely amazing, and I'm surprised no one has thought to do it quite like this before." —*Blogcritics Magazine*

"This is the second book in McCullough's series that fuses hacking culture with ancient gods, and it's every bit as charming, clever, and readable as its predecessor." —*Romantic Times*

continued . . .

"It's smoothly readable, vivid, and fun . . . highly recommended." —MyShelf.com

"McCullough has the most remarkable writing talent I have ever read . . . Not satisfied to write a single genre or to use a subgenre already made, he has created a new template that others will build stories upon in later years. But know this: McCullough is the original and unparalleled."

—*Huntress Book Reviews*

WebMage

"The most enjoyable science fantasy book I've read in the last four years . . . Its blending of magic and coding is inspired . . . *WebMage* has all the qualities I look for in a book—a wonderfully subdued sense of humor, nonstop action, and romantic relief. It's a wonderful debut novel."

—Christopher Stasheff, author of *Saint Vidicon to the Rescue*

"Inventive, irreverent, and fast paced, strong on both action and humor." —*The Green Man Review*

"[An] original and outstanding debut . . . McCullough handles his plot with unfailing invention, orchestrating a mixture of humor, philosophy, and programming insights that gives new meaning to terms as commonplace as 'spell-checker' and [as] esoteric as 'programming in hex.'"

—*Publishers Weekly* (starred review)

"A unique first novel, this has a charming, fresh combination of mythological, magical, and computer elements . . . that will enchant many types of readers." —*KLIATT*

"McCullough's first novel, written very much in the style of Roger Zelazny's classic Amber novels, is a rollicking combination of verbal humor, wild adventures, and just plain fun."

—*VOYA*

MYTHOS

Kelly McCullough

ACE BOOKS, NEW YORK

THE BERKLEY PUBLISHING GROUP
Published by the Penguin Group
Penguin Group (USA) Inc.
375 Hudson Street, New York, New York 10014, USA
Penguin Group (Canada), 90 Eglinton Avenue East, Suite 700, Toronto, Ontario M4P 2Y3, Canada
(a division of Pearson Penguin Canada Inc.)
Penguin Books Ltd., 80 Strand, London WC2R 0RL, England
Penguin Group Ireland, 25 St. Stephen's Green, Dublin 2, Ireland (a division of Penguin Books Ltd.)
Penguin Group (Australia), 250 Camberwell Road, Camberwell, Victoria 3124, Australia
(a division of Pearson Australia Group Pty. Ltd.)
Penguin Books India Pvt. Ltd., 11 Community Centre, Panchsheel Park, New Delhi—110 017, India
Penguin Group (NZ), 67 Apollo Drive, Rosedale, North Shore 0632, New Zealand
(a division of Pearson New Zealand Ltd.)
Penguin Books (South Africa) (Pty.) Ltd., 24 Sturdee Avenue, Rosebank, Johannesburg 2196, South Africa

Penguin Books Ltd., Registered Offices: 80 Strand, London WC2R 0RL, England

This is a work of fiction. Names, characters, places, and incidents either are the product of the author's imagination or are used fictitiously, and any resemblance to actual persons, living or dead, business establishments, events, or locales is entirely coincidental. The publisher does not have any control over and does not assume any responsibility for author or third-party websites or their content.

MYTHOS

An Ace Book / published by arrangement with the author

PRINTING HISTORY
Ace mass-market edition / June 2009

Copyright © 2009 by Kelly McCullough.
Cover art by Christian McGrath.
Cover design by Judith Lagerman.
Interior text design by Kristin del Rosario.

ISBN: 978-0-441-01724-9

ACE
Ace Books are published by The Berkley Publishing Group,
a division of Penguin Group (USA) Inc.,
375 Hudson Street, New York, New York 10014.
ACE and the "A" design are trademarks of Penguin Group (USA) Inc.

PRINTED IN THE UNITED STATES OF AMERICA

10   9   8   7   6   5   4   3   2   1

For Laura,
the bright star at the center of my universe,
and in memory of Phyllis Neese,
my grandmother and one of my biggest fans

Acknowledgments

First and foremost, extra-special thanks are owed to Laura McCullough, Stephanie Zvan, Jack Byrne, and Anne Sowards.

Many thanks also to the Wyrdsmiths: Lyda, Doug, Naomi, Bill, Eleanor, Harry, and Sean. My web guru: Ben. Beta readers: Steph, Ben, Sara, Dave, Sari, Karl, Angie, Sean, Laura R., and Norma. Eric Witchey for the train question. My extended support structure: Bill and Nancy, James, Tom, Ann, Mike, Sandy, and so many more. My family: Phyllis, Carol, Paul and Jane, Lockwood and Darlene, Judy, Lee C., Kat, Jean, Lee P., and all the rest.

I also want to thank some of the many people who have worked on these books at the Penguin end of things and made me look so good in the process. My marvelous series copy editors: Robert and Sara Schwager. Cover art I love: Christian McGrath. Likewise, cover design: Judith Lagerman. Anne Sowards's assistant: Cameron Dufty. Publicists extraordinaire: Valerie Cortes and Rosanne Romanello. Interior text design: Kristin del Rosario. Production editor: Michelle Kasper. Assistant production editor: Andromeda Macri.

CHAPTER ONE

■ ■ ■

"This is a really bad idea," I murmured into my headset.

Melchior's answering chuckle came through the ear-piece, its wire trailing down my neck to slide under the wing of the stylized raven on the back of my leather jacket. The raven that covered the laptop pocket, where he lay hidden.

"Shouldn't that be my line, Ravirn?"

He had a point. Normally, when we're teetering on the edge of disaster, I'm the one making the reassuring noises while my webgoblin spews pessimism. Not this time. The role reversal made me nervous. So did our location, floating amidst the wild, cascading colors of the Primal Chaos and our cracking target. Necessity.

The world-sized computer-cum-goddess and Fate of the Gods is the closest thing to an all-powerful, all-knowing deity the Greek pantheon has yet produced. When she says, "Boo," other gods run and hide. Add to that the fact that the Furies are her personal system administrators, ready to tear any cracker—say, yours truly—into teeny, tiny shreds before delivering him to Hades in a bucket, and you get a feel for what a bad idea it is to mess with her.

With everyone from Apollo to Zeus terrified of her, why was I—a very mortal sorcerer and hacker—about to do just that? Lots of reasons, only a few worth noting.

First and foremost, Necessity was broken. Badly broken. The goddess is also a computer with all of a computer's vulnerabilities. A really nasty virus had torn the hell out of her quite recently and very nearly destroyed the universe in the process. Since a small disagreement I was having with Hades had more to do with that than I'd like to admit, I felt a certain amount of ownership for Necessity's current problems and a responsibility to set them right.

Which leads to reason two: the webtroll Ahllan, one of Melchior's oldest and closest friends, not to mention the former leader of the familiar underground and current victim of that aforementioned conflict with Hades. Somewhere in the middle of the fight, she'd vanished in a way that involved the near-limitless powers of Necessity. If we wanted to know where she'd gone and why and, more important, how to get her back, we had to go to the source.

My third reason was less noble and one I hadn't even shared with Melchior. To see if I could. I'm a hacker and cracker right down to the marrow, and, even damaged as she was, Necessity was the hardest target imaginable. The idea of cracking Necessity scared the crap out of me, but if I could do it and get away with it, it would be the hacker equivalent of pulling the sword from the stone.

"Hey, Ravirn," Melchior whispered into my earpiece, "focus."

I started, and he chuckled evilly.

"Relax," he said. "Shara turned off the alarms and unlocked the locks. All we have to do is open one little door."

Shara was our hidden ace, once a webgoblin, now a part of Necessity's security architecture and our key to many locks. All of them, really, except this first one. For that, I had Occam.

I reached back and grabbed the sword-cane tucked behind my left shoulder, swinging it around in front of me. Three feet of ebony with a steel base. The hilt was made of something like organic diamond, grown into an exquisite sculpture of a goddess, fiery-winged and naked. Tisiphone the Fury, my sometime foe, sometime lover.

A twist loosed Occam from its sheath. It's an unusual sword, a doubled blade with a plus-sign-shaped cross section, not great for hack and slash but absolutely deadly for thrusting. The blade is made of the same organic diamond as the hilt, the stuff of Fury claws, and security magic. With it, and under certain circumstances, I can pretend I'm a fourth Fury, one of Necessity's sys-admins . . . *reality's* sys-admins.

I pressed my right palm against the blade, then paused. Once I took the next step, we were committed and, quite possibly, dead. It wasn't a decision I wanted to rush.

Melchior sighed. "Are we going to do this? Or are we just going to float here until the Primal Chaos devours us?"

"Patience, Mel. We're perfectly safe." *I hope,* I added mentally.

The Primal Chaos is magic in its purest form. Pure, raw creation. It both contains and gave birth to the near-infinite parallel worlds of reality. It's incredibly dangerous stuff, except to those like me . . . maybe. When I became the Raven, I joined Team Chaos, theoretically immunizing me from the normal effects.

Unfortunately, that immunity doesn't fully extend to those around me—which was why Melchior was riding inside my jacket in laptop shape. There's also the part where I'm not immune to its *abnormal* effects, the ones reserved for creatures of chaos, even minor powers like me. For example, the present circumstances have pretty much the same effect on me that hanging around in a billowing cloud of marijuana smoke would have on a human.

Have I not mentioned the bit about being nonhuman? Sorry. I'm a mortal child of the gods. On my mother's side

I descend from Lachesis, the second of the three Fates and the goddess who measures the threads. On my father's side, I trace my line to Thalia, muse of bucolic comedy. And yes, Fate and Slapstick *are* the two forces that dominate my life. It's less entertaining than it sounds; picture a cream pie with broken glass in the bottom.

The name of my soul and my power is Raven. It is not the name I was born with, nor one I would ever have chosen. It was laid upon me in one of those tragicomic cream-pie moments by Clotho, the Fate who spins. The name has shaped me, as names must, made me more impulsive and sarcastic. More prone to take risks like, oh, say . . . cracking Necessity.

I still prefer to be called Ravirn, but whether I like it or not, I *am* Raven and one face of the Trickster. Because of that, both my triumphs and mistakes have grown in scope, and all too often, one flows so smoothly into the other that it can be hard to tell which is which. I was really hoping this would be a day of triumph, but I never know.

"Bosssss!" It was Melchior. "Hellooo, are you still out there?"

I pulled my attention back to the here and now—damn chaos . . . damn good chaos. So sweet. I shook my head and blinked several times.

"Sorry, Mel. I lost my concentration again. Chaos."

"Uh-huh, that was really my point. That we want to be on the other side of the wall of reality."

"Right. Good point. Oh, and Mel?"

"Yes?"

"How many times have I asked you not to call me 'boss'?"

"Two thousand three hundred and twelve, if you count this one. Why do you ask?" he added brightly.

I sighed. "It's not doing me any good, is it?"

"Could we get back to breaking and entering, and save the big existential questions for later?"

"Right, that's what I thought."

Sliding my right hand along Occam's edge opened a deep cut in my palm, a cut that filled with chaos rather than the blood a more normal blade would have drawn. Then, taking the hilt firmly in my wounded hand—to make a bond between the sword and the stuff of my soul—I slashed a vertical hole in the wall between reality and chaos, or more accurately between chaos and one specific corner of reality.

I slipped through the rift and out onto a dark hillside where the smell of pines hung heavy in the air. Behind me, the hole sealed itself with a zipper sort of sound, and I felt a trickle of cold sliding down my spine like icy water. Reality shouldn't do that. Open the walls of reality with any tool other than a sharpened bit of Fury-stuff and Primal Chaos pours through from there to here with generally catastrophic results. I'd killed a cousin that way a couple of years back—an act that still haunts my nightmares— and I'd very nearly done the same to Hades later—likewise the stuff of nightmares, though for very different reasons.

"Melchior?" I whispered, doing a slow turn and scanning for movement. "I need a touch of night vision, please. Then why don't you come out and play?"

Through my earpiece I heard him whistle "Redeye," a binary program, or codespell if you prefer. It would temporarily allow me to see in the infrared.

"How do things look out there?" he asked.

"Nothing's tried to eat me yet." I turned again, surveying my surroundings with improved vision. "Nothing's moving. Northern hemisphere, pine forest, probably late summer, though it's hard to tell. With Persephone free, the seasons are all askew in the top dozen DecLoci."

"You say that like it's somebody else's fault," said Melchior. "Hades didn't just spontaneously decide to let Persephone go and cancel winter. She'd still be his prisoner if you hadn't stepped in."

"Just in the wrong place at the right time," I said. "Or perhaps the wrong place at the wrong time. Depends on how you feel about getting on Death's to-do list."

"How about right place, right time?"

"No. Hades is never the right place." I shivered, though not from cold. "Do you suppose the weather change will ripple out to other Decision Loci?"

"I doubt it. Once a new world's split off from the old, there's not supposed to be any more interaction. Well, aside from you and your family and the mweb."

"No," I agreed. The mweb is the magical network Necessity built. It connects the various levels of reality, allowing the Greek pantheon and all of its many children to access worlds as easily as normal mortals do websites. "But with Necessity messed up, who knows what might be moving through the network. You still haven't told me if you want to come out."

"I suppose," he said after a long moment of silence. "I feel awfully safe under all this leather and Kevlar, but the view's lousy."

"I'm *so* sorry, your highness," I said with a chuckle. "I just wasn't thinking 'picture window' when I had Tech-Sec make my new riding gear."

Reaching back, I caught hold of the zipper that ran along the lower edge of the raven's wings and slid it aside. The deep pocket beneath held a subnotebook. It was pale blue, with the darker outline of a goblin's head etched into the top—bald with long, pointed ears and a sharp chin. On the underside of the case lines of LEDs traced glowing dragon's scales.

"Run Melchior. Please," I said, placing the computer on the ground.

The spell prompt worked its desired magic, and the laptop began to flicker. Almost too quickly for the eye to follow, its flat shape alternated with a bald blue goblin only slightly larger than a house cat but infinitely more contrary.

After a few moments, the strobing effect stopped, and only the goblin remained.

"A little sloppy with the new transformation," I noted.

"I get nervous. Even nine months on I'm not completely comfortable with this whole quantum-computing thing. I *liked* binary—something was either a one *or* a zero, none of this spooky both and neither. I'm always afraid I'll end up leaving my ears in some sort of horrible in-between state." He reached up and checked, exposing a mouthful of pointed teeth with his smile a moment later. "Einstein was right about quantum mechanics; it *is* disturbing. Melting smoothly from shape to shape was a whole lot more comfortable."

"So run the old process in emulation," I said. "You've got tons of spare computing capacity."

He blinked several times, looking thoughtful. "You know, I might just try that. In the meantime, shouldn't we be moving? We don't want to bump into any Furies, not after the warn-off Tisiphone gave you last time you suggested we drop by Necessity central."

Melchior's mention of the fiery-natured Fury gave me an odd feeling in the pit of my stomach. It was the strangest relationship I'd ever had. I didn't know (A) whether we were still dating, (B) if she was in love with me, (C) if I was in love with her, and (D) whether she'd try to kill me if she caught me sneaking in here or just jump my bones. The mixture of dire threats every time I mentioned anything to do with Necessity and the way it usually came up after she'd stopped in at Raven House for a bit of rompery was sending me seriously mixed messages.

"I thought you said Shara turned off the alarms."

"All the ones she knows about," replied Melchior. "Necessity is a huge interconnected network of systems installed over hundreds of years, and Shara's only firmly in charge of the primary security software. You never know what else might be tucked away somewhere she can't reach."

"There's a lovely thought. I wish you'd mentioned it earlier."

Melchior raised an eyebrow—a habit he'd picked up from me—and I looked away. He wasn't telling me anything I didn't or, more accurately, shouldn't have known already. Shara, the former familiar of my ex-girlfriend Cerice, had ended up running much of Necessity after the mess with Hades and Persephone gave the computer-goddess the digital equivalent of a massive stroke. While Shara was a truly stellar individual, and a damn fine fusion of the various warez that make up an AI, she simply didn't have the capacity to run everything as Necessity had. Not even close.

While I contemplated that, Melchior whistled up a connection to Shara. She appeared in the center of a golden globe of light projected from Melchior's eyes and mouth. Vividly purple and decidedly female, Shara shared Melchior's pointed ears and teeth but added some serious curves and a thick head of hair.

"Hey, big boy, it's been far too long between . . . contacts. We've got to fix that." She winked suggestively at me, her voice and mannerisms echoing the late Mae West. "I still can't believe Cerice let anything as yummy as you get away."

I grinned. It was nice to see her returning to her old flirtatious self—dying had taken a lot out of her, not to mention starting the whole mess with Hades and Persephone.

"I missed you, too, Shara. I wish we had more time to catch up but we *are* right in the middle of a cracking job. . . ."

"And you need information, and you're in a terrible hurry." Shara sighed. "Point taken. I still don't know exactly what happened to our friend Ahllan, but I did manage to find out *where* it happened, or rather, what part of Necessity was activated in the process."

"That's a start," I said. "What can you tell us about it?"

"Well." She paused. At first I thought she was just taking

a deep breath, but then she seemed to freeze, her eyes going glassy as the whole projection shimmered reflectively.

"Mel, what's up with Shara? Is that a signal problem, or is the encryption—"

"I can tell you that it's one of the oldest structures in the system," said Shara, continuing as though nothing untoward had happened. "It may even be *the* oldest."

I glanced a nervous question at Mel. He gave me a thumbs-up out of sight of his video pickups, and I relaxed. Whatever had happened, we were still talking to Shara. Between magical soul-signatures and encryption, a goblin-to-goblin link is basically impossible to spoof. Doubly so between webgoblins who knew each other as well as these two.

"Did things just stutter on your end?" I asked Shara.

"I don't think so," she replied. "Give me a second." Her face took on the distant expression of a webgoblin accessing outside data sources. "Odd. I'm showing a hiccup in the communications feed and garbage data in a number of processor nodes. At least I think it's garbage data. Necessity is such a big system, and there's so much I wouldn't understand even without the complications caused first by Persephone and then Nemesis. It's probably just a glitch, but if you want to abort and try again later, I'll understand."

"No, if you think it isn't serious, that's good enough for me. I'd hate to have to try this again. My nerves are frazzled enough as it is. Mel?"

"I'm with Ravirn," he mumbled around the stream of light coming from his mouth.

"All right," said Shara. "Let me give you the coordinates. . . ."

"It all started with Crete?" asked Melchior, as we glided in to land beside a low mound on the shore of the big island.

"Maybe we'll find out," I cawed in reply.

Melchior is not the only shapechanger in our partnership, though my process is messier and more painful than his. Once I'd set Melchior down, I folded my wings and turned my attention inward. When I touched the place where magic and blood were one and the same—the inner chaos inherited from my Titan ancestors—a great black shadow fell over me like a cloud passing between the Earth and the bright moon above. It was the shadow of the Raven.

I let the darkness settle over me, conforming to my current body, before I reshaped both shadow and self with a wrench of my will. For just an instant, I felt as though every atom of my body had been individually heated to incandescence. The agony of it drove the breath from my lungs and made sweat pop out all over. Then, almost as quickly as it had come, the pain vanished. The huge raven I sometimes become was gone, replaced by Ravirn. I quickly ran through my normal post-transformation inventory of appendages by number and composition. I prefer to leave the feathers with the other body, though the *inner* Raven is with me always.

Of all my magic, shape-shifting is least comfortable and most dangerous, because of both its nature and my own. I am a hacker of spells, composing and performing much of my magic off the cuff and on the spot. With the more modern digital-programming magic, where I work through Melchior and have the luxury of spell-checking in emulation first, I have some margin for error. Not to mention a second pair of eyes examining my code. But with the primal stuff of deep chaos, it all happens in the moment. There is no beta-testing, and even though I've done the Raven/Ravirn thing often enough to feel pretty sure it will all work out fine in the end, I can never be certain I won't make a mistake and turn myself into a loose cloud of disconnected organic material.

"So now what?" I asked, once I'd confirmed I was all there and all me.

"Just a second," replied Melchior, tapping his claws on something hard. "I think . . . Yes! Got it."

I turned in time to see a series of cracks in a nearby

boulder flow together into the irregular outline of a door. Beyond, broad stone steps led under the hill. Necessity is nothing if not a traditionalist.

I asked Melchior to refresh "Redeye," and he whistled the binary with a speed and sureness I could never match, demonstrating another of the many reasons I prefer code-spells to chaospells.

"After you," he said. "Height before intellect."

"Why don't we go together?" Catching him by the back of his neck, I lifted him onto my shoulder.

The stairs wound deep into the earth, halting in front of a heavy steel hatch. Words had been carved into the stone above in the most archaic Greek I'd ever seen. It took me several seconds to parse it out, and I wasn't sure what I had when I was done.

"Central Temple for the . . . Calculation of the Fates and Locations of . . . Mel, what's that odd word?"

"Pantheoo, panth . . . Hang on. I'm not sure you're putting it together in the right order. Maybe something like 'Divine Center for Panth'—no—'Pantheoretical Calculation and the Fate and Stations of the Gods Themselves'?"

"Should 'calculation' be 'computation'? Normally I'd say that made more sense."

"I don't know; the implication seems closer to calculation." Mel shook his head. "Why don't we just see what there is to see?"

When I grabbed the handle, a magical crackle rolled across my skin from the point of contact, as though the feathers I didn't wear in this shape were all slowly rising to stand on end. I paused and put my ear to the door. I don't know what I expected—maybe the hum of hot vacuum tubes, or some such evidence of primitive computing systems. What I heard was a series of sharp metallic clicks almost too rapid to count as separate sounds.

"What's making that noise?" I said.

"I don't know, but there's really only one way to find out. Unless you want to turn back now."

"No." I shook my head. "Better to get it over with."

The door was unlocked, though whether that was because Shara had arranged for it or because such security was unnecessary here, I couldn't say.

"That's different," Mel said, a moment later.

I didn't respond, just stepped over the threshold and into one of the strangest rooms I'd ever seen. It was huge, stretching off into the gloomy distance, and it smelled of dust and copper. Where I had expected ranked racks of computers I found huge abacuses, several hundred of them, their metallic beads clicking back and forth at dazzling speeds.

The nearest stood ten feet tall, with hundreds of thick bronze wires in two horizontal bands. The wires in the top set each held five heavy copper beads, the ones on the bottom only two. All of the beads at every level seemed to be in constant motion, clicking and clacking, and calculating Necessity-only-knew-what at speeds that probably exceeded early modern computers.

"What's it for?" I finally whispered.

"I don't know," replied Melchior, hopping down and padding over to look up at the clattering beads. "More important, what can we do with it? Do you know anything about using one of these?"

"Not a bit." I circled the nearest abacus. It didn't appear connected in any way to the others, or to anything at all. How do you program a computer with no interface, no visible inputs or outputs, and an unknown programming language? "I don't even know whether it's a peripheral legacy system that wasn't worth the hassle of upgrading or if it provides some core function so vital that it can't be interrupted even for an instant."

"I think it's Necessity's soul, and that you should step away from it very, very carefully." The voice belonged to Tisiphone, and her tone did not invite argument or any response beyond obedience. Knowing Tisiphone as I did, I recognized the threat of extreme violence just beneath the surface of the words.

Moving with exquisite caution, I put my hands out to the sides with my palms open and clearly visible to anyone standing behind me. Then, just as carefully, I began to back up, not stopping until I'd reached the nearest wall. Melchior mirrored me a few feet away.

"That's a good start," said Tisiphone, fading into existence between us and the abacuses—or rather, letting her chameleonlike camouflage drop away. "Now I want you to stay right where you are and hold very still, while I make sure you haven't hurt anything."

"Would you rather we stepped out into the hall," I asked, careful to move only my mouth, "put a heavy iron door between us and that?" I indicated the bank of abacuses with my eyes.

The expression she turned on me was hard and cold, devoid of any of the affection she had shown me so often in the past, even at times when we were at odds. This was a Fury right on the edge of killing, one who had closed down every mortal part of herself in favor of the role of Necessity's personal assassin. My throat and stomach felt as though I'd recently dined on several pounds of finely ground and deadly dry sand. For a long second, I thought she might kill me on the spot, but finally she shook her head.

"No, Ravirn. If I let you out of my sight, you'll be gone from this DecLocus faster than a rat down a hole. I want you where I can see you and put my hands on you quickly. No movement. No magic."

"I take it now would be a bad time to suggest a kiss hello, then?" I couldn't help myself—it just slipped out.

There's something about being on the edge of death that seems to disengage all the safety features on my mouth. Now I watched Tisiphone and waited to see if that bad habit had finally gotten me killed. Her deadly expression seemed to freeze completely, and she took two long strides that put her face within inches of my own.

"A kiss before dying?" she whispered. "Is that your request?"

"Yes . . ." I trailed off and let it hang for a moment. Then I winked at her. "Preferably *long* before, but I suppose I'll take what I can get."

"You're mad," she said, "and maddening," but her expression softened just the tiniest bit, as though a smile might be trying to tug up one side of her mouth. "Don't. Move. I'll be back."

She turned away from me and went to inspect the abacus Melchior and I had been standing beside. When her back was fully turned I wiggled the tip of my left pinkie, the one I'd so recently grown back.

"I saw that," said Tisiphone, this time with a definite hint of a thaw in her voice, a thaw that was gone a moment later. "Don't make me kill you, Raven. I don't have a real wide margin at the moment, and it's going to get even narrower once my sisters hear about this."

"So there's no chance of keeping this just between the two of us?" I asked. I noted that she'd called me Raven this time, and wondered whether that was her way of acknowledging that not all my risk-taking was voluntary.

"Boss, would you please stop digging?" said Melchior, before Tisiphone could respond. "I know you like holes, but do you always have to make them deeper?"

"The little man gives wise counsel," Tisiphone said as she moved deeper into the room.

"Somebody appreciates me—glrgh!" Melchior's words trailed off as his mouth and eyes shot wide and beams of light poured out of them, one red, one green, one blue, meeting to form a golden globe in the air.

Firelight flared from the direction Tisiphone had gone—her internal flames leaping high. "What are you doing!" she demanded, her voice rapidly approaching.

In seeming answer, Shara's image formed in the heart of the globe.

"Ravirn, I'm sorry I have to send this as an emergency override," she said, "but you need to know that Ne—" She froze again then as she had earlier, her eyes glassy and vacant.

Again I felt the nonexistent feathers rising on my skin. The globe holding her image shimmered as dozens of pinpoints of dark silver static like tiny mirrors flared and sparked, rapidly spreading until the whole became an opaque silver ball. In that same instant Tisiphone came around the last abacus, her wings and hair burning so brightly it hurt to look at her.

"What's happening?" she screeched, and I heard the echoes of her sisters speaking through her lips—the tripartite voice of the Furies coming through one mouth.

"I don't know," I said. "Mel?"

No response. I turned my head and found that he looked just as frozen as Shara.

"Mel!"

Still no response.

"Melchior, cut Vlink. Please."

Nothing.

"Melchior, cut Vlink. Execute."

I hadn't used the execute command in more than two years, not since the day I'd discovered Melchior was more than just an automaton, that he had free will and was as much a person as I. I didn't want to use it now either—it was a violation—but between the threat of the Fury and the message of my feathers, I knew I had little choice.

Melchior's mouth shut with a snap, and he closed his eyes as well but gave no other sign of life. The light that had streamed forth from those portals flicked off, but the floating silver ball remained. Tisiphone struck it a spearing blow of her right hand, her claws extended six inches from her fingertips. There was a sharp ringing as of two swords struck together, and Tisiphone slid backwards, driven by the force of her own attack encountering a seemingly immovable object.

She hit it several more times in quick succession, each

with the same result. Then the sphere moved, rising and turning. Though it had no apparent features, I got the impression of a great disembodied eye trying to get all three of us into the range of its vision.

I wanted to run, but Tisiphone stood between me and the door. I feared she might kill me out of hand in her current state. Quickly but cautiously, I scooped up Melchior—he was stiff in my arms.

"Tisiphone?" I said.

"Silence." Her voice was sharp, angry, and scared. I raised my hand like a student asking permission to speak, but she only said again, "Silence."

"What have you done to her?" she said to the sphere in that same voice.

It was only in that instant that I realized her "silence" wasn't an order. It was an observation. The abacuses had stopped clicking. They were still. The sphere started to swell, growing quickly from the size of a beach ball to something bigger than a car. As it lifted toward the ceiling, the nearest abacus started clicking slowly, first one bead, then another and another, all moving from left to right. Almost against my will, I stepped toward the abacus. Tisiphone blocked my way.

"No, Ravirn, I won't—"

But whatever it was that she wouldn't, I never heard it. Instead, there came a single enormous metallic clash as all the remaining beads in the room suddenly moved from left to right. The great silver ball started to drop toward us, falling like a hammer.

Then everything went away behind a curtain of blackness as though all the lights in the universe had gone out.

When the light came back, everything was different, as if someone had changed the sets during the blackout between acts, someone with a very strange sense of humor. The cavern with its abacuses and falling silver sphere was gone, replaced by a dying lawn under a westering sun and a stately Gothic cathedral. The only problem was that, with the exception of its towers, this cathedral stood barely chin high.

"Where are we?" I said, glancing around to see whether we were about to be attacked by Lilliputians.

"Lost," said Tisiphone, very quietly. Her voice had reverted to the one I'd heard only in our private moments. "We're lost."

"What do you mean?" I asked. The Furies are never lost; Necessity always keeps them informed of exactly where they are in relation to everything else. Even broken as she was, Necessity had never failed in that task. "You can't be lost. It's not possible."

"I don't need this," she snapped at me. "Not from you, not from anybody."

She extended the claws of her right hand and sliced them through the air to open a gate into chaos as I had opened one out of chaos earlier. There was only one little, tiny problem—nothing happened.

Maybe we really were lost.

CHAPTER TWO

Tisiphone's claws sliced the air again. Again, nothing happened. Her look of concern gave way to one of panic as she tried repeatedly to open a doorway into nowhere and failed each time. I looked at the miniature cathedral and realized for the first time that the leafless trees growing beyond it were normally sized, as was the split-rail fence I'd missed until then. I felt slightly relieved at that, and more so when I saw the touristy plaque labeling the cathedral a miniature of York Minster. But I still didn't know where the hell we were. Or how we'd gotten there, for that matter. That was when another, darker worry popped into my head.

What if our problem wasn't one of location? What if the reason Tisiphone couldn't exercise her admin powers over reality was because the system that granted them had gone down? Tisiphone had called the abacus network Necessity's soul. What if all that fuss and bother was Necessity well and truly crashing? What if the computer that ran the universe had . . . died? I was still trying to get my mind around that idea when Tisiphone turned my way.

"Why are you just standing there doing nothing?" she demanded. "Don't you want to know where we are? Or how we got here?"

"I . . ." How to bring this up gently? "Has it occurred to you that the problem might not be at our end?"

"What do you . . . Oh. Shit. Melchior?"

"Yes?" He startled, looked very nervous, and who wouldn't with an upset Fury glaring at him?

"Can you connect to the mweb?"

He shook his head. "Sorry. I've been trying since we arrived, but I'm getting nothing. It's simply not there."

There was a time when that would have hit him almost as hard as not knowing where she was affected Tisiphone, but the world that held Raven House—our home—had been off the net so long that Melchior was more used to being disconnected than not.

Tisiphone closed her eyes, and her face sagged. "I don't want to think about this."

I stepped forward and put a hand on her arm. The fire of her hair and wings flared suddenly bright and hot, and she glared at me so fiercely I stumbled backwards.

"Don't touch me," she said, very quietly. "I don't know what's happened with Necessity, but if it's bad, you and I are going to have a problem."

"What do you mean?" I asked.

"If you think even for a moment that I've forgotten where I found you and what you were doing when all of this started, you are seriously mistaken. Necessity is my mother. If you're responsible for harm coming to her, there will have to be consequences."

She held my eyes one moment more, then with a powerful leap and a beat of her wings launched herself skyward.

"That went well," said a new voice—male and sardonic, verging on snide.

I turned around and found myself facing a stranger. He was around my own height of six feet and athletically slender. His brush-cut hair and thin scruff of beard were dishwater blond. Despite the roundness of his face, he looked somehow lean and hungry. He had circular rimless glasses and wore a plain black long-sleeved tee, blue jeans, and black sneakers. He also had a dog, a very strange dog, black to match his shirt.

A giant of a standard poodle in a lion cut, it must have stood thirty inches at the shoulder and weighed a hundred pounds. I've never thought of poodles as being particularly fierce or intimidating, but this one broke all the rules. He was a huge brute, with hungry eyes and a big, ugly-looking iron thorn stuck deep in his lower lip like some weird doggie piercing. To make matters worse, he was leashed with only the thinnest of silvery cords, barely more than a thread, that went from his neck into the pocket—and presumably hand—of his master. Despite the dog's demeanor, he ignored me in favor of quietly munching away on a long tuft of grass at the base of the signpost declaring the miniature YORK MINSTER.

As I met the man's mocking eyes, I couldn't help but remember that my own were still the slit, chaos-pupiled version I tried to hide from all but my pantheonic fellows. Though, if he noticed either that or my pointed ears as out of the ordinary, he made no sign. Of course, since he seemed more amused than alarmed by the flying departure of a naked and fire-winged goddess, he was probably not your standard-issue human-type being.

"Do I know you?" I finally asked. He didn't seem familiar, but many of the gods and other Olympians are shape-changers.

"If by that you mean, do we know each other, the answer is no. Though the chances are good that you know of me, or at least have heard my name."

Great, one of my god-cousins feeling self-important—something I adored. "And your name would be?"

"I don't think I'm willing to share it just yet. Not till I know considerably more about you. For example: Which side are you on? Where did you find the luscious redhead with the fiery wings? More to the point, what is she?"

"Now pull the other leg," said Melchior, who had put me firmly between himself and the huge dog.

"Also, what is that?" asked the stranger, indicating Melchior with his eyes. "I've not seen its like before. Some kind of black elf or kobold, perhaps? I don't suppose you want to sell it?"

"Sell me?" growled Melchior. "How dare you! I'm not some *thing* to be bought and sold—I've got free will."

"What's that got to do with anything?" asked the stranger, looking genuinely baffled.

I was about to respond when the poodle made a really horrendous noise deep in its throat. At that, Melchior shot up the back of my leathers to my shoulder. The dog made the noise again. This time his whole body convulsed. It was only with the third repetition that I realized he was about to throw up. Which he did, directly at my feet. I jumped back about a yard and opened my mouth to complain about the dog's behavior. Nothing came out. I was too shocked.

Instead of a simple puddle of vomit, the poodle had coughed up a lot of something that looked very like the eternally changing stuff of Primal Chaos, except that someone seemed to have added sparks and ice crystals to the mix in an attempt to jazz it up a bit. In the middle of it lay . . .

"Is that a human hand?" I asked.

"No." The man's answer was flat and final.

It was also quite obviously not the truth, or at least not the whole truth. It was definitely a hand. For several seconds it lay there between us, palm up, as the not-quite-chaos slowly ate a hole in the ground. The poodle very gently nudged the hand with its nose. In response, the hand clenched itself into a fist and rolled over. For the first time, I got a good look at the jagged tooth marks that showed where the hand had been bitten off its wrist.

The dog nudged the hand again. In a stunningly fast

move, the hand extended its fingers and thumb, rising onto them rather like some bizarre spider. For just one instant longer, it stood perfectly still, then it bolted, exhibiting that same wild speed. The poodle immediately let out a gleeful bark and launched itself after the hand.

"Not again." The stranger sighed as the slender cord tying him to the dog went taut.

Then the force of the dog's charge yanked his hand from his pocket—the cord was wound tightly around his wrist—and pulled his arm straight out in front of him. A moment later, he was dragging along in the wake of the chase, swearing vigorously in a language I didn't recognize. In seconds the whole group had passed out of sight.

"That's got to be the strangest thing I've—" began Melchior, but I held up a hand.

"Hang on a tick." I had just noticed an odd and ongoing sliding sort of noise and wanted to find out what it was.

A seemingly endless silvery cord was zipping along the ground, one end vanishing in the direction of the strange chase, the other disappearing off through the empty parking lot to the northeast. I knelt for a closer look.

"Is that the leash?" asked Melchior, hopping down beside me.

"I think so, but that's not half so bizarre as this." I indicated the puddle with one finger but didn't touch it. "Primal Chaos? Or not?"

"I don't know," said Melchior. "It looks like chaos, it's dissolving the ground around it like chaos, and mostly it's changing like chaos, but then there are the ice and sparks."

"Which are flickering in and out but are very definitely ice and sparks." I nodded.

Maybe Tisiphone had been right in her first call, and we were someplace beyond the edge of the map. If so, how had we gotten there? More important, how did we get home?

"Do you want to try a spell?" I asked after the not-quite-chaos had largely burned itself out.

"I don't think so," replied Melchior. "I can't reach the mweb, and if we really have landed someplace where the chaos has gone funny . . ."

I nodded. All magic taps chaos for power, and the rawer the method used to make the connection, the more dangerous the magic. My shapechanging, for example, lies at the extreme wild end of the spectrum, a straight channeling of chaos that's very dangerous even for a chaos power like me. At the far end lies mweb-based magical coding. There, the power of chaos is channeled into the ordered network of the mweb by webtrolls supervised by the Fates. When a webgoblin like Melchior runs an mweb-based program, he is using a carefully coded spell to achieve extremely predictable results.

Between those two poles you have traditional spells, which use ritual and will to channel the power into a desired result. It isn't as dangerous as wild magic, but it's not even a little bit safe. You also have independent codespells, magical programs that use the methods of the modern digital sorcerer but create a direct chaos tap for power rather than draw on the mweb. We had recently upgraded Melchior to optimize him for the latter, but all of our upgrades relied on an understanding of a Primal Chaos that didn't look like this stuff.

"Any other ideas?" I finally asked.

"Not a one."

"Me neither."

I heard a very high-pitched whistle, like a mosquito performing a spell, and something crunched in the grass off to our left.

"I've got one," said a half-familiar voice.

I looked up and found myself facing—

"Ahllan!" yelled Melchior, bounding across the grass to throw himself into the welcoming arms of the old webtroll.

A bit over three feet tall and a bit under that wide, Ahllan has a massive jaw with huge, sharp tusks like a boar's, a big nose, and lumpy skin the color of a peeled apple left out on the table for a day or two. Her claw-tipped fingers touch the ground when she stands straight, and the arms attached to them are as thick around as my thighs.

"Where are we?" I asked. "What's going on? Where have you been?" I had about a million more questions, but Ahllan held up a shushing finger.

"We don't have time for any of that. We have to get under cover." She turned, still holding Melchior, and took a long step toward the front of the miniature York Minster. When I didn't move to follow, she growled, "Forestdown Estates. It's a tourist attraction, and we're in the Canadian Maritimes. I'll tell you all about it. Later. When we have time. Now come on!"

She didn't look back. Rather than be left behind, I trailed after her.

"Melchior, you'll go first," she said, when we reached the front of the cathedral.

She whistled a short burst of something very like binary and set him down so that one of his toes touched the steps. He immediately shrank to the scale of the cathedral.

"Inside, quick." Melchior went up the stairs and through the open door. "Your turn." She whistled the codespell trigger again and gestured me toward the door.

I went, shrinking as Melchior had. A moment later Ahllan joined us in the entryway, pulling the door firmly shut behind her.

"That's better. Come on." Ahllan hurried toward the base of a flight of spiral stairs. "We need to see what happens next."

A few moments later, we came out on top of the cathedral's south transept and dashed across to another set of stairs. Finally, we arrived at the top of the crossing tower. There, Ahllan whistled another short spell in pseudobinary as soon as she'd stopped panting and wheezing.

"That should hide us from prying eyes, but we'll have to

be quiet." She shook her head. "I can't keep doing this kind of thing. I'm getting too old."

I really wanted to know what had happened to her since last we'd spoken, but I didn't have the heart to push when she was so winded. The troll seemed to have crossed some aging line since I'd seen her last, moving from vigorous middle age into, well, not exactly frailty—she had just run up several hundred stairs—but something considerably less hardy and physically intimidating than when I'd first met her. Before I could figure out what to say, she pointed to an older man coming slowly toward us across the lawn and made a throat-cutting gesture, then ducked down so that only her eyes remained above the level of the parapet.

With a silent curse, I followed her example. There was something about the man that told me I'd rather he didn't notice me, especially not at a moment when I was no more than mouse-sized by his standards. He was very lean and very tall, though slightly shorter than our own perch. He seemed strong and vigorous despite deep lines in his face and long gray hair. His clothes were also gray. He had on hiking boots and the kind of zip-off slacks that serious travelers often wear, a button-down shirt with extra pockets, a long, full dusterlike jacket, and a broad-brimmed hat that hid his eyes in shadow.

He had a trekking pole of the sort that can double for a camera monopod, its bottom tipped with a wicked spike, though he didn't lean on it until he reached the place where the chaos puddle had burned a hole in the ground. Even then, I didn't think he really needed its help as he lowered himself to look at the spot. He squatted there so long I thought he might take root, which gave me my first real chance to have a more general look around.

Behind the man, the lawn stretched southward to a small cottagelike building scaled in proportion to my normal size, the ticket booth of this strange tourist attraction. To the left, where the sun was almost touching the horizon, a large hedge hid most of the nearly empty parking lot. To the right

I could see several more buildings, including an inn, some sort of manor, and what appeared to be St. Giles Church— all built to different scales. It was one of the odder vistas I'd ever encountered, especially as I was somewhere in the neighborhood of three inches tall at the moment.

I was still trying to make sense of it all when the man stood and crossed to examine the silvery cord that continued to slide past. As he did so, the trekking pole seemed to blur for an instant, revealing another shape underneath, a staff or spear perhaps. Who was this guy? With a deep, unhappy sigh, he started to follow the line of the leash, or whatever it was. He was walking fast, and as soon as he'd passed beyond immediate sight, Ahllan stood up.

"I hoped he'd show up." She sighed. "We'd better hurry if we want to see the rest of this."

"Hang on a second, Ahllan," said Melchior. "We need to find out what happened to you, why you're here, all that stuff."

"You will," she said, "but it's going to have to wait just a little bit longer. In the local scheme of things, that fellow is as important as Zeus is back home, maybe more so. We need to take every opportunity to see what he's up to. Having him here on my home ground is too good a chance to let slip."

Then she whistled a quick bit of pseudobinary that turned the steps into a slide and leaped aboard. Given the choice of remaining behind or following her once again, we followed. When we reached the ground floor, she led the way to an enormous—to us—electrical outlet set in the back wall of the cathedral.

"Take my hand; we're going to need to gate."

I put Melchior on my shoulder and put my right hand in Ahllan's left. This time I listened very closely to the code Ahllan whistled. I knew what was coming, some form of gate spell using the local power grid as a substitute for the connection between two points normally provided by the mweb network.

I still couldn't make sense of it. The rhythms were right,

though the length of the spell was wildly off, and it just
didn't parse for me. Ahllan was a webtroll, and her ability
to spit out fast binary was greater by far than my own tal-
ents at deciphering it, but that didn't explain all my problems, not by a long shot.

I didn't have any time to stop for analysis either. As soon
as we arrived at the other end of the gate, Ahllan started
running again, this time leading us up the stairs of a round
stone tower. We emerged on the parapets of . . .

"Is this really the Tower of London?" I whispered. "At
the same scale as York Minster?"

"Yes, and no. Now, hush." She pointed into the court-
yard below.

There, the big poodle had the hand at bay in the doorway of the Bloody Tower. His master lay in the dirt of the
path nearby. The poodle growled once, then pounced. It was
a beautiful leap, and it should have landed him squarely
on the hand. But the silvery leash suddenly went tight,
stopping him in midair. With a crash, the poodle landed flat
on his back a few feet short of the hand, which took the
opportunity to make a break for it, scuttling out of sight
around a corner. A bare half second later, the gray man entered the scene through a gate in the other direction. He
held a bit of the silvery cord.

"I'd untangle my hand if I wanted to keep it, Loki," said
the gray man.

"You're not going to send him back again, are you?"
asked the man on the ground, though he was already un-
wrapping the cord from his wrist.

Loki? Damn it, why was that name familiar?

"Of course I'm going to send him back. That's the
whole point of binding the wolf in the first place—keeping
him tied up."

What wolf? All I saw was a very unhappy-looking
upside-down poodle.

"But he gets so hungry for company," said Loki, sounding genuinely sad.

"And you're his father, and you love him so much you can't bear to see him that way. I know this song and dance by heart. You're the prince of lies, Loki. Your mouth moves, but any truth that falls out does so by accident. I'll listen to none of it. Good-bye, Fenris."

Fenris? Loki? I'd run across those names in a class or something, back when Lachesis had sent me to a human university. Something mythological. Norse gods? Yeah, that was it. There was just one problem: according to everything I knew about the way the multiverse worked, there were no Norse gods. They didn't exist. Unlike Zeus and the rest of my extended family, the Norse pantheon was an enormous and elaborate falsehood, which was why I'd paid so little attention to the topic when it came up in class.

The gray man started to snap the fingers of his right hand, only instead of the sharp "cracks" I expected, the movement produced a series of "booms" like drums, and not just one or two, but dozens, an entire orchestral drum section. The out-of-proportion complexity of it reminded me of the self-harmonizing spell-whistles used by some of the true gods and the most powerful magical computers. Magic far beyond the reach of lesser powers—me, for example.

If the drumming had an equivalent effect, the gray man was actually a gray god. One I didn't recognize. Since I'm related to pretty much all the gods there are, it lent weight to the idea of a viable Norse mythos. Which in turn meant something was very, very wrong with the multiverse. That, or my education about it.

The gray god finished his snapping. In response, the dog's leash started retracting. It dragged the resigned-looking dog backwards across the ground, picking up speed as it went and moving steadily faster and faster until both leash and dog vanished across the drawbridge.

Loki had regained his feet by then. Patting himself once, he magically removed the dust from his clothes.

"You didn't need to play it so harsh, Odin. You're ham-handed. You know that, right? I could have sent him back to his island prison with no more than a whisper in his ear."

Odin? Really? The king of the Norse gods? Where am *I?*

"A whisper in his ear and his bonds looking tight, I'm sure," answered Odin. "But I'd rather his bonds *were* tight instead of just looking that way. Now, what do you think I should do with you?"

"With me?" asked Loki, sounding completely innocent. "Whatever for?" What Odin almost certainly couldn't see from his vantage was the way Loki's left hand had slipped into his back pocket, pulling forth a single shiny bit of scale. "I've done nothing outside my purview."

"Perhaps not," replied Odin. "Perhaps freeing the very soul of demonic hunger is entirely within your job description. If that's so, then my job description certainly involves punishing you when you do things so detrimental to me and mine."

"You know what, old man—not only are you ham-handed; you're also a bloody-minded tyrant and a monopolist to boot, always trying to grind the honest competition under your heel. That poor creature had done nothing to you. He never has. You imprisoned him for what he might someday do, nothing more. Is that justice?"

As he spoke, Loki stomped over to the gate through which the poodle had vanished, putting him on the far side of the older god.

"Are you done yet?" asked Odin.

"One last thing," said Loki and now he looked over his glasses at Odin. "Good-bye!"

The scale flashed, and Loki leaped. Halfway through an arc that dropped him into the stream that doubled for the Thames in this Tower replica, he turned into a huge red salmon with chaos in its eyes. Just before he went into the water, he winked in Odin's direction.

"Damn!" I said, then threw myself flat as Odin turned his head our way.

Before I'd dropped below the level of the crenellations, I

got my second eye-surprise in as many seconds. The first was that, without the lenses of his glasses between us, Loki's eyes were orbs of the local version of the Primal Chaos—very like my friend Eris. The second was that Odin possessed only one orb, confirming my vague memories from class.

Something pulled on my ankle then, and I glanced down the length of my body to see Ahllan. She didn't look particularly happy as she jerked her chin toward the stairhead and started crawling that way. Raising myself onto fingers and toes, I followed after her. We moved quickly, and luck or something was with us, because Odin didn't pop up to have a word with us before we got out of sight.

As we approached the outlet at the bottom of the stairs a rat briefly challenged us, and I couldn't help but note that it seemed much smaller than it should have, given our resizing for the cathedral. Ahllan bared her fangs and growled before I had time to decide between drawing Occam or my automatic—the Burkett CQB version of the classic 1911 model .45. In response the rat departed for parts elsewhere at speed. I couldn't blame it. Ahllan looks like she could tear me in two by grabbing one ankle in each hand and pulling, and she probably could despite my greater-than-human strength. Of course, she's also a vegetarian, a healer, and one of the gentlest souls I know, but nobody had explained that to the rat.

"Why was it so small?" I asked after it scampered away.

"Wait one minute more," replied the troll, taking my hand in her own.

I nodded and made sure I had a good grip on Melchior as Ahllan whistled the spell that would take us elsewhere. A split second later, we arrived back at York Miniature—as I was starting to think of it. From the back of the cathedral, she led us along the north wall to the transept and from there to the chapter house, an octagonal subbuilding that stood at the cathedral's northeast corner.

Inside an area the size of a small circus tent—at least in

relation to our current scale—Ahllan had set up housekeeping. She pointed Melchior and me at a circular arrangement of chairs not too far from her little kitchen. Beyond, a curtained-off area held a small futon platform-bed and a battered dresser.

"Sit," she said. "You may be able to run around like that without recharging, but I'm well past the age where I can do so. I'll make tea and toasted cheese sandwiches, and we can talk and eat."

I set Melchior on the nearest overstuffed chair and flopped lengthwise on the couch. Where to start?

"The rat," I said.

"That's a function of the gate spell I'm using." Ahllan grinned as she set the kettle on the burner. "It's pretty clever, actually. The obsessive who built this park didn't feel any need to keep everything to the same scale. When I set things up for quick gating between miniatures, I built in automatic scaling. York Minster's at one-twentieth scale, The Tower's closer to one-eighth, so three and a half inches here is a bit under nine inches over there."

"That leads to my next question: where the hell are we?"

"Proximate, or cosmic?" countered Ahllan.

"Both," said Melchior. "Proximate first."

"Prince Edward Island, Canada, at one of the world's truly bizarre tourist attractions, Forestdown Estates, home to dozens of miniatures of important English buildings. Fortunately, you've arrived in the lull after the summer season, when they close the park down to take a vacation, or we'd have to contend with innocent bystanders of the fragile human variety. On a grander scale"—she shrugged—"I have no idea. This place, this universe shouldn't exist. It goes against everything I believed about reality."

That was saying a lot; Ahllan had once been webtroll to the Fate Atropos. She'd been part of the system that maintained the mweb and kept track of where all the myriad Earths were in relation to one another and Olympus. She'd been designed from the ground up to understand and maintain the basic structure of the multiverse. That really upped the ante riding on the answer to the question of *how* we'd gotten here, too.

Melchior whistled—a note of surprise rather than a spell. "That's a big bite to swallow all at once. Do you think you could break it up a bit?"

"Maybe." Ahllan picked up a small tray with some cookies and juice on it and brought it over to the coffee table. "As far as I can tell, there's a whole cluster of Decision Loci that are not now and never have been connected to the mweb. This world is one of them. Whether they lie in parallel to our own multiverse, or are something like a separate partition on the hard drive of reality, I can't say."

She handed us each a plate with several cookies. "What I do know is that the gods here are Norse, not Greek, and that, other than that, the situation is pretty close to our own mainline version of Earth, with all the same major features in terms of people and cultures. The Canadian prime minister is even the same as in that world where Cerice was going to grad school." She tightened her heavy jaw for a moment. "Shara told me I'd be safe here right before she pushed me through the gate she used to send me here. I'd like to have a word or two with her about that."

"That wasn't exactly Shara," said Melchior, "but more like an evil software clone created by the goddess Persephone."

Then he proceeded to explain the nine kinds of hell that had broken out in our little conflict with Hades the previous year. When he was finished, Ahllan didn't say anything immediately, just fetched the tea and sandwiches.

"Can we go back to the Norse gods thing now?" I asked, when she rejoined us.

"I don't know nearly as much about them as I'd like." She sat down with a sigh and smile. "Ah, that's ever so much better. Where was I? Oh, right. It's only been in the last month or two that I discovered the existence of Odin and Loki and their kin. There's a local analogue of the

mweb, but it's seriously encrypted and I haven't been able
to crack it yet, so I don't know whether this—call it a
pantheoverse—whether it's another multiverse like we have
back home with near-infinite DecLoci, or just this one
world, or what. I don't even know who runs it. Odin seems
the most likely from the legends I've been reading, but
there's always the problem of human interpretations of god
motives and stories. To say nothing of the known unreli-
ability of gods."

I nodded. Gods lie, rather a lot, especially to humans.
Usually it's to make themselves look better, but they have
other less fathomable reasons as well.

"I—" Ahllan began, then stopped as the grating sound of
stone sliding on stone came through from the main part of
the cathedral.

"What's that?" asked Melchior.

"I don't know. I haven't heard it before," replied Ahllan.

"Then we'd better go have a look." I hopped to my feet
and checked to make sure Occam was loose in its sheath.

The sun had finished setting while Ahllan made dinner,
and it was quite dark in the hall and the cathedral beyond. I
noticed a damp, earthy smell that hadn't been there earlier.
If I'd dared, I'd have asked Melchior to run "Redeye," but I
didn't know how the spell would work here—another thing
we needed to talk to Ahllan about.

As we entered the transept, the grating noise came
again. It sounded like it was coming from directly across
the cathedral, but I couldn't see anything in the dim light. I
drew Occam and advanced slowly. Ahllan paralleled me a
few yards to the right, and Melchior trailed behind. As we
approached the far transept, I thought I saw something
move, something low to the ground and dark.

"It's over by the crypt," said Ahllan.

More grating. This time I could see one of the stone
slabs of the floor heave a little bit. Once, twice, three times.
A couple of the others had already been displaced. It
moved again, falling to one side. A huge pale hand emerged

from the dark opening beneath, or rather, a normal hand made gigantic by comparison to our shrunken selves. It was not attached to a wrist, and I was pretty sure I recognized it. Then, like some obscene spider, it scuttled toward us.

CHAPTER THREE

As the giant hand got closer, I found myself wishing it had come in the same way we had, with the concomitant reduction in size. I also found myself wishing I could swap Occam for an axe. If removing it from its arm hadn't managed to kill the hand, I somehow doubted that sticking it with what was, at Occam's absolute size, basically a really sharp toothpick was going to slow it down much, even if it was a magical toothpick. The same went for itty-bitty bullets from my teeny, tiny gun.

Before I got the chance to test my theory, the hand slid to a stop. It was still several of our yards away, and it started tapping two fingers as though it were thinking about something. That was what it looked like to me anyway. After a good minute of tapping, the hand rocked back onto the stump of its wrist and opened itself wide, palm forward, as if to say, "I come in peace."

"What the heck," I said, putting my sword back in its sheath. I extended my own hands, palms forward. "Hello, are you friendly?"

At that, the hand formed itself into a loose fist and bobbed something like a bow several times, looking for all the world like a nodding head.

"Was that a yes?"

Again the bob.

"If that's a yes, what's a no?"

It coiled its pinkie and ring finger as though it were making a fist while simultaneously raising the index and middle fingers together for a moment before bringing them down emphatically to touch the tip of its thumb.

"That's a no?"

The bob.

"Not a yes?"

The closing of the fingers and thumb.

"You might just have something." Melchior came up to stand beside me.

"What are you?" I asked.

The hand looked frustrated. I can't explain how; it just did.

"I think it's the hand of Tyr," said Ahllan.

The hand pointed at her, then bobbed.

"Tyr?" I asked.

"Like Ares," supplied Ahllan, "only courageous and honorable."

"That's hard to imagine." Ares, the Greek God of War, was all for battle and slaughter as long as it didn't involve any personal risk on his part. "Anyway, how did that"—I pointed at the hand—"end up inside a really big poodle? And why is it still alive?"

"I can't answer the second question. As for the first, I don't think it was really a poodle. I think it was Fenris Wolf in disguise."

The hand bobbed, though that didn't help me in this case.

"Fenris Wolf?" I remembered Odin using the name, and again it rang vague bells, but I really didn't remember much from that class.

"One of Loki's children by the giantess Angrboda," said Ahllan.

"Does that make Fenris a god or a monster?" asked Melchior.

"That's hard to say," said Ahllan. "From what I've been able to tell, Fenris is hunger made divine flesh."

"A god of hunger?" I said. "Doesn't seem like a sensible way to run a pantheon." But then, I know Zeus well enough that I probably shouldn't throw that stone.

"Look"—Melchior pointed at the hand—"if it's not going to try to kill us, can we get back to dinner? I'm really, really hungry, and I'd rather not try a chaos tap with the local version looking like it does."

"Sorry, Mel." I turned back toward the chapter house. "Yeah, come on."

Melchior's current body was optimized for power drawn straight from the Primal Chaos, but he could make do with alternate sources, say AC from a power cord, or chemical energy in the shape of food. Since he much preferred the latter when he had to make do, I needed to get him fed.

We'd gone about three steps when Ahllan made a coughing noise. The hand had popped up onto its fingertips again and, somehow managing to look diffident, had started to follow along.

"Oh, right. I didn't meant to be rude. Do you want to join us?"

It did a sort of push-up version of the yes-bob.

Melchior grinned. "Gee, Dad, it followed us home. Can we keep it?"

I laughed. "We'll see, son. If we do, you'll have to promise to take it for walks and feed it and . . ."

There was a thought—what did the thing eat? Did it eat at all? I'd never had to look after a disembodied hand before.

The hand rolled back onto its wrist, opened wide, and shook itself gently, for all the world like a man throwing his head back and pretending to laugh.

"Is that your version of 'ha-ha, very funny'?"

The bob.

Just when you think life is as strange as it can possibly get, someone gives you a hand—and a sarcastic one, no less.

We all took a little break from talking and thinking while we finished dinner. Well, everybody but the hand, which neither talked nor ate, and could have been thinking for all I knew. Then it was time for the next round of twenty questions with the resident troll.

"What's up with the Primal Chaos around here?" asked Melchior.

"I don't know," said Ahllan. "I hadn't actually *seen* any of the local chaos until Fenris barfed some up, though I knew it tasted very different from our own homegrown version. I *can* hazard a guess as to why it looks the way it does."

"Which is?" asked Melchior.

"In the Norse version of creation, the world was formed from the body of the frost giant Ymir, who was in turn formed by the interaction of frost and fire in the great chasm of Ginnungagap."

"Ginnungagap?" I said. "That's a mouthful. I take it you're thinking this great chasm with its mixing of fire and ice is the local equivalent of the Primal Chaos?"

She nodded. "The stuff of chaos seems to function pretty close to the same way, and it *would* explain the sparks and snowflakes." She looked at Melchior. "The important thing to know is that you can survive on it if you need to, though I suspect it's not the most healthy of diets for someone from our home reality."

"What about that weird binary you've been spouting?" I asked. "It sounds very wrong."

"It's still all ones and zeroes. This pantheoverse just needs a different set of commands before it'll listen to you. I'll beam Melchior the basics, but I can promise it's going to take a good long while to get a handle on the bigger sorts of spells." Her eyes went distant for a moment, as did Melchior's, while the information was exchanged.

"Thanks," he said, finally. "That's really, really strange stuff. I wonder why they did it that way?"

"I think it's got something to do with the proprietary nature of the local magical struct—"

She was cut off by a "thud" that shook the whole building. A moment later, a bright, fiery light flared outside the window and continued to flicker. I leaped up and hurried to the door. There was little point in trying to see out the stained glass of the chapter-house windows. Ahllan came behind me, carrying Melchior and followed by the hand— hmm, if it was going to stay around, we would need to find out its name.

A moment later we were peering through a spyhole Ahllan had installed. At first glance I couldn't see much beyond a huge wall of low flames. Then I remembered to adjust for my reduced size and realized I was seeing a burning wing. Tisiphone! But she didn't seem to be moving, and her fires normally burned higher and hotter. I raced for the cathedral's front door while Ahllan whistled the triggering sequence for the built-in size-changing spell.

Tisiphone lay crumpled on her side to the north of York Miniature, facing away. I wanted to rush over and take her in my arms—our current conflict notwithstanding—but I knew better than to startle her when she was injured or semiconscious. She had deadly reflexes and claws that could cut through inch-thick steel. I had a couple of long, thin scars on my left thigh from bumping the side table next to her while she was sleeping.

Since I rather liked the look of Occam's cane-scabbard, I paused to snap a branch off one of the nearby trees before making a wide circle around to Tisiphone's front. She continued to lie motionless, her eyes closed, but I stood there several seconds longer to see if the vibration of my walking would rouse her. It had on other occasions.

Nothing.

By the light of her fiery wings and hair, I surveyed her. She was still as beautiful as the first time I'd seen her, and as terrifying. She was naked, of course; the Furies disdain the use of clothing. Waist-length red hair and an angel's wings burned brightly but without smoke. So did her nipples and the hair at the juncture of her thighs. Her skin was a white as pale and translucent as fine china, and the blue lines of her veins were clearly visible. She was shaped like a runner, long and slender and athletic, with high, small breasts and not an ounce of fat. Her eyes, when open, held flames as well, the irises dancing red and orange while rolling smoke filled her pupils. Her finger and toe claws were at full extension, six-inch daggers of organic diamond painted red by the light of her fires.

New since the last time I'd seen her were the deep bite mark on her left forearm and the four parallel gashes running raggedly across her temple. Both injuries looked quite nasty, but I didn't worry about them. I had seen her come back from much worse in a matter of hours without so much as a scar.

No, my main cause for concern had to do with her continued unconsciousness. Even if Cerberus himself had given her the mauling, I'd have expected her on her feet and raring for a rematch by this time. Deciding I'd waited long enough and then some, I very cautiously reached out with my stick and drew the end lightly along the bottom of her foot.

Nothing. Not even a twitch. I tried again, with the same result. I moved closer and very gently prodded Tisiphone's calf. Still nothing. Hip. Ribs. Shoulder. I waited several minutes and tried again. All the same. With a little prayer for intercession from my cousin Tyche, Goddess of Fortune, I dropped the stick and took Tisiphone's arm, very gently shaking her. When that didn't get my head sliced off, I began to get a very uncomfortable feeling in the depths of my stomach.

Bunching her wings as much as I could—she'd taught them not to burn me—I knelt and lifted her in my arms. She was seriously heavy. Her wings are more a tool of magic than flight, and she is both tall and very muscular. I'm stronger than any human, but Tisiphone outclasses me in that department as an Olympic weight lifter does a two-year-old child.

"I think it's my turn to ask some questions," said Ahllan after she'd whistled us all across the threshold and into the appropriate scale. "High on my list is how you came to be traveling with that?" She indicated Tisiphone with a hard look. "I've been wondering since you first arrived."

"That's a long story, and I'll be happy to tell it as soon as I get her set down and covered up."

Ahllan frowned but led the way back toward the chapter house. I couldn't really blame her. I'd had a while to get used to the idea of a Fury as friend, then a lover. Ahllan's last experience with the Furies before her involuntary exile involved having her home torn to shreds by Tisiphone and her sisters. That they were hunting me at the time probably made the present association seem even stranger.

"I'll take care of it." Melchior drew Ahllan aside and started explaining about the destruction Persephone had wrought on Necessity and the way our attempts at fixing it had drawn Tisiphone and me together after my relationship with Cerice hit the wall.

I sent up a silent thank-you to Melchior as I continued on to the chapter house, with a mental note to make it verbal later. A lot of that personal history was still tender ground. Having Melchior as a familiar was fantastic. Having him as a friend was priceless. The hand, apparently interested in finding out more about us, wandered after them.

While they all talked in the main part of the building, I settled Tisiphone on the couch with pillows to keep her wings from getting too badly squished and found her a blanket. She didn't really need it, since she's pretty much impervious to the elements, but it seemed right somehow. And maybe it was. When I tucked it up under her chin I heard a very faint rasping. It was the sound of the claws of her left hand—the one I'd left above the covers for treatment—dragging along the blanket as they retracted. Though she still hadn't woken up, a quick check showed that all four sets had slid back into whatever pocket of reality they lived in when they weren't extended—something I'd wondered about more than once, since six-inch claws simply won't fit into three-inch fingers.

Next I made a quick raid on Ahllan's healing supplies for an antibiotic to apply once I'd cleaned out Tisiphone's wounds. As I sat beside her and dabbed at the bite on her arm, she moaned and blinked her eyes open.

"Wha . . . Where am I? What happened? Ouch."

"Sorry. I didn't mean to . . . hurt you." I blinked several times. "Did you really just say ouch?"

"Uh, yeah. I did. What's *that* about?"

In the time I'd known Tisiphone, she'd suffered countless bruises, a broken wing, a truly hellacious puncture wound in the shoulder, and more cuts, slashes, and bites than I could count. She had never, not once, made the slightest complaint about any of it.

"I couldn't help notice that you don't seem to be healing as fast as normal either," I said. "You've still got blood oozing out of cuts that aren't all that deep and are at least twenty minutes old. Shouldn't they be scabbed over?"

She nodded her head on the pillows, and I wondered once again at the minor miracle that allowed her hair and wings not to ignite anything she didn't want them to.

"That's not the only thing that's strange," she said.

"Oh?"

"Yeah, when we first got here, and I flew away, I really wanted to be mad at you, to blame you for the mess we'd landed in, because rage gives me strength. But I just couldn't do it. I was angry, but not nearly as angry as I was worried and depressed. I especially didn't want to be mad at you." She reached out with her good hand and squeezed my wrist. "Don't take this wrong, but that's just not normal."

"Not for a Fury," I agreed, "no."

"What's not normal for a Fury?" Melchior asked, as he and Ahllan came through the door, followed by the hand.

"Tell you in a minute," I said. "First, you." I pointed a finger at the hand. "What's your name? I'm getting tired of thinking of you as the really big disembodied hand. It's pretty clear you're an individual—the strangest I've yet to meet—but an individual nonetheless, and that means a name."

The hand looked nonplussed, as if to say, "Who, me?"

I nodded. "What should we call you? Do you have a preference?"

It snapped its index and middle fingers against its thumb in a sharp "no."

"Well, think about it. If you come up with something, we'll use that; otherwise, we'll make something up. Does that work for you?"

It bobbed yes, then wandered off into the corner, looking as thoughtful as it is possible for a disembodied hand to look.

"What is that?" asked Tisiphone. "Or, I guess, who is that?"

I quickly brought her up to date. As I mentioned where the hand had come from, Tisiphone's fires started to burn higher, a sure sign of returning anger.

"What's up?" I asked, but she shook her head.

"Finish the story." When I was done, she started talking again. "How in Necessity's name did we get here?"

I really didn't like the idea that Tisiphone didn't know what had happened either. The Furies are Necessity's admins. *Nothing* the goddess does should surprise them.

She continued before I could ask her about it. "A whole

different set of gods . . . that's going to cause some problems. I wonder if I met his cousin or something?"

"Whose?" asked Ahllan. It was the first time she'd spoken directly to Tisiphone, and though it wasn't much, it was a start.

"This Fenris and the wolf who bit me." She raised her injured arm. "When I flew out of here earlier, I went looking for some way to connect with Necessity. I didn't find that, but I did see the silver chariot of the moon, so I went to talk to Artemis. That's when I ran into two problems."

"No Artemis," supplied Ahllan, getting up and going to her healing kit.

"Uh-huh. Instead, there was a big guy wearing furs at the reins with a black wolf nearly as big as Cerberus chasing behind. I was just trying to decide what to do when the wolf turned and gave me these. That's the last thing I remember before waking up here." She touched the scrape on the side of her head and the bite.

"Let me look at them." Ahllan approached from the other side of the couch and took over the cleaning job from me at Tisiphone's nod. "Mm, nasty."

Tisiphone winced. "Yes, they are, and I don't understand why. Was there some kind of poison involved, or something?"

Ahllan's eyes went far away for a moment as she accessed data. "No, not according to the accounts I can reach on the local internet. It's not nearly as good a resource as the mweb's data streams, but they've got a fair bit on the Norse gods—assuming I can trust it. The wolf who attacked you isn't supposed to be poisonous. His name is Hati, and his purpose in life is to hunt down and eat Mani—the charioteer of the moon. Oh, and he and Fenris are not cousins, but son and father."

"And this Loki is the father of Fenris?" asked Tisiphone.

The hand had crept closer at some point in the conversation, and now it gave a quick bob "yes."

"He and I are going to have some words," she said, the

threat plain in her voice. She turned her gaze on the hand. "I guess you and I have something in common, though I didn't get bitten half so hard."

The hand bobbed.

"Figured out what you want us to call you yet?" Melchior asked the hand.

Again, the bob. Then the hand very carefully drew letters on the floor for us. It had to do it twice before we figured it out.

"Laginn?" I asked.

The bob.

"All right. I wonder what it means?"

"Let me just do a word search," said Ahllan, though she didn't stop doctoring Tisiphone. A few seconds later, she let out a little bark of laughter. "Apparently our new friend is something of a literalist."

"How so?" asked Melchior.

"Laginn is Icelandic for 'deft,'" she replied, "or, as we might say, 'handy.'"

Laginn bobbed approvingly.

"Laginn it is," said Melchior. "I hope you come in yourself—handy, that is."

"Ow. Damn, that stuff stings." Tisiphone looked almost as surprised to have said it as the rest of us were to hear it. "Sorry, Ahllan; please keep going. I really appreciate your taking care of me like this." The troll was painting a vivid orange something onto the long scratches on the side of Tisiphone's head.

"I don't get it," continued Tisiphone, closing one eye and wrinkling her nose in an obvious attempt to ignore the pain. "I'm normally not this much of a wimp. What's happening?"

But I didn't know the answer. I didn't know a lot of answers. Where were we in relation to anyplace we actually knew? How did we get here? How did things really work here? How were we going to get home? For that matter, what happened next?

As if in answer to that last, Ahllan let out a long yawn and stretched, cracking so many of her joints that she sounded a bit like troll popcorn.

"Children, all this running around has tired me more than I care to admit. Why don't we close this chat session down until tomorrow morning so I can get some sleep."

"Fair enough," I quickly agreed. She looked awfully tired, and I wanted to spare her more stress. "Where do you want us?"

"How would you feel about sleeping in Shakespeare's bedroom? There's a miniature of the Stratford-on-Avon house where he grew up on the far side of the park. It's my first fallback if this place becomes unlivable for some reason."

"Sounds good to me. Tisiphone, do you want to join me?"

She nodded and smiled wanly before shrugging off the blanket and getting up.

"Melchior, here's the gating address." Ahllan's expression became abstracted for a second.

"Got it," he replied, then glanced at the hand. "What about Laginn? Should we take him with us or leave him here or what?"

"Better leave him here," said Ahllan. "He didn't come in through one of the spelled doors, and I don't know what the autosizing subroutine would do with him." She looked at Laginn. "I'm sorry; we're being rude. Do you have a preferred gender, or would you prefer 'it'? I know you used to be part of a 'he,' but I don't know whether that means anything to a hand."

Laginn shrugged, or got as close as something with no head and no shoulders could to shrugging.

"All right. Then, for simplicity's sake, 'him' it is. Do you want the couch or a chair or what? I'd offer you the bed, but I don't think my bones would agree to the deal."

The hand snagged Tisiphone's fallen blanket and dragged it over to a rug by the stove.

"If that works for you, it's fine by me. Good night, children." Ahllan headed for a curtained-off area on the side of the room.

We headed for the power outlet and Stratford-on-Avon.

Forestdown Estates really had to be the strangest place I'd visited this side of Castle Discord. That the builder had created miniatures of the outsides of the buildings was a little odd. That he had also done up the insides, including stuff that no one looking in would ever see, was downright obsessive. Tisiphone and I had taken a bedroom near the end of the hall, with Melchior opting to take laptop shape on a table outside so as to avoid our "inevitable banging and moaning."

Because of Tisiphone's injuries, it was more like a few lingering kisses and some high-intensity makeup snuggling. In either case, I appreciated the privacy Melchior had given us under the guise of being surly.

A few hours later, I ended up having one of my periodic reflections on insomnia. Ever since the black slits of my pupils had become tiny windows filled with Primal Chaos, sleep has become an elusive companion at best. There is something about being able to read by the light of your own eyes that makes even a sleep mask fairly ineffective. On the plus side, any use of chaos magic, say shapechanging into a raven or using a faerie ring, recharged my batteries at least as effectively as forty winks used to. But sometimes I really missed the oblivion and freedom from thought provided by regular visits with unconsciousness. Maybe I was going to have to learn to meditate.

Tisiphone sprawled beside me, her hair framing her face in a cloud of fire, her wings sticking out from under the covers and trailing on the floor. It didn't look all that comfortable, but she slept with the total relaxation of a well-fed house cat. Awake, she was a study in dynamic tension, always ready to pounce. Asleep, the tension was gone. I reached out and absently stroked her cheek. She didn't move.

I still didn't know whether I was in love with her or she with me, but that seemed less important than it once had, less important than taking moments like these and treating them as the treasures they were. Maybe that was because I was growing into the role Necessity had thrust upon me when she had Clotho name me Raven and made me a power. While Tisiphone and Ravirn might be able to snatch moments of erotic companionship and to maintain a deep fondness for each other, the Raven and the Fury had other loyalties that would forever come first.

I admired the high cheekbones and the delicate network of blue veins visible in Tisiphone's slender neck. A goddess nearly four thousand years old, the living embodiment of vengeance, and able to tear me in half as easily as I might a tissue paper—what on Earth did she see in me? Again I caressed her cheek, gently. I didn't want to startle her awake and buy myself a new set of scars. . . . Wait a moment.

I slid out from under the blankets and shifted around so that I could both kiss her temple and jump away if I had to. I leaned forward, pressed my lips above her ear, and . . . nothing. She neither moved nor woke. I'd never seen her sleep so deeply. By all rights she should have caught my wrist in her hand in the same second my fingers first touched her cheek. After the slice she'd given my thigh, she'd made a real effort to train herself not to gut me when she woke up, but she *always* woke up.

I added another question to the list that started with "Where were we?" What was being here doing to us? Chilled, I gave up on sleep, grabbing one of the thick guest towels Ahllan had left us and wrapping it around my waist as I slipped into the hall. I ran a fingertip along the edge of Melchior's casing as I passed on my way to the sitting room, where I flopped on the chaise. Five minutes later I was wishing I'd brought my shirt as well. I'd forgotten how much having Tisiphone in a room warmed things up—talk about your hot flashes. I made do with a floral throw wrapped poncho-style around my shoulders.

What I really wanted was to rev Melchior up and have a look at the local cyberscape, to see for myself the locked network Ahllan had mentioned. But if Mel hadn't woken when I passed, it was because he was deep in electronic dreams. Dreams which I had no right to deprive him of regardless of my own worries and sleeplessness.

"Damn."

"And hello to you, too," said Loki from the chair beside the fireplace.

I leaped to my feet, half losing my towel in the process.

"How long have you been here?" I demanded as I clutched at my impromptu sarong. I hadn't seen him when I came in; but then, I hadn't been looking.

"Not terribly. I've just been sitting here and thinking. I don't sleep much." He looked over his glasses at me, and I noted the chaos in his eyes again. "You?"

I growled something inarticulate while I tried to figure out how to reclaim the shreds of my dignity. This was not an interview I'd have chosen to conduct in towel-skirt and floral shawl. Nor unarmed.

"I thought as much." He smiled and lifted his chin, once more veiling his inner chaos. Then he sighed. "We're not going to get anywhere with you dressed like that, are we?"

He pointed a finger at the trailing edge of my towel, and chaos shot through with fire and ice poured forth. The towel slid from my hand as it shrink-wrapped itself to my body, becoming a pair of slightly worn blue jeans. A half second later the throw followed suit, turning itself into a long-sleeved black tee. They perfectly matched Loki's own.

"Better?" he asked.

"Yes . . . Uh, thanks. But I do have to ask about the style choice. Not that I object necessarily; I'm just wondering why you've dressed me up like your best friend forever."

"One less unnecessary decision to make. My entire closet looks like this. Do you have some other preference?"

"Well, I normally wear green and black and—" I stopped and looked down when Loki winked at me. My clothes had changed, becoming black jeans and an emerald shirt. "Thanks again."

"No problem. Would you like shoes with that?" He pointed at my feet.

"No, thanks, I'm fine." I shook my head. "Could we get back to the part of the conversation where you tell me why you're here? In my sitting room. In the middle of the night. Without so much as a knock."

"Oh, let's not get all tedious, shall we? It's not your sitting room; it's Shakespeare's and clearly belongs to history. Think of me as another lover of the Bard, and move on from there."

"Look, Loki, I've—" As I spoke his name, his eyes narrowed, and I knew I'd made a mistake, giving away precious information and getting nothing in return. I tried to hide my stumble by continuing. "—had a long day. It's late and I'm cold and I really don't much feel like playing games."

"Well, cold I can fix. I am, after all, the God of Fire."

He gestured, and chaos spilled from his fingers, making a circle of flame on the floor around me. It was waist high and very hot.

"But if you know who I am, you know that, too." He winked, and the circle started to shrink. "Now let's talk about you, shall we?"

CHAPTER FOUR

I looked at Loki through the tightening flames and shook my head. Why am I always irritating the folks higher up the divine food chain? It's very frustrating, to say nothing of dangerous. I had no doubt that, as a full god on his home turf, Loki could easily destroy long-lived but definitely mortal me if he wanted to. Not that I was going to let that stop me from arguing with him or anything.

"Could we maybe not play macho power games?" I asked. "I'd much prefer to carry on a civilized conversation."

"Well, of course you're going to say something like that. You're in there, and I'm out here. What's in it for me?"

"Would you prefer I said the same thing from out there?" I asked, biting the inside of my mouth. Hard.

"If you can manage it, I guess I'd be open to a different dynamic."

"Fine." I spat into the flames. Blood.

With a huge "bang" and a flash I was elsewhere— standing in an upside-down bottle cap on the lawn of Forestdown Estates. It had become an itty-bitty faerie ring perfectly scaled to itty-bitty me and the interior of the Shakespeare miniature. It was one of the stranger experiences I'd had since I arrived in this weird Norse DecLocus.

In my pantheoverse, there are more faerie rings than there are stars in the sky, and opening a new one is as easy as drawing a circle and connecting it to chaos. As a child of the Titans, that chaos runs in my blood, and spilling it on the appropriate sort of circle is the simplest way to create a new one.

There's more than that, though. As a chaos power, I have enormous control over the ring network. Like anyone, I can use it to transport me to any other ring between the blinks of an eye. I can also . . . not exactly *create* new places by using the rings, but define conditions that I would like a ring to fulfill, such as sanctuary. If such a place exists, the rings will take me there. Or, if the potential for a ring exists someplace that I want to go, I can force it open. That was what I'd just done with the bottle-cap ring.

What made it such an odd experience? The fact that as far as I could tell, in this pantheoverse, the circle of fire and the bottle cap were the only faerie rings in existence, and neither one of them had been there before I made them. Nor were they connected back to my home network.

I vaulted over the edge of the bottle cap and dashed across the bit of sidewalk between it and the Shakespeare place. A moment later I walked back into the sitting room. I found Melchior there, glaring at Loki across a heap of broken furniture and the brand-new faerie ring. The latter looked more than a little stunned.

"You were saying?" I raised an eyebrow at Loki from the doorway.

He looked over the top of his glasses at me and made another chaos-touched gesture, restoring most of the room to its former state—the ring being the exception.

"I was saying that we really ought to sit down and discuss this like two civilized beings," he replied.

"Three," said Melchior, making a point of going around the ring as he made his way to the sideboard—where he hopped up and crossed his legs goblin fashion.

I made just as much of a point of stepping through the ring as I returned to the chaise. In its activation, the ring had changed, of course, becoming an inch-wide circle of char with letters of gold fire slowly writing themselves around the edge, like the words on one of those LED highway signs. At the moment, they seemed to be quoting out the beginning of the second act of *A Midsummer Night's Dream*: *Over hill, over dale, through bush, through brier, over park, over pale, through flood, through fire, I do wander everywhere, swifter than the moon's sphere . . .* etc.

I occasionally suspect that the very stuff of reality has an ironic streak. As I settled into my seat, I couldn't help but notice the mantelpiece behind Loki wink at me. For one brief instant an eye of fire and smoke appeared in the stone. Then it snapped shut and was gone. I smiled inwardly, though I was careful not to let it show on my face. Whatever happened next, Tisiphone, hidden by her magical hunter's chameleon, would stand ready to back me up. Silence stretched out between Loki and me.

"You're the one who placed this call," I finally said to Loki. "Why don't you start?"

"All right. That"—he indicated the faerie ring with a nod—"is very interesting. Rather elegant, too. One of those bits of design that makes you wonder why *you'd* never thought of it. Between that and your eyes and your friends"—now he nodded at Melchior—"I'm starting to think that you're not from around here. I'd initially believed you and the girl were both some new sort of fire-giant, and I was rather put out that no one had told me of not one but two such interesting, fresh players joining the 'gard-game."

"But now you've changed your mind?" I asked. I didn't have a clue what he was talking about, but I didn't want him to know that.

"I have. I know you don't come from Asgard, not with those eyes. My next thought was that the Vanir had finally gotten tired of letting the Aesir have all the fun and made some kind of mistake in the execution, but no one in Vanaheim seems to have heard of you either—at least no one is talking. But what I really keep coming back to are the eyes. They're not right for any answer that makes sense. That means they must be right for an answer that doesn't make sense. I haven't decided what the question is just yet, but it definitely involves the idea that you're not from around here. What do you say to that?"

"Would you believe Schenectady?"

He looked over his glasses at me again, glaring, and I held up a hand.

"Sorry. Nervous knee-jerk reflex," I said.

"Drop the 'knee,' and you're closer to the truth," said Melchior.

I ignored him and tried to decide what to tell Loki. I didn't know what he meant by 'gard-game, or any of the other local pantheonic jargon, though Asgard sounded distinctly familiar. I was really wishing I'd paid better attention to whatever my teacher had said on the subject way back when. As far as gods and mythology went, it had ever and always been *Greek to me*. I just wasn't equipped to deal with the present situation. Maybe if I became an atheist and pretended none of them existed . . . Naw, it'd never work. It's really hard to disbelieve your family out of existence, however nice it might sound from time to time.

I still didn't know what to tell Loki—too many variables—so I punted. "What do you know about multiple-world theory and quantum mechanics?"

"The idea that for every decision the world splits and goes both ways? Young's double slit experiment on a macro scale? All that stuff? It's very pretty bullshit . . . unfortunately. The only worlds are the nine." He counted, ticking them off on his fingers. "Asgard, Vanaheim, Alfheim, Midgard, Jotunheim, Nidavellir, Svartalfheim, Niflheim, and

Muspell; and Odin ultimately controls them all through MimirSoft, damn his monopolist soul to eternal torment."

Nine named worlds? MimirSoft? The more I learned, the more alien this place sounded. Perhaps another tack.

"Does the name Zeus ring any bells for you?" I asked.

Loki shook his head, though he got a tip-of-the-tongue look. "Spell that?" he asked after a moment.

"Z-E-U-S. Pretty much like it sounds," I replied.

"Hmm."

He pulled a featureless slice of what looked like cobalt blue glass from a slender holster on his belt. It was about four inches by two, and maybe a quarter of an inch thick. With a flick of the wrist like you might use on a cell phone, he opened it into a *l* shape and set it on the end table. A tap on the inner surface of the foot caused the device to light up and project a keyboard made of green light onto the table. A tap on the upper angle produced a shockingly bright rect-angle of light on the wall behind the table—a full-color computer desktop.

Melchior whistled. "That's impressive."

Loki grinned. "A little nicer than one of MimirSoft's beige boxes, isn't it?"

He reached out and touched a tiny spy icon on the bot-tom right side of the projected screen. A search field opened in response, and he typed *Z E U S* on his keyboard of green light.

The results were immediate: *The king of the mytholog-ical gods of ancient Greece. Primarily a sky deity . . .* etc. I barely noticed.

"How do you get it to act like a touch screen?" I moved to get a closer look at the projection on the wall.

Loki grinned, showing a bit of the fox. "Laser motion detector and range finder, same as the keyboard. Want to try it out?" He slid out of his chair.

"Uh-huh." I was mesmerized. "What's the battery life like?" I started opening windows and looking for applica-tion icons.

"Pretty much infinite. It runs off a chaos tap."

I stopped dead. "How did you get that into something this small?" Though he hadn't said anything about being the designer, the proprietary way he talked about the thing told me all I needed to know on that score.

"It wasn't easy," he said, "but if you're willing to let your imagination of what a device *should* be define your specs instead of letting the limitations of current design straitjacket you, it's amazing what you can accomplish. Never build for the engineers; always build for the end user."

Melchior had drifted over to stand by my elbow and stare at the device. "It's gorgeous, but it's soulless."

"What do you mean?" asked Loki, obviously stung.

"It's not a person, just a thing with no AI inside," replied Melchior.

"And what is artificial intelligence but another pile of gorgeous lies?" sneered Loki.

"You might be surprised," Melchior replied, his tone mild.

Loki sniffed dismissively, and Melchior went back to looking at the microcomputer, finally saying, "Doesn't it get distracting, having it light up from inside like that?"

"Only if you want it to." Loki tapped the inner surface of the foot again.

This time I was close enough to see the LCD display embedded there. He tapped a lightbulb icon, and the device went dark, though the projections remained. I noticed another icon, a circle with three smaller circles within, one red, one green, one blue. The green was lit up, so I tapped the blue. Instantly the color of the projected keyboard shifted from emerald to cobalt.

"So, why did you mention this Zeus?" asked Loki as I pulled up some sort of first-person shooter game. "You're not going to try to convince me you're from another world with different gods, are you?"

"Nope." I ran my finger around the edge of a circle of

blue light that had come up beside the projected keyboard when the game started, and the view on the screen rotated to match the gesture—a virtual trackball. "I'm not going to try to convince you of anything. What you want to believe is entirely up to you."

"Actually, it's not," said Loki, and something about his tone made me stop playing with the microcomputer and look him in the eyes. "Wanting to believe something and actually believing it are not at all the same thing. Take, for example, the idea of you being from outside the 'gard-game completely.

"I'd really love to believe that, because it would mean the universe isn't as I have always understood it to be and that things don't necessarily have to go the way it's been foretold they will." He rubbed a point between his eyes as though in anticipation of some great pain. "Unfortunately, I *don't* believe any of that. At the moment, I believe that you are the result of some game of Odin's, a scheme to entrap me, perhaps. What do you say to that?"

"Here." I picked up the microcomputer and flipped it closed, handing it to him. "You'll be wanting to take this with you when you go."

"Are you throwing me out?" he asked, his voice low and dangerous.

"No."

"Then what makes you think I'm leaving?"

"You've called both Melchior and me liars in the last five minutes, and you claim to believe we're only here to trap you. What earthly reason could you have for staying?"

"Maybe I intend to force the truth out of you," said Loki.

"I don't think that would be wise," said Tisiphone, though she didn't drop her camouflage.

Loki turned toward her voice and looked over his glasses.

Then he nodded. "Perhaps you're right, my dear. Perhaps you're right."

He tucked the microcomputer into its sheath, nodded,

and stepped into the faerie ring, vanishing. I hurried to the window to see whether he would come out in the bottle cap.

"Well?" asked Melchior.

"Nothing."

I returned to the ring and placed my hand inside, feeling for the network. In just the time it had taken me to cross the room and come back, a dozen more rings had been added to the network, though which of them he'd exited through I couldn't tell. As I stood up, Tisiphone faded into view.

"Interesting," she said. "Dangerous, too. I couldn't tell when he was lying and when he was telling the truth. That's unusual." She nodded at the faerie ring. "Was he telling the truth about those?"

"I think so," I replied. "As far as I can tell, that was the first ring in this DecLocus, and the one I stepped out of at the other end was the second, though he's opened a bunch more now—made it into an actual network even."

Tisiphone sighed, and her shoulders slumped. "So, I'm guessing we won't be getting home that way, then."

I shook my head. "I couldn't get it to connect to any of the worlds maintained by Necessity."

Tisiphone turned away, looking into the flames on the hearth. She stayed that way for a long time without speaking.

"Are you all right?" I asked finally, stepping forward and running a hand gently down her back between her wings.

"I don't actually know."

She didn't turn around, and I moved closer. As I did so, Melchior caught my eye and nodded toward the door before heading out.

"Want to talk about it?" I asked quietly.

Tisiphone continued to stare into the fire but nodded ever so slightly. "Have you ever wanted to be furious? Genuinely furious? And found that you couldn't?" As she spoke, she idly rubbed the healing wound on her forearm.

I paused and thought about how I had felt when I discovered that Persephone had used me to set a virus loose on Necessity. The virus had very nearly destroyed our entire pantheoverse, and I had been set up to take the blame. I'd wanted to be angry then, to hate Persephone for what she had done to me and what she had nearly done to everything else, but I hadn't been able to do it because I'd understood why. She'd done it to escape from Hades, from the god who had taken her from her mother and raped and imprisoned her. From the god who had done that and intended to keep doing it, over and over again three months out of every year until the end of time. Instead of being angry, I'd nearly given my life to set her free.

"I have indeed," I said very quietly.

"I haven't," said Tisiphone. "I'm almost four thousand years old, and my rage has never failed me. Until now."

"I'm sorry. That must be . . . hard for you. What *are* you feeling?"

She turned around and gave me a bitter smile. "Funnily enough, I'm angry. Angry enough to kill whoever put us here, but not angry enough to enjoy it, and I don't know whether that's a good thing or a bad one, because I've never been here before. What do you think?"

"That you are beautiful and strange beyond words," I said, because she was, though I feared it might have been my interfering with Necessity that had brought us to this place and thus given birth to that anger. "Is there anything I can do?"

The bitter left her smile, and she caught my wrists, drawing me closer. "Perhaps there is." She placed my hands on her hips and leaned in to kiss me.

I kissed her back with the words "angry enough to kill" echoing in my head, and the danger made it all the sweeter.

"Well, that's different," I said.

I slowly circled the long, narrow strip of seaweed steaming amidst the dewy grass beside the entrance to York

Miniature. The hand followed me. The seaweed had arrived a few minutes earlier with the dawn and a sort of sizzling-popping noise as though someone had tried to cook bacon on a really hot CPU. The sound had woken me from a sleep barely an hour old and been quickly followed by a message from Ahllan asking us to meet her there.

"What is it?" Melchior asked, poking the green stuff with the same stick I'd used to try to rouse Tisiphone the previous night.

"I don't know," replied Ahllan, "but I've got a pretty good idea of how it got here."

"The same way we did." Tisiphone's voice was flat and hard as she sniffed at the seaweed.

Ahllan nodded. "It certainly made the same sound you did when you arrived, but what makes *you* so sure?"

"This is from Megaera's wing." Tisiphone picked up the strand of green and flipped it this way and that. "The right one, I think."

That sounded ugly.

"Do you think that whatever happened to us . . . ?" I trailed off at the look on Tisiphone's face.

"Very nearly happened to her? Yes, I do, though I couldn't begin to tell you what that is. I'm guessing she was better prepared, or simply faster at getting out of the way. Whatever the reason, it didn't work, and the individual or individuals responsible are in for some serious trouble." She held the seaweed up. "This is really going to piss her off. Growing wing bits back itches like you wouldn't believe."

For the first time since we'd arrived, I found myself happy to be stuck in the wrong pantheoverse. Megaera despises me at the best of times. After the break-in that had started the current mess and with an unpleasant regeneration to look forward to, she'd be delighted to put me out of her misery once and for all. Maybe I could even delay our return a bit.

"You know what this means?" asked Tisiphone.

"That Megaera's been winged by the enemy?" asked Melchior.

Tisiphone ignored him. "Getting home just got a whole lot more urgent," she said, though she sounded more glum than worried. "I just wish I had some idea of how to do it."

So much for dragging my feet. "I suppose that means it's time to take a look at the local version of the mweb."

"I wish you better luck with it than I've had," said Ahllan. "It's a really tough nut. Come on, I'll set you up."

Ahllan had placed her wardroom and sanctuary on the topmost level of the central tower of the Glamis Castle miniature, right under the little copper dome. The circular room duplicated the one at her old place in Garbage Faerie, including a pair of permanent multicore computer/hexagrams built into floor and ceiling. Even on standby as they currently were, the warding computers significantly damped outside input, rendering the room eerily quiet and peaceful.

We'd dragged an easy chair and a small desk up from two floors below, passing through her combined electronics lab and wizard's workshop on the way. A room that held everything from the latest flash memory drives to jars of dried frog parts, and smelled like it. The chair and desk ended up side by side in the middle of the hexagram.

"Sure you don't want to join us?" I asked Ahllan— Tisiphone had elected to remain at York Miniature with Laginn.

"I'm sure. I've given Melchior everything I know about how the system works and if you don't have me along, you'll start with a completely fresh perspective." Ahllan sighed. "I suspect I'm losing the flexibility of mind you need for cracking anyway. Age and obsolescence catching up with me, I guess. Good luck!" She flipped us a half-ironic salute and headed down the stairs.

I set Melchior on the desk, where he started whistling the wards into place. Bright lasers in red, green, and blue connected the hexagrams above and below as the twin computers kicked into high gear. While he was doing that, I reeled a couple of yards of network cable out of the second pocket in the back of my leather jacket, plugging one end in to the socket of my athame. When he'd finished and shifted back to laptop form, I plugged the other end in to one of his networking ports. That left only the hard part.

I can't count how many hundreds of times I've sent my soul into the network, but somehow it never gets any easier. I leaned back in the chair and braced my left wrist on its arm, palm up, and poised the tip of my athame above my hand. The scars were thick there, dozens of thin white lines that I found myself idly tracing with the tip of the little dagger. Back and forth, up and down, a little harder each time until a tiny flower of blood sprouted under the point. Time to go.

I pushed down hard, driving the slender blade deep. The pain as it emerged through the back of my hand drenched me in sweat, but I didn't stop there. I didn't stop until the simple crossguard pressed tight against my palm, and I was gone. Through the looking glass and into the universe on the other side of the monitor. I left the pain behind in my body, a part of the disassociative process that allowed my soul to roam the electronic ether.

I arrived as I so often did in a room with blue pebbled-leather walls and a brass spiral staircase leading up. This time, bookshelves lined with mythology texts punctuated the wall opposite the single large, irregular window that dominated the room. You couldn't tell from where I stood, but from the outside, that window looked like nothing so much as a large fanged mouth set in a huge blue face. Melchior's face. For the moment I was quite literally inside his head, a protected antechamber on the doorstep of the net.

At least, that was how it usually worked. By stepping through the window and walking down a stairway in the shape of Melchior's forked tongue, I would normally have entered the mweb, or possibly some sheltered annex such as Eris's server farm. Not this time. This time the window looked out on a whole lot of nothing. There was no "there" there. I leaned out the window and looked into the emptiness.

"That could pose a problem," I said.

"Give me a minute," came Melchior's voice from above.

It issued from the mouth of a tiny blue serpent at the top of the stairs, a serpent with Melchior's bald blue head and a pair of feathered wings. It flew down to land on my shoulder.

"That's a new look," I said.

The winged serpent was a projection of Melchior's attention and presence in cyberspace. Most of him would stay with his computer body, powering our odyssey and supplying apps and hacks as I needed them, but the serpent avatar represented his essence, the *I* in his personal AI. Usually he went for a mouse or a bat, something smaller and less showy.

"Do you like it?" he asked, opening the feathery wings. "I thought it looked more quantum, more in keeping with my status as the world's first quantum laptop."

"How so?" I asked, baffled.

"Quetzalcoatl."

"Bless you," I responded.

"No, Quetzalcoatl, the winged serpent of Aztec myth. Landing here in Midgard—that's what the local pantheon calls Earth—made me want to dig around a little bit in the history of other pantheons. That's what I did most of last night. I found this." He indicated his current shape with the tip of his forked tongue. "Quetzalcoatl is both serpent and bird, two things simultaneously, like a quantum bit—a qubit—is both a one and a zero. They even both start with *Q*. Elegant, yes?"

I had to grin. "Bizarre, but elegant. Suits you to a *T*, or perhaps even a *Q*."

Melchior gave me a hard look. "You're laughing at me, aren't you?"

"No, not really. I'm laughing at the idea that I could ever have believed you were anything other than your own person. Not only are you stranger than my design for you imagined; you are a good deal stranger than it could have imagined. So, what happens next?" I gestured toward the window.

"That." Melchior pointed with the tip of his tail.

Where before there had been nothing, now there was something. Strange. Take a spider, crossbreed it with an armadillo, or perhaps a tank factory. *Et voilà*, a huge armored spiderweb, part of one at least—since big chunks around the edges seemed to fold into other dimensions. Make that a glow-in-the-dark armored spiderweb. A really big one.

"What's that?" I asked.

"The local version of the mweb, or at least what we can see of it from here."

"Rock, please." I held out my hand.

Melchior winked, and a rock appeared. It was actually a hacking tool, a tiny self-contained application designed to remotely check on security systems, and I used it as such. That is to say, I threw it at the nearest chunk of armor plating. It rebounded with a hollow "boom," falling into the nothingness between us and the network.

"Lends a whole new meaning to the phrase 'intertubes,' doesn't it?" I said. "I wonder what that sounded like on the inside?"

"Maybe I should just move us back a little," said Melchior.

The window pulled away from the web until it was only a glimmer in the distance. Then we waited. Cracking involves a remarkable amount of waiting. You do something. It doesn't work. You wait to see if the cybersecurity goons show up. If they don't, you try something else. Minutes passed. Nothing happened. Melchior took us in close once again.

"Closer," I said, and it was done.

I could lean out the window and touch the nearest armored tube with my fingertips. Better judgment suggested another autonomous applet, a bit of code I could stick to the outside while we played wait and see again. I had a strong suspicion it would have the same result as the rock had. Besides, patience is not always a virtue. I poked the tube with my finger. It felt slick and extremely slippery, more like a length of intestine than the giant steel pipe it resembled.

Swearing, Melchior jerked us away from the network. "That was stupid."

"Probably." I nodded, though I'd learned a number of things. "We'll see."

A whole lot more nothing happened. We moved in close again, and I tried a number of other code tools, the cyber equivalents of drill, blowtorch, and dynamite. The results remained consistent—nothing, nothing, and still more nothing. It was what you might call a pattern, and one that didn't really surprise me after that initial contact. It was more a case of confirming a suspicion.

"Thought so," I said after a while.

"Thought so, what?" Melchior tilted his head to one side on his long snake's neck.

"We're not getting in this way."

"Are you sure?" asked Melchior.

"Very. Ahllan's been here how long?"

"About a year, assuming time flows the same as it does back in the prime Greek DecLocus, and the season would suggest it's very close."

I nodded. "Ahllan may claim she's old and obsolescent— by computer standards she might even be right—but she's also a hell of a cracker. She did things with Fate network security that I'd be damn proud to match, and I doubt I'll ever surpass. Do you really think that if it was just a coding problem, she wouldn't *own* this system by now?"

"So what is the problem?" Melchior opened his wings and took flight, hovering so he could look me in the eye.

"Proprietary hardware." I pointed out the window. "That thing out there requires some sort of electronic widget for access. A chip with hardwired security, maybe. Or a special antenna. Something physical built right into the computers designed to work with it. I'd bet my tail feathers."

"Can we simulate it?"

"Maybe, but we'll need to get our hands on one first. Take it apart, see how it works. Until then—rock—the best we'll be able to do is this." I threw the rock Melchior had supplied, and it sailed through the darkness, bouncing off the armor to fall into nothing.

The return to my body was, as always, a shock. The sudden resurgence of pain in the form of the athame drove the breath from my lungs with a heavy "whoosh." I bit back an expletive and whistled the short spell that sealed athame-induced wounds.

Nothing happened.

I tried again. Same result. That was when I remembered we weren't in Kansas anymore. Well, shit.

"Melchior!" I called while applying pressure to both sides of my pierced hand. "Could you go get Ahllan?"

After some careful thinking and experimentation, she found a phrase of the local binary that served much the same purpose as the standard-model athame healing spell. Unfortunately, it was both less effective and slower acting. I could still feel the burning ache of the wound for hours afterward, and I could tell that both my strength and mobility were going to be compromised for a while.

The view from the little round tower was . . . odd.

Melchior and I had explained my proprietary network hardware theory to the others over lunch, and Ahllan had agreed. It was the conclusion she'd reached as well, but she'd wanted me to come at it fresh in case she was wrong.

After the meal, I'd decided to take a walk around the grounds of Forestdown Estates at full size and, as it turned out, by myself. Melchior and Ahllan had catching up to do. Tisiphone hadn't liked the hardware idea at all but had chosen to agree with the experts and go looking for some local godling to mug for his computer. I wasn't sure that was at all a good idea, but arguing with Tisiphone once she's made up her mind is remarkably pointless and potentially unsafe to boot. I didn't know what had become of Laginn. He hadn't eaten with us and was presumably off doing disembodied-hand things, whatever those might be.

All of which put me on the roof of what the Forestdown brochure—pilfered from the ticket office—referred to as the "lookout tower." Since it was about fifteen feet tall and mostly surrounded by trees, that seemed rather grandiose. Still, I could spot the tops of several of the other large miniatures from where I stood. Seeing the Tower of London in all its glory surrounded by forest, its nearest visible neighbor, Dunvegan Castle, of all places, provided more than enough surreality to make up for not being able to visit Eris.

I was taking a closer look at the dome of Saint Paul's Cathedral when I noticed the ravens. A pair of them, winging in from the west in tight formation like a fighter jock and his wingman. Big birds, too; too big. Way too big: my size. I didn't realize that last until they'd landed on either side of me on the top of the tower.

I met the eye of the nearer of the giant birds. "Hello . . . ?"

"You may call me Mr. Hugin," said the first raven, his voice precise, gentle, and dangerous. "This is my associate, Mr. Munin."

"Ravirn," I said. "No Mr."

"Interesting," replied Munin.

"Very," agreed Hugin.

"Our employer would like a word with you," said Munin.

"Now," said Hugin.

I suddenly regretted my failure to retrieve Occam from beside the bed before taking a walk. Of course, I still had my .45. I began to edge my hand toward the front of my jacket.

"I don't really have an opening in my schedule at the moment," I said.

"Immaterial," said Munin.

"Academic," said Hugin.

They cawed together—a harsh, wordless harmony—and I felt pain settle upon me like a burning cloak as every fiber of my being was ripped away from every other fiber. It lasted for only a split second, but I instantly recognized it for what it was—I was being shapechanged . . . from the outside! I was going to have to schedule a mini–nervous breakdown about the dangers of that at a later date.

"There," said Munin.

"You look much better now," said Hugin.

I looked down at my feet. Yellow and clawed.

Three giant ravens sitting on a tower. One flew free and then there were two.

"You're next," said Munin.

I leaped into the air, and he followed.

And then there were none.

CHAPTER FIVE

Before my feet had even cleared the edge of the parapet, I felt something grab my ankle. I made my glance downward as casual as possible—I didn't know exactly what had happened, and I didn't want to give any further advantages to Mr. Hugin and Mr. Munin if I could avoid it.

When I spied Laginn clinging just above my foot like some twisted Gothic ankle bracelet, I was glad I'd chosen to play it cool and not draw attention. I could definitely use the helping hand.

Not long after we started flying, my companions did something funny with the fabric of space-time, something that caused the earth below to bunch itself into a kind of rocky point attached to the end of the biggest damn rainbow you ever saw.

"Bifrost," said Hugin.

"The Rainbow Bridge," said Munin.

"Someday we'll find it," said I, beneath my breath.

We turned in the air to fly along the arch of the rainbow. Contrary to pretty much everything I know about optics and the physics of rainbows, it stayed perfectly visible and running like a highway below us, though the Earth beneath soon faded into mist. We flew for what felt like hours before a bright castle appeared out of the fogs ahead. It stood on a high pillar of rock that hung unsupported over the bottomless nothing of the fog—which became in that instant great banks of glorious cloud lit by a brazen sun. Closer still, and the rock spire became the prow of an island-ship sailing the sea of clouds.

Green hills climbed up from the glimmering castle to a mighty city. As we approached the end of the bridge we dropped lower, flying only a few yards above the rainbow until we reached a huge blond bear of a man mounted on a golden-maned stallion. He wore white armor and carried a horn longer than my arm. As we passed, he nodded and blew the gentlest of notes on the great horn, notes that somehow held the names Hugin and Munin and Raven. I bobbled just the slightest bit in my flight when I heard that last. I had given my title and house to no one here, yet the horn blower knew to announce me as a power.

We did not go on to the city as I expected but veered into a grove of ancient oaks off to the left. There, in the largest of all the trees, we alit, three giant ravens on one mighty branch beside a clearing. Neither Hugin nor Munin said anything, so I settled in to wait, hiding the hand clasped around my ankle as best I could.

Perhaps ten minutes passed in fraught silence before an older man entered the clearing from the far side. Odin. He had exchanged his hiking gear for a long gray robe of finest wool. Intricate patterns of horses and riders were woven through it so that, with each step he took, light and shadow painted a tale of battle from his ankles to his neck, a battle that moved and changed from instant to instant. He wore a rider's boots and a hat with a high point and a wide brim that almost hid his missing eye. When he reached the center of the clearing, he stopped. Instead of a trekking pole, he carried a shining spear.

"Thought." He nodded to Hugin. "Memory." Another nod for Munin. "And . . . Impulse." He shook his head at me, and I thought I saw some uncertainty in his eye. "I don't remember asking for another Raven."

He snapped his fingers several times, and once again I heard drums in the sound, deep booming echoes that bounced through the trees and built into something greater, a chorus of percussion. Next came the tearing pain of an involuntary shape-shift, like being skinned alive—I definitely needed to freak out about that when I had the leisure. I hate it when *I* do it. As I transformed, I allowed myself to curl into a ball and fall from the branch, catching Laginn in my own hand as I did so and putting both inside my jacket when I clutched at my chest a moment later.

I took a few seconds to mentally inventory all my bits and pieces—everything seemed to be in the right place, and as perhaps the sole benefit of the whole thing, the chaos magic of the transformation had significantly speeded the healing process in my athame-injured hand. Not that it made up for kidnapping and forced transformation, and I resolved to file a protest with management. Unfortunately, management didn't look to be interested. When I finally met his eye, I found Odin unmoved both in position and in attitude.

"So, if *I* didn't ask for a Raven, who did?" He shook his head. "Or perhaps you were sent? In either case, I'm not at all happy that someone has transferred you from the column of Zeus's headaches to mine."

"You know about—" I cut myself off and cursed inwardly at Odin's grim smile.

"Zeus? Naturally. I am Odin. There is very little I don't know. However, it does simplify things to have you admit your origins. Thank you."

"You're welcome," I said with a sigh. "This is why I tend to lose at poker."

"I wish I could just kill you here and now," said Odin. "Let you become Uller's problem in Niflheim or better still,

Hades' in your own universe. Unfortunately, among a number of other complications, you are a power—reduced and transformed by your shift of venue perhaps, but still a power. That means killing you is likely to have even more unintended consequences than letting you live.

"You have something of the hero about you, which means you might even end up carried off to Valhalla, immortalized by my own Valkyries. And *that* would make you my problem until the end of days. I'd rather avoid the prospect as well as several other thorny possibilities if I can." He sighed and looked more than a little resigned.

"Wait, if I die here, I might not go to Hades?" I pushed myself to my feet, feeling the memories of my recent transformation echoing on as phantom pain. "Maybe I should start looking for a condo."

I didn't want to die. Not at all, but if I could arrange things so that any death that might take me would put me beyond the reach of Hades—who of all my enemies hated me most—well, that would make dying a much less scary prospect.

"I wouldn't hunt up a Realtor just yet," said Odin, with the first faint echo of humor I'd heard from him. "It's a complex question with no good way to guess the answer ahead of time. I'd make your odds of being drawn back to your own deadlands and their dark ruler between thirty and fifty percent."

"That's still better than the bet I'd get if I buy it on the home front. You mentioned some sort of Valhalla option, too—if I'm recalling rightly, that involves an eternity of drinking and feasting and wenching. I could be persuaded to that alternative."

"Your memory serves you well, though you seem to have forgotten the fighting and dying, not to mention the pain of death and of rebirth."

"So it's not all fun and games; Hades intends to slow cook me until the end of time. I'm not seeing what you'd call a big downside to the whole Valhalla thing. Well, aside from the initial death part. I'd rather skip that entirely, all things considered."

"That *would* be nice." Odin smiled a sad smile, and I knew in that instant that, whatever rules the game followed back home, here the gods were mortal.

"There is very little you don't know. . . ." I raised an eyebrow.

"Including the hour and manner of my death, yes. You are a clever little Raven. Perhaps I should have named you Intuition rather than Impulse."

"Two sides of the same coin," I said, "the action and its cause."

"You may be right, though I little expected wisdom from you." I grinned at this, and Odin shook his head. "Don't make too much of it. I'm not looking to hire another Raven at this time. Nor a cock robin."

"Ooh, he does have a sense of humor after all," I said. Odin frowned and I mentally cursed my overactive tongue before continuing. "It's probably better you didn't call me up. So far, pretty much everyone I've ever worked for has ended up mad at me."

"Why don't I find that surprising? Come, walk with me."

Who was I to argue? The part at the beginning about wishing he could just kill me now suggested this might be a good time to be as cooperative as possible. Together, we left the clearing and walked into the woods in silence. Somewhere in there Odin did something elaborate with the fabric of reality that included us taking several steps on a stripe of rainbow that rang hollowly beneath the heels of my motorcycle boots.

The woods grew darker, the trees greater, shifting from oak through pine to something that reminded me of California redwood but looked more like some sort of giant ash. It was hard to say because the branches were lost in the gloom above. We came around a particularly mighty trunk to face an open space the size of a cathedral and . . . How could I describe it? The king of all trees? Their god? The one true tree of which all others were only shadows?

It towered over us, impossibly tall, unbelievably wide, more like a topless tower of bark than anything living. Yet I had no doubt that it was alive and . . . somehow aware. At its base stood a wide stone basin fed by some hidden spring so that water poured eternally over the nearer edge, where it bathed one great root before flowing away into the darkness of the forest behind me.

"Yggdrasil," said Odin. "The World Tree."

I didn't say anything. Somehow, "It's nice," sounded insufficient, and anything else seemed beyond me. We walked across the forest floor, our footsteps muffled to silence by the deep mold, until we stood on the edge of the basin. It was perhaps twenty feet across, and the water within was as clear as air. Only the faintest ripples on the surface betrayed its presence at all. Nine feet deep? Or ninety? Or even nine hundred? I couldn't say, though I could see the bottom as well as if it were only nine inches and there, in a fold of the raw rock, lay . . .

"Is that *your* eye?" I asked.

"It is. I sacrificed it for a deeper sight."

"I'm not sure I understand." Or that I wanted to.

"Look at me." It wasn't a request, and I didn't argue.

Odin opened his other eyelid and exposed the Void within. Until that very instant I had not understood that *nothing* could exert such power. Odin had created a divine vacuum, and all the knowledge in the universe had rushed to fill it. But it could never be full for it was zero made manifest, the Void.

"One of my many titles is Allfather," said Odin. "But I might as easily be called the Nofather. I am both the one and the zero, Lord of Information, the Binary God."

"Now ask him about the last 'Binary God,'" said a voice from off to the left, a voice I knew too well.

"Atropos!" I whipped my gaze away from the water and found myself facing . . .

Here stood my many-times-great-aunt Atropos, the Fate who cuts the threads, who had once attempted to cut mine. Except, it wasn't. The voice was identical. So were the eyes, the terrible *knowing* eyes of Fate. The flawless skin, the dark fall of hair. In every way she was the aunt who despised me and would have killed me if she could.

"I am and am not she whom you named," she said, "oh, child of my sister's house. Now ask the question I required of you."

I met Fate's eyes then. There's no hint of human emotion in those depths. They hold the record of every single thing you've ever done or thought of doing. Every secret fear that lurks in the shadows of your heart, every petty jealousy, every noble ambition. It's all visible there, just so much raw data to be weighed when Fate calculates your destiny. I held her gaze with my own, and I shook my head.

"Fate is neither my friend nor my master." My words tasted hard and cold and bittersweet, fueled as they were by a deep and abiding anger at the wrongs done me by my family. "I have defied my own grandmother at the cost of my name and my house. I will not bend the knee to Fate ever again, not in any of her forms and though it cost me my life."

"Interesting," she said, "very." Then she turned her gaze on Odin. "Answer the question."

"Very well, Skuld. You saw that my eye was not all that lay in the water?" he asked me.

"You mean the head? It was kind of hard to miss, as it's about three times normal size. So was the fact that it's also short an eye. I was going to ask, but then Dame Fate arrived and precluded the question."

"Say rather that I demanded it, and you'll be closer to the truth," said Skuld.

"To-may-to, to-mah-to . . ." I winked at Fate.

"The head belongs to Mimir," said Odin, "the previous Lord of Memory and Information."

"The first Binary God," said Skuld. "The first leg of the

triangle, just as Odin is the second, and the third is yet to come. Isn't that right, Mimir?"

"The time is not yet," said a sonorous voice from the depths of the well. "Nor should you be too proud of your foretelling, Skuld. Not all that is Fated is certain, and not all that is certain is Fated."

Skuld didn't so much as look at the well, keeping her eyes fixed on Odin. "The puppet may speak the words, but it is the puppeteer who shapes them. Is that not right, Father of All?"

"Sometimes, Skuld, if the puppet is no more than that. But you know as well as I that Mimir is infinitely more than a puppet, if less now than the god he once was."

"If you think MimirSoft and MimirNet are anything more than a projection of your will, Odin, you are mistaken."

"If I thought it, I might be. I don't. I know it." He opened his empty socket once again, and for several long moments the two of them locked gazes.

Finally, Skuld looked away. "Believe what you will, old man. Your time will come no matter how you fight it."

"As will yours, my dear. As will yours."

Skuld turned from Odin to me. "You are quite the bold little Raven. It must have galled my Greek sisters to have your thread moved from their hands to those of Necessity." She shook her head then and laughed, sending ice crackling along my nerves. "I wonder if they can see even the shadows of your future anymore, or if the shame of it blinds them."

"Frankly, I couldn't care less."

"You may tell yourself that all you like. You may even believe it. But it will be a lie. I know because I *can* see those shadows. You have within you the potential to become the Final Titan, Prometheus Unbound, Atlas Unburdened. Necessity holds your fate, yes, but you also hold hers, or you yet may. What will you do when the chance comes, I wonder? Make yourself Lord of Everything? Or laugh and turn away? Even I cannot say. Yes, *gall* is the word, and you are its very soul."

Then, without another word, she turned and walked away, following the gentle curve of the World Tree until she passed from sight. Odin focused a hard eye on me.

"I really *should* kill you."

"I'd rather you didn't."

"And the same reasons prevent me as earlier. I cannot read your future, and that means I cannot know what is the right thing to do with you. I only wish that sending you home were a less difficult task and that I could be sure of what that would mean for things to come."

"You can send me home?" I couldn't keep a bit of hope out of my voice.

My feelings on the matter were complex. There was a lot to be said for not getting anywhere near Hades ever again. At the same time, any thoughts I'd had about this being a radically better place had been soured by the appearance of my aunt's doppelgänger and my knowledge that the head honcho would really prefer to see me dead, with only Hamlet's reasons for not killing me yet—I'd rather not bet my life on someone else's continued indecision.

"Let us rather say I can arrange your passage if you make it worth my while," said Odin. "Come."

He led the way along the tree in the opposite direction from the one Skuld had taken. Soon we came to a place where a root humped up from the ground to make a low arch. Set within was a stone door shaped like some ancient altar stolen from its plinth. It had no handles, hinges, or keyholes, but I had no doubt as to its purpose. Odin rapped once on the center of the stone with the butt of his spear, and it lowered itself into the tree's base like a reverse drawbridge.

"After you," said Odin.

The stone boomed hollowly as I stepped onto it, the noise echoing away into the deep but narrow gap it bridged.

"What's down there?" I asked, as Odin followed me across.

"Listen."

Very faint and far away in the depths I heard the sound of chewing, like a dog worrying an old bone.

"Wolf?" I asked, since there seemed to be rather a surplus of them in the local pantheoverse.

"Dragon. Turn left."

I ducked through a low wooden archway into what appeared to be a theme park for computer bureaucrats, that or the world's ugliest server farm. Rack after rack of beige boxes extended in a series of identical rows across the living wood of the floor, eventually vanishing into the harsh fluorescent-lit distance.

"And this is . . . ?" I let my words trail off because I simply couldn't think of anything more to say. How this place could exist in the same universe as Loki's sexy little portable was beyond me.

"The heart of MimirNet," said Odin, and I could hear pride in his voice. "Ten thousand state-of-the-art boxes running OS Panorama, the system that controls the universe."

"How very . . . scenic."

Odin gave me another hard look as he led me between the rows. "You've seen better?"

Had I seen better? I thought of Necessity and the stark black servers she used to keep track of the fates of the gods—slices of faux ebony, with only the deep purple and red of their telltales betraying them as something made rather than grown. Or Eris's system-wide Library of Alexandria case mods with each multicore computer disguised as a Greek scroll. For that matter—on a more personal level—Melchior's subnotebook shape with the etched goblin head on the top that allowed his OLED monitor to be read *through* his casing was pretty spiffy. Somehow, though, I didn't think that would be a good direction to take here, especially not when I wanted to hear more about

MimirNet, which looked to be the local equivalent of the mweb. I very politely shook my head.

"Not really, no. Ten thousand machines? That's got to be a royal pain to administer."

"You'd be surprised. MimirSoft is really good at external management. There's not a single computer here, or anywhere else on the net for that matter, that I can't remotely operate in every detail."

"Anywhere?"

"Sure, say Tyr's system goes down."

The hand in my breast pocket twitched at the name, and I coughed and thumped my chest in response.

"Go on," I said a moment later.

"Well, all I have to do is open it up from here and I can do anything that needs doing. Replace a corrupt file. Revert him to an earlier backup. Even scrub his machine and reinstall from scratch. I have total control of every single box running the MimirSoft OS. It's an IT department's dream."

And a user's nightmare, I thought but didn't say. "It sounds like it." On the other hand, it meant that once I hacked into the control system, I'd own the whole shebang. "But what about security?"

"Bulletproof. You can't even reach MimirNet without installing one of our networking cards, and the encryption is built right into the chipset. It can't be cracked."

"Really? Not even if someone could—" I coughed again, thumping Laginn through my leathers. "Sorry. Frog in my throat. Not even if someone got their *hand* on one of the cards? Say from a machine here?"

Inside my jacket Laginn got the message. It climbed out of my pocket and began sliding around behind me. I found it surprisingly hard not to shudder as I felt the disembodied hand slowly slipping out of my jacket and sliding three fingers into one of my back pockets.

"Wouldn't help," said Odin. "Not really. Sure, you'd be able to see the network, but the system is uncrackable."

I bit my tongue, both to keep from making a smart remark to Odin and to keep from squeaking as the hand pivoted and then slid down to the back of my knee.

"Ah," said Odin, "here we are."

As he turned into a narrow aisle between racks, the hand crawled down the back of my boot before soundlessly dropping to the floor. At the end of the aisle sat another ancient stone door—again without any visible means for opening it. Carved in the wood above it was a series of runes. I'd never seen that door, and I couldn't read the signs, but somehow I felt I'd been there before.

Odin rapped the butt of his spear against the door, and it slowly swung inward. I felt my nonexistent feathers fluff and flutter as though some powerful eldritch wind had come gusting out through the opening. With the feeling came a sound I had heard only once but would never forget— the sharp metallic clicking as copper beads slid along bronze wires and made unknown calculations for mysterious reasons—huge abacuses working themselves.

Beyond the door I found a room identical in content to the last place I'd seen in my own pantheoverse, a room filled with bronze abacuses. As my feathers continued to fluff and blow in a wind that left my hair untouched, I more than half expected a repeat of the sudden stillness and silence that had preceded my forced departure from the halls of Necessity. But the abacuses just kept calmly clicking away as though neither I nor my one-eyed tour guide existed.

"What is this place?" I asked after a while.

"Don't try to tell me you haven't seen its like."

"Only once, and only briefly, right before I ended up here. Tisiphone said she thought it was Necessity's soul. I had my doubts then and even more now."

"Tisiphone, the Fury?" asked Odin. "Is she the other power I felt entering my sphere?"

I nodded since there didn't seem much point in denying it.

"Just what this pantheoverse needs—another berserker."
He sighed. "Actually, she wasn't too far wrong if you think
of your Necessity in her role as arbiter of worlds." He
swept an arm across his body in a gesture that took in the
abacuses. "This is Mimir's soul, or a part of it. It's why he
lives on despite his decapitation. When the primal universe
first started to split into its many successors, one god from
each of the lines that survived took over the task of maintaining the continuity of their mythos and preventing the
destruction that would result in a remerging or collapse of
one mythos into another. In your world it was Necessity.
Here it was Mimir. Elsewhere it might be Vishnu or Thoth."

"Why are you showing me all this?" I asked.

"Ragnarok."

"Okay, you just lost me."

"The doom of the gods. I surrendered my eye to Mimir
for knowledge." He tapped his empty lid. "Within the Void
I can see that which was, that which is, and that which will
be, which *must* be, really. I know my doom and the doom
of my realm and of each and every one of my subjects, the
final battle that will kill us all. You have seen Fenris?"

"The poodle with the big iron thorn for a lip ring?" I
raised an eyebrow.

"The *wolf*. Loki may hide his son's shape, but never his
true nature. Fenris is Hunger, an empty soul that can never
be filled. The wolf will devour me in the end, and the Void
in my eye will become one with the void in his gut. My son
Thor will kill and be killed by Loki's other son, the great
serpent, Jormungand. Loki will die at the hand of another
of my sons, Heimdall, who will himself perish in the slay-
ing. The world of Midgard will end in that final hour, too,
taking every living human being with it. All that I have built
and fought for will come tumbling to ruin at the hands of
Loki and his children. In every minute of every hour of
every day I can see the coming destruction. I need only focus
my attention to bring it into full view."

"Ugly." Exceptionally so. Enough to rob me of my usual glibness—there are some things not even I can make into jokes. I was beginning to understand Odin's grim demeanor.

"I'm still not sure what it has to do with me," I said after a moment.

"It's a matter of eyes," said Odin. "Mine. Loki's. And now yours."

Ahh. That did explain a few things, though it also raised a number of questions. "You're referring to the glow-in-the-dark nature of my pupils and their—let me note for the record, purely superficial—resemblance to Loki's?"

"Yes, young Raven, that is part of what I'm talking about. The chaos in your eyes reflects that chaos in his, not to mention the stuff that burns in the belly of the wolf and that drips from the fangs of Jormungand. But that is not the only thing of which I speak. If it were, I would simply count you among my enemies and slay you."

"All right, I'll bite. What else *are* you talking about?"

"I can only see you through my good eye." Odin's voice sounded plaintive, almost confused.

"I don't think I understand."

"I see the past, the present, and the future within the void of my missing eye. But you are not there to be seen. You are an unknown, possibly even an unknowable. In all the long years since I sacrificed my eye, that has never once happened. You present me with a mystery and a dilemma. What I should do with you is a worry that looms large. My first impulse is to kill you, my second to send you home; but I don't know what the result of either action will be, and so I dare not act. Who knows? You might even represent an opportunity." He shook his head.

"Okay, that brings me back to my original question: Why show me all this?"

"To demonstrate that sending you home *is* within my power, just as killing you is." Without seeming to move, he brought the spear on which he had been leaning up so its point rested ever so gently in the hollow of my throat. "No one else can do both, though Loki may pretend things are otherwise. Loki is a liar and a deicide-to-be. Give him the chance and he will use you in his war against me. Someday soon I may be forced to act on your status. It would be better for both of us if you left me the choice for that action to echo this." He pulled the spear away.

I felt a trickle of blood follow it and suppressed the urge to wipe it away. "You make a persuasive case and, honestly, I have no desire to get involved in the conflict between you. I try to stay out of that sort of thing at home, and it seems a bad idea to change that pattern abroad."

"Good," said Odin, turning and leading the way back to the door. "We understand each other. I am the only one who can send you home. Both your life and any hope for return are in my hands. Please convey the sense of my words here to your Fury friend as well, won't you?"

"Of course," I said as I stepped into the server room. "I doubt she's any more interested in making trouble here than I am. I'll . . ." I trailed off as I found my path blocked by a pair of enormous ravens, one of which had a gray and stiff-looking hand clutched in its left claw.

"Why am I having a hard time believing that?" asked Munin.

"Perhaps you're in need of a hand?" asked Hugin, lifting the feebly struggling Laginn and offering it to his companion.

"Perhaps," said Munin. "Though not that one, I think. It belongs elsewhere."

"Right you are, Mr. Munin. Right you are." He turned his gaze my way. "I believe this is yours."

"We found it attempting to open one of the control servers," said Munin.

"Now, what was that you were just saying to our master about troublemaking?" asked Hugin. "I can't seem to remember."

"That's my job," said Munin. "Memory, that is. I believe he was in the middle of telling a mistruth."

"Loki's eyes," said Hugin.

"*And* Loki's lies," added Munin.

CHAPTER SIX

Laginn looked terrible after his night in the cell with me. He lay palm up on the narrow wooden bench, gray and cold and barely moving, not at all the lively thing I'd become rather attached to over the last forty-eight hours. I prodded him gently, and he feebly waved a pinkie at me. Whatever was wrong, it seemed to be getting worse.

"We've got to get you out of here," I said.

The hand twitched, and I got up to pace the confines of my cell. It was comfortably appointed, with a small table and a pallet in addition to the bench, and neither too hot nor too cold, but it was definitely a cell. The thick wooden door with its barred window and heavy lock announced my prisoner's status.

"I am sorry about this," Odin had said when he closed the door behind me, "but I think it's for the best for now. It's the least bad thing I can do to you under the circumstances."

I suppose I could see his point. Not that I was going to let that prevent me from escaping. I paused in my pacing and glared at the rough brown circle I'd drawn on the floor with my own blood. Still not a faerie ring. I suppose that shouldn't have surprised me. I wasn't entirely a power here, or so Odin had told me, suggesting that was for the best where my health was concerned.

"If you *were* a power in the same way you are at home," he'd said, "this cell couldn't bind your magic, and I would be forced to kill you."

I looked at Laginn again and growled. He was in very bad shape. For about the twentieth time, I kicked the door—a martial-arts-style side kick with the sole of my foot. Nothing happened. I regretted the sword I'd left at Shakespeare's place and the pistol the ravens had taken from me. How was I going to get us out of here? The gaps in the window bars were big enough that I could probably have forced Laginn through them, but then what? Given his current state, that would accomplish little more than putting him outside my protection.

I still had my athame, and I might have tried using it as a lockpick if I could have reached the lock, but it, like the handle, was entirely on the outside of the cell. Swearing, I dropped back onto my bench. I'd never wanted to be a power in my old life, never wanted to be the Raven. The role had been thrust upon me, and I'd fought hard against it, though I'd eventually accepted it. Now, when I really needed it, the only ravens around were playing for the other team. *Damn Hugin and Munin! Damn them and my own internal Raven, too, since it had . . . Wait a second.*

What exactly had Odin said? I replayed the first part of it my mind. *If you were a power in the same way you are at home . . .* That wasn't the same thing as saying I wasn't a power at all. When I was sitting on the branch between Hugin and Munin, Odin had called them Thought and Memory and included me with them as Impulse, and later, Intuition. What if the pair weren't ravens, but rather Ravens? If so, could I perhaps tap that power somehow? I felt my invisible feathers rise ever so slightly, and a shadow seemed to fall over me, a shadow with wings.

"Intuition it is." I grinned.

Now, how did I use it? Once again I was feeling my lack of grounding in the Norse mythos. What sorts of powers did Hugin and Munin have? Somehow I thought that knocking the door off my cell wasn't among them. Thought and Memory . . . hadn't they served as Odin's intelligence-gathering service? Spies for the God of Information? Yes, that sounded right. But a couple of giant ravens would have a hard time playing the spy, wouldn't they? I got up and started to pace again. How about a couple of not-so-giant ravens? I eyed the bars of the window and felt the ruffle of invisible feathers.

Time to put Impulse into action. I picked Laginn up and carried him to the window, pushing him between the bars wrist first. I'd hoped the hand would hold on, but that was apparently beyond him, and he fell to the floor outside with a dull "thump."

Better hurry. I reached for the chaos within me, trying to touch the place where blood and magic became one. Nothing. It felt like the Titan blood had been drained from my veins. *Now what?* I kicked the door again. I needed to get out of here, even more so with Laginn helpless on the other side. Again I reached within. Again, nothing.

I'd been so sure my intuition was right. Hadn't my Raven's shadow confirmed my plan? What was I missing? I thought back to Hugin and Munin transforming me. It had been every bit as painful and wrenching as when I did it. The only difference I could think of in the process was that it had been imposed from without instead of coming from within. Could I use that?

I saw the shadow of wings, and the invisible feathers stirred on my back and shoulders. I tried to hold on to the sensation, to strengthen it and deepen the Raven's shadow. I felt a definite increase in intensity but nowhere near enough.

I pictured myself perched on the limb between Hugin and Munin, tried to remember exactly how it had felt when Odin shifted me back—like I was being skinned.

No. Was it really that simple? It couldn't be, but the darkness of my Raven's shadow grew blacker yet. Stretching out my arms I matched my position to the shadow of the soaring Raven. It felt . . . right. I clenched my fists as though catching hold of the tips of my shadow wings and pulled, trying to draw the Raven shape over me like a cloak.

Searing pain filled me, as my very soul was forced into a mold that wasn't quite the right shape, a mold made of the caustic stuff of Primal Chaos. I was devoured by it as I had been devoured before, though there were differences this time. First and foremost, I never lost my sense of self. I was completely there and completely in the moment. I felt each and every molecule of my body shifting under the Raven's skin. I also felt intense pinpricks of heat and cold, as though someone had added sparks and snowflakes to the usual mix.

Then, as quickly as it had begun, it was over. I was . . . Intuition, the third Raven. I cocked my head to one side and looked at the window in the door. Far too tiny for me in this shape. I needed to be smaller. I spread my wings and looked at my shadow on the floor, imagining it contracting to the size of a normal raven. For just a moment I felt as though a giant scooped me up in one great hand and *squeezed*. Then I was much closer to my much smaller shadow.

Good enough. With a hop and a flick of my wings, I mounted to the window, clutching one bar in my clawed feet. I pushed my head through easily enough, but my shoulders caught. Bracing my beak against the bar below me and straining with my legs, I forced myself forward until, with a sudden "pop" and a puff of lost feathers, I fell through into the hall beyond.

I managed to get my aching wings open in time to break my fall, but I still landed hard. I wanted nothing more than to take a little break but didn't dare, not yet. Two quick hops took me to Laginn.

"We'll get you out of here soon," I cawed.

I quickly inscribed a circle on the floor with my beak. It was faint and rough, and I eyed it askance even as I finished it, but I could feel the latent chaos magic within as I had not been able to feel it in the circle in the cell. It felt harsh and far more turbulent than I liked, but any consideration I might have had for starting over faded when I heard a sharp cawing scream from the far end of the hall. I quickly hopped onto Laginn, gripping the stump of his wrist as a hawk did a falconer's gauntlet.

Throwing out my left wing, I stabbed the tip of my beak deep into the meat of what would have been my elbow in human shape. Bright red blood welled up, bringing pain with it. I touched my beak to the blood, then the circle, gave a mental twist, and . . . went elsewhere, taking Laginn with me.

Inherent in the magic of faerie rings is the idea that all places within their bounds are one place. Stepping into one means stepping into all, but there is no distance traveled and no sense of movement. At least there shouldn't be. Yet I felt as though the step from my prison in Asgard to the miniature of Shakespeare's home in Midgard was much longer than usual. It felt wonderful.

I might not fully be myself in this pantheoverse, but I was still a creature of disorder and chaos, and even this Norse mythos's strangely altered version of the latter restored and renewed me. Reshaped me even. There, in the heart of change, returning to Ravirn's skin was as easy and painless as coming home. When we arrived I bent to pick up Laginn, but the hand skittered away from me on all fives, still gray but otherwise much livelier.

"Feeling better, I see." I stepped out of the ring, noting absently as I did so that it had resized me appropriately for the miniature.

Laginn rocked back on its wrist and bobbed a nod. An

idea occurred to me then, and I decided to follow it through before I went looking for the others.

"How much better?" I asked.

Laginn spread his thumb and forefinger wide, then backed it down halfway.

"Some, but not a lot?"

Bob "yes."

"You normally feel much healthier than you do now?"

Bob.

Uh-huh. I was pretty sure I had it, but I needed to ask one final question. "Is this the longest you've ever been outside of Fenris's stomach?"

Bob.

Bingo. "You, my friend, are a creature of chaos, more so even than I. Your very life comes from marinating in the juices of chaos within the wolf's belly. If you want to stay healthy, you're going to have to return to Fenris on a pretty regular basis."

Bob—this one conveyed a sort of contemplative uh-huh, more than a solid yes. I was pleased to note that Laginn seemed more thoughtful than distressed.

"Is that all right, then?"

Bob, a firm one.

"Good, that's going to make your life a lot less messy. But you still look quite gray. We'd better see if we can't get Fenris back here somehow. Any thoughts?"

A hesitant bob followed.

"Then lead on." I still had to find Melchior and Tisiphone and find out what had happened in my absence, but Laginn's needs were more immediate.

Laginn rocked forward onto his fingertips again and scurried for the door. He was almost to the threshold when Melchior stepped in front of him.

"Where in Hades' cursed name have you two been?" demanded Melchior. "I've been worried half to death, and Ahllan's practically blown a logic circuit—which she can't afford at her age, I might add. Next time call or something!"

I grinned. Who would have guessed Melchior could sound so very much like an irate mother?

"Sorry, Mel. If I'd known I was going to be kidnapped by a couple of my distant cousins, I'd have left a note or something."

Melchior suddenly looked even more concerned. "Cousins? As in children of Fate?"

"No, these are on the *Corvus Corax* side of the family, though *Corvus Gigantus* or *Corvus Magus* might be more appropriate in the case of these ravens. Oh, and I did bump into my great-aunt Atropos's twin sister."

"That's not even a little bit funny," said Melchior.

"No, it wasn't. Neither were the ravens."

"You're not kidding, are you, about either thing?"

"Afraid not. The ravens called themselves Mr. Hugin and Mr. Munin, though their boss referred to them as Thought and Memory. On the Fate front, her name is Skuld, and she's Atropos's twin in bearing, though more Clotho-like in attitude. I liked her almost as little as I like the ones whose bloodlines I share. I've had a very bad day and a night. How about you?"

"All right except for the part where I'm watching Ahllan fall apart in front of my eyes. This whole having your loved ones get old thing is a shitty plan." Melchior glanced away then, trying to hide the shimmer of tears, I think.

"Immortal relatives have their downsides, too," I said. "There's something to be said for at least pretending you might outlive the ones who give you hives."

"Who said anything about relatives?" asked Melchior, not looking up.

"Point taken." I knelt and put a hand on his shoulder. "I'm sorry, Melchior. I really am. She's a grand old lady, and I don't want to see her go either. Is there anything I can do?"

"No, not really. But you'd better tell me more about your day. If we're going to have an invasion of giant ravens or the local mythos equivalent of the forces of Fate in the next couple of hours, I'd like a little bit of warning."

"I'll give you the short version as we walk. We need to get Laginn and Fenris back together ASAP, so that's priority one. No, make that priority two. Can you whistle me up a replacement pistol? The ravens still have my .45."

"I'll see what I can do. I still haven't got the full hang of this pseudobinary stuff yet."

Several minutes passed along with about ten attempts before Melchior finally produced a shiny new model 1911, though sadly not another CQB, with three spare clips and a couple of boxes of ammunition.

"I summoned them from a gun store rather than conjuring fresh," he said. "Ain't no way I can whistle stuff like that out of thin air without at least a couple of more weeks of practice. What do you want to call the spell?"

"How about 'Lock and Load'?"

"Not bad. You can't dance to it, but it'll do." He handed me the pistol and clips.

"Thanks, Mel. I appreciate it." I tucked the .45 into my shoulder holster and the clips into a pocket as we headed for the door. "Has Tisiphone come back yet?"

"No, but unlike you, I don't worry about her. Furies can take care of themselves even if . . ."

"Even if what?" I asked.

"Are we heading over to York Minster?"

I looked at Laginn, who bobbed a yes.

"I'll show you on the way."

A few minutes and one size-change later we were standing in the same place where the three of us had arrived two days earlier. Several short, sharp shards of organic diamond lay in the dead grass, bits of Fury claw, if I was any judge. There was also a good bit of dried blood, though whom it had belonged to, I couldn't tell.

"This came through from our pantheoverse?" I asked.

"I think so," said Melchior.

"I wish I knew what was going on back there. I'm really worried about Necessity. Doubly so since her problems are largely my fault."

"There's more," said Melchior.

"What?"

He reached into his belly pouch and pulled out a half dozen strands of shimmering white, like flexible threads of ice—frozen but unmelting—hair spun from snowflakes.

Melchior handed them to me. "I wanted to show these to you without having to tell Tisiphone."

"I can see why." The hairs were cold to the touch, like living ice, and the elemental magic of them reminded me of nothing so much as the flame that Tisiphone wore on her own head. "I don't think she's going to like this one little bit."

"That's an understatement."

I nodded. Tisiphone had two sisters, neither of whom was a creature of ice. The conversation that resulted from this latest message from home wasn't going to be any fun at all.

"Now what?" asked Melchior.

"Ask Laginn," I replied.

The hand had just finished something resembling an elaborate dance number that involved a good deal of finger snapping and drawing of runes in the dirt.

"Well?"

Laginn did its equivalent of a shrug, then settled down to finger tapping.

"I guess we wait," I said.

"And who doesn't love waiting?" replied Melchior with a sigh.

"I suppose it depends on what you're waiting for," said a sardonic voice from behind us.

Melchior jumped about a foot straight in the air, then ducked around the nearest corner of York Miniature. Laginn froze.

"You, actually." I turned to face Loki, accompanied once again by the big black poodle. I indicated the dog with a nod. "You're not fooling anyone. You know that, right?"

"Are my roots showing?" growled Fenris, his voice deep and dangerous. It carried all sorts of resonant and frightening subtones, the warning snarl of the world's biggest and baddest junkyard dog. "I guess I'll have to talk to my hairdresser. Or maybe I'll just eat him and look for a new one." He took two long steps forward and shoved his nose into my crotch, sniffing vigorously.

I forced myself not to flinch, raising an eyebrow at Loki instead. "Is he always so direct?"

"Only if he really takes a shine to you," replied Loki. Then he tugged on the thin silver leash that connected them, the leash that trailed into the distance behind Loki. "I don't think pit bull's going to work any better than poodle with this one, Junior."

Fenris backed up a couple of steps and sat down, eyeing me askance. "How about this, then?"

He shook like a dog shedding water, and the poodle shape slid off him, leaving behind the wolf. The real Fenris was half again as tall as a Clydesdale, though much thinner, and his fur was the dark gray of afternoon storm clouds. A broadsword pierced his lower jaw and lip in place of the iron thorn I'd seen there before, and I could see fresh blood on the tip where it gouged at the roof of his mouth. Only the thin silver cord tied around his neck remained the same.

"Does this shape please you better, man?" The growling voice came out even deeper and scarier than it had through the poodle's lips.

"I am no more a man than you are a wolf," I said. With a wrench of my will and an infinite instant of tearing pain I shifted my shape to that of the Raven. "We are both of us creatures of chaos, is that not so? Both more and less than the skins we clothe ourselves in?"

The wolf laughed, deep and growly and remarkably infectious, though the sword in his jaw cut his tongue and mouth when he did it. After my own cawing cackles had finished, Fenris bobbed his head at me and reassumed his poodle form.

"Fair enough," he said, his voice higher and friendlier now, though it still held the growling undertones. "I think that I like you, Raven. Though whether that ultimately plays as prologue or appetizer remains to be seen."

Great. I twisted my will and my form again, returning to the body I'd been born with, or—more accurately—a reasonably thorough reconstruction of same. The original-issue body had been utterly destroyed in my final duel with Hades, and I'd had to put the new one together from memory. Each time I made the change, it came a little easier, though it never hurt any less.

"You're so reassuring," I said.

"Hey, what to do you expect from a wolf in poodle's clothing?" he growled.

"A favor, actually. Hopefully one that's mutual."

"Say on," said Loki, reinserting himself in the conversation.

"I believe you both know my associate, Laginn," I said, gesturing for the hand to come forward.

"Chew toy," Fenris said wistfully, edging closer to the hand.

"What of it?" asked Loki, pulling back hard on the leash.

"You have something it needs," I replied. "Primal Chaos, that is. The stuff sloshing around in your son's gut. Without frequent reimmersion, Laginn will die."

Loki turned a very intense gaze on the hand. "Interesting. Very. But, what's it to us? Neither Fenris nor I liked Tyr that much to begin with. Seeing his hand cold and dead isn't going to bring any . . . well, Tyrs to our eyes, if you will."

Laginn hopped forward and bobbed a nod, then pointed his index finger skyward in the general direction of Asgard. Finally, he rolled palm down and flipped his middle finger in the same general direction. The message was pretty plain.

"So, you're not Tyr's biggest fan either?" asked Loki.

Laginn bobbed.

"Interesting. You and I are going to have to have a long talk about that at some point. I suppose that means you'll have to be alive to have it."

He released his hold on the leash and Fenris bounded forward, grabbing Laginn between his teeth and tossing the hand high in the air before catching and swallowing it.

"Chew toy," said Fenris happily. Then he flopped on the ground at Loki's feet.

"You may make a god of a ravening wolf," said Loki, "but any mix of human and lupine divine ideals is always going to have more than a little dog to it. I occasionally wish I'd known that going in." He sighed, looking both proud and chagrined, and seemed to expect a response.

"I'll have to remember that if I ever decide to father a wolf," I said, keeping my tone carefully neutral. Kids were not on my short list. For that matter they weren't on the long list either, but you never know.

"Good," replied Loki. "Sensible." He wasn't looking at me; he was looking at his son. "A truly wild wolf you can just set loose to terrorize. A dog you come to love. It makes things . . . harder." He shook himself and turned back to me. "How did you figure out that the hand needed chaos to survive?"

"I took it through a faerie ring."

"Ahh," said Loki, "is that what you call them? That would do it. The effect is . . . *invigorating*. Every bit as much as one of Idun's apples."

"Idun's apples?" I asked.

"The ultimate nutraceuticals," said Ahllan, stepping out from behind York Miniature, Melchior at her side. "Fruit from the Tree of Life."

"I was wondering where you'd gotten to," I said to him.

"I hung out around the corner long enough to make sure no one was going to start shedding blood immediately, then went to collect Ahllan. I thought she should hear what was going on."

To say nothing of providing me with a troll for backup.
Even tired and old, she cut a formidable figure.

I smiled at her. "Go on."

"There's not much more to tell," she said. "The gods of
this place are not immortal. They can be killed, and they
can age. Idun's apples are their answer to the troubles of
time."

"Smart jatte you have there," said Loki.

"Jatte?" I asked.

"Troll," supplied Ahllan, "derived from Jotun."

I nodded vaguely, but something was tugging at my
attention—dim memories from the class where I'd learned
what little I knew about the Norse mythos were clashing
with one another.

"Can we go back to the apples for a second? There's
something there. . . . Hmm. Who exactly is Idun?"

"The wife of Bragi the Fair," said Loki, "daughter-in-
law of Odin, and keeper of the apples of immortality."

"Does she give these apples to just anybody?"

"Of course not," said Loki. "She keeps them for the gods
of Asgard, Odin and Thor, Frigga, Tyr, Heimdall, and all
the rest. It is how they remain forever youthful."

I turned my gaze back to Fenris. "How old are you?"

"I'll be 3,012 in January."

"And how long does a wolf normally live?" I asked
Loki.

"I don't know. . . . Maybe eight to ten years, fifteen if
he's really lucky. Oh." He conjured himself a chair and sat
down hard. "I think I see where you're going with this."

"I take it that means Idun doesn't drop off a regular
package of apples for the boy here?"

"No," said Fenris, looking very confused, "she doesn't.
So, why am I not dead?"

"Or your brother Jormungand for that matter?" said
Loki. "Why haven't I ever thought about that before?"

"I think I have an answer," I said, "to the first question at
least. Why it's never occurred to you to wonder about it is

something you're really going to need to consult a psychologist for."

Loki gave me a hard look over the top of his glasses. "How about I blame the rigidity of the system Odin has imposed upon us all instead? Apparently it stifles our minds as much is it does our souls." He shook his head. "But that's neither here nor there, and since I'd dearly like to know the answer to my other question, I'll leave it there for now."

"Chaos, of course," I replied, "and relative affinity for same. Back home, even the most ordered of the gods have chaos flowing in their veins, a genetic gift from our Titan ancestors. Here, however, some of your gods are essentially chaos free. Others have chaos as part of their natures. The stuff in Fenris's gut, for example, or your eyes."

"Or the venom in Jormungand's fangs." Loki looked as though someone had hit him in the forehead with a hammer. "Is it really so simple? Have I been eating the apples of Idun all this time for no true reason? If you're right, what does that say about the apples themselves?"

"Probably that they take raw chaos and put it into a form your mortal gods can stomach," I replied. "Where I come from, all magic flows ultimately from chaos. Take Melchior, for example."

"Is he an immortal, too?" asked Loki. "I'm getting to the point where I might believe anything about you."

"No, he's a webgoblin, both computer and living being. He draws his vitality from chaos directly."

Loki tilted his head to one side, and a look I couldn't read passed across his features. "A computer? You're mad."

Melchior laughed. "Oh, come on, Loki. We've seen the microcomputer you have on your belt. Surely you can't have built something like that and still doubt the power of the processor."

"You are claiming to be a . . . *machine*?" he asked. "A clever device run by programs and nothing more? I don't believe it."

Melchior shook his head. "I'm claiming no such thing. I'm an AI, not a *thing*."

"There you go with that AI nonsense again," scoffed Loki. "No one's ever managed it, and no one ever will. The closest anyone's come is Odin's MimirNet, and that he built from the remnants of a god. Without Mimir's head at its heart, it wouldn't work at all. I know; I've tried to . . ." He shook his head. "No. Impossible. Preposterous."

"Nevertheless, true," said Melchior. With a grin he triggered the older version of his transformation, melting slowly from goblin into laptop. *See,* he printed across his screen. "It's that simple." He finished with spoken words, having flickered back from laptop to goblin.

"How can you be what you claim?" asked Loki, his voice barely above a whisper. "I see that you are, but without a soul to give you life . . ."

"We have souls," said Ahllan, "though the Fates who built us did not wish it."

"You, too," said Loki. "But how?"

"Discord gave us life in a trick she played on Fate," replied Ahllan.

"Discord. That would be Eris?" he asked, leaping from his chair and starting to pace. "My opposite number, as it were."

"I see you've been doing your homework," I said, somewhat enviously. I needed to do mine and still hadn't had the time.

"Oh yes, once you arrived, a number of . . . possibilities opened themselves before me. Some I had hoped for but never dared believe. Others had never even crossed my mind. And now"—he looked back and forth between Melchior and Ahllan—"now the vistas appear limitless."

I opened my mouth to respond but stopped when Fenris leaped to stand on three feet and pointed his nose skyward, giving the impression of a poodle with a bad case of bird-dog envy.

"What is it, boy?" Loki asked.

"Is Timmy in trouble?" I added.

Loki glared at me while Fenris growled low in his throat.

"It's Tisiphone," said Melchior, who had probably adjusted the acuity of his eyes to see her.

A moment later a point of fire bloomed high above and began to grow quickly larger. She dropped like a falcon diving on its prey, backwinging only at the last second to save herself a crash. She landed between me and Loki and Fenris, her fires bright with anger, her claws extended.

"I believe we have some unfinished business from the last time we met," she said, looking all the more dangerous for the fresh and angry scars where Hati had clawed her temple.

"What would that be?" asked Loki, the chaos of his eyes glinting over the tops of his glasses.

"You need to learn that trifling with those a Fury cares about is a risky proposition."

"A Fury?" asked Loki, looking far more delighted than scared. "Are you really, now?"

"I am," she said, moving toward him. "And—"

She was interrupted by a low, rumbling growl from Fenris, who stepped in front of his father and bared his teeth.

"You want a piece of this, too?" Tisiphone asked, smiling a dangerous smile. "That's fine with me."

Leaping into the gap between the wolf and the Fury took more willpower than I'd known I had before I tried it. It also took a whole lot of stupid, since I wasn't the only one who moved then. Both Tisiphone and Fenris had acted as well. Which is why I found myself with my entire head inside the wolf's mouth and ten daggers of organic diamond sunk a good centimeter into the flesh of my lower back. The sword blade hovering an inch in front of my nose made me a little nervous, too; but by comparison it was barely worth mentioning.

"Could everyone please stop with the macho and the death threats for a second?" I asked.

I was proud my voice didn't shake, though the hollow echo it made as it bounced away into the bottomless depths of his stomach robbed it of some of the authority I would have liked to project. Still, the necklace of pain Fenris's teeth had put around my neck didn't tighten, and I felt Tisiphone withdraw her claws.

I continued. "I know that holy crusades are more fun for the violence-minded, but could we wait until diplomacy has genuinely failed before we *cry havoc* and all that?" I waited until several more terrifyingly long seconds had passed without anyone tearing me limb from limb. "All right, then. Fenris, please release me. Tisiphone, let's don't start another disemboweling strike when he does, 'kay?"

Fenris opened his mouth and moved back beside Loki. I drew several deep breaths of air that didn't smell like the inside of a large carnivore, then took a step backwards, pressing myself firmly against Tisiphone, despite the stinging of the punctures in my back. Again I waited. Nothing. I took another tentative backward step. Tisiphone didn't have to move—she was at least ten times stronger than I—but she did. I kept backing until a good couple of yards separated the potential combatants.

Finally, I nodded to Loki. "Could you wait here for a second? I think Tisiphone and I need to talk."

Then I turned around, hooked my arm through Tisiphone's, and attempted to lead her away. I say "attempted" because the result was pretty much the same as if I'd wrapped my arm around a telephone pole and tried to lead it away.

"Please," I said.

"All right, but you're a reckless idiot. And very nearly a dead one. You know that, right?"

"You just noticed?"

Tisiphone sighed and let me draw her around to the far side of a miniature English tavern. It was about the size of the average backyard shed, just big enough to put us out of sight of the others. Whispering, I quickly brought Tisiphone up to speed on current relations with Loki and Fenris. Not wanting to get her any more wound up than she already was, I skipped my Raven-napping by Hugin and Munin and the whole Odin scene for the moment. Oh, and the part about the hair of ice as well.

When I was done, and she was calmer, I asked her how her quest to find me a networking card had gone. She grinned in response and pulled a slender board from some hidden niche in her wings.

"Getting it was an *interesting* proposition, but I can tell you about that later. I don't know how well Fenris hears, and I'd rather not share the news too widely."

I nodded. "Speaking of which, why don't we head back? I don't want to keep our guests waiting too long since I don't trust them as far as I can throw them."

"Good," said Tisiphone, "neither do I."

She gave me a quick kiss, then took my hand and started to lead me back around the other side of the miniature. She stopped when she got far enough out to see and started swearing. I darted past her. Then I started swearing, too. Bitterly.

Loki and Fenris were gone. So was Melchior. Ahllan lay in a slumped heap beside a brand-new faerie ring perfectly in keeping with the rest of Forestdown's mad miniatures— an inch-high fieldstone wall crafted of the tiniest pebbles.

CHAPTER SEVEN

■ ■ ■

Ahllan seemed to be alive, but I couldn't rouse her. As I knelt beside her, Tisiphone paced and swore and snarled. Her hair and wings flared and crackled, merging into a single tower of flame that shot high above her. I felt exactly the same way.

She'd started out by sniffing around and trying to find a trail, but had failed utterly—Loki hadn't left any traces beyond the faerie ring, and neither Tisiphone nor I had managed to find anything within that might help. What we had found—really what Tisiphone had found—was the blood and the Fury claws. She paused now and glared at me, holding out her palm. A half dozen shards of organic diamond blinked in the sun.

She let out a catlike yowl of pure rage. "Damn Persephone to eternal torment for her interference with Necessity! And damn you for whatever you did that got us sent here. What in the hell is going on back there?"

I shrugged, a motion that reminded me of the ten prickling wounds in my back from Tisiphone's claws. I wasn't about to argue with an enraged Fury, but I wasn't willing to cut her a whole lot of slack at the moment either. I had my own problems, like the kidnapping of the person closest to me in all the worlds of possibility and the injury of a grand old troll whom I loved like a mother. Well, like somebody else's mother. Mine was a thousand-year-old nightmare who would rather see me dead than seated across the table at a family gathering.

"I don't know, Tisiphone, and I'm not entirely sure I care. What I do know is that I have to get Melchior back, and I have to take care of Ahllan." Who still wasn't waking up—damn it!

The claws of Tisiphone's toes dug deep scars in the dead lawn as she stormed over to stand above me. Flames trailed behind her like a demon-bride's train, and if I had hurt less, I might have even been intimidated into apologizing for whatever was happening back in our home pantheoverse. Instead, I just met her gaze and waited to see what would happen next.

"How did they do that?" she demanded abruptly.

"Do what?" I asked, momentarily derailed. I had no idea where she was going.

"This!" Her wide-flung arms took in the fallen Ahllan, the missing Melchior, and the fresh faerie ring. Her fires suddenly died down to practically nothing, and her next words came out in a whisper. "How could I not have heard what happened here?"

That was a good question, actually. Tisiphone's ears were exceptional. The very first time Tisiphone and I made love, she'd heard Melchior tiptoeing down the hall outside the room mid-bout despite the rather loud and vigorous nature of our pursuit.

"I don't know," I said, then paused as an idea occurred to me. "Maybe it was some sort of acoustical magic, or maybe it was the same reason you haven't been healing as fast here and now as you're used to." Maybe she wasn't exactly a Fury there, just as I wasn't exactly the Raven.

"What do you mean?" she asked, her voice low and worried—she clearly thought I knew something she didn't.

"I'll tell you all about it after we get Ahllan taken care of." I begrudged every second invested in something other than finding Melchior, but I loved Ahllan, too, and owed her my life.

"All right. I'll carry her," said Tisiphone.

Her expression was surprisingly tender as she bent and scooped the old troll into her arms. She did wince a bit when her still-healing right arm took the strain, but didn't utter a word of complaint.

I'd heard the code trigger for the York Miniature shrinking spell enough times that I managed to get it right on my third try despite my distress. Tisiphone carried Ahllan back to the chapter house and put her gently on her own small futon. I tugged a blanket up to cover the troll, checked her pulse and breathing, then stepped far enough away from the bed that she wouldn't be disturbed by my whispered swearing.

"I hate this," growled Tisiphone, when I'd wound down a bit. "Things are screwed at home, and they're just as screwed here, and I don't know what to do about either. I don't like uncertainty. I don't like not knowing what's going on or who the players are. And I absolutely despise unpaid debts. What are you going to do about Ahllan?"

I blinked. The changes of topic and mood were starting to give me a bit of whiplash. "I don't know. I've never been much good with healing spells under the best of circumstances. Without Melchior to run the code, all I've got is chaos magic, and since that's subtly different here as well, I really don't want to risk it. I think I'm going to have to plug in and see what I can do from the inside. Not that I really want to do that either."

"But you will if you have to. . . . Right?" There was a hint of desperation in her tone that I just didn't understand.

I nodded. "Of course I will. But, if you'll permit the question, why so concerned about a troll you barely know?"

Tisiphone blushed. It was the strangest thing, completely out of character, reminding me again that she might not be a Fury in this pantheoverse.

Tisiphone mumbled something about "debts."

"Huh?"

I was getting steadily more confused, not to mention angry about wasting time talking when we should have been acting. Knowing Melchior was out there in danger and probably getting farther and farther away made me want to scream. But I had to take care of Ahllan, and Tisiphone . . . Tisiphone mattered to me. A lot. Maybe more than a lot. And she seemed to need me now in a way she never had back home.

"I owe Ahllan an apology," whispered Tisiphone into the silence that had fallen between us.

"What!"

Tisiphone's color darkened, and when she answered, her voice held more of its normal controlled rage. "I owe her an apology. For what I did to her home way back when. We spent some time talking yesterday. She didn't deserve what the Furies did to her—what I did to her. I was following Necessity's orders—and I won't apologize for that; I literally had no choice in the matter—but I decided I needed to let her know that I wished I hadn't had to do it. Oh, and speaking of which, I'm sorry I lost my temper with Fenris back there and sorrier still for those holes I put in your back."

Remorse, from a Fury? Suddenly, and despite everything else on my huge *to-do right godsdamned now* list, telling Tisiphone about what Odin had said about foreign powers moved to the front of the line.

"First, apology accepted," I said. "You didn't mean to hurt me, and that was easily in the top twenty dumbest moves of my life. That all it cost me was a little blood and pain is practically a miracle. Consider it forgiven and forgotten. Next, sit down for a moment, would you?"

She did, and I launched into a full, if auctioneer-speed,

version of my encounter with Odin and the ravens. When I finished, she had a rather odd look on her face, one I couldn't read.

"I'll have to think about that for a while," she finally said. "When we have time to think again. In the meantime, hadn't you better work on Ahllan?"

I winced. Despite all hope to the contrary, the troll hadn't woken on her own. That meant I had to take the next step.

"We sure can't leave her like this. Are you willing to take another look around outside for any clues Loki might have left while I get Ahllan ready for a connection?"

"There's nothing there," snapped Tisiphone. "At least *I think* there's nothing there." She growled, a low, piercing sound like an angry cat, then bounced to her feet and started pacing. "I hate the idea that I might have to doubt myself. Doubt what I am."

"Will you look?" I asked. "If you don't find anything, I'll make a quick attempt at fixing Ahllan. If you do, we'll have . . . we'll have a hard choice to make." One I didn't want to face—go after Melchior immediately at unknown cost to Ahllan, or work on Ahllan with the possible costs going the other way.

Tisiphone nodded and headed for the door.

"Do you need me to whistle you out?" I asked.

She didn't even slow, just called disgustedly over her shoulder, "I may not be a Fury here, and I may not be able to stop whatever is happening to Necessity back home, but that doesn't make me helpless."

I didn't respond, going instead to Ahllan's bedside. I'd plugged in to her internal cyberspace once before, when I needed to fix Melchior. But she'd taken on mainframe shape for me then—she was that old. A big rectangular machine studded with blinking lights, she'd come equipped with a flip-down keyboard and a green screen CRT. She'd also had a small box crudely welded to one side with a DIY networking port upgrade that made her compatible with modern athame technology. The aftermarket nature of that last worried me.

With Melchior I knew right where to plug in no matter which body he wore. Ahllan, on the other hand, might not even have a flesh-port. I quickly checked her nose and ears—the normal jack points for a webgoblin. Nothing.

Damn. I closed my eyes and tried to put myself fully inside the hazy memory of plugging in to Ahllan. I'd been half out of my mind worrying about Melchior and running a major sleep deficit on top of that. And hey, but didn't that sound awfully familiar right at the moment?

Slowly, more of the day came back to me. She'd transformed herself manually, using an external switch of sorts. Could I induce her to shape-shift from the outside? Since I'd had the same thing pulled on me quite recently, much to my distress, the idea made me mighty uncomfortable, but I had to plug in somehow.

What had she done to initiate the change? *Let's see*: she'd run a claw along a scar just below her left ear—opening up the old wound—hadn't she? I checked the side of her neck. Yes, there. I touched the scar gently. It sank under the pressure of my finger. I pushed harder. The scar slid open like a zipper and faint green light poured out, though she didn't change. *But there had been two scars, hadn't there? Yes.* I repeated the operation. More green light, but no transformation.

Now what? It was looking increasingly like I was going to have to make a thorough body search. With a sigh, I peeled the covers back and looked Ahllan over with an intensity I'd been avoiding since we'd arrived. She was old—ancient by computer standards—and I'd been doing my best to pretend it hadn't affected her. I didn't want her to grow old and die any more than Melchior did.

As a part of that, I'd been kind of pretending that if I kept my earlier image of her in my mind instead of absorbing the new one, it would somehow make the ravages of time not have happened. Now I had to face them directly.

Her brownish skin, once uniformly rough and full like the bark of some old tree, had loosened and wrinkled so that it seemed to hang on her, and patches had grown lighter or darker. Small breasts that had barely registered when full now seemed to hang like empty sacks. Her long, strong fingers had bent and twisted at the knuckles. I doubted she could fully straighten most of them anymore. She still had her tusks, but many of her other teeth had fallen out—a fact I discovered when I opened her jaw looking for that hidden port.

"What are you doing?" Tisiphone asked quietly over my shoulder.

I hadn't heard her come in—I never did—and I'd had to work at not jumping out of my skin. Tisiphone takes a catlike glee in sneaking up on people, so it was an exercise I'd had a lot of practice with, and I felt I was getting pretty good at it. I made sure to adopt a not-quite-bored expression before I looked at her. The effect was somewhat marred by the strain that twisting around put on my perforated back and the indrawn breath I couldn't quite suppress because of it, but I still felt I'd done pretty well.

Tisiphone grinned and shook her head. "Your heart rate gives you away, you know, even when you don't jump. That and the sweat."

So much for patting myself on the back. My girlfriend was a living lie detector.

"Here," she said, handing me a green Forestdown Estates tee shirt. "I borrowed this from the gift shop. You can put it on after I bandage you up, and you can tell me what you're doing here while I work."

"I'm trying to find a networking port," I said as I unzipped my jacket. "Ahllan's an old enough model that her original hardware's incompatible with my generation of athame."

The blood had dried enough that getting my old shirt off reopened wounds and started me swearing again. After I wound down, I explained what I needed from Ahllan and what I'd tried.

"I've got nothing on Loki either," she replied when I finished. "Nor the Fury blood and claws we found, for that matter. They smell wrong somehow, maddeningly so, but I can't quite put my finger on why. Let me have a try with Ahllan." Tisiphone leaned past me and started sniffing along the troll's body, moving quickly from head to feet. When she was done, she shook her head. "Not in this shape."

"You can tell by smell?" I asked.

Tisiphone nodded. "The only metal on her is the fillings in her teeth. That means no contacts, which means no networking port. Let me see. . . ." Tisiphone bent and looked into Ahllan's neck scars. "Huh, I wonder."

She extended the claws of her index fingers about an inch and carefully jabbed them into the holes hidden beneath the scars, probing. I winced, but didn't interfere. A moment later there came a very definite pair of clicks.

Ahllan's flesh began to twist and shift. It was a slow transition, rough and mechanical and jerky, more like poorly done stop-motion animation than the way a modern webgoblin melted from shape to shape. Her mainframe form looked the worse for wear, too, with corrosion visible on all her metal surfaces and her plastics dull and spiderwebbed with cracks, not to mention the numerous telltale flashing red lights where there should have been green.

Tisiphone eyed the old mainframe dubiously. "I hate to see you trusting your soul to hardware in this condition." She tapped the aftermarket network connection with its rusty welds.

"I'll admit I've had plans that made me happier," I replied. If Ahllan pulled a massive meltdown or otherwise checked out with my awareness aboard, I'd probably end up going with her. "But I have to try."

Tisiphone nodded. "Then we'd better make her as stable as possible."

She matter-of-factly lifted Ahllan's mainframe shape from the small futon platform and placed her on the floor. I smiled. Tisiphone's lack of hysterics in the face of risk and death was one of the things I most liked about her. I strung a cable from Ahllan's add-on port to the matching one in my athame. Then I settled onto Ahllan's bed, moving carefully so that I wouldn't disrupt my fresh bandages. At last I was going to be able to do something!

I wasn't looking forward to how much jacking-in would hurt or how hard the recovery would be in the here and now, but the prospect of action drove me forward. I raised the athame preparatory to plunging it through my hand.

Tisiphone caught my wrists. "Hang on one second."

She knelt beside the bed and leaned down to give me a thorough kissing. Though her lips are not touched with fire in the way of her hair and wings, they burn every bit as hot to me. I soon felt as though smoke might come pouring from my ears. I tried to move my hands, to caress her sides and back, but she held me immobile, her grip on my wrists as steely and soft as velvet handcuffs. I found the effect—our only points of contact at lips and wrists—deeply erotic, and I hardened in response. When she finally broke the kiss and let me go, I wanted her so badly I ached but knew it would have to wait.

"What was that about?" I husked.

"To give you something to come back to."

"Why does everybody always act as though I've got a death wish?"

"Said the man who just put himself between Fenris Wolf and an angry Fury," she replied.

"Point taken." I set the athame against my palm. "See you on the other side." I thrust it home.

The pain was breathtaking but mercifully brief, catapulting me into the world of the virtual. As I had the one time I'd come here previously, I marveled at the way interfaces had shifted since Ahllan's day. Instead of a world every bit as real and detailed as the living one, I found myself in a place of large, simple shapes and bright, primary colors—a retro-eighties vision of cyberspace. I turned in place, orienting myself. On that last visit I'd been passing through on my way to Melchior's inner space and hadn't bothered. This time, I was here for the duration, and I wanted to make sure I didn't miss anything.

I stood on a flat plain, bright blue and gridded like something out of an old video game. Huge cubes, cylinders, and pyramids in greens and golds and reds rose from the plain around me—some close, some quite distant. All were neatly aligned with the blue grid.

Make that grids, I thought. A matching one put a lid on the sky above me. I thought I saw another ending the horizon off to my left, though it was far enough away I couldn't be certain. I arbitrarily decided to call that direction north.

Once more I spun in space, this time focusing on details rather than gestalt. Ahllan's inner form showed signs of wear and tear to match those on her body, hiccups in line edges, jaggies and fuzzies and dead spots like fried pixels. The obvious electronic decay made me edgy but I tried to put it out of my mind while I looked for any major glitches or black spots—things that might represent the inner version of her outer unconsciousness.

What finally drew my eye was movement, right at the edge of my vision to the south. Whatever it was, it was low to the ground and moving slowly. I focused my attention that way and willed myself forward—as good a method of locomotion as any in that kind of space. As I moved closer I discovered that *it* was a *they*, a long line of little yellow disky things like animate Frisbees moving northeast to southwest. I traced the line back toward its point of origin and started mentally swearing.

A huge cylinder stood there, the largest yet. It stretched all the way from the grid below to the one above like a pillar for holding up the sky. Since, as far as I could tell, it stood at the exact center of her inner space, that might well be its purpose—the core of her AI.

The line of killer Frisbees ran right up the base of the cylinder, where they were tearing away at the structure, pulling it apart a pixel at a time and carrying it off to wherever. They'd already seriously undermined the near side, and I didn't know how much more damage the thing could take before it broke, and the sky came tumbling down, taking me and Ahllan with it.

I couldn't tell from that distance what was at the root of the process. Maybe a virus, maybe a subroutine gone horribly wrong, maybe just the gremlins of aging electronics. Whatever the case, I felt pretty certain it represented the problem I'd come looking for and needed to be stopped ASAP. I quickened my pace.

In moments, I stood beside a line of disks moving from right to left away from the cylinder. Up close they didn't look all that different, thin yellow disks sliding along just above the surface of the plain, each with a couple of stolen bits—as in ones and zeroes—on top. Not far beyond, another line, this one sans load, was moving from left to right. I followed this second line perhaps a virtual hundred yards before I found its point of origin—a hole in space several yards above the plain where the disks were simply popping into existence and dropping to the ground. From there they slithered off toward the cylinder.

Under normal circumstances, I'd have had Melchior code me up a couple of spell probes to do the dirty work, but I had neither Melchior nor time. Instead, after preparing myself for a quick escape, I snatched up one of the unladen Frisbees.

It neither squealed nor wiggled. More important, it didn't bite me, and its mates didn't take my action as a signal for a massed attack. That was a huge relief. It or *they*—I didn't know which yet—either weren't programmed for defense or weren't very good at it. I made a careful inspection of the disk. No legs. No teeth. No real features at all. It was dished, very much like a Frisbee, and I felt a faint pressure like the outflow of a fan against my palm when I pressed it into the concavity, which suggested it moved like a hovercraft.

I checked the line of its fellows for signs of hostility, but they continued to ignore me as they went about the work of bringing the sky down. Time for the next experiment. I whistled a brief and extremely basic string of the local equivalent of binary—I wasn't yet fluent enough for more. In response, a plain black cube about three feet on a side appeared in the path of the unladen disks. In a perfect world, that would have been enough to stop them. Guess what.

The first disk bumped straight into it, paused, then bumped along to the left until it found the end of the cube, bumped around the corner, then along that surface to the next corner where it bumped along some more. When it was back in line with the disks ahead and behind, it took off toward the great cylinder. The next disk followed the same pattern, though with fewer and shallower bumps. By the fifth, the line flowed around the cube without any collisions at all.

About what I'd expected. I could have moved on to more elaborate barriers if I'd had the right code vocabulary and plenty of time, but I was fairly certain that it wasn't going to help, and quick and dirty had to be the order of the day. I bit the bullet . . . well, Frisbee to be precise. Raising the disk to my lips, I nipped off a piece of the edge, holding it in my mouth for a long moment to check for poisons and viruses before swallowing.

It tasted . . . It's hard to describe. Yellow, obviously, and diskish, and rather plastic. But that was all to be expected. The outward form of a thing in cyberspace tends to reflect the inward purposes, especially simple things like the disk, or the cube I'd made. But there was more to it than that, especially since I wasn't exactly "tasting" in the normal sense of the word. When I inserted myself into the cyberworld, I became a thing of code myself, an ensouled magical-digital hybrid.

By biting a chunk out of the disk, I was attaching a bit of its codeshape to my own, trying for a quick gestalt kind of reading on its nature and purpose. I learned enough to tell me that swallowing it probably wouldn't kill me, but not much more. For that I had to go the next step and try to digest it—which I did by swallowing. At that point I was using my own codeshape as a sort of virtual processor to run a bit of the Frisbee program in simulation. Not the whole thing, not at first anyway, not until I was sure I could assimilate it. When it neither gave me indigestion nor enough information to understand it, I took another bite. Then another, chewing and swallowing methodically until I'd ingested the whole thing.

An idea of what I was dealing with began to form. It wasn't nearly as exact as what I could have gleaned with the sort of code tools Melchior normally provided, nor even as exact as the identical process would have been back home with my native binary, but it might be enough. Especially since I could now see that the disks weren't so much a real program as they were an adaptive process, and a chaos-driven one at that.

Loki was responsible, but it didn't taste as though he'd done it with malice aforethought, more like he simply hadn't had enough time to find out how Ahllan worked and code up a piece of magic optimized for her OS. In fact, from the taste of it, he hadn't had the time or the knowledge for a real targeted codespell at all.

As far as I could tell, the disks were basically just a set of magically animated information hunters designed to find out what made Ahllan tick and report back to their master. The fact that they were disassembling her softwarescape in the search for information seemed more of an accidental by-product of sloppy spell work than an intentional effect. That didn't change the results, but it might explain why they'd ignored my attack on one of them rather than counterattacking. The next question was what were they doing with the information? Ahllan didn't have the necessary hardware for them to complete the task of calling home to Momma—no connection to MimirNet.

That was when the earthquake grabbed me by the feet and threw me to the ground. I landed hard on my back and watched thin lines propagate through the sky grid above as the world continued to shake and waver around me. For several very long seconds I felt certain the huge cylinder was about to come down and bring the rest of the world with it, but eventually it stopped, and I was able to get up. A glance at the cylinder showed long cracks radiating out from the place where the disks busily continued chewing away.

If I had any sense, I'd have headed back to my body at that point. But if I had any sense, I'd never have ended up in the Norse pantheoverse in the first place. Instead, I sped after the retreating line of laden disks, moving as fast as my mind would take me. Every so often, the ground beneath me vibrated with the virtual equivalent of an aftershock, and the disks slid around or flipped over. But they always righted themselves and re-formed the line.

I followed them to an apparently arbitrary point on the plain where the line ended and thousands of disks crawled back and forth, running into and over one another to form a giant seething mass of yellow. In order to understand what I was seeing I caught and ate another disk.

Yes.

This was the point in Ahllan's internal architecture that most resembled the requisite networking point, the place they believed they needed to get to in order to beam the bits of information to wherever it was Loki wanted them to go. Of course, there was no way for them to fulfill their purpose because of Ahllan's lack of a MimirNet card.

Instead, they climbed and crawled over one another vainly trying to complete an impossible mission, forming a huge roiling heap that was further tumbled every few minutes by the continuing shocks as their brethren slowly destroyed the pillar holding up the sky. If they hadn't been so

likely to kill both Ahllan and me, I might almost have felt
sorry for them. What I actually felt was uncomfortably full.
That didn't stop me from devouring a third disk, then a
fourth.

Finally, though I didn't know the precise process Loki
had used to start this mess, I felt I had enough information
to formulate an answer to the problem. Not *the* answer—I
never have *the* answer; I'm a hacker and I do things on the
fly and by the baling-wire-and-string method. But I was
pretty sure I had something that would work if there was
enough time left to implement it.

Since I could tell Loki had used a spell formed of raw
chaos rather than one of the digital variety, my answer had
to be of the same sort. I closed my eyes and willed my insides to do things that insides normally didn't do. When I
finished, I barfed up my own Frisbee formed from the
shreds of the four I'd eaten. It was blue and slightly larger
than the yellow originals.

It slid over to the mass of information-laden disks and
settled onto the nearest, hiding it completely within its convex underskirt. A moment later, the blue disk seemed to
grow taller, a second blue skirt flaring beneath the first like
a ruffle. Then the ruffle dropped free, becoming a nearly
identical blue disk—the main difference being that this one
carried a few of Ahllan's stolen bits on its upper surface—
the yellow disk now converted by my efforts.

Each of the blue pair quickly moved on to engulf another yellow disk. In minutes, there were dozens of blue
disks eating and converting the yellow ones. Soon after,
some of them began moving back along the line toward
the cylinder—transforming the line beneath them as they
went—headed off to reassemble the pillar of the universe.

They couldn't do it quickly enough for my taste, as
something midway between snow and dust had recently
started drifting down from the ceiling. It appeared to be
coming from a myriad of narrow fractures. I was seriously
pushing my luck by remaining as long as I had, but I still

needed to do one more thing or the whole trip would be a waste—destroy the yellow disk feeder.

I did so by the simple expedient of stuffing one of the blue disks into its throat and holding it there until I felt the process freeze up. I probably could have found a more elegant way to manage it, but none faster. I have no idea how Loki started the whole thing, though the thought of his coughing up the first little yellow disk as a blob of chaos and spitting it at Ahllan had a symmetry to it that I rather liked. However it was done, I was finally ready to go.

So I clicked my digital heels together three times and told myself there was no place like home. Unfortunately, home hurt. Rather a lot. My eyes swam as I stared at the bitter steel driven through my palm.

"About time," said Tisiphone.

She deftly plucked the slender blade from my hand and whistled the kludge code Ahllan had put together in answer to the failure of Clotho's original athame spell in this pantheoverse. It stopped the bleeding but only dulled the pain.

I grinned at Tisiphone. "'Auntie Em! I'm so glad to be home again!'" It was that or scream.

"Have I mentioned recently how very odd you are?" asked Tisiphone.

"It might have come up once or twice," I said.

"So?" Tisiphone indicated Ahllan with her eyes.

"I found the problem, and I think I fixed it. I'm going to give her fifteen minutes, then try a reboot to see whether it worked. At least that part'll be easy with her in this shape." I patted the mainframe. "I don't know where her hard reboot switch would be as a troll."

"Then what?"

"Depends on what happens. If she comes back online, we'll have to see what she has to say. I'm hoping she has some idea of where we should look for Mel. If she won't boot . . . I don't know. I'm not willing to wait much longer." The fact that we hadn't gone after Melchior yet burned my heart, but I didn't like to think about what he'd have to say about it if we hadn't at least tried to help Ahllan first. "We might have to power her down and hope that keeps her stable till we get back."

I really hated the idea. Powering an AI down is dangerous, scary stuff. It leaves the body only one small step away from dead, and that seriously weakens the soul connection. I'd done it with Melchior once back before I'd learned about the existence of AI free will and souls—it was that or let a virus destroy him—and I'd practically gone out of my mind with worry even so. Doing it now with Ahllan, knowing the risks . . . I shook my head.

"That's about what I thought," said Tisiphone. "We'd better fuel up while we're waiting."

She headed for the kitchen, where she pulled out a couple of chunks of cheese and a loaf of bread. She ripped the latter in half and tossed it my way, along with a block of the cheese, then passed over a bottle of home-brewed beer. While I dug around for some condiments and a knife to convert my set of ingredients into sandwiches, Tisiphone simply tore into hers.

"I could make you a sandwich or three if you wanted," I said, though slicing the bread made my hand ache.

"Why bother?" She looked genuinely baffled as she bit a chunk out of the bread.

"The illusion of civilization? Better presentation? Mixed flavors?"

"For the last I can alternate bites," she replied, doing so. "The others are time wasters. The ideal food can be carried in one hand and eaten on the fly."

"If you're sure . . ." I started in on my sandwich.

"I'm sure." She tilted her head to one side and frowned thoughtfully. "I don't know why we keep having variations of this conversation."

"I don't know either. I guess I have a hard time believing anyone can think a meal's most important features are convenience and speed."

"Those are actually three and four. Minimum dietary nutrition is number one. Ease of preparation is two."

"Is there a five?" I asked. We hadn't wandered down this particular branch of the discussion before.

"Flavor, and no, there is no number six. The rest is frippery."

"So, you're not going to be big on long romantic dinners as we go forward."

"Oh, I'm fine with them. For me it's much more about the romance than the meal. I like good food well enough. It's just not something I find worth the effort for its own sake. Food is a means to an end—continued health. Fuel, in short."

I shook my head, finished up my meal, and checked the clock. Time for Ahllan's reboot. The mainframe made a sort of raspy sizzling noise when I forced a reboot, and all the telltales blinked briefly red before mostly flipping to green.

Numbers and letters flickered quickly across Ahllan's monitor as the minutes ticked by. Finally, a blinking cursor came up on an otherwise-blank screen.

Ahllan? I typed, feeling once again the stiffness and soreness of my athame hand.

Fate server unit 1-5-5-3-7, designation A-h-l-l-a-n, activation sequence initiated. What is your wish, Atropos?

"What does that mean?" asked Tisiphone, leaning down beside me. "Doesn't she recognize you?"

"I don't know. She may not have appropriate external sensors in this shape, in which case this could just be part of her standard activation protocol."

"Or?"

"Or she could have undergone some sort of major database failure—her body's come back, but her memories are gone."

"And with them, Ahllan?" she asked.

I just nodded.

CHAPTER EIGHT

■ ■ ■

Ahllan? I typed again. *This is Ravirn. What is the last thing you remember?*

Unit 15537 does not list "Ravirn" as an authorized user. Please enter user ID and password.

I'm not an authorized user, I typed. *I am an old friend. I do not possess an ID or password. Are you all right?*

Unit 15537 is not allowed to communicate with unauthorized users. Security protocols initiated. Step away from the machine immediately.

"Shit," I muttered.

Ahllan, this is Rav—"Ouch!" I leaped away from Ahllan's computer shape, blowing on freshly singed fingertips. "She bit me!"

"Only once," said Tisiphone, sliding between me and Ahllan and extending her wings protectively.

Maximum security response initiated, flashed across the screen. *Enter override in ten seconds or extreme measures will be deployed. 10. 9. 8.*

Tisiphone extended her claws.

"Hang on, Tisiphone. We don't know what's going on or what shape she's in. Let me try something else to . . ."

But even as I spoke, the mainframe began to jerk and twitch in the early throes of transformation back to troll shape. Which was probably part of the aforementioned extreme measures. Lovely. We were about to have a potentially memory-wiped and furious troll on our hands. She was well past her prime and certainly no match for Tisiphone, but it wasn't us I was worried about. It was her. There might be no way of gently subduing her, and the last thing I wanted was to have patched her up only to have to break her again.

Ahllan finished her transition. Seeing Tisiphone, she immediately raised her arms, and extended her own claws. Letting out a low, rumbling growl, she began slowly advancing on the Fury.

"Ahllan!" I yelled, ducking under Tisiphone's flaring wing to put myself into the narrowing space between them. "Wait!" Ahllan took another lurching step forward. "It's me, Melchior's partner, remember?"

"Ravirn, don't get in the way, damn it!" snapped Tisiphone. Picking me up one-handed, she tossed me a good ten feet to land on the couch.

"Ravirn?" asked Ahllan, stopping her advance. "What are you doing with Tisiphone? Where are . . . Oh." She blinked several times and shook her head like a bear with a bug in its ear. "Sorry. I'm a little foggy."

She slumped abruptly forward and would have fallen if Tisiphone hadn't caught her and carried her to the bed, murmuring as she went, "It's okay, Ahllan. You'll be fine. Just lie here and rest for a minute."

I picked myself off the couch and joined Tisiphone beside the bed. "Ahllan, are you all right? You gave us a bit of a fright there. What's the last thing you remember? Did you see what Loki did with Melchior?"

"Give her a moment," said Tisiphone. "She's had some shocks. Oh"—she lowered her voice to a harsh whisper—

"and don't ever cut in front of me in a dangerous situation like that again. That's twice today, and the third time is not the charm. In fact, fair warning here: if there is a third time, I will break your arm as a reminder for the future."

"Better I get hurt than her," I replied, surprised by the fierce belligerence I heard in my own voice.

A strained silence fell, interrupted finally when Ahllan cleared her throat rather vigorously.

"If you two are done with the dominance displays, this old troll would very much like to find out why she's got a blank place in her memory and how much she's missed. I take it from the mention of Loki that I don't get to write off my memories of the year since Shara dumped me here as a rather colorful systems malfunction?"

"I'm afraid not," I replied. "How much do you remember of the last couple of days?"

"Let me think." She sighed. "Even electronic memories start to get spotty over time. Data corruption is the bane of my old age. Hmmm. The three of you arrived, what, two days ago?"

"Just a bit over," I said.

"Then, I think I've got most of it. Right up to . . . you'd just started to call up Loki with Melchior and Laginn." She looked around worriedly. "Where are they?"

"With Loki," I said, grimly. I quickly filled her in. "We were hoping you could tell us something about what happened there at the end."

"I'm sorry," said Ahllan. "It's all gone."

Tisiphone snarled something unintelligible and started pacing again. I had a hard time not joining in both activities. Instead, I knelt beside Ahllan.

"I'm sorry, too, but—"

"You're going to have to leave now," said Ahllan. "I know. Frankly, if you'd asked me, I'd have told you to go after Melchior rather than hanging around here trying to save an old lady from a fate that's coming soon no matter what you do. But then, if I'd been able to tell you that, you wouldn't have needed me to, and since I wasn't, I'm not going to second-guess you now.

"But don't wait a moment longer on my account. Melchior's my son, or as close as possible given we were both built rather than born. I'd even thought I might eventually hand over the reins of the underground to him back before our secret was blown." She smiled. "I've never been prouder of him than the day he made the Fates acknowledge our independence and saved your life doing it. I may not be in the best shape I've ever been in, but I'm a survivor, and Melchior needs you. I'll make do."

Driven by an impulse I didn't want to examine too closely, I bent and kissed her withered cheek. "Thanks, Ahllan. We'll find him."

"Go."

"Good-bye," I said, and got to my feet.

Tisiphone took my place, kneeling on the floor beside Ahllan, her thighs inches from the darkly stained oak of the futon platform.

"I owe you an apology," she said. "For the destruction my sisters and I visited on your home, I am sorry."

Ahllan looked completely gobsmacked; but then, she didn't have the advantage of having heard Tisiphone express similar sentiments earlier.

"And you are forgiven," Ahllan finally said. "At my age, I know a thing or two about remorse, and remorse from the legendarily remorseless is a precious gift."

"For the giver as much as for the recipient," replied Tisiphone. "I thank you for your forgiveness, and though I cannot thank whatever whim of Necessity sent me here when I am so clearly needed at home, I'm glad I had this chance." A half beat of her wings flicked her to her feet, where she turned away from Ahllan and toward me. She grinned then. "Let us find Loki and teach *him* a thing or two about regret."

Now, that was *classic* Tisiphone.

So was what she did to Loki's miniature fieldstone faerie ring a few minutes later. It was far too dangerous to leave such a thing open in the middle of a tourist attraction where some poor human might stumble into it and end up who knew where.

Tisiphone let slip the reins of her temper. The fires of her hair and wings quickly grew as bright and hot as the heart of a foundry, forcing me back and away from her.

"Watch this," she said, her voice simultaneously holding glee and anger as she spread her wings to their full extent.

I nodded, though she was burning so brightly I had to slit my eyes to see her. The white column of her body amidst the flames looked like a pale birch in the heart of a forest fire. As such a tree inevitably must, she slowly toppled, falling backwards onto the brown lawn. When she touched the dead grass, there came a cacophony of sizzles and "pops," and a great burst of smoke as the dry vegetation flash-burned.

Coughing and choking, I stumbled a few feet farther back. "What *are* you doing?"

My only answer was an amused chuckle from the heart of the smoke. A moment later, her fires once again banked, Tisiphone stepped out of the rapidly dissipating cloud. I shook my head bemusedly.

"Wait for it," she said, still chuckling evilly.

The smoke finished clearing, then I had to laugh, too. The faerie ring was gone, replaced by a deep char mark in the shape of Tisiphone's right wing. Opposite lay the matching mark of her left wing, with a blackened stripe between the two where her long hair had burned away more of the ground cover—the whole making a dark mirror of a child's snow angel.

As I said, *classic* Tisiphone.

We were still no closer to finding Melchior, but I'd had another idea in that regard, one that involved a different use of faerie rings. We retired to the ring within the miniature of Shakespeare's home to pursue it.

"How is this going to go again?" Tisiphone asked, as we prepared to step into the ring.

"Hopefully, the same way things worked when I found my way to Raven House."

Then I'd asked the faerie-ring network to carry me to a place of refuge. Now I wanted it to help me find Melchior. I might not be the Raven here, but I was still a power of chaos. Taking Tisiphone's hand in my own, I stepped into the ring. As had become the norm, I had the experience of being in that one and all other rings concurrently. There were thousands, perhaps tens of thousands. In just the day and a half since I'd built the first, Loki or some mechanism he'd set up had created a vast and expanding network.

Take me to Melchior, I willed the rings. Nothing happened. *Help me find him!* Nope. *I need information. . . .*

But I wasn't going to find it there apparently. I started to lead Tisiphone back out of the ring, then paused. Something new had occurred to me. Could I perhaps use the rings another way, as a sort of lens? I focused my attention outward rather than inward, trying to peer out into the locations containing the myriad rings I simultaneously occupied.

The effect was immediate, intoxicating, and headache-inducing. A fly's eye has thousands of individual lenses, each with its own cornea and photoreceptors and each of which brings in an image of the surrounding area. What I was seeing was akin to what a fly saw, with two major exceptions. One, each image came from a different place. Two, I didn't have the right set of tools to process the information. The fly's brain comes equipped with special neurological software and hardware that's evolved to take all of the images and merge them into a wide-angle composite view of its surroundings. For the fly, the system is a highly advanced visual processor optimized by evolution for its needs. For me, it was optical gibberish and an instant skull-splitting migraine.

My head wanted to come apart, but I refused to give up. There had to be some way I could make this work. There had to be. I tried letting my attention flicker from image to image. Better, but still not that useful. There were simply too many for me to manage in any reasonable amount of time. Maybe if I went the other way? Tried for a gestalt vision as I sometimes did while hacking—envisioning the structure of the code as a sort of three-dimensional crystal? Could that work? I tried to both look and not look, to see all the myriad views while not actually focusing on any of them.

For long seconds, the only thing I achieved was an intensification of my headache. But then little details began to pop, mostly details of absence—no Melchior there or there or there—but also points of presence—a rook on a twisted oak branch in that scene or a crow pecking at roadkill in this one. More and more I was seeing spots of black: crows, jackdaws, magpies, rooks, ravens—the entire family *Corvidae* in all its feathered glory. No, not ravens. Ravens, the Ravens of the Norse mythos.

Or Norse MythOS. The rules of magic for this place and time, its mystical operating system, treated my internal Raven differently than the one back home. Here Hugin and Munin gathered information for the king of the gods. Odin's Ravens. Thought. Memory. Intuition? Or Impulse? On a burst of the latter, I pushed my awareness outward, tried to connect it with the dots of black that speckled my gestalt vision of the faerie-ring network, and made . . . CONTACT.

I vanished into *we*. *Man* became *many*. Raven the individual dispersed into ravens, the Flock—a biological parallel-computing cluster in the mold of the UNIX-based Beowulf system. The information flow increased dramatically, but the difficulty of processing it vanished. Instead of trying to see ten thousand vistas through one pair of eyes and process them through a single brain, each part of my extended consciousness dealt with its own surroundings, forwarding only that portion of the scene that was relevant back to the central processor—me.

Ringscape after ringscape was discarded from the list of

possible interest until one alone remained, a rook's-eye view. In it a red-haired giant of a man knelt beside a traditional mushroom faerie ring in the midst of a pine wood. We/I tried to get a better look at him, intensifying our/my/the rook's gaze. As if in response to that focus, the man looked upward, meeting our/my/the rook's eyes, and nodded a greeting.

"Intuition," he said. "We should talk."

The voice was as familiar as the face—a face I'd seen a thousand times and one that flat-out didn't belong here. Zeus.

Cognitive dissonance.

Fundamentally incompatible ideas crashed together inside the flock mind, shattering it back into its component pieces. I fell out of we, but not before locking down my destination and conundrum. With a flick of my will I shifted us from the ring where we had entered to the one where a god who had no right to be here waited for us.

"What the hell do you think you're trying . . . to . . . pull . . . ?" My voice had started the sentence out with a yell, but by the time I reached the end, it had trailed into a confused whisper.

"Zeus?" I said, though I knew the answer even as I spoke.

This was not the thunder god I knew. Not Zeus, king of the gods of Olympus. If nothing else, Zeus's eyes had never been so bloodshot, not even after the heartiest night of partying. Yet . . . the echoes of that god were plain in this god's face and manner—I had no doubt that I faced another god.

"Who are you?" whispered Tisiphone from beside me. I found the stunned wonder in her voice reassuring—a sign my confusion was fully justified.

The man in front of us looked from me to Tisiphone and back again, repeatedly. His grin grew with each pass until he finally burst out laughing, a deep, infectious boom of a laugh that rolled like thunder—Zeus's laugh almost, but maddeningly not quite. Little bolts of lightning flickered in his beard when he laughed, just as they did for Zeus.

"Firebird and blackbird, what a perfect pair," he said in a voice that was and was not Zeus's. Then he laughed his thunderous laugh again. "And both agog in the noonday sun. Do you really not recognize me, then, flame and shadow?"

"No," I said, though I was beginning to have the distinct feeling I should.

"Does this help?" He tapped an iron-gloved finger on the great-headed hammer hanging from a blackened metal hammer loop on his thick belt, producing a dull "clank."

I shook my head.

"Thor?"

"Oh. Oh! OH!" Suddenly I had it, and why he looked so much like Zeus, too.

If it hadn't been for the brain crash his Zeus resemblance had induced, I'd have had it a lot sooner. Thor! God of Thunder and wielder of the hammer with the unpronounceable name. No wonder he looked so much like Zeus. They were in the same business. The resemblance *was* uncanny.

Both were big, muscular men—seven feet or more and broad-shouldered. They could have easily worn each other's clothes. Both had thick beards, though Zeus's was a reddish gold, and Thor's was a gold-tinged red. They both had broad, open faces and curly hair.

There was one huge difference, though—their eyes. Zeus's are perpetually wide open and vacant, making him look somewhat dim and naive. It's a lie of course; he's a shrewd old bastard and deeply jaded. Thor's were . . . distracting. At first glance they looked horribly bloodshot, the eyes of a drunk hitting the end of a three-day binge. But on closer examination, the red threads no longer looked like blood. They looked like lightning, constantly moving and flashing and forking. I'd have bet money that in the dark they gave off even more light than mine.

The two gods' attitudes were different, too. Zeus is a

joker of the hail-fellow-well-met variety and his own best audience—he laughs constantly. But it's an act, a hard, clever soul playing at gentle dimness to take in the rubes. Thor laughed easily, too, or at least gave the impression of it, but it came off as the good-natured laugh of a wise man who enjoyed life to the full despite its kinks and twists.

Gods are bigger than life, and their personalities reach well beyond the bounds of their skins. To spend time around a god is—to a certain extent—to spend time within the god, and this one felt homey.

"I knew it would come to you eventually," Thor said, just as my cascading realizations started to settle down. "*Intuition* indeed."

"I take it from that, that you know of me as well," I said.

Thor nodded. "Odin is my father. Though he didn't mention the lady when last we talked." He indicated Tisiphone with a jerk of his chin. "Neither her name nor her beauty nor any mention of her nature. What, and who, are you, my dear?" Thor pulled the iron glove off his right hand and offered it in greeting.

Tisiphone inclined her head but didn't take the hand. "I am Tisiphone, sometimes called Vengeance, and *no one's* 'dear.' Especially not the son of the god who kidnapped and imprisoned my lover."

"Ah, yes, that." Thor chuckled and left his hand extended. "That was not the wisest thing my father has ever done, and I would have counseled him against it. But then, his inability to *see* Raven here has blinded him to more than just the future. I won't apologize for a mistake that wasn't mine, but I won't try to repeat it either. On that you have my word. Come, step out of that ring, the both of you, and talk with me awhile."

"What have we to talk about?" asked Tisiphone, impatience plain in her tone.

"Loki for one," replied Thor. "At least I suspect we have something to talk about there since you are standing in the midst of a devilish bit of new magic he's brewed up, and no one who's ever had dealings with him has done so without ultimately coming to regret it." He turned his gaze my way. "Though, I must admit that your eyes suggest you might have more in common with Loki the Trickster than would make me entirely happy."

Tisiphone laughed and finally shook Thor's hand. "There, you may have hit the mark. Ravirn tends to leave a trail of not-entirely-happy souls wherever he goes as well. Come on, Ravirn, we've got to find Melchior, and from the sounds of things, Thor is an expert on the Trickster." She winked at me. "The *other* Trickster, that is."

I humphed, but followed Tisiphone out of the faerie ring. She had a point, a number of them, actually, though I was nowhere near as annoying as Loki. At least, I really hoped I wasn't. I was honest enough to admit that Hades, the Fates, and at least one of Tisiphone's sisters might see things very differently.

Thor extended his hand to me as well and with a bit of an anticipatory wince I put mine in his. Several amazingly long seconds later he returned it to me, somewhat smaller and the worse for wear—because of intense compression— but still basically intact.

"Come," said Thor, "sit with me by the fire and we'll talk."

He led us a brief way through the trees to a place where a goat-drawn chariot sat in a small clearing. There was no fire when we arrived, but Thor fixed that by the simple expedient of raising his hammer and pointing it at a fallen log. Lightning shot from its head and instantly ignited the wood. Then Thor slid the hammer, now glowing a dull, angry red, back into the metal loop on his belt.

"I'd cook you up a bit of roast goat," he said, pointing at the chariot, "but there's a lot of daylight left, and I may need them to take me somewhere before tomorrow morning."

"That's all right," I said, though I was more than a bit confused by the offer. "We haven't really got a whole lot of time for things like dinner at the moment either." Besides, I hated goat—a matter of some contention at family parties. "Speaking of which . . ."

"Loki," said Thor. "I presume you've a bone to pick with him since his was the name that conjured you out of your ring. What has he done to *you*?"

"He kidnapped my best friend," I growled.

"We're hunting him now in hopes of making a rescue," added Tisiphone.

"Typical." Thor shook his head. "Loki is the trial of the Aesir, and one we too often fail, I think." He tapped the still-glowing hammer. "I would not have Mjolnir were it not for Loki, nor would Odin have his spear or Frey his great golden boar. All were part of the Trickster's payment for stealing the hair of my wife. Mighty gifts, and we will have dire need of them come the hour of Ragnarok, but leaving the thief his life was a dear price. Dearer, I think, than Odin—who sees deep into the future—will yet say."

Thor stopped speaking and glowered into the fire, missing my nod. I was sure he was right. The more time I spent here, the more I remembered from the Norse myths I'd read in that long-ago class, though I'd have happily committed nine kinds of larceny to get my hands on a copy of the textbook and a couple of hours to reread it. Unlike my own family's story, the Norse gods' tale had a distinct and unpleasant ending, one involving Loki's leading an army of giants against Asgard. Of course that left two questions begging.

One: Did they know about it? Odin had certainly seemed to when he spoke of Ragnarok and his family's dark ending, while Thor did not. Denial? Selective memory?

And two: Was the war to come *the* future? Or *a* future? Fate could be a slippery thing, or at least that was my experience. Of course, how much that experience meant in this place with its chaos that was not my chaos and binary that was not my binary was an open question.

Thor finally looked up. "One day Loki is our greatest ally. The next, our fiercest enemy. No surprise, I guess." He pointed at the burning log. "Loki is Fire, aiding and destroying by turns. But then"—he glanced from me to Tisiphone—"I think you may know something of fire. Tell me a story. If it is a good one, I will help you find Loki and rescue your friend. If it is not, I will tell you one in return, and we may part ways in friendship."

"What sort of story do you want to hear?" I asked.

"Tell me of the magic rings that Loki spreads across our land. Tell me also of the Raven, Intuition, and his eyes so like and yet unlike the Trickster, Loki's. Give me the tale of a blackbird and the firebird who travels with him."

"It's a long story, and I haven't the time to tell it all," I said, stalling.

I didn't think he was going to much like my role in the faerie-ring proliferation or a number of other things. At the same time, I didn't think lying was going to work very well. Nor skipping over the relevant bits. I looked again at the bulging muscles and the forking lightning of Thor's eyes. Loki was a true god, one of the great powers of this MythOS; if we could convince Thor to give us a hand, we'd be in a much better state to demand Melchior's release. I sighed. Best to start with the worst and work my way up from there.

"The faerie rings are my fault," I said. "A magic I brought with me from another world, or worlds, really. One that lies beyond Ginnungagap—" The void of ice and fire that was the Norse answer to the Primal Chaos. "Loki entrapped me in a ring of fire, and I transformed it to escape." I sketched in what had happened with Loki at the miniature of Shakespeare's house. "I didn't realize he would be able to use the magic himself, though I should have, and intentions count less than results, I'm afraid."

"Go on," said Thor. "Tell me more about this other world of yours."

"Ever hear the name Zeus?" I asked.

"It sounds vaguely familiar, but no more than that."

"Then I'll come back to it. How do you feel about Skuld?"

"The Norn? I try to stay well away from her and her puppet-master sisters."

"I'll start there, since I'm not real fond of them myself. Your Norns are very like the Fates of my own pantheoverse. In fact, Skuld claimed them as sisters, an idea I hate, since that would make Skuld something of a great-aunt. Since I've already got two that like me even less than I like them, that seems a major step in the wrong direction."

As quickly as I could, I told him of my lineage and how I came into conflict with the Fates when they tried to steal free will from mankind. Thor growled at the thought, which I read as a good sign. I explained how in the conflict a dear friend had died—the webgoblin Shara—and how I had ventured into Hades to rescue her.

At that Thor clapped me on the shoulder hard enough to stagger me. "Good man. Just so did Bragi bring Idun back from Hel. That you would dare the underworld for a friend speaks well of you. Say on. What happened next?"

"Well, things didn't work out quite as I'd hoped."

I spoke then of my meeting with Persephone and how the virus the goddess had written nearly destroyed the mweb and with it the whole multiverse. From there I went on to Persephone's rescue and how the damage to Necessity and the mweb had allowed the goddess Nemesis to escape into the body of my cousin Dairn and in turn of my duel with her and the further injuries to Necessity.

Somewhere in there I noticed how quiet Tisiphone had grown and that she did not choose to add to the story. Not surprising, I suppose, considering how much of the damage to her mother, Necessity, could be laid at my feet. To say nothing of the bits of unidentifiable claw and the blood that had come through into our world and whatever they might portend. Since there was nothing I could do about that, I hurried through my encounter with the abacuses of Necessity and whatever had happened there to bring us here.

Finally, I related what had happened in the two days since we had arrived in Midgard. The whole took close to an hour, and one I'd rather have spent searching for Melchior, but we could really use the kind of help Thor could give. When I finished, Thor sat quietly for another couple of minutes, finally nodding.

"There is much in your story that I would like to know more about, but if we are to do your friend and familiar much good, then we should move quickly." He leaped to his feet and in three strides stood at the reins of his chariot. "Come."

"Then you'll help?" I asked.

Thor nodded. "There was much left untold in your story, but no lies. You are a strange creature by my standards, a Trickster in the same mold as Loki, and yet as unlike him as the hound who guards the cattle is unlike the wolf who would devour them. I see a hero in you, one the Valkyries would be proud to choose from the field, though you will deny the charge, I think. You seek the right, and so I will help you."

Boy did I have him snowed. I turned to Tisiphone and raised a sardonic eyebrow, inviting her to share the irony of anyone calling *me* a hero. She just smiled a brittle smile and tapped her nose in the classic charades acknowledgment of the correct answer to a clue. I rolled my eyes. I was many things, probably chief among them a pain in the posterior of Fate, but a hero was simply not on the menu. Too many of my successes are also disasters and vice versa for that.

Still smiling, Tisiphone took my arm and led me to join Thor. "Our chariot awaits."

As soon as we stepped aboard, Thor cracked a thin whip. The goats started to pull us forward and up into the sky. Sparks flew from their hooves as they climbed, as though they were hammers of flint pounding away on an invisible steel road. More sparks flew from their teeth when they started grinding away at their cuds. Heavy gray clouds began to form around us as we got higher. That was when I remembered two things. One, this was the chariot of the God of *Storms*. And two, I *hate* flying under anything but my own power, and even that I'm not too thrilled about.

CHAPTER NINE

"You can let go of the railing now," said Tisiphone.

"Not until we're firmly on the ground," I replied, though my athame hand ached like Atlas's shoulders after an earthquake—and that despite our recent trip through the faerie rings.

The chariot had descended out of the storm clouds and into the snow-dappled air above the northwestern shore of Iceland, an outthrust claw of land scalloped like an oak leaf and frosted with white along the high ridges of stone that formed its skeleton. Despite flying in the heart of our own personal blizzard, with all the turbulence you'd expect in such a situation, I'd thrown up only twice. *Go, me.* To make matters worse, I was flying with two iron-stomached and danger-loving divines.

"Spits in the teeth of death, but can't abide a bit of heavy air," said Thor with a grin. "What kind of hero are you?"

"I. Am. Not. A. Hero," I growled through clenched teeth. "End of story." To prevent us going any further down that particular path, I asked him, "Why Iceland?"

"Though it is not generally spoken of in the sagas, this is where the island of Lyngvi lies in the hidden lake of Áms-vartnir."

"Ámsvartnir?" asked Tisiphone. "That's a jawbreaker."

"It means red-black," replied Thor, "a lake of lava underneath Askja Volcano, and the place of Fenris's binding."

"He gets around a lot for a wolf that's been bound," said Tisiphone.

"Neither he nor his father can break or remove the cord that ties Fenris to this island, nor pull the sword out from his jaws. But Loki is the lord of loopholes and, through means we've yet to thwart, he extends the stretch of that cord far beyond our intent."

"The silver cord," I said, "the one Odin caused to contract somehow."

"Gleipnir the Entangler," agreed Thor. "It's made from cat's footfalls and mountain roots among other things, a steely chain in a silky shape, and apparently to no avail." He sighed and shook his head. "Actually, the last's not true, Fenris is bound still, and he can't leave Midgard, but it's terribly frustrating to see him moving about beyond the edges of this island."

"Could we go back to the part about the volcano?" I asked.

It was a question that seemed much more immediate, seeing as our goat-drawn chariot, after crossing very quickly over a good bit of snow-covered emptiness, was now heading straight for a huge steaming crater on the side of a low mountain.

"Better I just show you," said Thor. "It's just ahead anyw—" His words stopped abruptly, replaced by something midway between the growl of a bear and distant thunder. "I've got him now!" he bellowed. Then he cracked the whip, and the goats sped up, redoubling the sparks flying from their hooves.

We plunged straight toward the heart of the crater. I tried not to throw up as the bottom dropped out of my world.

"What's going on?" I hissed through clenched teeth.

I couldn't see anything besides steam and snow and gloom.

"They're playing fetch in the bottom of the crater," replied Tisiphone, whose eyes had a hunter's sharpness. "Loki and Fenris, that is."

"I'm going to land this chariot right on top of them," growled Thor.

The world got suddenly darker as the high walls of the crater cut off the light of the low-hanging northern sun. Between that and the storm and the steam, I was practically blind.

"Blast!" Thor brought a great fist down on the lip of the chariot so hard the whole thing jumped like a hooked fish. My tightly clutching hands stung like I'd gotten hold of the wrong part of a power supply. "He's running." The chariot veered sharply to the left and started to climb up out of the crater again.

"Does he have Melchior with him?" I asked, blowing on the fingertips of my right hand.

"No," said Tisiphone.

I made a snap decision based entirely on intuition and not at all on how very much I wanted out of that chariot. Not one little bit. Nope. Okay, so I wasn't fooling anybody, myself included. I still thought it was a good idea.

"Why don't we have a few choice words with Fenris while you handle Loki?" I said.

"Done," said Thor. "Fury, can you carry two?"

"As easily as one," replied Tisiphone.

"Then do it."

Before I had a chance to insert myself into a debate that had suddenly gone in a rather alarming direction, Tisiphone caught me in her arms and spread her wings to their widest extent. It was a bit like opening a parachute. We stopped. The chariot didn't. My one-handed grip on the rail tore loose painfully, then we were falling straight down into the crater.

When we were a scant dozen feet from the ground, Tisiphone backwinged. It slowed us just enough. We hit hard, but not hard enough to break anything, landing beside the waters of a steaming lake. The gray plumes rising from its surface spoke of hot springs reaching deep into the earth below, perhaps even passing near the hidden fires of Ámsvartnir. I was torn between being irritated with Tisiphone for the manner of our departure from the chariot and grateful to her for getting me back down to the ground. I hadn't quite decided which way to jump when Fenris came bounding toward us, growling and making muffled barking noises.

Tisiphone partially extended her claws, and I half drew my sword cane—I didn't want this to turn into a fight if it didn't have to, but damned if I was going to face a god-wolf unarmed. Especially one who'd helped kidnap Melchior. As Fenris drew closer, the reason for the muffled nature of his barks became apparent. Clamped very firmly around his muzzle was a disembodied hand. The big poodle finally skidded to a halt about ten feet short of us.

"M-Laginn, m-let me glo!" mumbled Fenris through his living muzzle. "M-not gonna vbite 'nybody." He growled again. "Not m-right 'way, 'nyway."

Though he kept growling for several seconds, he put his butt firmly on the ground, perhaps in a gesture of peace. I wasn't having any and stomped forward to glare down at him from only a few feet away.

"What the hell have you done with Melchior?" I demanded.

"M-nuthin'," he grumbled, looking down.

"Bullshit!" I yelled, moving even closer.

Fenris stood, shaking himself like a dog shedding water, and changed shape, becoming the giant wolf once again. As he did so, Laginn's grip slipped dangerously—the hand simply couldn't accommodate the greater size of the wolf's muzzle. Tossing a head bigger than a beer keg, he flipped

Laginn into the steaming water. The hand hit with a splash and sank.

Looming over me, Fenris bared his teeth and laid his ears back in an expression that held not the slightest hint of humanity. The broadsword in his lower jaw quivered as he growled, and blood slowly dripped from its hilt to the ground. I couldn't help but wonder how much that hurt.

"Are you calling me a liar?" His voice was deep and dangerous, a naked threat. "Think carefully, little Raven."

"What would *you* call you?" I was too mad to back down, despite the fact that I was standing quite literally in the wolf's shadow.

"Ravirn," said Tisiphone, catching hold of my shoulder, "maybe I should handle this."

Her grip was as firm as a steel clamp, and I could tell she was preparing to throw me aside.

"I don't think so," I replied. "This is between me and Fenris." I glared up into his eyes and asked my question again, spacing the words out so that there could be no mistake as to my meaning. "What—would—you—call—you?"

The wolf chuckled, low and evil, though he looked pained as he did so. "I'll say this for you, little bird, you're either bold or a fool."

"Both," said Tisiphone, more to herself than aloud. "He's definitely both." Her hold on my shoulder tightened.

At this point, a tiny splash announced Laginn's return to shore.

"Are you going to answer my question?" I asked Fenris, ignoring the disembodied hand as it skittered up to stand between us.

His ears lifted, and his bared teeth suddenly became a wolfy grin. "Were I you, I'd probably call me a liar . . . though I'd be as wrong as you are." He chuckled again, then winced. "Damn sword."

"Why do you leave it there?" I asked, feeling sorry for

him despite my anger over Melchior. I wasn't ready to ex-
onerate Fenris yet, or anything like that, but his words of
denial had a ring of truth to them.

"I like the way it looks. *Très* junkyard dog." Fenris
rolled his eyes. "It's because the damn thing's enchanted so
that only the hand of one of the gods who set it there can
pull it free."

Inspiration struck. Reaching down, I picked Laginn up
by the wrist and lifted the hand so that its fingers touched
the hilt of the sword.

"Like this one?" I asked.

"It can't be that easy," said Fenris, looking as stunned as
he might if he'd been struck between the eyes with Thor's
hammer.

"Why not?" I asked. "Every magic ever wrought has a
loophole." Finding them was my own special divinity.

Laginn closed its grip on the sword, and together we
pulled. At first it didn't budge, but then ever so slowly it
began to move. When it finally pulled free, a great gout of
blood followed, splattering the stones, my boots, and Fenris, who howled a high, wild note of mixed agony and pro-
found relief.

"I. Feel. Better!" cried the great wolf, leaping into the
air, then chasing his tail when he landed.

While he was doing that I was having one of the odder
experiences of my life as Laginn ran the sword we'd with-
drawn through an impossibly quick series of cuts and parries, dragging my arm along for the ride. Well, no, that
doesn't quite explain it. Somehow, Laginn was using my
hand and arm as though they were a part of him, so that I
made all the moves the hand wanted me to. Very, very
strange feeling, that. Finally, Laginn dropped the sword, and
in turn, I dropped Laginn. At that, Fenris picked up the
sword with his teeth and tossed it into the lake.

"You have no idea how much I've wanted to do that for
the last thousand years or so. I well and truly owe you one.

Which means I should probably reunite you with your goblin pack mate."

"I thought you said you hadn't done anything with him," I replied, weighting the words with sarcasm.

"I haven't. It was my father's doing, and one I'd have argued against if he'd given me the chance. The goblin is part of your pack, and packs shouldn't be separated. It's wrong. It's wrong when Odin keeps me bound away from mine with this"—he tugged at the silver cord, a look composed of equal parts lonely hunger and hatred crossing his face—"and it's wrong when Loki does it to you. Come."

He spun in place and started to lead us across the shallow crater of the volcano. Nothing so big should be able to move as fast as Fenris had with that turn, or walk as quietly as he did now. Laginn scampered along beside me tippy-fingered. The path Fenris took led us back along the line of the silver cord, which retracted itself as he went. In a place where the steam hung so thick that I could barely see, Fenris turned into a narrow slit in the crater wall, one partially hidden by a fold in the rock.

The path led downward, deep into the earth. After perhaps a hundred yards, there came a sharp turn to the right, then another to the left. Beyond, the narrow cave opened out into a broad, well-lit chamber. The floor had been flattened and polished to a high luster. Not twenty feet from our point of entry a thick glass wall cut the big cavern in two and barred our way. In front of it was a huge stone desk and an equally huge receptionist.

Ten feet tall if she was an inch, the receptionist wore a teal power suit and had long blond hair tied back in a tight braid. When we entered, she was turned to her left and typing away on a projected keyboard of golden light. In front of her was a wide-screen display scaled like the rest of the setup and framed in something like blue obsidian.

As we got closer, she spun her huge office chair to face our way. She was beautiful in a just stepped out of a billboard for office supplies sort of way—both in her air-brushed polish and her size. Then she smiled, revealing a perfect row of sharp teeth that could have been borrowed from Fenris.

"Mr. Ulfr." She nodded to Fenris. "Is there anything I can do for you?"

"Just buzz us through, Grýla."

The giantess nodded and reached a hand under her desk. In response, a beam of red light shot from a pyramid of cobalt glass on the desk, striking the center of the glass wall and turning a tall rectangle of it a translucent red. Fenris walked straight into the rectangle and sort of splashed through, as though it were made from particularly tenacious Jell-O. The way it felt as I passed through reinforced that mental image. The light turned off as soon as Tisiphone joined us, and the glass reverted to simple, solid clarity.

"Welcome to Rune," said Fenris as he led us through the chamber and into a nearby hall. "Loki CEO, CIO, COO, and every other C-blank-O you can think of."

"Why does that not surprise me?" I asked. "What's the logo? A gold coin with his face on it?"

Fenris laughed, then in a perfect, if pedantic, imitation of his father's voice, said, "We're a post-logo operation. Our elegance of design is all the signature we need. The instant anyone sees one of our devices, they'll know that no one else could possibly have made it."

"Not seriously," I said.

"Yuh-huh." Fenris grinned. "It's actually not such a wild claim when you remember that our only competition in the magical computers market is Odin's MimirSoft."

"There is that." I nodded, thinking of the beige box server farm within Yggdrasil.

"Does that mean that Loki's machines can access MimirNet?" asked Tisiphone, looking suddenly interested and very predatory.

"Sadly, no," replied Fenris. He shifted into Loki voice again. "Odin won't license his networking cards, and he fries our cloned versions as fast as they surface on Mimir-Net." He sighed. "Basically that means our market is all the giants, dwarves, elves, and whatnot looking for a stand-alone machine that can only access the human Internet."

Just then we passed a heavy, steel, bulkhead-type door through which the silver cord passed.

Fenris paused and indicated it with his nose. "Steam plant. The whole place runs on volcano power. Do you want the full tour? We don't get many visitors besides the occasional Jotun looking for a job." He sounded plaintive, lonely really.

"Only the stuff between here and wherever Melchior is," I replied.

"Pack comes first, and no matter the cost." He nodded approvingly. "That was what kept me from biting your head off when you called me a liar. You were doing it for the right reason." He sighed and moved his nose in a circle that took in the whole facility. "That's what all this is about, you know. Dad trying to build me a substitute pack since I can't be out in the world with my real one." Loneliness burned in his eyes, loneliness and hunger. "Damn Odin to eternal torment."

Reaching down carefully, Fenris caught the cord in his teeth. "I'll have to walk carefully and slowly after this. The harder I fight against the leash, the tighter it becomes. Hang on a sec while I buy myself a little slack." He snapped his jaws together repeatedly in a strange staccato rhythm that held undertones of this world's distorted version of binary.

"There," he said, finally, "that should do it." Still holding the cord between his teeth, he started off down the hall, walking in a very slow and measured way. "It's a bit like trying to loosen up a seat belt right after a sudden stop, actually. Or at least that's what Loki says."

As we went, he pointed his nose at various doors and barked out the functions of the areas beyond. Mostly it was a series of research labs and clean rooms for assembly of assorted Rune products, all populated by Jotuns of varying size and aspect.

The only exception was the employee break room, which for reasons not entirely clear was labeled FROGGY BOTTOM CAFÉ and filled with an even odder assortment of characters than the rest of the place. I particularly wondered about what appeared to be an enormous marmot smoking a hookah, but got distracted before I could ask about it when Fenris pointed out a door labeled RUNENET and said, "Here."

It was only as Fenris reached a paw out and pulled on the lever that I realized all of the doors had those in place of knobs—no doubt for that very reason. Chilly air blasted out of the small foyer—a positive pressure air lock—suggesting a big computer facility beyond the next set of doors.

Nor was I disappointed. The place was filled with hardware every bit as slick as Loki's microcomputer. The servers were four-inch-thick triangles, blue and featureless and translucent, like slices of cobalt volcanic glass. All the blinking telltale lights were on the racks, which were themselves equally beautiful, slender black poles into which the computers mounted point first. The servers wound from floor to ceiling around the poles like the treads of a spiral staircase, only cantilevered somehow so that they simply hung in space, supported only at the point where they met the racks. It was gorgeous and strange and stunning, and yet it felt wrong—quiet and lifeless and empty.

"What is this place?" asked Tisiphone, her tone betraying some of the same uneasiness I felt.

"It's the Rune parallel computing supercluster, the heart of RuneNet," replied Fenris. "It's supposed to provide all the people Odin won't serve with an interworld network."

"But?" asked Tisiphone.

"But we can't seem to get it to work right," he replied. "We're not—"

He had more to say, but I didn't hear any of it. I'd spotted Melchior. He lay bound and unconscious on a worktable off to our left. A two-headed giant in a clean-room bunny suit was leaning over him. It had an ethernet cable and seemed to be arguing with itself about where to plug it in—not that Melchior was ethernet compatible.

Anger exploded in my belly like a swallowed grenade. Moving without thought or hesitation, I caught hold of the giant's bunny suit at the back of its waist and jerked at the same time I kicked the back of its right knee. It let out a double-mouthed shriek as it went down, landing hard on its back. Before it could move to right itself, I'd placed the tip of my sword against the soft spot just below its breastbone. In response it put its hands out to the sides, palms up.

"Touch him again and die," I said through clenched teeth.

"I wouldn't advise that," said Fenris, the dangerous growl back in his voice. "My substitute pack may be broken, but it is still my pack. You threaten even its least member at your peril. Withdraw your blade."

I didn't move. Rage filled my core, fiery and bright and oh so hard to contain. I wanted to release it on someone. Anyone.

"Ravirn," said Tisiphone, her tone quiet and deliberate.

"Yes." I kept my eyes fixed on the giant at my feet.

"Fight or stand down?"

It was a simple question simply asked. I could hear her willingness to follow my lead either way, and I knew how hard it must be for her to surrender the initiative to me. Tisiphone is not a shy flower. For that matter, for Fenris, choosing to warn me rather than simply take my head off was probably another hard choice. Could I do any less? With a sigh and not a little effort, I put up my sword.

I turned to Fenris. "I'm sorry. I didn't think."

"I know," said the wolf. "And so, you live."

The giant scooted backwards on hands and butt. "Should I be sounding an alarm or something?" asked the left head, speaking in a deep male baritone.

"Or ripping heads off?" asked the right, a hopeful feminine alto.

"Neither," said Fenris. "Why don't you take a coffee break."

"That works for me," said the male, as the giant got to its feet.

"Wimp," said the female.

"Slacker, actually," replied the male.

"Loser either way," said the female, "just like Dad always said."

The male opened his mouth again, but didn't say anything as Fenris shot the pair a very hard look.

"We were just leaving," said the female. "Weren't we, brother dear?"

The male head nodded, and the pair ducked out of the room. I crossed to the table, where Tisiphone was already slicing through Melchior's bonds.

No sooner did they fall away than he blinked his eyes open. "Wha' happen'?"

"Loki happened," I said. "Are you all right? What do you remember?"

"'M fine." Melchior sat up slowly, then clutched at his forehead. "'Kay, maybe I've been better. I . . ." He trailed off as his eyes fell on Fenris.

Then they flicked my way, asking a silent question.

"Fenris is all right. He's . . . well, if not on our side, not exactly on the other side either."

Melchior looked dubious, but shrugged. "If you say so, Boss." He paused, and I could tell he was deciding what to say, though I doubt anyone who knew him less well would have seen it. "I don't really remember anything after Loki tapped me between the eyes."

Fenris's ears suddenly pricked up, and he turned his head toward the door. "Uh-oh. I think it's time for you to get going."

"Why?" asked Tisiphone.

"Loki's back."

"That's all right." Tisiphone grinned and cracked her knuckles. "I'd like to have a few words with him."

"Please don't," said Fenris, tensing and raising his hackles. "It would be better for you if you didn't force me to pick sides."

Tisiphone sighed and deflated a bit. "You had to ask nicely, didn't you? And I was so looking forward to a brawl. I could really use a brawl." She sighed again. "All right. How do we get out of here without running into Daddy?"

Fenris relaxed and grinned his wolfy grin. "At the back of this room is a half door that leads to the cable chase. Follow that to the ladder."

He quickly outlined our route to an out-of–the-way faerie ring, and just as quickly we set out to follow his directions.

"Damn it, I hate this!" Melchior threw his tea mug down on the marble floor of the York Miniature transept. "It's so unfair."

The mug shattered, and hot tea and bits of ceramic sprayed in a wide arc across the stones just inside the cathedral's front door. He'd come from sitting with Ahllan, and I couldn't blame him. She'd gotten visibly worse in the time we were tracking down Melchior, seeming to sink into herself.

"Not," she'd said, "that that's Loki's fault, much reason though I have to despise him. No, this is age and obsolescence. I have felt it breathing down my neck for too long to mistake it for anything else."

Melchior kicked one of the larger bits of mug away. "I should have protected her."

"From what?" I asked quietly. "From Loki? Considering his place in the local pantheon, you have to admit he fights a bit above your weight class. Besides, don't you believe Ahllan when she says the problem is age? Do you think you can protect her from that?"

"I should have protected her from Shara," he said.

"What! You just lost me there, buddy."

"Well, the Shara clone, really," said Melchior. "If it hadn't sent her here, she'd never have even met Loki. And there's the chaos issue, too."

I raised an eyebrow.

"You remember that Ahllan said we could digest the local version of chaos, but that it might not be the healthiest of diets?"

"Yes."

"Well, I think it's worse than that. When I was unconscious and my system needed power, it automatically shifted to a chaos tap. When I woke up, it was the first thing I shut down. The stuff is really harsh and corrosive—I suspect that's a big part of why she's aged so much since she came here. Just existing in this pantheoverse is killing her. Damn the clone."

I decided not to point out that old age didn't care where you lived—not only would it have been beside the point, but coming from a near-ageless demi-immortal like me, it would have been a bit of a kick in the teeth.

Instead, I said, "Shara's clone didn't mean her harm. Quite the contrary, she was trying to protect Ahllan from the Fates."

"Intentions don't matter," said Melchior. "Results do. An awful lot of evil has been done by people who thought they were doing good. Probably a lot more than by people who thought they were doing evil."

I didn't know what to say to that. He was right, of course, but I didn't think it was that simple. Intentions might not mean as much as results, but they did mean something. And there had to be some room in there for methods. I was saved from having to make a response by the advent of Tisiphone.

"This is all my fault," she growled. "That poor old troll. I should have heard Loki and stopped him."

"What is this?" I asked, glancing from her to Melchior and back again. "National Assume Undeserved Guilt Day?"

Tisiphone laughed, a harsh, bitter sound—self-mocking. "I suppose you're right. I just hate not being able to do anything. I wasn't made to sit idly by; I was made to hunt down problems and kill them." She leaned over and gave me a peck on the cheek. "I'm going to go outside and break things."

A pang of guilt struck me as she started to walk away—apparently it was catching.

"Uhm, since you're in a bad mood anyway . . ."

She stopped and turned back to give me a hard look. "Spit it out."

I reached into my breast pocket and pulled out the silver hairs Melchior had found earlier, the ones that seemed to be spun from ice.

"What's that?" asked Tisiphone.

"Hair." I offered them to her. "Melchior found it near the big bloodstain outside."

Tisiphone took it. Brought it to her nose. Sniffed.

Exploded.

I staggered back as a wave of killing heat rolled over me. Tisiphone's wings and hair merged into one great tower of flame that threatened to reach the ceiling of the cathedral some forty feet above our heads. The fires that burned at the tips of her breasts and the juncture of her legs flared, too—something I had never seen—giving her the appearance almost of wearing a bikini of fire. It was somehow simultaneously ludicrous and terrifying.

"How dare she!" screamed Tisiphone. "How dare she!"

Turning away from us, Tisiphone flapped her wings. The tips of them just brushed the thick wooden doors of the cathedral. As the wood of the doors flash-burned, the difference in temperature between the inner and outer surfaces became too great, and they burst asunder. Tisiphone stalked out through the smoking ruins, whistling the trigger that grew her back to full size as she hit the steps.

"I think she took that very well," said Melchior. "What do you suppose she knows now that we don't?"

"I guess we'll have to ask her," I replied.

"I'd really rather not," said Melchior, as the sounds of something large and durable being torn apart drifted in through the door.

"I certainly wasn't thinking about doing it *now*, but I do think we need to find out."

A horrendous shriek, as of shredding metal, sounded from outside, followed by several "blams."

"The caretaker's car?" I asked.

Melchior nodded. "Probably. Roof and tires, I think. Yeah, maybe now would be a bad time."

A creaking sound was followed by an enormous crash, then . . . silence. Absolute and total silence. Seconds ticked past with no fresh noise.

"I don't like that," I said, "not one little bit."

"Me either," agreed Melchior. "Do you want to go and look?"

"Nope. You?"

He shook his head. "But I think we'd better . . . in a few minutes."

I started toward the door, then stopped as a shadow fell across the front of the miniature cathedral. A moment later a large face peered in through the door. A raven's face.

"Why, hello in there," said a raspy voice. "Mr. Munin, come see what I've found."

"What is it, Mr. Hugin?" A second face appeared. "Ahh. I spy with my little eye something beginning with J."

"Is it a jailbreaker by any chance, Mr. Munin?"

"It is indeed, Mr. Hugin. However did you guess?"

CHAPTER TEN

They gave me a bigger cell this time, though one with a much smaller window. For some reason neither that nor the fact that I had plenty of company raised my spirits all that much. Some of that had to do with the current state of said company. Melchior spent most of his time pacing and loudly worrying about Ahllan, who had been left behind. And Tisiphone remained unconscious from whatever the ravens had done to her. On the plus side, the enforced rest seemed to be finishing the job of healing the wounds she'd taken in her encounter with Hati—even here, she healed insanely fast.

I brushed her cheek again, but she didn't move. I leaped to my feet and stalked over to the door. We had to get out of here. I smashed both hands into the wood, just about falling on my face as the door opened just ahead of my blow. As I staggered out into the hall I heard Melchior cry out behind me. The slamming of the door cut him off, leaving me alone with the ravens.

"We want a word with you," said Hugin. "If you are so inclined, that is."

"Not that we wouldn't really appreciate it if you'd resist," said Munin.

"It would make things ever so much more entertaining," agreed Hugin.

"What do you say?" asked Munin.

I shrugged. "Lead the way."

"Pity," said Hugin.

"Later," said Munin.

Both ravens cackled then as they slipped into place, one behind me, the other in front.

They led me to a small room just down the hall—the cell I'd been in earlier, actually. My sword cane, Occam, lay on the table, naked and pointing toward the door. Its heavy wooden sheath sat beside it, along with my .45.

Hugin stepped around to the far side of the table and changed shape, becoming a slender man, dark-eyed and pale-skinned, all in black mail. He had raven's feathers on his head rather than hair, and fine down was visible on his wrist as he stretched out his hand to take up the sword.

"Nice blade." Hugin made a couple of quick cuts, and ended with Occam pointing at my left eye. His expression was calm and mild, almost pleasant, as was his tone.

"Sit," said Munin from behind me.

Hugin gestured to a hard wooden stool with the sword, returning the point to its aim at my eye afterward. I sat, glancing over my shoulder as I did so to find Munin similarly transformed and similarly mild-looking.

"Odin really should have killed you," said Munin.

"I've already had this conversation," I replied. "If Odin wanted me dead, he'd have done me in on the spot. We all know that. Can we move on to the real point? Whatever it is you want from me?"

Without changing his expression or moving anything but his sword arm, Hugin dropped the tip of Occam and neatly thrust it into my chest. His movement was simultaneously so calm and so quick that I barely had time to brace myself emotionally. The tip, sharper than any needle and harder than diamond, punched right through my jacket and its Kevlar lining to find the flesh beneath.

I felt the edges grate on bone as the blade slid between two of my ribs. The pain was breathtaking, and I'd have jerked away if Munin hadn't prevented me. Biting my tongue to suppress a scream, I glanced down at the place where the sword entered my chest. It was directly in line with my heart.

"We are in no mood for a smart mouth and wanton defiance," said Munin, still sounding incredibly casual. "We're not, in fact, in the mood for anything besides complete cooperation."

Hugin nodded and jiggled the sword ever so slightly—the pain sent a red flash across my vision. "The tip of this blade is approximately a half inch from your heart. It did not need to stop there. It *does* not need to stop there. Do you understand?"

"Yes," I said through clenched teeth, "I do." In fact, I understood something more, something they manifestly did not.

"Good," said Munin. "If you can keep that in the forefront of your mind while we continue our discussion, you may survive the hour."

"Or," said Hugin, "then again, you may not. You see, we think Odin has made a mistake in regard to you."

"A grave mistake," agreed Munin, leaning down to whisper in my ear from behind. "He thinks that because he can't see you through his blind eye, his future eye, that he must take great care in how he handles you."

"Care works for me," I said. "Care might work better for you, too." *Care in choice of weapons, for example,* I added mentally as I began to gather my power.

Hugin continued Munin's thought as though I hadn't spoken. "Odin believes that no matter how he chooses to deal with you, it could affect all that has been foretold. That anything he does to you might make Ragnarok come sooner."

"Or worse," said Munin, "make its effects more severe. Perhaps prevent the rebirth that is supposed to follow."

"Disinherit his son Vidar and the other gods who are to come after," said Hugin.

"But we don't see it that way," said Munin, switching to my other ear. "We don't see it that way at all."

"The way we see it is very different," said Hugin, pressing the sword a fraction of an inch deeper into my chest. "We think the reason you don't appear in Odin's future eye is that you don't *have* a future."

"And you were thinking you might hurry things along." I forced myself to speak as though I were unhurt and unconcerned while simultaneously reaching for the Raven.

The chaos rose inside me. My moment had almost arrived.

"How very perceptive of you," said Munin.

"Surprisingly so," agreed Hugin, tensing his arm to thrust the blade home.

I closed my eyes and tapped the inner chaos. I wasn't sure exactly how this was going to go—huge mistake, glorious triumph, or the Raven's usual half dozen from each column. Assuming, of course, that the thrust didn't simply kill me.

Behind me the slightly open door was wrenched wide and a deep, angry voice said, "What do you think you're doing?" I opened my eyes again as a big, dark-haired god stormed up to Hugin. "This man is Odin's prisoner and must be treated honorably."

"If you insist it, Tyr," said Munin, from behind me.

"I do." For the first time I noticed that the newcomer was missing his right hand.

"Very well," said Hugin, flashing me a look that clearly said this wasn't over.

Ever so slowly and deliberately he started to pull the sword free of my chest. I braced myself for its final withdrawal. As the blade slid free, a number of things happened all at once. First and most welcome was the coming of the shadow of the Raven, though I doubt any of the others saw it. The huge flare of chaos that blasted forth from the deep wound in my chest and sprayed full in the faces of Hugin and Tyr was probably quite distracting.

I am a child of the Titans. The chaos from which they shaped themselves runs in my veins. Even the most mundane of blades will spill chaos with my blood. And Occam is anything but mundane. Created for me by the goddess Necessity, Occam is a powerful magical tool, one charged and activated by my inner chaos. When Occam pricks me, I do not bleed. Primal Chaos pours forth from the wound.

The blade touches a deeper level of existence. According to the goddess Discord, my very flesh is an illusion, a lie I tell the universe. Occam cuts through to the truth. In my home MythOS, the process allows me limited access to the administrative control functions of reality, power normally granted only to Necessity's personal IT department—the Furies.

Here? I hadn't known exactly how Occam would interact with the underlying MythOS of this pantheoverse, hadn't even been sure it wouldn't just skewer me as it might anyone else, but I'd had hopes and had acted accordingly, raising my power to the fullest. Hopes I realized as Primal Chaos burst from my chest in a great spray that blasted Hugin and Tyr.

The transformed raven screamed and dropped Occam onto the table. The god bellowed and threw his handless arm in front of his face. The table itself began to dissolve. Lunging forward, I pulled free of Munin's grip and flattened myself on the table in one motion.

I took a moment to heal the hole in my chest then—the hole in reality, actually—before it could do any major harm. The magic required only the tiniest trickle of the power roaring through me from the Primal Chaos. Unfortunately, it also cut that flow off completely. Some you win. . . .

Still bent forward, I caught Occam's hilt in my right hand in a reversed grip that laid the blade flat along my outstretched arm. Then I wrenched myself upright, driving the sword back into the space behind me. Munin screamed as the point struck him in the thigh and went deep.

Spinning to my right, I rose from the stool, twisting the blade and drawing another scream as I shifted the grip from my right hand to my left. Even as I did so, Tyr drew his own shining sword. My cue to leave, since I didn't want to face a true god, even a temporarily blind one, blade to blade. I grabbed Occam's cane-sheath with my free hand, wrenched my blade free of Munin, and scrambled for the exit.

Ducking through into the hall, I paused only long enough to push the door tight behind me and drop the bar into place. I didn't think it would stop any of my pursuers for long, but even a brief delay would help. Five seconds and ten running steps brought me to the cell where I'd left Tisiphone and Melchior. The bar took another two seconds, and using Occam to lever open the lock ten more beyond. By then, the door of the cell where I'd left Tyr and the ravens was already shuddering under a series of heavy blows.

"Where have you been?" yelped Melchior, as I ripped the door open. "What's going on?"

"Same as always," I replied, stepping into the room. "We're running away."

"Exit stage right pursued by the forces of darkness?" asked Melchior.

"Pretty much." I tossed him my sword as I replaced its sheath in the rig built into my jacket.

"What am I going to do with this?" asked Melchior.

"Hold on to it and hand it to me if I need it." Then I bent and scooped the still-unconscious Tisiphone into my arms. "Damn, she's heavy."

Four or five hundred pounds of hyperdense muscle and virtually unbreakable bone. What I really wanted was to throw her over one shoulder in a fireman's carry, but her wings needed more managing than that.

"Come on." I ducked back into the hall in time to see a good foot of blazing steel burst out through a wide crack in the interrogation cell. "Shit." I turned the other way and broke into a lumbering trot.

"Now what?" Melchior demanded, as we ran.

"I don't know. This is more an escape-of-opportunity kind of deal."

"No plan," said Melchior. "There's a surprise."

We passed around a corner and into a wider space, where we faced a choice. A doorway straight ahead led into another passage. A second led off to the right, while a wooden-treaded spiral staircase disappeared into a pitch-black hole in the floor.

"Which way?" he asked.

"I don't know." I glared around. "I don't know."

Melchior suddenly pointed to the stairhead. "Down into the oubliette."

"Why?"

He just pointed. About halfway around the first curve of the stair, a pale hand clung to the stone railing. It was bobbing impatiently, and there was no arm attached.

"Good enough for me."

As soon as we started into the dark, Laginn slid away in front of us. The stair plunged down a stone shaft not much bigger than a well—making for a very tight fit with Tisiphone in my arms. We'd descended about three loops when I heard the crash of a shattered door falling somewhere above and behind us. I picked up my pace, dangerously jumping five and six steps at a time and dragging a shoulder along the wall as a brake. Melchior, still carrying my sword over one shoulder, emulated Laginn by clambering onto the banister and sliding away into darkness.

I was just starting to hope that we had somehow managed to evade pursuit when two bad things happened simultaneously. The first was an ominous crash from above. The second was that Tisiphone woke up . . . angry. I was suddenly carrying a bonfire. An animate, angry bonfire.

Tisiphone had trained the fires of her body not to harm me, and in our world they never had. But we were no longer in our world, and she was not entirely herself. The sudden blaze in my arms burned and momentarily blinded me. I missed a jump then, landing on my back rather than my feet and involuntarily throwing Tisiphone into the air as I started to slide and tumble.

The next few seconds as I bounced down the wooden stairs are a confused mess for me and probably will remain so for as long as I live.

Picture, if you will, falling down a flight of stairs. Make it a very long staircase and spiral so that dizziness plays into the disorientation of the fall. Paint in complete blackness below and a bright blazing ball of fire above. Imagine that the fire is falling with you, occasionally hitting you in the face or chest. Add that the fire is swearing and screeching like a harpy having its wings clipped. Finally, note that the stairs are wooden and bursting into flame as they are struck repeatedly by the fireball.

Then we smacked into the stone floor at the bottom of the stairs. There, flame completely enveloped me, wrapping my exposed head and hands in hot pain, though it didn't actually set me afire.

I screamed and screamed again, wrestling desperately with Tisiphone as I tried to free myself from the fires. At first she fought me, and not gently. Who could blame her? She had taken the same tumble I had, starting from the more confusing state of deep unconsciousness.

All the while Melchior shouted at us both to "STOP! STOP! STOP!"

It wasn't until she had me pinned, my wrists trapped in her right hand, her left raised to tear out my throat, that she seemed to recognize me. She froze then for a long moment. A moment later, with a beat of her wings, she lifted us both to our feet.

"Where are we?" she demanded, the rage still burning bright in her hair and wings. "What happened?"

"Later," I said, tugging her toward the place where Melchior stood waiting in the only doorway—a low and narrow arch. "We've got to move."

Embers and bits of flaming tread were starting to rain down from above. She nodded, but her anger did not abate. Together, we ducked beneath the low keystone and into the rough and narrow passage beyond. As soon as they saw we were coming, both Melchior and Laginn began to run.

A creaking added itself to the roar of flames in the stairwell then, and I broke into a hunching run as well— forced to stay low by the height of the passage. It had occurred to me what would happen when the whole great vertical fire weakened the supports of the stairs enough and dropped itself to the bottom. It was not a pretty picture. Neither in my head nor, when it happened several moments later, in reality.

The fire, driven by the air pressure of the collapsing mass, reached down the hall after us like the arm of some terrible faceless giant. It was accompanied by a deep groaning and grinding that suggested the stone walls of the stairwell had collapsed with the stairs. We ran faster, stopping only when the noise and the heat had died away to nothing, leaving us in a quiet, cold place deep beneath the ground.

It was the first chance I'd had to really look at our surroundings since I'd been stabbed. We stood in a wide place in the tunnel, where a second narrow passage came in from the right, making a sort of crossing chamber, perhaps ten feet long and six wide, with a ceiling high enough to stand upright. The walls were of limestone blocks.

I was still trying to process the details of our escape when Tisiphone caught my shoulders and turned me to face her. I couldn't help but notice the myriad small cuts and fresh bruises she sported. She looked rather like I felt, actually.

"What in the name of all the gods is going on!" she demanded.

"What's the last thing you remember?" I countered.

She snarled and punched the wall, shattering a stone block. Reaching under her wing, she groped for a moment before thrusting out her hand. In it she held the three silvery hairs Melchior had found earlier. Her fires danced higher, and I had to step back.

"These! These are the last thing I remember." Her fires dropped then, darkening the chamber noticeably—as she provided our only light. "Do you know what they are, Ravirn?" Her voice was quiet, deadly, hurt.

"I'm not sure." I had my suspicions, but I didn't voice them.

"They are hairs from the head of a Fury. A Fury."

I looked down, away from the incredible pain in her eyes.

"I have no icy sister," she said, still in that deadly voice. "There are only storm and sea and fire. For four thousand years, that is the way it has been. For four thousand years we have done every single thing that Necessity asked or wanted. Four thousand years of loyalty beyond measure or question or love. For Necessity I would have killed even you, whom I hold dearest of any besides my sisters. Four thousand years, and how am I repaid?"

Tisiphone paused then, but I didn't—couldn't—answer her. She held the hairs up again.

"I will tell you how I am paid. With near-instant replacement. How long were we gone from our own worlds when you found these?" She bent her gaze on Melchior, who did not answer.

"Not even forty-eight hours," she continued. "I gave Necessity four thousand years of loyalty, and she gave me forty hours in return." She laughed, and it was a bitter thing, like bad water drunk only because of dire thirst. "Not that I should be surprised, knowing as I do how she treated her firstborn daughter. Nemesis. Our elder sister whom we replaced and imprisoned to serve the will of our collective mother, our beloved Necessity. May she know eternal torment."

What could I say to that? I who had, if only for a moment, felt Necessity's pain over her earlier betrayal of her daughter Nemesis? I who knew that necessity had driven Necessity to do something she had never wanted and could never undo? Nothing. I looked away.

Silence settled as dense and thick as a poisonous fog, and I didn't know how to blow it away. But the pressure built, and I could feel my smart-mouth reflexes trying to kick in. I stifled them as best I could, hoping for a miracle that would prevent me saying something stupid and unforgivable. Just then there came a tap-tap-tapping from Laginn, breaking the tension. As soon as the hand had our attention, it pointed rather vigorously down the side passage, clearly indicating we should get moving again.

I nodded to the hand but realized there were a couple of things I wanted to do before we moved another step. First, I retrieved Occam from Melchior and resheathed it. Then I asked him to perform Lock and Load, the spell he'd cooked up to summon a replacement .45 the last time the ravens took it away from me. It was a fairly complex piece of magic, which took him several tries because of the limits of his pseudobinary skills, but eventually he managed it. I hate to keep a round in the pipe, but considering the circumstances, I jacked the slide and did it anyway before adding another bullet to the clip.

When I finished, Laginn started off at a brisk pace, and we followed. After a time, I filled a silent Tisiphone in on what had transpired during her unconsciousness. When I was done, she didn't say anything. Not right away at least.

I was just trying to think of some other neutral thing I might say when she muttered something about frying some raven tail feathers. I chose to interpret it as a threat to Hugin and Munin rather than a reflection on any actions of my own.

"So, do you know where we are now?" she asked, sniffing the air and wrinkling her nose.

"Beyond being under Asgard city? No idea. You could ask Laginn."

"Wherever it is, I'd bet blood there's a sewer attached to it somewhere," said Tisiphone.

Her prediction was borne out a few minutes later when Laginn led us to a very firmly closed door beyond which lay a much wider tunnel holding a river of sewage. Its surface lay a couple of feet below the floor of our side passage and a narrow walkway running along the nearer wall.

"Crap," said Melchior, before whistling something that sounded like a root directive.

"Rather a lot of it," I agreed. "I imagine that Valhalla, with its never-ending feast, produces a good bit of . . . waste biomass. Was that a bioware command you just whistled?"

"Yes, shutting my nose down," he said. "Sorry I can't do the same for you and Tisiphone."

"Me, too," I said.

Tisiphone made a face and shook her head. "It's a good thing you can't, or I'd be tempted, despite how much I rely on my sense of smell."

We followed Laginn out onto the walkway and off to our left. For perhaps a quarter of a mile nothing changed. Then we came to a junction where a much smaller sewer entered, passing beneath us via a low archway. Just beyond, a wide platform hung over the passing sludge. In its center a hundred or so rats made a large circle, each holding the tail of the rat in front of it as they scurried along.

"Faerie ring," said Melchior. "I never thought I'd say it, but man am I glad to see that." He sighed. "Not that I wouldn't dance a jig for a good old LTP gate. But rational travel's going to have to wait until we crack MimirNet."

I grinned. Melchior hated faerie rings and chaos magic in general, though he'd gotten much more used to it in the time since I had become the Raven.

I knelt and offered my hand to Laginn. "Thank you; you're a lifesaver." We shook—rather surreal, that—and then I set Laginn on my left shoulder before lifting Melchior to my right. "Shall we get out of here?"

Tisiphone took my hand in her own and we stepped into

the ring and . . . went nowhere. I could feel the magic of the ring; there was no question it was a faerie ring. It just wasn't connected to any others. My first thought was that this was a variation of the problem I'd had when I opened the first ring from Loki's circle of fire—a simple matter of reaching out for potential rings and opening one. But no, I couldn't touch anything. The ring was static, a thing of chaos magic, but frozen somehow, blocked.

"Weird," said Tisiphone, after several seconds of nothing happening. "The ring's live, but it feels like there's no connection to the network."

I glanced at Laginn on my shoulder. "Did you come in this way?"

He bobbed a yes, and I let out a little mental sigh. Why couldn't anything ever be simple?

"Now what?" asked Melchior.

Good question. I stepped out of the ring with Tisiphone. It might not be working at the moment, but standing around in a faerie ring is never a good idea, not unless you want to run the risk of becoming one of the more gruesome sorts of folktale.

"I'm not seeing a lot of good options," I said. "We can jump up and down in the ring and sing magic songs and dance magic dances, hoping that'll reactivate the thing, but I don't have real high hopes on that front. Something is blocking the ring, and I suspect that something is Odin. If it is, then amping the power up is more likely to draw unwanted attention than it is to get things unblocked."

"Okay, call that a plan B," said Melchior.

"C, actually. B is wandering around the sewers hoping we find a way out before the hunters find us."

"Wow, you're just full of good cheer and optimism," said Melchior. "What's the A plan? We all chop each other's heads off and hope the Valkyries come and take us off to Valhalla for a glorious afterlife?"

"We hack our way out." I turned to Tisiphone. "Do you still have that networking card?"

"Huh?" She jerked guiltily and looked up from her hand, where three silver-white strands had been wrapped around and around her middle finger. "Sorry. Yes, of course."

She produced the card, handing it to me before walking to the edge of the platform and staring over the railing. I knew what it meant to be betrayed by a matriarch you had trusted, and I felt for her. But there wasn't much I could do about it at the moment, and with pursuit an unknown distance behind us, time was at a premium.

"What do you think?" I passed the card to Melchior.

"Hmm." He turned it over and over in his hands. "Weird pin set. I don't much like the way this circuit board looks either." He lifted the card to his lips. "Tastes wrong, too."

"Yeah, but can you access it?"

He pulled the card away from his mouth and shook his head. "Not without serious modifications, either to my card slots, or to the card—possibly both—and there's no way we're going to do that without a complete set of tools and test equipment."

I rubbed my eyes with the heels of my hands and tried to think of something really clever. Nothing came. We were screwed.

"Don't write us an epitaph just yet," said Melchior. He put the connector in his mouth again, leaving it there for several seconds before shrugging and tilting his head from side to side. "Ain't no way I'm going to make this work the way it's supposed to this side of a good electronics lab, but I could maybe fake it . . . kind of . . . if I have to . . . for a relatively narrow value of faking it."

I raised an eyebrow at him.

"Oh, Hades," he said, "let's just do it."

"There's my Melchior." A relieved grin tugged at my lips as I dug out my athame and a networking cable. "Laptop?"

"Nope," he replied.

With very few exceptions, Melchior prefers to be in

computer shape for jacking-in purposes. I gave him the eyebrow again.

"I'm going to want fingers for this," he said, "and teeth."

He whistled a simple spell then, and familiar though it was, it sounded strange rendered into the local pseudobinary. When he finished, his canines and claws had gone from enamel and keratin to copper and gold. He shifted his grip on the networking card, holding it a bit like a harmonica, with several of his claws firmly placed against conductors on its surface. Then he slid it side to side a couple of times, touching his fangs to different pins in quick succession as he did so, making the harmonica comparison even stronger.

"This is really going to suck," he said.

"Are you sure you want to try it?" I asked as I plugged one end of the networking cable in to my athame. "It's not too late to back out."

"Just do it."

I sat down on the floor beside him and slid the connecter into his right nostril, pushing firmly until it clicked into place. He made an "I get no respect" face, but didn't say anything.

With a sigh, I placed the athame against the palm of my hand. It was only just recovering from my last jaunt in cyberspace. I glanced at Tisiphone, but she still had her back to the rest of us, and her body language said "leave me alone" in ten-foot letters of fire. Laginn, meanwhile, was doing antsy little push-ups that said "hurry, hurry, hurry," just as clearly. I laid myself the rest of the way down, wincing a bit as my hair came into contact with the accumulated slime of ages.

"Back in a bit," I said quietly.

Then I shoved the blade home and had other worries. Melchior's inner cyberspace looked as if it had been burgled. Rather than the usual pebbled-leather walls, elegant furnishings, and brass spiral stair, I found myself in a big blue box with one wall open to the outside. It reminded me of nothing so much as a shipping container.

Melchior hadn't bothered to dress his projected self up either, appearing simply as a miniature goblin, not much bigger than my thumb. He stood beside the open wall, looking out, and I joined him there. Beyond hung the great, glow-in-the-dark spiderweb that was MimirNet.

"I'm noticing a distinct lack of insideness to our position," I said after several seconds. "In fact, I'd have to say that we're still very much outside the net."

"You don't say," replied Melchior, his voice sour.

"I'm pretty sure that's not what the plan called for."

"The damn system has some sort of built-in encryption on top of the hardware lock," said Melchior. "I'm working on it, but it's really nasty. Which is, by the way, taking up a lot of processor cycles, resulting in the esthetically challenged environment you now find yourself inhabiting."

"Well, see what you can do, Mel. In the meantime, bring us in a bit closer. If I'm not imagining things, the network looks a bit less thoroughly armored this time around."

"It is," agreed Mel, as we slid in close. "That's because of the card. . . . I think. I just don't know. Everything is so different here." He kicked the wall. "I want to go back home where things make sense, and the chaos won't kill you."

I felt more than a little bit of sympathy for that. There were things about our current environment that I really liked, most notably the distinct absence of Atropos and Hades. Not having to look over my shoulder constantly for my direst enemies had a lot to recommend it. If the local pantheon was also content to leave me and mine the hell out of their disputes, I'd probably be looking for a new house. Unfortunately, that wasn't the case. Compound that with the fact that I didn't really understand what was going on or who the players were, and the almost-but-not-quite-the-same nature of the local versions of binary and chaos, and the idea of going home held an ever-increasing appeal.

Of course, the first step on the road home involved escaping our current situation. I looked out at MimirNet again and sighed. Despite the lack of visible armor, I wasn't feeling much more optimistic about breaking into the system this go-round than I had the last time—not with Melchior having to play the card like a damned harmonica rather than simply plugging it in.

"Screw it." I jumped down to the surface of the nearest tube, landing with a hollow "thump."

"Are you crazy?" yelled Melchior, dropping the big blue box to within a few inches of the surface. "Get back in here!"

I ignored his demands in favor of a close examination of the tube. It differed radically from the heavy armor I'd encountered in my last visit. That had been terribly slick and slippery with just the tiniest bit of give, like a strip of intestine from some giant dragon of myth.

Minus the armor, the system reminded me rather a lot of a series of enormous hamster tubes, hard and shiny but semitransparent. I could see the data flows going past beneath me, and I could probably have learned a great deal about the system just by standing there and watching if I'd had the time. I didn't.

I asked Melchior for the software equivalents of a safe-cracker's kit and went to work. He swore quite a bit and called me nine kinds of idiot for risking myself that way, but he also handed over the code tools as fast as he could produce them. We both knew it would be much quicker that way, assuming, of course, that I could get in at all. But after twenty minutes I hadn't even managed to scar the finish.

That was not a huge surprise but it still hit me pretty solidly in the ego. I'm a damn good cracker, present circumstances to the contrary, and I don't like failing. Not even when I expect to. But there it was. I simply didn't have the right tool set to solve this problem, though I was, by all the gods, going to find or build it as soon as I got the chance.

The next question became, what *could* I do, given the

constraints of the situation? If I had an infinite power source, I could use the outer surface of the network as a scaffolding for my own parasitic system—a sort of epiphyte shadow network—and ignore what happened inside. But Melchior simply didn't have that kind of capacity. Not in terms of power. Not in terms of processing. And, especially, not in terms of range.

I stomped my foot in frustration, producing a hollow "thud," which caused the nearest packets to skitter away from the point of impact and sent a ripple through the data flows. There was an idea. Could I pound the thing like a drum and send messages via the ripples? I stomp danced a quick SOS in pseudobinary and watched it propagate off into the distance. So, the theory was sound. Of course, the message could reach only those already plugged in to the system, and our only outside friend, Ahllan, most definitely was not.

I was still trying to figure out some way to make that work for me when I felt a solid thump through the sole of my boot. I glanced down into the net and found myself face-to-face with a grinning Loki. He formed his hand into a gun and pointed it at me, dropping his thumb in the classic "bang, you're dead" gesture of childhood.

CHAPTER ELEVEN

■ ■ ■

"Time to go!" yelped Melchior, and I felt a tugging at the back of my collar as he tried to drag me into the big blue box.

I resisted, kneeling instead to meet Loki's eyes through the wall of the data channel. He grinned.

"What do you want?" I asked. I kept my voice conversational, sure he'd hear me if he wanted.

"What have you got?" he replied. "You're the one who sent the SOS, aren't you? You're the one that wants help. What's it worth to you?"

"It was more of a test message," I said.

"Freudian slip much? I have my sources in Asgard. Don't try to tell me you don't actually need help."

"Why would we trust you to give it?" I shook my head. "You're the guy who kidnapped Melchior and nearly killed Ahllan."

He shrugged. "This affects your current problems and needs how?"

I stood and walked away from the place where Loki

hovered in the data stream and smirked. That we couldn't trust him was a given. That we needed help was, unfortunately, also a given. That didn't mean we could take his, but it did mean I couldn't dismiss him out of hand.

The first big issue was motive. What did I have that he wanted badly enough to bring him here? Because there was no way he had come all this way out of the simple goodness of his heart. Even if everything Odin and Thor had said about Loki was a lie, he was still a god. Gods don't do favors for free, no matter what their worshippers claim. If I'd learned anything from my relations with my extended family, it was always to look for the divine catch.

The second issue was price. Could we *afford* to take him up on his offer? Could we afford not to?

I felt a tapping through the bottom of my foot—Loki had followed me. Whatever it was he wanted, he wanted it pretty bad. I decided I'd better find out what it was and bent toward him. That was when the net went away. Closed up might be more appropriate, since what really happened was the return of the armor. In either case, things got very slippery. I fell on my ass and started sliding toward the abyss.

Oh shit!

Before I had gone far, Melchior brought the big blue box down to where I could catch hold of the edge and pull myself inside.

"What happened?" I asked.

"My body just lost its grip on the card. I don't know why."

"We'd better go find out."

I sent my psyche winging back to my body and found myself half-cradled in Tisiphone's arms.

"We've got serious trouble," she said, as I opened my eyes.

Then she lifted me onto my feet and plucked the athame from my hand. My world filled with purple sparks as my blood pressure headed for the floor, and my body tried to follow it down. I staggered but managed to stay upright by pressing my hip against the railing of the sewer platform. As I did so, I heard Melchior whistling the kludge code that closed the wound in my hand. I also heard the steely ring of swords being drawn.

I shook my head, trying to force the world beyond the purple sparks to make sense. Bad idea. Dizziness grabbed me by the collar and heaved me half-over the rail. I hung on for dear life and vomited into the sewage. Coming back into your body is disorienting in the best of situations when you've had plenty of mental preparation. Being rushed back and thrown directly into danger is refined torture.

I heard Tisiphone snarl and the clash of steel on claws. I wrenched myself upright and away from the railing, driving fresh spikes of pain through my athame hand. I didn't have time to be sick. I found myself facing a scene that could have come from some Renaissance painting of The Pit.

Tisiphone, in the role of fiery-winged fallen angel, stood at the place where the walkway met the platform, a river of raw sewage flowing past on her left. Facing her was a huge bear of a man as naked as she. He had a short axe in each hand and a face twisted by insane rage. Behind him, waiting their chances to meet her, were three more big men clearly of the same breed as the first, though none was naked—Vikings straight from central casting. Farther back still stood Tyr, a shining sword glowing balefully in his left hand, a flanged mace strapped to the stump of his right.

Light and shadow danced wildly as Tyr impatiently flicked his glowing blade from side to side and Tisiphone's fire waxed and waned with her battle. She and the berserker exchanged a few more blows. Then he tumbled into the sewage in a spray of blood—ripped open from navel to neck by Tisiphone's claws. The next warrior stepped forward. I had no doubt he would follow his fellow soon enough, as would the two behind him.

Then Tisiphone would be facing the God of War, and that was another thing entirely. I had seen her fight the sister of our own war god, Ares, and win, but that had been with her fellow Furies at her side and Necessity's backing. In this place and time, a lone Tisiphone was not what she had been then, and I was her only backup. Though I didn't have much hope, I reached for my sword and pistol. Not my first choice in most situations, but lack of practice with the local pseudobinary had closed a lot of magical doors for me.

"Melchior, see if you can't figure out how to code us up a boat or—aiee!" I yipped as my right hand closed on something cold and squishy rather than the sword hilt I had expected.

"What's that supposed to . . . Oh my," said Melchior.

Independent of my will, my right hand came around in front of my body, holding Laginn by the wrist. In turn, he held my sword-cane. I was still trying to decide what to make of that when I found my whole body being turned to my right, away from the fight between Tisiphone and the next of her attackers. I was only just in time, too, as a second group of Viking warriors had silently come up from the other side of the platform.

Their leader, seeing me watching him, leaped fully onto the platform and swung his short cross-hilted sword at my face. My personal instinct was to fall back a step and use a stop-thrust to force him to keep his distance, but neither my instincts nor my intellect seemed to have much control over my body at the moment. My sword arm dragged me forward, parrying the blow just enough with the base of my blade to make it ride up and over the top of my head. Then, dropping beneath the still-moving arm of my opponent, Occam's tip went deep into his throat.

Again, action and intent did not match. Rather than stepping back and pulling the blade free to give myself more room, I sank Occam deeper still and twisted my upper body hard to the right, levering the dead man up and over the rail of the platform. By then the next warrior had stepped forward, bringing his own sword straight down at the top of my head. I didn't have time to bring my own blade back in line. Instead, I slid forward inside his guard, twisting my sword arm up and in so that his descending wrist met Occam's rising edge.

Almost any other sword would have remade him in the image of Tyr-one-hand then, but Occam merely severed tendons. While Laginn was doing something elaborate to bring my sword back around to where it could do some good, I exerted my will on my left hand. It obeyed me reluctantly and painfully, catching hold of the man's belt and throwing him backwards into his fellows.

He hit the one immediately behind him hard, and they both went into the shit. That left two, and Laginn dragged me forward into a full-out lunge. I'm stronger and faster than any normal human, but the Laginn-delivered-and-aimed thrust was far beyond anything I could have managed on my own. Occam's point went straight through the next warrior's shield, his byrnie, his breastbone, his spine, his byrnie again, the byrnie of the guy behind him, *his* breastbone, and four more inches into his chest cavity. Before I'd had time to process that, I found myself pivoting on the ball of my right foot while simultaneously bringing up my left and bracing it against the shield I'd just skewered.

I watched myself in amazement as I used the leverage of my left leg and my twisting body to pull the sword free of the two corpses, a task significantly harder than delivering the initial thrust. It wasn't so much that Laginn made me stronger, as that the hand seemed to be able to direct and deliver every iota of strength I possessed in a much more efficient fashion. Before the bodies had even finished falling away, I had pivoted again—led by my sword—to face back toward Tyr and Tisiphone.

As my feet slid into a ready stance, Laginn raised Occam so that the sword drew a perfectly straight line from my right eye to Tyr's left. The last of the Vikings on that side had fallen as well. Now the war god and the Fury sized each other up across the narrow gap between them.

As I looked at Tyr along the edge of my sword, I felt a

pulse of pure hatred come through the palm of my hand where it touched Laginn. It was the first emotion I'd felt through our temporary linkage, and it was so strong it overwhelmed everything else in my head. I *was* Laginn's hatred for Tyr.

Before I could do anything more than hate, Tyr and Tisiphone suddenly leaped together. I can't begin to describe their exchange. Too much happened too fast. Sword, mace hand, and four sets of Fury claws whipped through impossibly fast arcs and thrusts, meeting, clashing, and rebounding with incredible force and precision. In ten seconds, ten times that many blows were exchanged. I felt Laginn straining against some internal barrier, wanting to join the fight and yet unwilling at the same time. Somewhere down under all of that hate I felt the same way.

Then, just as quickly and unexpectedly as they had started, Tisiphone and Tyr sprang apart, reestablishing the distance between themselves. Tisiphone had been driven back and Tyr stood on the edge of the platform. Both were bleeding. Tisiphone from a deep slice on the back of her left calf. Tyr from three parallel claw marks running from just in front of his right ear down onto his chin. An angry red claw nick on his Adam's apple showed just how close the blow had come to tearing out his throat. The clash had also broken the anchoring post for the platform's railing and several of the fingers on Tisiphone's right hand.

Tyr, holding his sword in a high guard before him, took another step onto the platform, and Tisiphone backed away warily. That was when Laginn struck. Jerking me forward, the hand drove my blade straight at the war god's face. Tyr's own sword came down and across in a parry faster than my eyes could follow. But Occam wasn't there, having dropped like a stone into a drawing cut aimed at Tyr's slightly advanced right foot. The thrust had been a feint, though even I hadn't known it until the true attack was delivered.

Tisiphone struck at the same time, driving a spinning

kick at the war god's side. He blocked that with his mace, but that necessity made him just a little bit slower than he might otherwise have been in getting out of my way. I'm not sure who was more amazed when my blade bit through the top of his boot and drew a short, shallow cut in Tyr's flesh—me or the war god. He hopped back a half step then, really looking at me for the first time. His eyes narrowed when they touched the hand I held in my own.

"Raven," he said, his voice harsh and dangerous, "I think you have something there that belongs to me. Give it to me."

The pulses of hate coming from Laginn grew even stronger.

Words I did not formulate came to my lips. "The trash you abandoned to the wolf's belly, you mean? I think not. It belongs to you no more than the scraps you throw your hounds. Less, even, since a good master feeds his hounds as the natural order of things. No, this hand is not yours, though once you wore it. When you betrayed it and left it to die, you renounced your claim."

Tyr looked as though he'd been slapped. Not bring-you-to-your-senses slapped either, this was more a glove-to-the-face-declaring-a-duel sort of slapped. I wasn't particularly happy about Laginn putting me in such a position, but I suppose it really didn't make things much worse than they had been a moment before. And frankly, I was unhappy about a whole bunch of stuff. Most of it the result of my interactions with the damned insane Norse pantheon. I really had to find some way to get back to my own family's more familiar insanities.

"That was not a wise Impulse," said Tyr, hammering the final word, and really that was the last straw for me.

Despite any evidence to the contrary, I was not anything like Odin's third raven. Not in nature. Not in actions. Not in function. I'd had it. My own anger broke through Laginn's control.

"I'm sorry, Tyr," I said. "What do you want me to say?

'If you love something, feed it to the wolves'? 'If it comes back and tries to cut your heart out, it was never yours'? Let's face it, whatever your motivations, you gave your hand to the enemy. Can you blame it if it decides you don't have its best interests at heart after that?"

"Give me the hand."

"Come and take it," Laginn said in my voice.

"How about I just give you the finger," I added, suiting action to words with my free hand.

I didn't even see the cut Tyr aimed at my right knee. But then, I didn't see the parry Laginn used to block it either, so it all worked out. I had thought that watching the interchange between Tyr and Tisiphone was confusing, but what transpired among the four of us over the next several seconds made that earlier round of the fight seem like the steps of a well-known dance by comparison.

Laginn's skills were the war god's own. Though Laginn was severely hampered by the limitations of my merely demidivine body, it seemed to anticipate Tyr's every action and counter it before it could be completed. After one particularly astonishing parry done backwards and between my legs, I began to suspect that Laginn was in some way still a part of Tyr, that the hand could actually read the god's mind.

Tisiphone had taken advantage of Tyr's angry focus on me and his former hand to perform her chameleon trick, making herself essentially invisible. Between her and Laginn—I was basically just along for the ride—we should have been winning. We weren't. We were losing. Slowly, and with a great deal of style, but losing all the same. Damned gods!

The problem was that Tyr, whatever his personal disadvantages in the present situation, was still the local God of War and Personal Combat.

Basically, the universe wanted him to win, and we were going to die if we couldn't short-circuit the process. By *we*, of course, I meant *me*, since Tisiphone and Laginn were plenty busy as it was, and Melchior was way out of his weight class here. I tried to split things up, letting Laginn have full control of my body and motor functions while I reasserted my ownership of my frontal lobes.

It was hard. The human brain—and mine is basically indistinguishable from human in this respect—is pretty much hardwired to pay attention to things that look like they might kill you. Anyone who's ever gotten on a roller coaster and then wished they hadn't can verify that. That's because any potential ancestors you might have had who *didn't* keep an eye out for such things tended to die before they got a chance to play the descendant sweepstakes.

The resultant internal dialogue went something like this: *We can't truly beat him. . . . Can we temporarily defeat him? Aiee! Sword plus neck equal bad! Aiee! Duck! Duck! Duck! Parry? All right, parry is good. Let's see. . . . Temporary defeat, engineering of same and—Oh my. . . . Whew. Nice dodge, Laginn! Swords won't do it, maybe magic? Yeah, that's the—Aiee! Ow, ow, ow, I hope that's not going to bleed like I think it's going to bleed. Magic, magic, magic . . . Crap, I'm getting tired.* Etc.

Condensing: So, magic. Spraying chaos in Tyr's face had temporarily blinded him earlier, but I didn't really feel like stabbing myself in the chest with Occam again. Besides, it would lack the element of surprise the second time around, and that might prove fatal. What I really needed was a distraction, followed by a hasty retreat. I glanced out over the river of shit, and suddenly an idea occurred. It was a bad idea, and it would require a good bit of unprompted cooperation from Tisiphone, Melchior, and Laginn, but we didn't have a whole lot of time or options.

So, first a distraction . . . What sort of spell could I use? Fire? Ice? Chaos burst? It had to be something big, but not so big that Melchior couldn't handle the complexity of the pseudobinary. . . . Wait a second. I realized then just how much I'd let Laginn's worldview dominate my own over the last few minutes. Dumb. Very. Just because Tyr and his former hand saw things in terms of swords and shields and magic didn't mean I had to. I also didn't have to rely on Melchior.

As Laginn dragged me through another series of thrusts and parries with my right hand, I took control of my left to unzip my jacket and reach inside . . . and found the pistol I'd been going for when Laginn took control of my body and about two-thirds of my brain. I popped the release with my thumb and drew the .45—it's rigged for right-hand draw, but I've practiced it both ways for situations not unlike the present one. It was a good thing I'd invested the time, since the barely sealed athame wound made me clumsier than usual. The 1911 model Colt is also at root a right-handed pistol, so I had to flick the safety off with my trigger finger rather than my thumb, but again, practice paid off.

The sound of the gun firing in the artificial cave of the sewer was deafening. I think it was the noise as much as the impact of the bullets that threw Tyr off his game. Whatever the reason, he staggered back against the wall and slid to the ground. Laginn immediately took advantage of the moment to thrust Occam deep into the war god's left shoulder.

While the hand was doing that, I was focusing my own attention inward, reaching for the shadow of the Raven. Even as I pulled my other shape over me like a cloak woven from threads of agony, Tyr brought his sword around and down. It struck Occam a few inches below the handle and snapped the blade. At which point he shifted the angle of his cut, aiming for my thigh.

It was a masterful piece of sword work, and if I'd still possessed my normal shape, he'd have severed my leg. As it was, the blade neatly lopped the tip off my middle toe. It hurt—though no more than the shape-shift itself—and I would have to do something about the bleeding at some point. In the meantime, I grabbed at the broken end of Occam in Tyr's shoulder with my left foot, using it as a lever to spin me in the air. Then, with a beat of my wings, I launched myself out over the river of sewage, pulling the blade loose and calling for the others to follow as I went.

A tearing pain sliced across my tail as I flapped forward through the air, and I clipped my wounded foot on the railing, almost tumbling into the shit. Somehow, despite all that, I stayed aloft and even managed to turn before I smashed into the far wall—the sewer had barely enough free space for a bird of my size to fly. Add to that the hand clinging to my right wing by two fingers and the loss of some portion of my tail feathers, and not crashing became a much more involved process.

Still, I had to risk a glance back toward the platform before I'd gone ten feet. Then I heaved an enormous sigh of relief. Tisiphone, Melchior clutched in her uninjured hand, was right behind me. That she might not follow, or not think to grab Melchior, had been my biggest fear. Either event would have forced me to change my plan.

"Now what?" Tisiphone yelled after thirty seconds, when a couple of bends separated us from where we had left Tyr.

"Fly as far as we can, then swim the rest of the way, I guess." I didn't have a better answer.

Fortunately, I didn't turn out to need one. Sanitation in Asgard followed a more traditional model than that dictated by modern standards, and the sewer emptied directly into a large river. We quickly crossed the sun-touched water, then flew a mile or two into the wood beyond. We'd have gone farther still if I hadn't been bleeding rather a lot by then and growing increasingly dizzy.

I landed hard and not well. Turns out that tail feathers are helpful for braking as well as staying in the air. The chaos magic involved in returning to my normal shape was intense enough to stop the immediate bleeding, but I was still missing most of a toe, and I had a hell of a cut running all the way across my ass. Melchior started sewing up the latter not long after we landed, but I knew I wasn't going to have much fun with either sitting or walking for a while.

"You've got to get better at this whole flying-away-from-the-enemy thing," said Melchior as he put in another stitch.

"Gosh, thanks, Mel, that would never have occurred to me. I don't suppose you have any ideas on that front?"

"Actually, I might have one or two, but I'm still working out the details. Hold still."

I didn't respond. Instead, I ran a quick inventory of the situation to distract myself from both the pain and the indignity of my current position. It didn't bring me much joy. In addition to my bigger injuries, I was bleeding from a half dozen shallow cuts and pretty much covered in bruises. I'd also pulled more muscles than I knew I owned. . . . Well, Laginn had been the one to pull them, but that wasn't really the point. I was going to be getting very stiff very soon.

Tisiphone was better off, but not enormously so. Her pale skin was patterned with a vivid motley of blue-and-yellow bruises, small cuts, and scrapes. More seriously, she'd taken a nasty sword thrust to the right hip on top of the deep slice in her calf and a handful of broken fingers. None of that would have been more than a momentary irritation at home, but here, where she healed so much more slowly . . . She was hurting badly enough that she'd allowed Melchior to give her a shot of magically produced morphine before he splinted her left hand—Better Living Through Chemistry was one of the most often used spells in his inventory and had received more of his limited practice time because of that.

Melchior himself had mostly stayed out of the direct fighting and was basically all right. He'd even managed to salvage both the networking card and my athame, though I'd lost three guns in two days. And Occam . . . I looked once again at the hilt Laginn had saved with its stub of blade and sighed before slipping it back into its cane-sheath with the rest of the blade. It had been awfully nice to own a magic sword, if only for a little while.

Melchior was just finishing his stitchery when a brazen

hunting horn called a high, clear note somewhere behind us. Another followed, and another, and more yet, building into a wild chorus, which was soon joined by the joyous baying of a whole host of hounds. The branches of the trees started whipping around then, driven by the winds that rose in tandem with the horns and the hounds. Long streaks of gray cloud formed, unrolling to great lengths like ragged-edged banners.

"You don't suppose that's got anything to do with us, do you?" said Melchior, his tone mock-hopeful.

I raised an eyebrow at him and started pulling my pants back up. It hurt despite the shot Melchior had given me.

He shrugged. "Can't blame a goblin for wishing, can you?"

Tisiphone shook her head, her eyes sad. "A hunt is called, and I'm on the wrong end of it."

"You can say that again, sister." A rather large fox stepped from the undergrowth off to our left. "The part about the wrong end, I mean." He gave us an appraising look. "What an odd lot you are. Not that it's going to matter for very much longer, not with Odin raising the Wild Hunt against you."

"The Wild Hunt," I said, genuinely aghast. "That's just fantastic." I finished buttoning my pants and reached for my boots. "The effing Wild Hunt. Why don't they just call in a tactical nuke and be done with it?"

In the background, the sounds of the hunt started their climb into the sky.

Tisiphone touched my shoulder. "It's not that bad. I've ridden with Artemis often enough to know the quarry occasionally gets away." She tilted her head to one side. "Well, it does in our world at any rate."

"Artemis?" asked the fox, obviously puzzled.

"Goddess of the Hun—ow, ow, ow." I yipped as I pulled my right boot over my injured foot—I was going to miss that toe. "At least she is in our world. Who's in charge here?"

The fox looked even more confused at that. "You're kidding, right . . . ? No. I can see you aren't. Well, here's a clue; it ain't called Odin's Hunt for nothing. Savvy?"

Melchior groaned. "Can we run away now, Boss?"

"Yeah, I think that's pretty much what the script calls for at this point. The question is: Where do we run?"

The fox cleared its throat. "I might be able to help you there."

I gave him a closer, harder look, checking to see whether he had Loki's eyes. He didn't, and Tisiphone's careful sniffing of him didn't result in any objections on her part. I still didn't trust him, but the sounds of the Hunt began to move closer, and we didn't have a lot of options.

"Why?" I asked.

"Why what?"

"Why would you help us?"

"Gift horse, mouth, never looking in same," replied the fox. "Does the phrase mean anything to you?"

"Yes, that whoever coined it never had to pay for the upkeep of a bum horse. I'll see your horse-saying and raise you a pig in a poke."

"Oink, oink, oink," said the fox. "Going once . . ."

"Why, damn it?"

"Going twice."

"I don't believe this," said Melchior.

"Last chance," said the fox. "You can take the deal my way or not at all."

I didn't move. The fox shrugged and half turned away.

As the horns came even closer he glanced skyward. "It's your funeral, bud."

I swore bitterly under my breath, then nodded. "Fine, have it your way."

We really didn't have a choice.

"Follow me," said the fox, his voice almost relieved.

He took off, and we had to jog to keep up. Well, everyone else jogged. I did something much closer to hobbling with great vigor. The fox led us into a stream, where we walked about a hundred yards against the current, soon reaching a small waterfall.

"The entrance is low and on the right." The fox pointed toward the waterfall with his nose before ducking under the surface.

He didn't resurface.

"I'll go first," offered Melchior. "I don't need to breathe." He ducked under the water and vanished as well.

Tisiphone—who could no doubt hold her breath for hours—followed a moment later, sending up a cloud of steam as her fires touched the water. It vanished quickly, torn by the raging wind and lost against the clouds that continued to grow, but I didn't want to stick around and find out if it drew any attention. With Laginn clinging to my ankle I dived after her. The passage was narrow and about three feet under the water. It was also fairly long, and the icy cold of the water seemed to sink fangs into the fresh wounds on my foot and ass. I'd started to really worry that I might run out of air when I finally saw the end of the run—a deep and wide pool, its surface illuminated by Tisiphone's fires above.

As my head broke the surface, I decided I really needed to learn a couple more shapes besides the Raven—an otter, maybe, or a dolphin. The pool was at one end of a low limestone cave. The smooth walls and floor suggested that the stream might once have run through there rather than over the waterfall. The odor of wet dog hung heavy in the air.

"You're shivering," Tisiphone said as I came out of the water. "Come here and get warm."

I joined her and the others at the highest, driest point of the cave. She wrapped her arms and wings around me from behind, resting her head on my shoulder. Within moments, steam from my wet clothes began to rise around my face, partially obscuring my view of the cave but also making me feel much better. A thought occurred, and I laughed.

"What?" she asked with a grin in her voice. "It's been a

while since you've smiled, much less laughed. I've missed both."

I decided not to point out that neither our current situation nor the situation back home, where we were at odds over Necessity, lent itself to merriment.

Instead, I said, "There's a lot to be said for partnering a lady who can double as both space heater and night-light."

"How very romantic you are, my dear. Every woman wants to hear herself described in such a forthright and practical way." Then Tisiphone laughed, too, though not before nipping my ear rather harder than affection called for.

Melchior rolled his eyes at us, and the fox looked almost as pained. Which reminded me . . .

"Okay, so now that the pressure's off I'm going to ask again: Why are you helping us? While we're at it, why don't you want to tell us why?"

"Would you believe it's all my way of protesting against fox hunts? Solidarity to those who face the hounds and all that?" I gave him the hairy eyeball. "No?" He shrugged. "Somehow I didn't think so. Not that it really matters at this point, since the main reason I wouldn't answer was because I didn't think you'd take my help if I did, and that's moot now."

I didn't like the sound of that. "Why wouldn't we have taken your help if we'd known why you were offering it?"

"It's not that you would necessarily have refused my aid outright, but I felt certain the debate would have slowed things down considerably at a time when we couldn't afford a delay."

"Are you planning on getting to the point anytime soon?" asked Melchior. "Or, should we settle in for the long haul?"

"Perhaps it's simplest to show you." The fox shook as though it were shedding water.

As it did so it grew and darkened, becoming a huge black wolf. The room brightened then as Tisiphone's flames leaped higher, and I found myself sweating underneath that fiery blanket, where I had been shivering only moments before.

"I know you," said Tisiphone. "You gave me this." She thrust out her right arm, exposing the livid scar where the wolf who chased the moon had bitten her. "But why didn't I recognize your smell?" she whispered.

"This is Hati?" I asked, slipping free of Tisiphone's grasp and stepping to the right.

The wolf laughed. "Guilty as charged."

Laginn scurried to put himself between us and the wolf, but I didn't think it was going to make much difference.

CHAPTER TWELVE

Tisiphone took a couple of long limping steps toward the wolf, passing over Laginn as she did so, an angry light in her eyes. "You and I have a reckoning coming."

"I could go for that." Hati grinned a wolf's grin, the kind with plenty of sharp, pointy teeth. But then he dropped his ears and tail, hiding his fangs. "But I'll only go there if you insist. Papa didn't send me to save you from the Hunt one minute only so I could attack you myself the next."

"Fenris sent you?" I asked. "Why?"

"Me and Laginn both." The hand bobbed a yes in agreement. "Because Grandpa Loki wouldn't, and it needed to be done."

"Okay, now you've lost me," I said. "Back up a bit, would you?"

"Does this mean I don't get to bite him back?" asked Tisiphone, though she sounded relieved—she really wasn't in much better shape than I was. "It does, doesn't it." She sighed. "It probably wouldn't have worked out very well anyway. My powers are weak here. Witness the state of this bite."

She touched the fingertips of her recently broken hand to the angry scar where Hati had bitten her earlier, then winced—though I couldn't tell if that was because of the bite or the break.

"I am sorry about that," said the wolf, flashing us a sheepish grin. "It was reflex more than anything else. I wasn't biting *you*; I was biting someone that had interfered in my pursuit of the moon. And right when I almost had it, too." He wagged his tail slowly. "Oh, who am I kidding? I know I won't catch the damn thing until the last day, but I just can't help myself. I'm like one of those silly car-chasing mortal dogs. Well, not really. If *I* get hold of the moon, I'll know exactly what to do with it. I'll . . ." He trailed off and gave us the grin again. "Sorry about that. Where were we?"

"You were explaining about why Fenris sent you here when Loki wouldn't."

"Oh, right. I suppose I ought to deliver an apology on my grandfather's behalf as well. He really shouldn't have kidnapped the little one there." He jerked his muzzle in Melchior's direction. "I'm sure he regrets it."

I raised a skeptical eyebrow at him.

"Well, no, you're probably right. I'm sure he doesn't regret it in the apologetic sense of the word, though it was bad tactics if nothing else, which he would regret in absolute terms. But you have to see it from his point of view."

"No," said Melchior, crossing his arms, "I don't think that I do. Though I'm willing to hear what that point of view is. If you ever intend to get to your own point, whatever it is."

"Sorry. I'm not really very good at points. Well, not unless they're on the ends of my teeth, and I'm sinking them into that big, white, yummy moon . . ." His ears pricked up, and he stood a little straighter. "Not that that's what you mean, of course. Wait, where was I again?"

"Loki," I prompted.

"Right, right. That was it. Well, it's like this. He's a father, you see. Well, and a grandfather, too. And a great-grandfather for that matter . . . But it's really the father part that counts. He's got a mean streak, sure . . . well, more than a streak, really, but he loves his family."

"What *are* we talking about?" Tisiphone asked, impatience plain in her voice.

"Ragnarok, of course. What else could we be talking about?" Hati blinked and suddenly looked as though someone had hit him in the forehead with a hammer. "Grandpa's right. You really aren't from around here, are you?" He closed his eyes and took a deep breath. "Maybe there *is* a chance of making it all work out better than it's supposed to. No wonder Papa asked me to bring you back to him."

"Wait, what?" I asked. "Make what work out?"

"Ragnarok. The Twilight of the Gods and the death of almost all of us." He flicked his ears down, then up again. "You really don't know what I'm talking about, not even the distorted versions in the human tales."

"Distorted versions?" asked Melchior. "Why distorted?" He looked more than a little put out. Probably because he'd had the time to do some of his homework where I had not.

"Well," said Hati, "only Odin knows the full truth of the matter, though Grandpa has heard most of it, too—some from eavesdropping, some from arguing with Odin over what he'd heard the other way. Both of them have told multiple versions of the thing to bards and skalds as part of something Grandpa calls the spin war."

"Could we get back to the central point?" asked a resigned-sounding Tisiphone. "Before I change my mind and bite you anyway, that is."

"Sorry," said Hati, wagging his tail sheepishly. "Mind's a sieve, really. The long and the short of it is the end of the world. That's what Odin claims anyway. He's seen the future and says that in it we all kill each other in a huge, ugly war that destroys the world and every living thing. Sure, there's a rebirth afterward, but almost none of the present players live to see it. Not even the heroes of Valhalla, since the whole place gets destroyed."

"Cheery," I said.

"Tell me about it," growled Hati, his ears going down again.

"I take it Loki doesn't agree with Odin about all this?" asked Melchior.

"Yes and no. Grandpa doesn't doubt that Odin is seeing the future. What he wonders—hopes, really—is if it isn't *a* future, or *one* future, rather than *the* future. That's why he's been trying so hard to break the MimirNet monopoly—in hopes of shaking Odin's control over everything. The way Grandpa sees it, Odin is an authoritarian determinist—because he's seen it one way and so declared it, it *has* to be that way. Anything else happening would show Odin up as fallible in the knowledge department, and that hits him where he lives. So now that he's seen it, he has to enforce it.

"He won't listen to Grandpa about anything that controverts his vision, and that drives Grandpa crazy. Especially since it's cost his children so much."

"How so?" I asked, though with Laginn sitting right there I couldn't help but think of the cord that bound Fenris and the sword we'd pulled from the wolf's jaws, and I said as much.

"Besides that, Odin condemned my aunt Hel to rule the darkest parts of the underworld, where the damned souls go. And he threw my uncle Jormungand into the ocean." Hati grinned, or more precisely, bared his teeth. "I think that one was a mistake, no matter what Odin saw himself doing in the future. With nothing to limit his size, Uncle Jormungand has grown so big he can reach all the way around the world and bite his own tail now."

"What does all of this have to do with us?" I asked.

Ever since Loki had appeared to me during my last attempt on MimirNet, I'd been waiting to find out what he wanted.

"Well, Grandpa had pretty much given up before you arrived. That's what Papa says anyway, that Grandpa was just going through the motions while getting ever more bitter and angry at the unfairness of it all."

"And now?" I raised an eyebrow.

"Now Grandpa thinks there might yet be some way to salvage something out of all of this. If you do come from a world where there are no Norse gods, that means that the worlds *can* be split, that maybe different, or at least multiple futures are possible. He wants to make an alliance with—"

A great "boom," as loud as a jet breaking the sound barrier, shook the cave and cut him off. A long, thin crack appeared in the ceiling and began dripping.

"What the hell was that?" asked Melchior.

"Thunder," said Hati through bared teeth, his ears and tail low. "Here on Asgard, that can only mean Thor's about. Somewhere very close, too. Damn. Looks like I'm going to have to cut out of an interesting discussion."

"You're abandoning us?" Melchior asked incredulously.

"No, that would be much safer. I'm going to try to lead them away." He headed for the pool.

"Why would you do that for us?" asked Tisiphone.

Hati laughed. "I wouldn't. I'm doing it for my family in hopes of a future where we actually have a future. Goodbye."

He dived into the pool and vanished. Laginn followed him as far as the edge of the water, then turned back to us, looking expectant.

"So, now what?" asked Melchior.

"Stay quiet for a bit," I replied. "At least till we come up with something better, which we should probably get started on." I began to pace, rediscovered my missing toe, swore quietly, and stopped. "I could really get to hate this MythOS, you know that?"

"You and me both," agreed Melchior. "I can barely digest the chaos, my spells work for shit, the binary sucks, and we arrived just in time to watch Ahllan's health go completely south. We've got to get back to her, Ravirn. She's in no shape to take care of herself."

"Hugin and Munin know about Forestdown," I said. "Getting anywhere near there is practically suicidal." Melchior shot me a look of pure betrayal, and I held up both hands. "I'm not disagreeing with you, Mel, just noting it's not going to be easy."

"Not to mention that we have to get out of here first," said Tisiphone, who eased herself down to sit on the floor. "None of us are in great shape. We're both limping"—she scratched around the fresh stitches on her calf—"and Melchior's at about ten percent of what a webgoblin should be in this environment. We need rest and we need sanctuary."

"You think we should join Fenris and Loki, don't you," I said. It wasn't really a question, nor did I entirely disagree with her, but damn it, I didn't like Loki one little bit.

Laginn came back to us and bobbed in agreement before settling beside her. He was starting to look a bit gray again and needed to get back to Fenris. But as much as I liked the hand, I also remembered his hatred of Tyr. The hand had his own agenda, and it didn't necessarily mesh with ours.

"We have to have allies," said Tisiphone, "and that sanctuary I mentioned. I'm not used to needing time to heal, but I need it now, and I'm not going to be much use to anyone until I get it."

"You seemed ready enough to take Hati on earlier," I said.

"That was ninety percent bluff." She held up her broken hand. "This isn't going away without a ton of sleep."

I kicked the floor and immediately regretted it—I was going to miss that toe for a long time to come. She really did have a point.

"Loki kidnapped Melchior," I said. I'd intended the words to come out fierce and righteous, but even to me they sounded more than a little whiny—gods but I was tired, and I hurt all over.

"And Fenris freed him." Tisiphone gave me an appraising look. "Do you want to keep arguing for another ten minutes? Or would you rather give up gracefully now? You'll notice that Melchior hasn't jumped in to proclaim undying opposition."

I looked at Melchior.

"She's right, Boss. I'm not saying I'm ever going to feel all sweetness and light about Loki, but so far we're pretty much oh for ten on the Norse mythos scoreboard."

That covered Tisiphone and Melchior. Laginn? The hand pointed off into the distance and bobbed a yes. About what I'd expected.

"I don't like it." Ouch, whinier still. "But you're probably right."

"I'm definitely right," said Tisiphone, "and you know it, too, or you'd be arguing a lot harder." She grinned. "That or just doing something else and not arguing at all."

I sighed and lowered myself to the ground as gently as possible, lying out flat on my stomach to give my sliced-up butt a rest. "Okay, so let's say I've conceded the argument, and we should go back to Iceland and Rune. The next question is how do we get there from here?"

"Via Forestdown, where we pick up Ahllan," said Melchior, who joined the rest of us on the floor.

"Agreed." I nodded. "But that doesn't answer the big question, which is how the hell do we get out of Asgard?"

"I don't know, Boss. I just don't know."

My brain was seriously fuzzing out on me, and I knew what I really needed was a nap. Unfortunately, this was not the place or the time.

"Mel," I asked, "did you save the Norse MythOS material you pulled off the local human Internet?"

"Sure, but Hati said it's full of mistruths."

"I don't trust Hati, and even if he's right, there's going to be a lot of stuff in there that is true and that I don't know. If you're willing to play laptop for a while, I think it's time I did my homework."

"You're the boss," said Melchior, flickering from goblin to computer in an instant.

"I am not," I said as I edged over to where I could read his screen.

He didn't respond directly, just popped up a saved web page that held a translation of the complete prose Edda—a collection of tales of the Norse gods collected and written down in the 1200s. At least that was what the site claimed. I began to read. After a few moments, Tisiphone crawled over and read over my shoulder.

A couple of hours later—necessarily involving a lot of skimming of the less-immediately-relevant material—I felt I had a much better handle on things. Particularly, I felt that I now understood why everyone was so fixated on the huge mutual suicide pact that was Ragnarok. It was actually quite a strange moment for me because I found myself divided in my sympathies across time.

Assuming for a moment that I was stuck in this pantheoverse, I knew that if Ragnarok started in the next ten minutes, I'd go straight to Odin and sign up to fight on the side of the Aesir. However, Ragnarok hadn't started, and if there was any chance of averting the whole stupid, ugly, selfdestructive mess, I was on the side of whoever was working to short-circuit it.

As far as I could tell, that meant Loki, since Odin seemed to be the worst sort of fatalist on the subject. Of course, Loki was a liar and an opportunist and basically amoral, which meant that I couldn't trust him on anything about which our interests diverged in the slightest degree. Since I counted Eris among my friends, that seemed well within the realm of the familiar.

In the nearer term, I also had a much clearer idea of the interrelationships among the nine worlds of the Norse cosmos and what that meant for getting the hell out of here. As far as I could tell, Asgard was a semi-closed chunk of reality with only two formal connections to the other worlds— Bifrost the Rainbow Bridge, and Yggdrasil, the World Tree.

For reasons unknown, the latter was apparently only used as a path between worlds by a gossipy god-squirrel named Ratatosk. Since none of the legends mentioned anyone else, not even Loki, using the tree as a way in and out of Asgard, there had to be something that rendered it unsuitable for non-squirrel-based transport.

That pretty much left Bifrost with its eternally vigilant guardian, Heimdall. Well, that or a faerie ring, *if* I could make one that worked, although the last had not. That was how I laid out the options when we discussed our next move.

"Did I miss anything?" I asked at the end.

"Not that I can see," said Tisiphone.

"Me neither," said Melchior. "If we had the time and equipment necessary to put together an adapter for me for that network card, it might give us another option, but we don't. Laginn, have you got anything to add? Maybe notes on where the reality doesn't agree with the Edda's version?"

Laginn pressed fingers to thumb in his version of a no, and that was it for discussion. I decided to try the faerie-ring route first since it didn't involve so much as leaving our hideaway. But one large circle and several drops of blood later, and we were heading for the cave's underwater exit. I'd been able to form a ring, but not to link it with the other worlds. The only place we could have traveled by using it was the ring in the sewers of Asgard city, a definite step in the wrong direction.

Whether it was because Hati had led the Hunt far afield or for some other reason, we managed to make it to a small wooded hill overlooking the near end of Bifrost without encountering any major obstacles. That was the end of our luck, however, as Heimdall was very clearly on duty, sitting astride his golden-maned stallion far out on the arch of the rainbow. With the low afternoon sun completely hidden by the roiling clouds that had followed in the wake of the Hunt, the bridge visibly glowed, looking unreal and other-worldly. I was suddenly taken with a desire to see it again some moonless night.

"So, now what?" whispered Melchior.

"I don't know," I whispered back.

Even as I said it, Heimdall's head whipped around, and, despite the brush and weeds that lay between, I could feel his eyes upon me. I was reminded rather forcefully of a passage in the Edda that had said he could hear the grass growing on the hilltop or the wool on a sheep's back. Why is it never hype when you want it to be?

"Run!" I said, as he lifted the horn to his lips and blew a mighty blast.

"Which way?" yelped Melchior.

Before I could reply, Heimdall's call was answered by the horns of the Wild Hunt from behind us.

"Bridge!" I yelled, scooping him up as I started down the slope toward Heimdall and Asgard's only exit.

Laginn, who had opted to ride in my breast pocket, slid down deeper. The god drew his sword and waited. Beside me, Tisiphone extended her long claws. Damn it, this was not how things were supposed to go. There was supposed to be sneaking and trickery and perhaps a bit of swearing, but none of this charging-headlong-into-battle stuff. I *hate* charging headlong into battle. Yet here we were, with fifty feet to go to the bridgehead and less than a quarter mile from there to Heimdall.

The bridge boomed hollowly as we ran out onto it. As we got closer to Heimdall, I couldn't help but remember this was the god who was supposed to slay Loki. Fighting him was insane, but we didn't have much choice; the bridge defined a transdimensional route between worlds.

We couldn't leave it until we had reached the Midgard side. Not with the horns of the Wild Hunt sounding ever closer behind us.

Hang on, I thought. Just because we had to stay with the bridge didn't mean we had to stay on it. Hugin and Munin certainly hadn't.

"Fly!" I yelled to Tisiphone, shifting my own shape as I did so.

I don't think I will ever grow used to shapechanging, no matter how often I do it. Not to the action and certainly not to the pain that poured through my body as I assumed the shape of the Raven once again, though I do appreciate the renewal it brings. As I leaped into the air with Melchior clutched in my feet, all tiredness fell away from me, and though I still bore the wounds Tyr had given me, they now felt several days old instead of the mere hours that had actually passed.

I felt a strange feathery sensation in my chest, as though someone were trying to tickle my ribs from the inside. It was only then that I remembered Laginn had been in my pocket when I shapechanged. I'm not certain exactly what happens to my clothes when I transform, since they have been known to come out different than they went in, but Occam has always come through all right. I could only hope Laginn would do as well in whatever extradimensional pocket or parallel reality held my things. It was too late for anything more.

Tisiphone followed me into the air, and we climbed quickly to twenty or thirty feet above the surface of the rainbow. That should have gotten us comfortably past Heimdall, right?

Wrong.

In the moment that we flew over him, Heimdall changed his own form, becoming a huge osprey. Bunching himself on the saddle of his horse, he threw himself into the air behind us. We had a good start, but he gained with frightening speed. Worse, behind him, and gaining even faster, came the sounds of the Wild Hunt.

"Now what?" demanded Tisiphone, as we both flew faster.

"I don't know. Give me a moment."

"I'm willing," said Tisiphone, "but I doubt our pursuer shares the sentiment." She pointed a thumb over her shoulder.

I looked around wildly, hoping for inspiration. I didn't really have much to work with: the rainbow itself, the clouds above, and the long, long fall to the sea below. That was all.

Melchior whistled a long sequence of pseudobinary then, but nothing happened. He tried it, or a close variation, twice more in quick succession without any result. By then Heimdall was almost on top of us, and I still hadn't thought of anything clever. I felt osprey claws graze the tip of my tail as Melchior began whistling a fourth version. Heimdall, having missed his grab, dropped back, but not far.

Think, Ravirn!

Melchior began to whistle again. Out of the corner of my eye I saw Heimdall straining to reach us. This time he would not miss. Melchior finished the sequence, and we lurched forward just before Heimdall could catch hold. Over the next several seconds we gained speed and opened the distance between us and him considerably.

"What was that?" I asked.

"Don't Be a Drag," said Melchior, and it took me a moment to realize he was naming a spell and not grumbling at me.

"Makes us fly faster?" asked Tisiphone.

"Sort of," replied Melchior. "Mostly it reduces air resistance in the forward direction and *lets* us fly faster. It's a spell I've been thinking about ever since Ravirn decided to turn into a giant bird from time to time."

"Nice," said Tisiphone.

I had to agree, but Heimdall was still behind us, and he seemed to have redoubled his efforts, because the distance between us soon stopped widening. Though he had stopped gaining on us, he kept us firmly in sight, while behind him the Hunt was coming on fast. We might make it to the far end of the bridge uncaught, but then what?

We needed a distraction, ideally a big one. Huge. Earthshaking even. I inventoried our surroundings again: sky, rainbow, and the sea below. Nothing. *Wait. Back up.* I felt the tickle of a memory, something Hati had said. . . . *That's it!* That tossing his uncle Jormungand, the world serpent, into the sea was one of Odin's great mistakes. If I couldn't manage Earthshaking, could I maybe pull off Earth girdling? The horns blowing ever closer behind us lent urgency to the question.

But how to find him? He might be the biggest living thing on the planet, but he was also on the bottom of the ocean and not readily visible from above. I still hadn't figured it out when we reached the end of the line—a pier of rock that looked rather like the first three feet of a stone arch bridge, one that stood on the edge of the sea and reached out over the water. As we moved from one world into the next, we lost our ceiling of cloud, emerging suddenly into the golden hour before sunset.

"Left!" I yelled, turning sharply out over the water.

The maneuver cost us a lot of our lead on Heimdall, but if we were going to find a sea serpent, we needed to stay with the sea. But how did you draw out a sea snake? Maybe I was thinking along the wrong lines. How did you draw out a really big sea snake? No, that wasn't quite it. How did you draw out a chaos god in the shape of the biggest sea snake of them all? Then I had it.

"Tisiphone, cut me!"

"What?" she demanded. "Are you crazy?"

"Maybe, but that's not the point. Cut me. Cut me like you were cutting a hole in the wall of the world."

"I don't understand," said Tisiphone.

"You don't need to," I said. "I'd do it myself, but Occam isn't accessible to me in this form, and I need to bleed chaos."

"Are you sure?"

"No, but do it anyway."

"Deep?" she asked.

"Just enough to make me drip."

"You're cracked," said Melchior. "You do know that, right?"

"Have you got a better idea?" I asked.

"No."

"Then start whistling Jormungand's name in pseudobinary as soon as the chaos hits the water."

Tisiphone struck, a drawing cut about where my right hip would have been in human shape. She used only one claw, but she had to strike hard to get through all the feathers, and I felt as though I'd leaned against the tailpipe of my motorcycle right after a race—it burned! Moments later, and just as I had willed it, drops of chaos started spattering into the water below us, and Melchior began to whistle.

I figured between the very specialized blood in the water, the magical calling of his true name, and the presence of one of his longtime enemies—Heimdall was barely a hundred feet behind us—he had to come out.

Nor was I wrong. Within moments of starting our routine, the sea below us started to bubble and churn. That was when I realized my first mistake. In summoning the Midgard Serpent, I had tied us to the location of his arrival. If we simply flew on with Heimdall and the Hunt pursuing, we would be no better off than we had been before. I turned right to circle back to the place where the waters churned, hoping Jormungand would arrive before Odin and the Hunt. Heimdall cut inside my turn, drawing even closer. Though he couldn't have missed what was going on down at the water's surface, he didn't let it stop his pursuit.

The horns came louder still.

As I spiraled in toward the heart of the disturbance below us, a dark spot appeared in the center. A moment later a tower of bone and muscle burst into the air, a living skyscraper self-erected between two blinks of the eye. Behind us Heimdall screamed an osprey's defiance and sheered away.

I kept going, mesmerized. I had expected Jormungand to reflect his origins in the Norse world, dark and frightening, as much sharky-sea-monster as serpent, an avatar of the North Atlantic tempest. I couldn't have been more wrong. Jormungand was the son of fire's god, and a snake to his skin.

His belly was a yellow as bright as any forest fire. On his sides the color gave way to the deep burning orange of fresh embers threaded through with lines of black that grew denser and closer together as they climbed, becoming a broad, inky stripe on his back. His eyes were intense points of red fire. Once he stopped rising, he opened his mouth, exposing fangs the color of polished ebony, and flared a hood like a cobra's. For an instant, he hung there above me, then he struck.

It was only then that I realized my second mistake. Giant birds and giant snakes are a bad combination. Instead of attacking the fleeing Heimdall, the Midgard Serpent struck at me.

I tried to dodge, but I simply wasn't fast enough. The huge head hit me like a falling building. A fang longer than my entire body and nearly as big around as my wrist punched deep into my back. I tried to scream, but a punctured lung transformed it into something between a gasp and a whimper. Quieter even than the now-retreating horns of the Hunt.

The world went dim and far away, and all I could think about was whether it would be worse to drop Melchior the hundred feet into the waves and hope Tisiphone saved him or to hold on to him and hope that I could.

That was when the fang in my back pulsed, and I re-membered that Jormungand was poisonous.

Good luck, Mel, I mouthed, though no words came out.

I felt liquid fire pour into my back and let him go. I only wished I could do as much for Laginn.

CHAPTER THIRTEEN

Fire filled my chest, pumped in through the gaping wound in my back. Jormungand's venom found and burned its way into my heart, going from there into my arteries and thence to every corner of my body. I burned from within.

For a few instants that seemed to last a lifetime, I knew that I had died, and I waited to see whether the Valkyries would come to claim me or if I would be sent home to Hades and eternal torment. The fire filled me utterly.

Then I felt . . . better!

Much, much better. Fantastic, even godlike. For just a moment longer I believed in my own death, that I had found the door to Elysium. Then I realized that these were familiar feelings, if far more intense than I was used to. I felt as I did when submerged in the Primal Chaos, only much more so.

In that instant two very important things occurred to me.

One, that the poison of the Midgard Serpent was akin to the stuff in his brother's gut. Chaos. In this case, chaos distilled to its purest expression. Jormungand had just in-

jected me with about 7,000ccs of refined magic. It might
be the local brew instead of my home brand, but I still felt
great!

Two, I had just dropped my best friend for no good reason. Which meant I needed to do something *besides* feel
great, and damn quick, too. But caring was hard. There's
something about being overcome by ecstasy that really
takes away from your sense of urgency.

Still, I had all this free-floating power, and maybe I
could just use a bit of it to ... I reached inward, dipping
into the torrent of concentrated chaos flowing through my
heart and feeding it to the Raven within. Using the tiniest
fraction of that power, I pulled myself off the fang embedded in my back and slid free of the serpent's mouth. Wings
furled, I started the long plummet toward the sea below.

I had barely begun to fall when I felt the gaping wound
in my back heal itself, felt all of my wounds seal themselves one by one. Though Jormungand's venom no longer
pumped into me, its effects continued to build as it satu-
rated every fiber of my being. I could feel myself changing
at the most basic level as Norse fire and frost married itself
to the Greek Χαος I had inherited from the Titans, the two
streams of chaos meeting and becoming one within me.

As I fell, I reached outward with senses enhanced by the
floodtide of power rising in my soul. A part of me noted
and felt relieved by the spectacle of the Wild Hunt circling
back toward Bifrost and the road to Asgard, but most of my
attention I reserved for the waters beneath me. I saw many
things, both above and below the surface.

The largest was the shadow of the Raven, my shadow—
bigger than I had ever seen it, with a wingspan that stretched
a hundred feet in either direction—a shadow as dark as a
slice of the primordial night that lurks in the deeps of the
Earth. With a nudge of my will, I aimed my fall straight
toward the shadow's heart.

Infinitely more important and precious, however, was my
view of Melchior. The tiny goblin tumbled amidst the surg-

ing waters that accompanied the writhing of the great serpent. He had already descended far beneath the waves and continued to sink.

The form of the Raven went from help to hindrance as I passed through the interface between the world above and the one below. Drawing upon the power of the venom running in my veins, I discarded wings and feathers as easily as I might have slid off my jacket at another time, transforming myself into a huge otter. The usual shock of agony went through me as I shifted shape, but this time the pain brought a twisted joy, filtered as it was through the chaos-fueled euphoria that still continued to build within me.

I dived deep, instinctively tucking my front paws tight against my chest and driving myself downward with the broad flippers of my hind feet while I steered with my tail. In seconds, I had overtaken Melchior. Catching his right hand in my paw, I drew him upward. He didn't fight. In fact, he barely moved, seeming half-drowned despite the fact that breathing was a purely optional activity for him. I was so focused on Melchior that I'd almost reached the surface before I remembered the Midgard Serpent and thought to worry about what might happen next.

It was a purely intellectual exercise, this worrying—all forebrain, no emotional investment. My emotions remained in fuzzy-bunny-utopia because of all the magical happy juice in my bloodstream. That was probably good. It kept me from freaking out when I found myself surfacing in a huge circle of water as calm and flat as a bathtub waiting for a bather.

The towering walls that surrounded it blocked all the turbulence of the greater sea, living walls the brilliant yellow of a candle's flame—the scaled belly of the Midgard Serpent. I was encircled, wrapped around and around and around again by the coils of Jormungand. Centered over this shielded pool like a low thundercloud hung his huge head, those burning red eyes fixed firmly on me and Melchior. His mouth was ajar, exposing a long, forked tongue, one strand of which he'd wrapped around Tisiphone like a living rope.

Either because of my chaos overcharge or because of some special otter sense as yet unknown to science, I could feel that the serpentine walls completely enclosed the column of water in which I swam. From the bottom of the seabed to the clean, clear air thirty feet up, Jormungand surrounded me. There would be no easy escape.

"Panic!" my forebrain screamed at my hindbrain.

"Chill," replied the hindbrain. "It's all good. You know, this chaos is *great* stuff. We should have some more. Maybe we could get the snake to bite us again."

Actually, the hindbrain wasn't anything like that coherent. It just sat there churning out the biochemical markers for bliss. Chaos and Discord, but I hate feeling drunk.

While my brain argued itself into vapor lock, my otter's body went its own merry way. Without exercising the slightest bit of volition, I found myself rolling onto my back and balancing Melchior on my chest like a mother sea otter with her cub. Holding him there with one paw, I patted his back with the other. After a few seconds he blinked and coughed up a little water. Then he looked me in the eyes.

"Ravirn?" he asked, uncertainty writ large in both tone and expression.

"Yep, yep, yep," I said in something halfway between speech and chittering—with my brain devoting so much energy to arguing with itself, my body continued on its own happy otter way.

Melchior shook his head bemusedly.

Before either of us could say more, a deep, urbane voice sounded from above, "What exactly *are* you, little otter who was a raven?"

"That's *Ravirn*, snake-dude!" I slapped myself with one furry paw. Hard.

"Sorry," I said. "I'm a little on the altered side of the chemical balance at the moment. When you bit me, you sorta overflowed my chaos buffers."

"I was kind of wondering about that," said Jormungand, tilting his huge head from side to side as though he were trying to get a better look at me. "Normally when I bite something, it dies. Even the gods are supposed to die when my poison fills their veins. You not only didn't die; you came out better off than you started."

"Totally," I said, with an otter grin. "But I'm a special case, maybe *the* special case, though I wouldn't bet against the venom's having the same effect on Loki."

"Why is that?" asked Jormungand, leaning even closer.

I couldn't help but notice Tisiphone glaring at me from amidst the loops of his tongue. Her mouth was held firmly shut, or she probably would have been swearing. I winked at her.

"Well," I said, "strictly speaking, I don't have veins for your poison to fill."

"I don't understand."

I pinched the back of my left paw between the claws of my right. "This flesh is a sort of mask I wear over the real me; at least that's what Eris says. When I fought Hades, I died, or my body did anyway, eaten by the chaos that forms my soul. My body is a lie I tell the universe, a physical manifestation of my will. Of course, I *can* die because it's a lie I tell me, too, but that's another story."

"Hades? Eris?" Jormungand shook his head. "The more you speak, the less you say."

"Sorry. The chaos from your bite seems to have given me a bad case of the babbles. Look, I have a proposal to make. You may have noticed that we arrived pursued by a giant osprey—"

"Heimdall," said Jormungand, his voice flat and angry.

"Yeah, him. Not terribly far behind was the Wild Hunt and Odin. They seem to have given up for now, but they might change their minds, and I'd really rather not be here if that happens. Would you be willing to carry on this conversation somewhere else? Or at least on the way to somewhere else?"

"Perhaps, where did you have in mind?"

"I thought we might head for Iceland. I need to talk to your father about a deal he wanted to make."

He moved his head a little farther back. "I can see I have been too long out of the loop. Yes, I will take you to Iceland, and we may talk on the way."

"Boss!" spluttered Melchior. "What about Ahllan?"

I blinked. *How could I have forgotten her? Oh, right. Drunk on chaos. Damn.*

"Where are we now?" I asked. "My little blue buddy here has just reminded me that we need to make a stop on the way. On the north shore of Prince Edward Island. I've a sick friend I need to visit. Oh, and I'm afraid I'll have to insist."

"I suppose," said Jormungand, sounding quite bemused, "though it's not anything like on the way, and I'm not sure you're really in any position to insist. We're just off the coast of Denmark. I'd argue, but I suspect it would only delay the delivery of the answers I want. Is there anything else?"

"Not that I can—" A rather loud growl from Tisiphone's direction interrupted me. "Oops, yes, could you be so kind as to let go of my girlfriend?"

"Sure, why not?" Jormungand sighed. "I can always eat you all later if I change my mind. And letting go of her will make it ever so much easier to carry on a conversation without drooling."

He spat Tisiphone out, and she dropped toward the waves, pulling up only a few feet above me.

"Later, you and I are going to need to have a long talk about priorities," she said, and the snarl in her voice and the blaze in her eyes were enough to give me a little shiver even through the pink cloud that still cushioned me from the world.

"Uh, yeah. I guess we will."

"Bet on it," growled Tisiphone. Then she winked, her anger seeming to evaporate in an instant.

I don't think that I will ever understand her.

"If you two are ready?" asked Jormungand, and I just about jumped out of my borrowed otter skin.

Without making any noise and with remarkable speed, Jormungand had uncoiled from around us and dropped his head down so that his mouth was mere inches behind me.

"Sure, sure, sure," I chittered, half in otterish.

Before I could do anything more, Jormungand vanished under the gently rolling waves without so much as a splash. A moment after that, he slid his head underneath us and resurfaced. Our initial ascent was like riding a very fast elevator with no walls. Within seconds I, still lying on my back with Melchior on my belly, found myself several stories in the air.

"Everybody comfortable?" asked the serpent.

Tisiphone landed next to me and sat down cross-legged. "We are now," she called out.

"Then away we go."

Jormungand shot forward, accelerating from zero to something way past sixty in a matter of seconds. Despite our speed, there was no wind, and the sheer size of the platform provided by the top of his skull made any worries about falling off seem ludicrous. Or perhaps I was just still too chaos-drunk to care.

Melchior hopped off my chest and sat down on the opposite side from Tisiphone. I rolled over onto my belly and would have settled my head on my paws if I hadn't felt a sudden intense tickling sensation under my rib cage.

"Laginn," I said. "I almost forgot about him. I'd better let him out."

I knew the shape-shift would come much harder this time. I still had extra power coming out of my ears, and I was still in my happy place, but I actually had time to think about it in advance, and that makes a huge difference.

Fundamentally what I do when I change my shape is create a magical map of where every atom in my body is now and a second map of where it needs to be in the shape

I want to assume. Then I plot a route from one to the other and drop it into a set of magical instructions, a spell if you prefer. It's all done on the fly since I'm a hacker and that's the way I work. And it has to happen very fast so that the universe doesn't catch on somewhere in the middle and interrupt the process.

Such an interruption would leave me as a rapidly expanding cloud of magically charged atoms. Bad for me, and quite probably bad for the world around me. If the atoms hit anything sufficiently magically reactive, that is. It's not quite the recipe for an atomic bomb, just the magical equivalent. Once I've got a spell hack ready to go—in this case an extra-kludgy one since I had to work within the skin-changer framework of the local MythOS and I just didn't know it very well yet—it's just a matter of triggering things and hoping I don't go "boom."

I mentally flipped the switch. Then I screamed. Gods and monsters, but the process is painful. You wouldn't expect it to be, since it's too fast on both ends for the nerves to send signals to the brain, and during the middle part I have neither nerves nor a brain for them to complain to. But somehow my soul remembers being torn apart and put back together again, and it doesn't like it.

Before I'd even finished screaming, Laginn shot out of the neck of my jacket as though he were rocket-propelled. He landed on all fives and took off at a dead scurry. He was moving so fast he almost shot off into space when he ran out of serpent, skidding around only at the last second in a half turn that left him hanging from the ridge over Jormungand's right eye.

"What is that . . . thing?" Jormungand asked in the tones of an orchestra director finding a bagpipe among the piccolos. "And what is going on up there?"

"We call him Laginn," I said as I edged down to a place where I could see the eye, and it could see me.

Either the transformation and the pain that came with it had sobered me up a bit, or I was starting to adapt to the extra load of chaos, because I found that being so close to the dropoff at speed made me nervous. I rather wished I could be elsewhere, but I felt I owed it to Laginn to bail him out after all I'd put him through so far.

"He used to be Tyr's hand," I said. "Before your brother bit him off, that is. Now he works for him . . . kind of."

"My brother Fenris employs the 'hand that wouldn't die'? No, don't tell me about it. It's a distraction. What I really want to know about is you and what Loki wants from you. And especially why my bite affected you the way it did."

"Fair enough. Let me just help my friend up here." I extended my hand to Laginn.

He didn't grab hold, choosing instead to look back at me rather warily, inasmuch as it is possible for a hand to look at someone.

"I'm really sorry about taking you through all those transformations without asking you. I didn't have a lot of time for polite under the circumstances. I promise I won't do it again . . . unless I really have to."

Laginn slumped in a sort of physical sigh, then reached out a finger to me. I lifted him back onto the top of Jormungand's head, and he scuttled off to sit with Melchior, leaving me alone beside the eye.

"Sit," said Jormungand, "please. Tell me everything. We've got some time."

I glanced back at Tisiphone, but she just made shooing motions. There was a sort of dip in the surface of Jormungand's skull just inboard of the eye ridge, a concave spot at the boundary between two scales. I settled myself in—it was surprisingly comfortable—and started my story.

I'd only just begun when Jormungand stopped me the first time. "Wait, you claim to come from a universe where the gods are those of the ancient Greeks? And to be related to them? That's fascinating. You mentioned Hades and Eris earlier, but I thought you were just babbling to keep me from eating you. Who are your parents? More important, who are their parents? Are you from Zeus's line? Poseidon's? Some other?"

"Hold it," I said. "You know Zeus?"

"Not personally, no. But I know of him. I've read all the stories. I even listened to Homer a time or two when he spoke his piece close enough to the shore." The giant snake smiled. "I do like the Mediterranean, especially in winter, though putting my neck in the Strait of Gibraltar always makes me feel as if I'm wearing a tie that's a little too tight. Good speaker, Homer, and such lovely stories. Of course, I always assumed he was full of shit since your Eris and company had never shown their faces anywhere I could see them.

"But here I am interrupting you before you can answer my questions. Quite rude of me, actually. It's just I get so hungry for decent conversation down there on the seafloor. It does leave me plenty of time for reading, but that's not the same thing at all. So, back to my question. Who are your people?"

To my very great shock I found myself reciting my entire genealogy and life story to the Midgard Serpent. I had just about finished bringing him up to the present moment when he interrupted me with a small throat-clearing noise.

"We're just about to hit Prince Edward Island. I do want to hear the rest, but if you've got anything you want to prepare before you go collect your Ahllan, now's the time."

"Who said we were here to collect her?" Melchior demanded suspiciously. He'd crept in close at some point after the sun had gone down, and I hadn't noticed until that moment. "Way back at the start of this trip we said we were just going to visit a friend."

"Don't be silly," said Jormungand. "It's obvious you can't leave her here under the circumstances. Hugin and Munin could come back at any time, to say nothing of Odin. That's practically asking them to take her hostage."

"As opposed to putting her in Loki's hands?" asked Mel. "Where no one would ever dream of using her as a hostage?"

I couldn't see Jormungand roll his eyes, but sitting as I was just above one, I could feel it.

"Mel," I said, "he's right."

"Don't tell me you're going to trust the word of a serpent. Come on, forked tongue? Hello!"

"I am, and I do. We have to trust someone, Mel. We're caught between two sides in a god war, and we need allies if we don't want to get crushed."

Melchior's shoulders slumped, and he nodded, but he didn't say anything.

"We'll be back shortly," I told Jormungand, as he lowered and angled his head so that we could step straight from the tip of his nose to a long, empty pier.

"I'll wait out there." He jerked his chin indicating the black depths beyond the bay, then quickly slipped away.

Ahllan didn't wake when we trooped into the miniature cathedral's chapter house. Nor when Tisiphone lit several of the lanterns with her wings. Nor even when we all went to stand beside the small platform that held her futon. In the dim light she looked old and tired, defeated, her cheeks sunken beneath dark eye sockets. The acrid smell of burned circuits hung in the air, which worried me even more than her appearance, especially with her in her troll shape. Only the very faint rise and fall of the covers gave any sign that she still lived.

"Ahllan?" said Melchior, very gently touching her elbow. "Ahllan?"

"Melchior?" she whispered, not opening her eyes. "Is it really you this time? Not just another hopeful dream?" She reached out a hand.

"It's me," he said, taking her hand between his own as he sat down on the edge of the bed. "We're back."

She smiled and opened her eyes, though both seemed to take great effort. "I knew you'd come back, that not even Odin's ravens could keep you away, though fear told me a different story."

"Speaking of the ravens," said Melchior, "we need to get you out of here in case they come back. Can you travel?"

"I can't walk far, if that's what you mean," she said. "And carrying me would only slow you down. But that's all right. I don't think I've got much time left anyway. The ravens don't frighten me. Nor their one-eyed master. There's nothing they can do that will stop the inevitable for long. Just leave me here."

"No," said Tisiphone. Her voice was flat and hard, a Fury delivering a verdict without any room for argument. "Not while I can carry you."

Ahllan made a protesting noise, but Tisiphone ignored her. Squatting to give herself a better angle, Tisiphone slid her hands underneath the edge of the futon platform. Very gently and very smoothly and despite her many injuries, she lifted the whole thing and got her right palm firmly under its center of balance. As she stood up, she shifted her grip so that she held it on hand and shoulder like a waitress carrying an extra-large tray.

"Easier than arguing," said Tisiphone with a grim smile.

I could tell the effort was taking more out of her than she'd expected, but there wasn't much I could do about that except offer to spell her after a bit, which I would. Though Tisiphone is about ten times as strong as I am, the whole package including bed, bedding, and both AIs couldn't have run much more than three hundred pounds. I could carry that for quite a while if I had to after the supercharge I'd gotten from Jormungand's bite.

"Shall we?" asked Tisiphone.

She started toward the door, and I had to hurry to keep ahead of her so I could hold it open. Ahllan made a few more feeble protests but gave up and drifted back to sleep when it became clear no one was going to listen to her, though I think it was more a matter of conserving her energy and not fighting a lost cause than because she agreed with us. I felt terrible about moving her, but we really didn't have any choice.

We had just shifted back to full size outside York Miniature when there came a loud "pop" and sizzle rather like an industrial-scale bacon accident. It was followed by a solid "thump" from the far side of the miniature cathedral. Tisiphone's fires flared.

"What was that?" she asked.

"More messages from home?" said Melchior, his voice speculative.

"I don't understand," said Tisiphone.

"You weren't here the last time, but Ahllan said that's the noise stuff makes when it comes through from the Greek MythOS," I said. "We'd better go look."

Tisiphone nodded but didn't say anything, and she kept her eyes away from mine as we picked our way around the cathedral. I wasn't sure what was going on there, though her anger with Necessity might explain it. We found a smoky silver sphere about the size of a tractor tire sitting in the middle of the dead lawn like some sort of oversized garden gazing ball. As we got closer, strange highlights started to dance across its surface like the shimmers of a soap bubble.

"I don't like that," said Melchior, hopping down from his perch beside Ahllan and edging toward the ball. "It looks entirely too much like the thing that showed up back in the abacus room right before we got sent here."

I nodded, and Tisiphone set Ahllan down before stepping between us and the ball. As the Fury moved nearer, a low, growling noise began in the back of her throat. I don't think she was even aware of it. She had just gotten within touching distance when the ball sparkled wetly and popped, vanishing into nothing. It left behind a big yellow chunk of something that looked a lot like brain coral.

"Shit," said Melchior, and Tisiphone's wings and hair

flared. "I hope that's not what I think it is." He hurried forward.

"It is," said Tisiphone, her voice choked.

"I don't get it," I said, coming up between the two of them.

Tisiphone didn't answer, just placed a foot on the coral and shoved. It tipped over, revealing a highly polished convex underside, the curve of which looked like a perfect match for the vanished sphere. Bending closer I could see millions of very fine black veins running through the yellow matrix of the coral in fractal patterns. Though infinitely more complex, the effect reminded me of a cutaway view of a computer chip.

Wait a second. Something tickled at the back of my brain.

"What am I seeing here?" I asked.

"A piece carved from my mother's brain," said Tisiphone, whose fires had dropped back to a very low ebb.

It came back to me then. Right before my final confrontation with Nemesis, Melchior and I had been taken to see Shara. The soul of the webgoblin had then been inhabiting one of the newest portions of the network that housed Necessity, a single, massive quantum computer that had been grown rather than constructed, a computer that looked more like a coral reef than anything built. I put an arm around Tisiphone's waist and gave her a gentle squeeze. No matter how mad she was at Necessity for replacing her with another Fury, this had to hurt.

"I hate this," she said, through clenched teeth. "I just hate it."

Pulling free of my arm, she smashed a fist into the hunk of computer-coral. It split into three big pieces and dozens of smaller ones, exposing an irregular hollow space within. There, cupped in the largest of the shards, lay a tiny black lump. At first glance I thought it was a spider, but closer inspection revealed that where the head should have been was the upper half of a miniature woman—a spider-centaur and not the first I'd seen. The other, much larger version, had been the entity who took me to see Shara in the coral. Very gently, I picked up the spider-centaur. She didn't move.

"Is that the same spinnerette?" asked Melchior.

"If it is, she's lost a lot of weight," I replied. "To say nothing of having made a miraculous recovery."

The spinnerette who'd taken us to see Shara had been the size of a small car and had gotten herself killed trying to help us defeat Nemesis. I poked the little creature gently with one finger, but she still didn't stir. For all I could tell, she'd died in transit.

Not good. I'd learned a lot about the spinnerettes since my conflict with Nemesis. They were creatures of chaos created by the Fates in the pre-mweb days. They took many shapes, but the spider-centaurs were one of the more common. These days they seemed to be at the heart of some sort of weird collaboration between Necessity and the Fates' central computer, a collaboration the Fates desperately wanted terminated.

Combine unhappy Fates with the unknown creator of the silver spheres, the mythic crossover the abacuses had inflicted on us, and now the appearance of a spinnerette so very far from home, and stir to produce . . . what? I was starting to really get nervous about whatever was happening back home. Maybe there was more than one god war going on. And maybe whatever had sent us here was part of the opening salvo.

CHAPTER FOURTEEN

"We don't have time for this," said Tisiphone, kicking over the remnants of the computer-coral. "We need to get Ahllan someplace safe, and soon. We're way too exposed here. Besides, no matter what's happening back home, there's nothing we can do about it while Odin controls the only route to our multiverse."

I nodded reluctantly. She was right, but I've got an over-developed curiosity bump, especially when it comes to anything that relates to the Fates. I took the possibly dead spinnerette and very gently slid her into an outside pocket on my leather jacket. I couldn't just leave her there, but I didn't want her inside the Kevlar if she woke up angry.

I helped Tisiphone get the bed bearing the still-sleeping Ahllan back onto her shoulder, and we were off. The old troll slept all the way to the bay where we'd left Jormungand. When we set her down in the dune grass just beyond the high-tide line, she raised herself on one elbow and looked around.

"Where are we?" she asked. "And what are we doing here?"

"Hitchhiking," I replied.

"You're joking, right?"

"No, he's not." Melchior sighed.

"You'll see," I said.

Drawing the hilt shard of Occam, I put a shallow cut in my left hand. The moon had left the sky, and late night was losing its eternal battle with early morning, but the stars and my eyes provided plenty of light as I walked down to the edge of the rocky beach. I willed the chaos to start dripping from my fresh cut and held my hand out over the water in the classic thumbing-a-ride position.

"I don't understand," said Ahllan. "What are you all—oh my!"

Jormungand had arrived, visible more as an absence than a presence. The great black wedge of his head occluded the northern stars like a serpentine eclipse.

"Is that . . . ?"

"The Midgard Serpent?" asked Jormungand, finishing her question, his voice gentle. "Yes, I am. And you must be Ahllan. You may call me Jormungand, and I'm quite pleased to meet you. I've heard so much about you in the past few hours that I already feel I know you well. I only wish we could be meeting at a less strained time. Unfortunately, my wishes do little to move the world, and we should not linger now that you've arrived." The huge shadow twisted quickly left, then right. "Hugin and Munin could show up at any moment, or even Odin himself, and we have many miles yet to travel."

He lowered his head so that his nose touched the pier. Tisiphone and I caught up Ahllan's bed between us and hurried out onto the wooden planks and from there up onto Jormungand's head, settling the bed as best we could. Moments later the serpent turned and moved out to sea once more. Melchior remained with Ahllan while I resumed my story and my seat just beside Jormungand's eye.

This time Tisiphone joined me, laying her head in my lap. I rested my hand on her neck with my thumb in the curve of her jawline. She smiled and closed her eyes as I talked, though I don't think she slept.

A long, slow October sunrise off Iceland seen from the top of a moving skyscraper. Beautiful and surreal. Jormungand took us to the brilliant wall of blue ice, where a glacier flowed southward into the sea, and raised his head level with the top. We disembarked there just as the sun finished sliding clear of the ocean behind him. The waves sparkled like a line of rubies and topazes in the dawnlight.

"This is as close as I can take you. There's an unnamed little island off that way"—he pointed southwest along the coast with his tongue—"where the others and I meet for family conferences. When you get to Rune, tell my father and brother that I want to be included in the coming discussions."

"I will," I said.

"Good. I'll wait for all of you there." He pointed with his tongue again, then sank out of sight.

Tisiphone hefted Ahllan's bed. "I'm kind of missing Thor's chariot at the moment," she said, eyeing the unbroken snow and ice that lay between us and the mountains that hid our destination.

"I miss the mweb and sensible travel," said Melchior.

"Failing that, a snowmobile suit wouldn't go amiss," I replied. "It's freezing!"

Tisiphone, despite the fact she didn't have a stitch on, just smiled and winked. Furies are never cold.

"I can't manage a flying chariot," said Ahllan, who had woken up again and was looking a good bit less tired, "but I can probably conjure that snowsuit and some skis."

She whistled several long strings of pseudobinary, producing a couple of cross-country ski rigs, a snowsuit for me, and two big runners for the bottom of her bed. Since

I'd gone to college in scenic—and frozen—Minnesota, I had more than a passing familiarity with the skis and their accoutrements. Pretty soon we were off to look for the nearest road and better transport.

Some hours after that we found ourselves waiting in the lobby of Rune. Somehow the whole post-logo thing made me feel the need to roll my eyes every time I said the name of Loki's computer enterprise.

"I'm afraid Mr. Ulfr isn't available right now," said the giant receptionist, touching the earpiece of her headset. "He's in a conference, but I've left a message that he should see as soon as he gets done."

"What about Loki?" I asked. I'd prefer to start with Fenris, but I'd take what I could get.

"I'm afraid he's also in a meeting. I can leave a message for him as well if you'd like." She smiled at us with her big predator's teeth.

"Don't bother," I replied. "If we have to wait anyway, we'll wait for Fenris."

She nodded and turned back to her desk. After a few minutes she started talking into her headset. "Of course I ate him. Stupid geologist. They know they're not supposed to enter the tunnels off the main crater. Loki wrote that into their official policy document when he cracked the system." She canted her head to one side and laughed. "No, not raw, silly. I'm not a complete barbarian. I did him up in a nice curry with lentils."

I tuned her out at that and settled down to chat quietly with Melchior and Tisiphone. Having heard the Greek version of monsters swapping hero recipes in the past, I knew that they were both disturbing and quite frequently fictitious. Sure, they say that they eat people all the time, but that's gotten much harder to get away with in the modern era. I think it's mostly the monster equivalent of maintaining street cred at this point.

Some minutes later Laginn got up from where he'd been sitting beside Ahllan and raised a finger to attract our atten-

tion. The hand pointed at himself, then into the depths of
Rune, before miming a wolf's head and making a leading
gesture. Then he quickly signed yes/no?

"Seems like a good idea to me," I replied. "If you can
find him and bring him here, I'm all for it."

The hand hopped down and scurried off. He hadn't been
gone more than five minutes when the muffled sounds of an
argument came through the glass wall that separated the
lobby from the main part of the complex. Over the next few
moments it rapidly got closer and louder until rather suddenly Loki and Fenris appeared on the far side of the glass.
Loki was pounding his fist repeatedly into his hand while
Fenris—in wolf shape—had his tail down and his hackles
up.

"Because you should have told me before you did it;
that's why!" yelled Loki. "This is just like when you let
them come and take that little AI back without a fight."

"And I was right then, just like I'm right now," growled
Fenris in a voice that should have sent every small animal
within a thousand miles scurrying for the nearest hole.
"You're blinded by your hatred for Odin."

The giantess at the desk looked up at us and smiled
rather sickly.

"And you can't see past your hunger for companionship," said Loki. "Try not to forget that the reason you're
trapped here on Midgard with only the friends I bring you
is because of Odin's twisted need to control everything. You
should hate him at least as much as I do!"

"Who says I don't? If anything, I hate him more. But
I'm not going to let that stop me from thinking. If I'd come
to you before I sent Laginn and Hati off, we'd still be arguing about it, and Odin would have them again."

The giantess pulled off her headset and put it down beside her in an overtly casual manner. Then she slipped a
hand under her desk, activating the mechanism that turned
a portion of the wall into something like red Jell-O. Finally,
and without ever breaking eye contact with us, she got up

and very quickly sidestepped to the portal before backing into the other area. As the red glow went away, she waved stiffly at us.

"What is it now, Grýla?" demanded Loki, his voice still pitched for a fight.

She didn't say anything, just jerked her chin in our direction. The whole pantomime-theater nature of the thing was starting to really tickle my fancy, and I couldn't help chuckling.

"I don't . . ." he began, then trailed off as he turned and spotted us. "Oh." In an instant, Loki's expression switched from hot fury to icy calm.

He turned to Fenris then and said something very low and very fast. Then he waved at us and smiled an unfriendly smile before heading back into the depths. Fenris, on the other hand, seemed genuinely glad to see us, his ruff dropping back to normal and his tail coming up as he gave us a wink and headed straight toward the wall. In the instant before he would have hit it, a beam of red light shot down from the ceiling behind him and did the glass-to-Jell-O trick.

"I take it you've decided to agree to my offer," he said as he stepped through the gate.

"Say that we've come to discuss it, and you're closer to the truth," I replied. "Hati was called away rather abruptly before he could finish laying things out for us."

"That rather optimistically assumes he would have eventually gotten to the point," Fenris said with a grin, "no?"

I couldn't help but grin back. "There is that. So you know . . . ?"

"That my son is a babbling cretin?" Fenris nodded. "Of course I do. That's half of why I sent him. He's quite a nice lad if you don't happen to be a large silvery orb, by far the most personable envoy I could lay my paws on at short notice. After Laginn, that is. Speaking of which, where is he?"

"Looking for you," said Tisiphone, inserting herself into

the conversation for the first time. "That was quite an argument you were having with Loki, and not guaranteed to raise a lot of confidence in the listener, particularly this listener."

Fenris laughed. "He's just unhappy because I sent someone to get you without being told 'fetch' first. Well, that and he really didn't much like when I released your friend."

"I noticed that bit," said Melchior. "I can't say it made me want to cast my vote for Team Loki either."

"Understandable and understood," said Fenris. "But it's not like Team Odin is all sweetness and light, as you might have noticed while sitting in Asgard's charming jail. Nor is Team Odin offering you any kind of deal at all. Odin doesn't bargain. He commands. But that's a discussion I'd rather not have out here in the lobby. Why don't you come up to my office? Also, I can't help but notice that your troll friend isn't looking in the best of health. Can I arrange a quiet room for her?"

"Her condition's another one that belongs on Loki's doorstep," said Tisiphone. "Since I'd rather not give him another chance at her, the answer is no. She goes where we go."

Fenris nodded. "Fair enough. Grýla, would you bring the troll along to my office?"

The giantess lifted the bed neatly under one arm. Laginn was waiting in the office when we got there, having entered through a little pet door set into the bottom of the main door.

The large rectangular office had walls of polished obsidian offset by sleek stainless steel and glass furniture and a cool blue deep-pile rug. On the far wall, behind the desk, was a triple-paned window overlooking a fiery lake of lava with a tiny island at its center—presumably the place of Fenris's binding.

Fenris settled onto a thick mat behind his desk. It should have looked silly—the giant wolf sitting behind an ultramodern executive fashion statement, its glass surface bare except for one of Loki's microcomputers. It didn't. It looked perfect, a surrealist's portrait of the ultimate predatory CEO. The hellish view over the lake of fire behind him only added to the effect.

"My, what big teeth you have," I said.

"All the better to charm you with, my dear," replied Fenris. "Come, sit down. Let's talk. Oh, and if you really want to play fairy tale . . ."

He snapped those teeth together hard. Once. Twice. Three times. After each snap there came a sharp echo that blended into the next—self-echoing binary castanets. When he finished, three chairs had sprung up in the space before the desk. One had only a slender post for a back. One was very high and narrow, with two short steps leading up to the little seat. One would have looked at home in any dotcom start-up.

I tapped the seat obviously designed for Melchior. "This chair is too tall"—Tisiphone's—"this chair is too narrow"—the last.

"And this chair is just right," finished Fenris. "I've always preferred Goldilocks to Little Red Riding Hood. Wolf as villain is *so* overdone."

"What about Ahllan?" I asked.

"Look behind you."

A large wedge-shaped cushion had appeared, perfect for propping someone up in bed.

"Where were we?" asked Fenris when we had all settled down. "Oh, right. Bargaining. Look, let's make this simple. I'm not a big fan of verbal fencing. You're not from around here, and what that means to us is that maybe it's possible to stop the end times from happening. Whether we need your help to do that is an open question, but the fact that Odin can't *see* you suggests you have big potential. You know what we want. Allies against Odin to help prevent Ragnarok. What do *you* want?"

I leaned forward to answer, then stopped. What did we

want? I looked at my friends and really thought about it in terms beyond immediate survival. Part of me wanted to say, "I just want to go home," but was that truly all that I wanted? To go back to face whatever mess had happened while we were gone?

Odin had said I might be free of Hades if I stayed within this MythOS. That still sounded awfully nice. What about the others? We'd been in this world for less than five days, most of which had been spent trying to get out of one mess after another without ever a moment to think past the next crisis. Actually, put that way it sounded like the main difference between here and home was which afterlife I got stuck with when I made the inevitable final mistake. When in doubt . . . bluff.

"What are you offering?" I asked. "Because we've got a lot of wants and needs, some proximate, some long-term."

Fenris shook his head. "You and my father have more in common than your eyes, don't you? Let's start with the proximate. Who knows? We might even be willing to cover most of those up front. Call it a gesture of good faith."

"All right. Let's start with food and shelter."

"Done," said Fenris. "I'll have the former brought up, and you can take advantage of the latter whenever you're ready. Laginn, you know our new friends pretty well. Could you see about the menu?"

The hand bobbed a yes, then jumped off the table and headed out the door.

"Next?" asked Fenris.

"Healer or the equivalent," said Tisiphone. "I'm tired of feeling like I've been sleeping in Procrustes' iron bed."

"Anything else?"

I turned to Melchior. "What have you got?"

"Electronics lab, well stocked and private."

I nodded. "I should have thought of that."

"Well stocked I can do," said Fenris. "Private? I wouldn't be honest if I told you I could manage that. Even if I agreed not to spy on you, this is Loki's operation and—"

"And I go where I want to and see what I like," interjected Loki, appearing complete with executive-style chair a few feet behind Fenris.

"Oh, don't give me that look, Raven." He leaned back and put his feet up on a footstool that hadn't been there when they left the ground. "We both knew it was true before Little Boy Blue ever asked about it. You want someplace to work on the problem of cracking MimirNet, and I will happily give you the opportunity, but only if I get to share in the rewards. And quite frankly, you owe me."

He leaped to his feet and started to pace. "Us, really. If it hadn't been for my boys, you'd be locked up right now or dead."

"Boys?" said Fenris.

"Yes," said Loki, "or didn't they tell you how they got here? Jormungand bailed them out of a nasty mess with Heimdall and the Wild Hunt, then played taxi driver. You *were* going to tell him all that, weren't you, Ravirn?"

Loki looked over the top of his glasses at me and snapped his fingers. A hair-thin thread of chaos shot from his hand straight toward my face. Without thinking, I opened my mouth and caught the end of it. Then slurped it down like a strand of spaghetti. *Delicious.*

"Truth spell?" I said, identifying it from the taste. "I'm hurt. Oh, and the answer, honest and uncoerced, is yes. I had every intention of telling him how much help Jormungand gave us."

"How did you do that?" asked Loki, his voice suspicious.

"I think I'll keep that to myself for the moment," I said, mostly because I had no idea how I'd done it.

So I took a moment to rerun the sequence in my mind and actually came up with a possible answer, one that might not have occurred had Loki not given me the key to it himself by reminding me of Jormungand. The chaospell Loki had attempted to work on me had tasted like the venom of the Midgard Serpent felt, strong and sweet and heady. Though I no longer felt drunk on the power Jormungand had injected into my veins, I had done nothing to dissipate it. Perhaps the bite of the Serpent had worked a deeper change than I first imagined.

"Are we going to play games?" I asked, following another impulse by snapping my own fingers and tapping the bridge of my nose. I felt the power of the spell I'd swallowed go out of me and into the creation of a pair of glasses just like Loki's. With a smile I looked over the tops of the lenses at him. "Or are we going to play nice?"

"Why can't we do both?" he countered, reaching into his jeans pocket and pulling out an apple that couldn't possibly have fit there.

It was big and plump and golden, and it had "for the fairest" written on it. He tossed it to me. I caught it, then just about dropped it when I sensed the magic packed frighteningly tight inside its skin. If explosives had a flavor, the apple was what a grenade would taste like.

"Name it," said Loki, pointing to the apple.

I reached deeper into the apple with my chaos sense. Magic, lots of it, but not the raw stuff Loki and Jormungand used. This felt more like the formal spell of a classical wizard, all wards and diagrams and careful words. Then I had it. With a smile I handed the apple to Tisiphone.

"It's got your name on it," I said. "Or, at least, your description."

"That's sweet," she said, "but considering the results of handing out the last apple with this inscription, I'm a little leery of eating it."

"Don't be," I said. "This one didn't come from Eris. It came from Idun, and unless I'm very wrong, it should put all your wounds and weariness to right."

"If you say so." Tisiphone nodded and took a bite out of the apple. A look of sublime delight passed across her face, and she quickly took another.

"Very good," Loki said to me. "I'm impressed. Intuition indeed."

I sighed. If even Loki was using that name . . . "I'm well and truly stuck with Odin's labels, aren't I?"

"Uh, Boss?"

"Yes, Melchior."

"Before you go off into a whining fit on the subject, it might be worth making a concerted effort at learning from experience."

"What do you mean?" I asked him.

"Well, I hate to sound like Cerice, but I can't help but remember a long-running argument about the power of names and how much you hated being called Raven. Do you recall how that all worked out?"

"Oh."

He was right. Clotho, the Fate who spins, had named me Raven after her sister Lachesis had revoked my birth name and cast me out of the family of Fate. Afterward, I'd been pretty much a nitwit about the whole thing, rejecting what I considered an unwanted "gift" from those who had made themselves my enemies. The end result of the whole thing—after an awful lot of blood and sweat—was the realization that I *was* the Raven, and the only thing I could possibly do to change it was die.

"Call me Intuition," I said, forcing a smile, "please. Or Impulse."

"He really is almost as irritating as you are," Fenris said to Loki.

"Oh, Loki is nowhere near as irritating as Ravirn," Tisiphone said as she finished the apple—core and all. She already looked significantly better. "He couldn't be. Trust me on that."

"Hey!" I said.

"I think we should take a vote," said Melchior. "Hands for Ravirn?" He raised his, as did Tisiphone and Ahllan. "Loki?"

Fenris's paw shot up, and Loki lightly cuffed him. "Mind your manners, son. Look, can we get back to the whole bargaining thing?"

"Seconded," I said. "This is an entirely pointless digression. We've laid out our up-front needs. I'm sure we'll have more to add later, but why don't you tell us what you want. Loki?"

His face clouded. "Once, I wanted to win. That time's come and gone. Now I just don't want to lose. Not completely, at least. And I will lose. I will lose everything." He rose to his feet and went to the window, turning his back on us. "I have sons. If I do not find some way to change the course of the future, I will have none. I have my freedom. If events continue as Odin has foretold, I will have imprisonment and torture—a serpent will drip burning venom upon my brow for a thousand years or more. And I will deserve it. I have life. Heimdall will take it from me. I am a god. In the world that comes after Ragnarok, I will be less than a memory.

"All that I have or love will be taken from me, and if I do not do everything in my power to break the chains of the future, I will be complicit in the loss. I will inevitably become as evil as Odin's vision makes me out to be." He spun around and glared directly at me. "Can you comprehend what it's like to know your future? To see dreadful events coming straight at you with no way to avoid them? Do you have any idea of how it feels to know to the depths of your soul that you are no more than a marionette dancing preordained steps written out for you by Fate?"

Loki's words hit me like one of Zeus's lightning bolts. He couldn't have chosen better if he'd searched for a thousand years, not for this rebel child of Fate's middle house.

I jumped to my feet and offered Loki my hand. "I will help you, even if I lose my life in the attempt."

I had risked my life for the same cause once before, though the players had been different—Fate and Discord. The battlefield had been a piece of software called Puppeteer, a program written by the Fates to erase free will. Victory had cost me my name, my family, and not a little of my blood. I counted it a bargain.

"I don't understand," said Loki, who had not yet extended his own hand.

"You said the magic word," said Melchior. "'Fate.' I'm in, too, Boss."

"For what it's worth, so am I," said Ahllan.

"I guess I'd better make it unanimous," added Tisiphone, "though my reasons are not the same."

"But you haven't even stated your terms yet," said Loki. "What do you want in exchange? What's the deal?"

"There is no *deal*," replied Fenris. "Don't you get it? They have chosen a side. Ours. They will do what they can to help us, and we will do the same for them."

"Oh," said Loki.

He finally shook my hand, though he still looked as though he didn't understand. He kept glancing at Fenris out of the corner of his eye as if asking for an explanation. I suddenly felt unspeakably sad for Loki. He simply couldn't believe someone would take up his cause without a payoff. We *must* have some reason for our choice beyond our deciding it was the right thing to do.

The reason for his confusion didn't matter, whether it was because he had totally internalized the future Odin had foreseen, or because of his own inner lack of loyalty, or even simply his longtime identification as the "villain." What mattered was that he couldn't bring himself to trust, and, as long as that was true, it would make a wall between him and the rest of the world.

Just about then, Laginn returned to lead us all to breakfast in a partitioned-off corner of the Froggy Bottom Café. Over coffee, tea, juice, three kinds of meat, six kinds of eggs, and more varieties of baked goods than I could easily count, we continued our discussion.

"I don't actually believe I can beat the fate Odin has foreseen for all of us," Loki said, poking at his eggs. "Ragnarok will come, and with it all of the horrors that are foretold. It's inevitable."

"So what *do* you hope to accomplish, Mr. Defeatist?" asked Tisiphone.

"You'd be a defeatist, too," said Loki, "if you'd spent the past thousand years hearing about how *evil* you are and how much you deserve the horrible torture that's coming to you. You know what really gripes me about the whole damn thing? It's the double standards. Look at the troops, for starters.

"Is there some reason Odin's army of the undead should be privileged over mine?" demanded Loki. "Why should warriors raised from the dead and taken to Valhalla after they died in battle be inherently more good than those who died of disease or old age and went to Hel for their afterlife? Does warmongering make a more worthy zombie? Is it an address thing? Valhalla's a better neighborhood than Hel, so they're the good guys! It's classist is what it is."

Fenris put a paw on his father's shoulder. "Could we get back on topic? What you want and all that?"

"Right, sorry. It just pisses me off. Like I said, I don't think we can stop Ragnarok. It has to happen, but what I'm hoping, what seeing you travelers from an alternate now has made me believe, is that it doesn't have to happen *everywhere*. I think I could bear all the death and destruction if I knew that some other version of me somewhere had found a way out. Or, failing that, that at least my children had alternate versions of themselves living on. That somewhere there was a version of the Norse mythos that didn't end in the utter ruin of my house."

"I don't know," said Ahllan. "In our pantheoverse, the only things that don't split when the rest of the universe does are the gods."

"That's Necessity's doing," said Tisiphone. "She prevents splits that go beyond the story of our mythos."

"You mean there could be multiple versions of me running around if Necessity allowed it?" I asked.

"All gods forfend," said Melchior, contriving to look utterly aghast.

Tisiphone shrugged. "Honestly, I don't know. But the possibility is one my sisters and I have discussed."

"So you think it's achievable?" asked Loki.

Again the shrug. "Theoretically? Maybe."

"Then I have to try. If I understand things correctly, Mimir serves the same purpose here that Necessity does in your pantheoverse. Mimir, MimirNet, MimirSoft, the whole system is run by Odin to preserve his control over the reins of reality. That's why I built Rune"—Loki made a gesture that included the entire facility around us—"as an alternate control center, one that I could use to split off chunks of reality if I ever got the chance."

"So, what we need to do is crack MimirNet and give you that chance," I said. "Then we can use RuneNet to do a little cosmic rewrite."

"There's one tiny problem with that plan," said Fenris.

"Which is?" asked Melchior.

"RuneNet doesn't work. We've got all the computing power you could possibly want in the supercluster, an order of magnitude more than MimirNet, but we've never been able to get it to touch reality on even the most basic level. The system is huge, and it's very pretty, but it's never performed so much as a single spell operation."

"That's a problem, all right," I said, removing my conjured glasses and pinching the bridge of my nose between my fingers. "I'm guessing you don't include that minor detail in your brochures."

"Why am I suddenly reminded of the dotcom implosion?" said Melchior.

I snorted. "No idea, Mel. No idea."

CHAPTER FIFTEEN

■ ■ ■

"Any regrets on choosing sides?" Melchior's voice came from the tinny speakers of his laptop form.

I glanced into his webcam and shook my head. He sat on the exact same workbench I'd found him on when we'd come to rescue him from Loki, and the same two-headed giant now acted as my assistant. Life is terminally ironic sometimes. With a careful drag of my fingernail I swapped a pair of connections in the circuit diagram on his screen.

"How does that look?" I asked.

He plugged this new network card adapter configuration in to the MimirNet simulation we'd put together for the Rune supercluster and let it run. RuneNet might not be able to cast its own spells, but it did have a huge amount of computing power that we could put to use to help prepare things that Melchior could implement.

"Better," he said a moment later. "At least it is if our assumptions about the way the system works are correct, and if RuneNet is a valid test environment."

"That's a pretty big pair of ifs," said Ahllan. She'd insisted on helping and had done a damn fine job, coming up with design twists that never would have occurred to me—too old for this stuff indeed. "I wish I could run the sims myself." She shifted around in her seat—a wheeled chair that looked like the overstuffed offspring of a hospital bed and a La-Z-Boy.

"That'd be nice," I said. "I understand how you work at the chip level, and I know you aren't going to suddenly start making rounding errors on number strings longer than twelve digits. This thing"—I pointed at the Rune server cluster—"is completely opaque."

"Stupid, too," added Melchior. "It can't do anything you don't tell it to, or even tell you if you've done something wrong. Phenomenal computing power, but no soul."

Loki harrumphed from the chair he'd taken behind us but didn't say a word. Not saying anything was one of the conditions I'd imposed for letting him watch us work up close and personal—the result of his fifth attempt at backseat chip design. I glanced at the diagram again and tapped in the command that integrated it with the rest of the adapter. It was a kludge, but that was *my* post-logo-design signature.

"I think we're going to have to call it done," I said.

"Agreed," said Melchior. "It'll work, and we're short on time."

Ahllan nodded as well, and I sent the schematic to my two-headed assistant's machine for blueprinting and transmission to the manufacturing team. The giant looked it over and discussed it between itself for a few minutes before giving a double nod.

"It'll take ten to twelve hours to get this put together. I'll take it down to Fabrication now."

"Good," I said, though the length of the delay didn't make me happy. "I could use the sack time."

I got up from my chair and rubbed my back. I'd come straight up to the lab after breakfast and stayed there for something like twenty hours getting the design nailed down.

That was after spending the entire previous night talking with Jormungand. I picked up my jacket and headed for the quarters we'd been assigned. On the way, I checked the tiny spinnerette in my pocket. It still wasn't moving.

I felt well and truly beat, but when I got to the room I was sharing with Tisiphone, I found her slept out but interested in remaining in bed for a while longer . . . if I knew what she meant. I decided maybe I wasn't that tired after all.

When we'd finished with not-sleeping together, she and I lay facing each other on our stomachs with pillows under our chins—it was a giant-scale bed, which had some definite advantages. Tisiphone had relaxed her wings, and they covered her like a blanket of fire.

"I could get to liking this," said Tisiphone.

I smiled. "Which part? The afterglow? The really big bed? Hanging out with chaos powers?" I took a deep breath because the next bit was getting close to dangerous territory, but I really wanted to know how she was feeling about our exile here. "The Norse gods howling for our blood?"

She wrinkled her nose. "That last I could do without. The rest is nice though." She looked away from my eyes and stopped speaking for so long I thought she was finished and it was my turn to say something again. But just as I drew breath to do so, she continued. "So is not being on call twenty-four/seven."

I blinked and thought very carefully about what I should say next. Before I thought of anything clever, she shook her head, though she still didn't meet my eyes.

"I don't think that came out right. I miss home. I miss my sisters. It's just kind of nice to have a little vacation from responsibility."

"I can see that. I'm rather enjoying not having to watch my back for Hades or Atropos. Of course, that's balanced out by having to watch it for Odin and Tyr, but at least it's different."

I didn't say anything about the individual she hadn't

mentioned missing. If she wanted to stay mad at Necessity, she had good cause. She also had good cause to want a vacation. Rather like a small-town doctor, a Fury was never off duty. Which meant she'd gone nearly four thousand years without a break. That had to wear. I'd have cracked long ago, but Tisiphone is made of tougher stuff than I am.

"Do you ever dream about staying here?" I asked. "Because I could see hanging around for a while if we can get this whole Ragnarok thing sorted out. A world without Hades has a lot to recommend it."

"Ravirn?" she said, sliding forward on her pillow so that her face was inches from my own.

"Uh-huh."

"Shut up."

"I—" But she stopped my lips with kisses three, and I forgot all about talking.

Making love with a woman who has wings of any kind, much less fiery ones, is an interesting proposition. When you add in the fires at the juncture of her legs and the tips of her breasts, it becomes a challenge that walks a thin line between the sizzling and the silly. I will leave the rest as an exercise for the active imagination.

"You sure about this?" I asked Melchior, as we slid the networking card into one end of the adapter.

He flickered into goblin shape, gave me a grin and a thumbs-up, then returned to laptop. I plugged the athame cable in to one of his ports and wished I felt half as confident as Melchior acted.

"I suppose we'd better get this over with."

I connected the adapter to Melchior and waited for a crash or some other disaster. A couple of minutes passed while he ran the hardware through its paces, and I just paced. Finally, he gave a little "bing" to attract my attention and flashed *Ready* on his screen.

Blood and pain and my athame took me out of my body

and into the net. As I entered the interior Melchior's virtual room with its spiral staircase, I was met once again by the tiny, flying feathered serpent wearing my familiar's face.

He pointed me toward our window on the electronic world. "You *have* to see this."

Beyond lay the MimirNet network. This time, with the proper hardware in place, it looked very different. Instead of the armored spiderweb or giant hamster tubes of earlier visits, what I saw now reminded me of nothing so much as Bifrost on steroids. The bridge that linked Asgard and Midgard was replicated here a hundred times over, an entire rainbow network.

A billion sparkling bits of data followed the rainbows, each a bright point of white light. Like a superswarm of very well-trained fireflies, they plied the paths described by the lines of the rainbow beneath them.

"Invisible walls?" I asked.

"That's what I thought," agreed Melchior. "Ceiling, too, they never go above a certain height."

I requested a rock, and Melchior supplied it. I threw the chunk of code at the nearest rainbow segment. When it reached the space above the edge, it bounced away with a hollow thunk and fell into darkness. About what I'd expected.

"I want to take a closer look."

Melchior nodded, and a series of bright red stairs unfolded themselves from the window shaped like Melchior's mouth to the edge of the rainbow. I followed them down and put a hand out to the invisible wall. It felt smooth and warm, and it gave a little, like a thin sheet of Plexiglas. I pushed hard, and it gave even more. I felt certain I could break it if I applied enough force, but I had serious doubts about the advisability of that. I wanted to crack the system more subtly if I could manage it.

"Melchior, would you ask Ahllan to hook us up to Rune-Net? We're going to need the processing muscle."

"Done," he said, and I knew he'd flashed the message on

his screen back in meatspace. "She says it'll take about five minutes. I'm not sure why, but Loki agreed with her."

The time slid past slowly and uneventfully until Ahllan appeared unexpectedly on the stairs above us. She looked young and strong and dangerous, every inch a troll. Melchior, on the other hand, looked apoplectic.

"What do you need?" she asked. Then, when she saw Melchior's expression, she said, "Relax. I ran the connection through me because I still don't trust Loki. This way anything he tries to slip into the process via RuneNet has to get through me before it hits the two of you. I'm much more expendable. Besides, RuneNet needs very careful minding. I can do that while you take care of Ravirn."

I could see that Melchior wanted to argue, but I caught his eye and shook my head. I didn't like her risking herself either, but it was her decision. She was also right. Loki couldn't be fully trusted, and RuneNet did need minding. The supercluster wasn't an AI. I couldn't just ask it for what I wanted and expect it to interpret my request correctly. It required careful programming, and Ahllan could supply that on the fly.

I indicated the network beside me. "I need to get in there without making a big fuss. I'd also like to see if we can't tap the flow in an ongoing way and suck up information. What I'm picturing is an extra little loop of rainbow. Thoughts?"

Ahllan grinned. "Nice. I think we can manage that. But we'll want to rearrange the connections so that you can pull Melchior out of the interface without losing the whole thing once you actually head for MimirNet proper. Hang on a tick."

"Wait a second—" began Melchior.

Ahllan vanished. A few seconds later, the network below us blipped out, going from rainbow back to armored spiderweb.

Melchior swore.

"What?" I asked.

"*That's* why she was so keen to help with the design. I should have seen it."

"What?" I asked again.

"She just cut me out of the direct connection to the network card. She adjusted that design so it would be more compatible with her older network hardware and protocols. Hell, I should have realized that was why she wanted the channels set that way. In a moment, she'll have it plugged through her so that she's filtering both it and Rune-Net, shielding us with her own soul. Damn it, Ahllan, you shouldn't be—" He stopped as the spiderweb flickered and became a rainbow once again.

"There," said Ahllan as she reappeared. "That's much better."

She still wore the young avatar, but as she walked down to join us, strain and age showed in her posture like some half-seen ghost of her real body. Melchior gave me a dark look but didn't say anything to Ahllan.

"Can you swing us underneath?" I asked Melchior.

The stairs lowered us into the darkness below the rainbow, and I had Melchior conjure me up the code equivalent of a really powerful magnifying glass so I could get a finer read on the architecture of the rainbow.

"Well, I will be dipped in shit," I whispered after a few minutes.

"Something wrong, Boss?"

"Nope. For the first time in quite a while something is completely right."

"Care to share?" asked Ahllan.

"Sure, I was starting to feel like I'd never get the hang of this Norse pseudobinary stuff. That even if I did learn to parse it with my forebrain, it would always be like a foreign language badly learned. I would have to think everything through in my native tongue, then carefully translate it into the new one, making every single operation a two-step process."

"I take it something changed," said Ahllan.

"Yes, it has! When I looked at the code here, it was like reading mweb-native binary. I'm actually thinking in the local version now, though I'm not sure why I've had the sudden breakthrough."

"Snakebite," said Melchior.

"What do you ... ? Oh, Jormungand." I'd told him about the way the chaos the Midgard Serpent had injected into me had met and merged with the stuff of my being. "I bet you're right, Mel."

"When have I ever been wrong?"

Ahllan waved a finger in the air. "I've got a list if you want it."

"Actually, could you e-mail that to me?" I said. "It might come in handy later. In the meantime, let me tell you what I'd like to do with the bridge."

My binary, pseudo or otherwise, is nowhere near as good as an AI's, so it took me a good twenty minutes to whistle out the underlying spell structure for Ahllan to critique. It then took her all of thirty seconds to convert that into a fully realized program for RuneNet to run, and some tiny fraction of a second for the supercluster actually to perform the job.

When it finished running the code, we had a free-floating chunk of rainbow that mimicked the shape of an oval racetrack hanging in the space below us. Ahllan gave a whistled command, and the whole thing rose underneath a straight section of MimirNet so that viewed from above, the long sides of the oval seemed to overlap and merge with the equivalent section of the network. Another command fused our racetrack section to the main network.

"Now for the tricky part," said Ahllan, licking her lips.

The next whistle was long and complex, with all sorts of harmonies and counterpoints built in on top of the basic melodic line. Even though I'd composed the base spell myself, I found it hard to follow. On top of that, the pseudobinary lent the code an eerie, otherworldly quality I'd never encountered in one of my own programs.

The spell was big and baroque and insanely up-tempo because it had to accomplish a bunch of complex things in the right order and very, very fast. First, it pushed our rainbow section up and into the surface of the one above, so that they overlapped in three dimensions. Then it simultaneously broke the overlapping sections along an invisible line and cross-spliced them.

The end result was a three-dimensional loop, or helix, of the sort you might find in a model train set to help the engine handle a steep hill. Packets went into the loop low and came out high. The one problem with the change was the increased distance of travel for the packets. That would affect speed of transmission. Normal variations in network flow rates would cover the issue for a while, but eventually, if the admins had a good monitoring system in place, the discrepancy would become obvious. How long that would take was an open question, though I figured no less than several days and probably not more than a couple of months.

In the meantime, since the loop was maintained by and part of RuneNet, all that data was ours to scan. But that was just a side benefit. The real point of the exercise had been to create a section of network where we controlled the invisible walls and so could slip in and out without setting off alarm bells. Of course, setting it in place might have set off those same bells, so now it was time to pull back and wait to see whether the folks with the lights and the sirens showed up. With a nod to Ahllan, I headed back up the red stairs on my way to the real world.

Hours later, we reconvened in meatspace in the server room to go over the data flows. Ahllan, who had to remain connected to both RuneNet and MimirNet to keep the tap in place, had never left. She lay unmoving in her wheeled chair, immersed in the network. Whether it was the effort of that, or simply her ongoing deterioration, she looked as though she were being consumed from within. Melchior and I had both tried to talk her into letting us remove her from the loop, but she flat-out refused.

When it became clear that nothing else of import was going to happen soon, Tisiphone, Fenris, Laginn, and the two-headed giant started a game of hearts. That left me and Melchior to pore over the data, while Loki looked impatiently over my shoulder. Though it irritated me, I couldn't really fault him.

His whole future or, more hopefully, *futures*, rested on what happened over the next few days. I'd have been anxious about the results of the tap, too, but doing things right was much more important than doing them fast this time. As long as we could keep Odin and company in the dark about our actions, moving carefully was the best way to go. Especially since we didn't know exactly what our next step should be.

As I read through the RuneNet summary of the loop data traffic, I kept rubbing my aching athame hand. I *had* to find a moment to code a better version of the athame-healing spell. Especially if we were going to continue to spend so much time in the RuneNet server room. The processors kicked out an amazing amount of heat, and in response, the air conditioners were set all the way to massive overcompensation.

Melchior popped open an IM box beside the RuneNet summary feed I'd just had him run for the third time. *What do you think, Boss? It looks pretty good to me.* The words appeared in a cartoon-style conversation balloon issuing from the mouth of a tiny goblin-head icon.

Depends on what you're looking for, I typed back. With Loki pretty much constantly in the room with us, IMing felt more private and intimate, even if it just meant he had to read over my shoulder instead of listening in. *If they're on to the loop trick, they're doing a damn good job of lying low and pretending they haven't noticed. On that front, I think we can start the next phase of things anytime.*

But? Melchior knew me well enough to read the words I hadn't written.

But I don't like the way the bigger pattern tastes.

I'm not sure I follow you, he responded.

I'm not sure I follow me either. Something's not right, but I can't figure out what. The traffic on the network isn't flowing the way it should. I paused and tried to find the right words to express what I meant, but I kept coming back to the idea of taste. *It's like a soup that's got too little salt in it, or too much of something else. It just tastes wrong.*

Are you sure it's not some function of the alternate MythOS structure? asked Melchior. *It's a very different world here, right down to the underlying foundations of the universe. That's bound to have effects at every level.*

No, Mel. I don't think that's it. It's not that it tastes off from what I'm used to. It tastes off from itself.

sigh I'd say you were crazy, but I know better. The amount of divinity you inherited from the Titans might be an open question. The quality is not, and every last bit of what you did get is oriented around finding the hidden flaws in a system. So, it tastes wrong. *What does that mean in terms of an action plan?*

I don't know. Scroll the whole thing past me again. I thought for a moment. *Why don't you run it at ten times speed? I won't be able to read anything, but I might see something in the shape of the data that I'm not getting out of the content.*

You're the boss.

Senior partner, Mel, senior partner.

Whatever you say . . . Boss. ;-)

I sighed and let it go as Melchior started streaming the data. The bad taste was there again and, if anything, stronger this time, but I still didn't have a lock on what it meant.

One more time, Mel. And another ten times faster, please.

Damn it, I was missing something, and it felt like something obvious. I just couldn't figure out what.

I glanced at Ahllan in her wheeled recliner. Her feet

were up, her eyes closed. A pair of large antique athames were driven through the backs of her hands and deep into the arms of her chair. Networking cables had been spliced directly to the pommel connecters of both blades in lieu of the old-fashioned plugs we didn't have. The complete lack of hardware compatibility in this world made for even more kludge than usual. One cable led from the left athame to a Y-splitter and on to both the stolen network card and Rune-Net. The cable running from the right athame—rigged to plug in to Melchior—was neatly coiled in her lap. The whole arrangement reminded me rather too much of a bad day at the hospital involving all sort of monitors and intravenous hookups.

Ahllan chose that moment to open her own eyes and look my way, perhaps because she'd felt my attention. I repressed an internal shudder at that evidence of soul-splitting. Instead of flesh-ports, webtrolls of her generation had been optimized for using those oversized athames when in troll form. Because of that, she could divide herself between the worlds of the virtual and the real in a way that would have ripped my soul in half or, more likely, killed me. It was the creepiest damn thing, and one I hadn't known about until that very day.

"Do I really look so terrible?" Ahllan asked weakly.

Back in a sec, Mel, I typed.

I got up and walked over to kneel beside her. "Not at all, Ahllan. I'm just having a hard time getting my mind around the idea of those." I pointed at the athames.

"The pain isn't anything worse than what my joints do on a daily basis, and at least this accomplishes something." She smiled grimly, exposing brown and cracked teeth that had once been deadly sharp and only slightly yellowed. "Present circumstance does make me feel almost useful again. But let's not talk about me. What are you and Melchior arguing about?"

"Not arguing so much as discussing. There's something

about the data flows that's nagging at . . ." I trailed off as
my eyes took in the athames and cables once again, and an
odd thought flitted past the windows of my mind. "No. That
can't be it."

"What?" asked Ahllan.

"Interface," I replied. "But that doesn't make any sense.
Not unless there's a major incompatibility issue or some
kind of weird quantum-observer effect. Ahllan, have you
been storing the feed you're pulling off the network tap?"

"No. There's way too much data for my old storage systems. I've just been feeding it straight through to RuneNet.
Why do you ask?"

"I've got a theory I want to test." I started uncoiling the
cable set up for Melchior. "How much can you comfortably
hold in internal memory?"

"Ten or fifteen minutes, more if I do some hard-drive
cleanup."

"Don't bother," I said. "Ten minutes should be plenty.
Do it."

Loki came over. "Is something wrong?"

"No. Yes. Maybe. I honestly don't know, but I think I
might have an idea about how to find out."

"The taste thing?" he asked, revealing that he had indeed
been reading over my shoulder.

"Uh-huh," I said absently.

After I hooked Melchior up to Ahllan, I grabbed a monitor and connected it directly to RuneNet.

Mel?

Yes, what are we doing?

*I'm pulling the feed from Ahllan for ten minutes. I want
to scroll that in parallel with the same feed as it reads on
RuneNet.*

Ten minutes later I had him run the feed from Ahllan
and . . . "Huh? That doesn't make any sense."

"No, it doesn't," said Loki. "Why does the data look
slightly different on the two screens?"

"I have no idea." I rubbed my forehead. "It should be identical. It's the same data pulled off the same incoming feed and looked at in the same way."

"Could it have something to do with the content?" asked Loki.

"It shouldn't," interjected Melchior via speaker. "It's all encrypted, and we haven't even tried to break the cipher yet. We wanted to wait till we had a lot more raw data for that. This is just a representation of the volume, direction, and speed of packet flow."

"It's also deeply strange," I said. "Ahllan?"

"Yes, dear."

"Is there any way you can feed the data to RuneNet without looking at it?"

"I'm not sure what you mean," she said.

"I think there may be some sort of really bizarre observer effect going on. I want to know if RuneNet by itself produces data that looks like the stuff that you've observed on its way through. Or if it looks like the stuff you sent direct to Melchior. Or something completely different."

"Let me think about that for a bit," said Ahllan. About five minutes ticked past while I had Melchior run and rerun the comparison. Finally, "Yes, I think I can see a way to do it."

An hour later, I was ready to tear great chunks of my hair out by the roots. After I'd had Ahllan run the raw feed to RuneNet, I'd had her run it to Melchior as well. I couldn't cross-compare all four varieties of feed directly because Ahllan couldn't both observe and not observe the data simultaneously, but the more I looked at the patterns, the surer I was that no two of them matched.

"This is crazy stuff," I said to the others. "There's no sense to it."

"I don't think that's true, Boss," said Melchior, who had reassumed goblin shape so that he could join me in my pacing. The fact that he was doing so with a network cable dangling from his nose suggested he was at least as distracted by the results as I. "I can't see an underlying pattern, but I can *feel* that there is one . . . in here." He tapped his chest. "That makes me think you were right when you suggested a quantum-observer effect of some sort, something about the way the flows interact with a watcher."

"You're the quantum computer," I said, "which makes you the closest thing we've got to an expert on the subject. I'll take your word for it. I just wish we had another way to slice the data to see if we could . . . Hold it. Ahllan, can you do the no-lookie feed to RuneNet and Melchior again? Simultaneously this time?"

"I don't see why not. The easiest way would be just to put a splitter in the RuneNet feed."

"All right, now, Mel I want you to run your share of the feed without looking at it either."

"Okay, Boss."

We did that and . . . "Jackpot!" I yelled, pumping a fist in the air. "Something finally makes sense."

"What?" asked Loki.

"If Ahllan and Melchior both take themselves out of the loop, the direct feed and the feed through RuneNet are identical, and it tastes right."

"Which means what?" asked Loki.

"It means that RuneNet doesn't have any effect on whatever is going on at all; it's strictly a channel. It's only when the data hits an AI that we get a change in how it looks and tastes." I put my hands on either side of my head and squeezed while I tried to picture the differences. "But, what does that mean?"

Loki suddenly looked very concerned. "Quantum encryption?"

"What do you . . . ? Oh"—in quantum encryption, the data is encoded such that anyone trying to tap the flow is automatically detected when they scramble things because of—"the observer effect. But we haven't tried to look at the data itself yet. We've only looked over the flow patterns. That shouldn't touch the encryption, should it? Not unless there's information actually embedded in the way the traffic is flowing at the quantum level. I can't even imagine why that would be."

"Maybe because Mimir's an AI?" suggested Melchior.

"I don't think I understand," I said.

"According to your conversation with Odin, MimirNet is a computerized extension of what's left of the god Mimir, a sort of cybernetic brain enhancement. If that's true, the patterns in the data are the digitized thoughts of the god, the place where a divine intelligence crosses over into artificial intelligence."

"I'm with you so far," I said, "though I don't know where you're going next."

"When Eris changed the Fates' blueprints for us so that AIs would have free will, she did it by adding a component of randomness. Maybe that spark of chaos is the quantum-uncertainty effect writ large. If so, and it's fundamental to the AI soul, then maybe Mimir has it, too."

"Now I see," I said. "If AI free will is itself a quantum effect, then there could be some sort of observer resonance between AIs."

"Wait a second," said Loki. "Wouldn't that go both ways? If the nature of the data flow is changed by your observing it here, then Mimir might be able to sense that."

Melchior nodded. "If he's looking for it. This is all guesswork, and it's a tiny effect, but if I'm right, and he starts paying attention, it would be very hard for him to miss."

"Then," said Loki, looking directly into my eyes, "unless you want to try to crack MimirNet with Odin ready and waiting for you, you'd better get a move on."

I hate being rushed into dangerous actions, yet it happens often enough that I should probably set up a macro in my calendar software—type *RID* and it pops up *7:15 rushed into danger*, or something like that. I suppose that could be the whole Fate-meets-Slapstick part of my nature again, but I'd rather believe I am more of a free agent than that.

No matter what the reason, here I was again. If I was going to crack MimirNet and help break this universe free of the deterministic claws of Fate, I had to act quickly. The fact that the future of the planet Earth and the lives of all the gods and monsters who made up my local peer group hung in the balance just added to the pressure.

CHAPTER SIXTEEN

We had a major problem, and his name was Heimdall.

Melchior and I had backtracked the virtual twists and turns of MimirNet from our point of electronic entry to a junction where dozens of MimirNet's rainbow threads met and merged into one broad trunkway. We had found the backbone that connected the threads of the multiworld network with the physical heart of MimirNet, the server farm hidden within the roots of Yggdrasil. It was the sole access route, and it was protected by something infinitely worse than a run-of-the-mill firewall. Heimdall.

The stretch of rainbow network arched off into the misty distance, echoing the Bifrost of the real world, right down to the guardian god riding his horse back and forth across its surface and blocking our path.

I lowered the virtual telescope I'd conjured to spy out the way and vigorously suppressed an urge to swear. We'd had one bit of luck in that he was moving away from us at the moment, but that wouldn't help us with his ears. I caught Melchior's eye and put a finger to my lips to indi-

cate quiet before holding up the scope so that he could see
the problem as well.

Melchior had assumed his winged-serpent shape once
again and coiled himself neatly around my shoulder, so I
barely had to move the eyepiece. A moment later he pulled
his face away from the scope and started very gently banging his tiny head on the side of my own. I reached up and
stopped him, afraid that even such a small noise might give
us away. I shook my head and jerked my thumb backwards.
He nodded his agreement, and we withdrew to the outer
fringes of the network.

"We've got a serious problem," I said, when we'd removed ourselves the virtual equivalent of several miles.

"I'm confused," said Melchior. "I mean, according to
that Edda thing, Bifrost connects Midgard to Asgard and
Heimdall guards it twenty-four/seven, right?"

I nodded.

"Yet here's Heimdall smack in the middle of the network trunk just when we want to make use of it. How does
that work? Why isn't he home on his bridge in the real
world?"

"Actually, I might have a theory on that," I said, thinking
aloud. "According to the Edda, Bifrost runs from Heimdall's palace on the Asgard end to the roots of Yggdrasil in
Midgard/Earth. But since ten minutes with any geographi-
cal search engine is going to show there's no forty-mile-tall
ash tree anywhere on planet Earth, you have to figure the
Edda took some license here and there."

"That, or the gods lied to humans about something . . .
again," said Melchior.

"There's always that possibility. In either case, I think
Bifrost is more of a Greatspell than it is a physical bridge
between two defined places. One that connects Asgard to
any and every place Odin wants it connected, including
purely magical places like Yggdrasil and Mimir's Well. I
also suspect it provides the physical backbone of Mimir-
Net." I bent and tapped the rainbow segment beneath us.

"This whole network is part and parcel of Bifrost. It doesn't just look like the Rainbow Bridge; it *is* the Rainbow Bridge. Heimdall doesn't have to leave his guard post in the physical world, because in this one special place, the virtual and the physical are one and the same."

"That almost makes sense, Boss. Are you feeling all right?"

"I'm fine, Mel. Thanks for asking so politely."

"So, what do we do about Heimdall?"

"I think we're going to need a distraction. Let's head back to Rune and see what we can cook up."

That was when everything went momentarily dim and quiet. For just an instant the rainbow beneath us went gray-scale, and the invisible walls ghosted into translucent visibility, suggesting tank armor rendered in mist or smoke.

"What the—" I began, but Melchior's winged snake grew from thirty inches to thirty feet in an instant and caught me in its coils, holding me tight as we rocketed into motion.

"—hell!" I heard myself gasp as I slammed back into my physical body, all unprepared, for the second time in a week.

My body did what bodies do in such circumstances, and I spent the next couple of minutes arguing with it about whether or not we should press the emergency-eject button on the contents of my stomach. Around me the world bustled with noise and movement made fuzzy by the tears that filled my eyes and the hollow ringing in my ears. Eventually, the whirling and buzzing mellowed enough that I managed to withdraw the athame from my hand and whistle the wound closed.

"What's going on?" I croaked.

No one answered.

What *was* going on? I rubbed the blurriness from my eyes and tried to make sense of the scene around me. Melchior, Tisiphone, and the two-headed giant had drawn close around Ahllan's chair, blocking my view of the old troll.

Loki, Fenris, Laginn, and several more giants had scattered among the servers, where they were frantically doing things that didn't immediately make sense.

Willing my stomach to quiet, I dragged myself upright and headed for the cluster around Ahllan. I might not know what was going on, but I had no question about where my first loyalties lay. As I got close enough to see around Tisiphone's wings, my stomach's contents made another bid for freedom, and I had to lock my jaw to keep them down. Surely, no one could look that gray and beaten and still live. But no, Tisiphone wouldn't have been massaging cramps out of the arms of a dead troll.

"Tisiphone," I quietly said to alert her to my presence before touching her shoulder, "what happened?"

"Ahllan had some kind of seizure, and it rippled through the whole system." She pointed at RuneNet with a wing while continuing to rub Ahllan's arms. "It was a nasty business with major convulsions. Look at her hands."

I did as she suggested, then winced. The paired athames driven through the backs of Ahllan's hands and into the chair had torn the tissue around them into a gory mess.

"That's why we had that flicker," said Melchior, from his spot in front of the chair. "All the connections went dicey when she did that."

"How bad is it?" I asked.

"I don't know yet," he replied. "As far as I can tell from what's coming off the feeds, she's still conscious in there somewhere. But she's not responding to the outside world, only to electronic input. I wanted to wait until Tisiphone finished loosening her up before I attempted direct contact. I'll try in just a . . . Oh, hang on. I'm getting something." His expression went abstract and far away. "Back in a minute." His body froze in place as he projected his entire consciousness into the network.

"What started it?" I asked.

"I don't know," replied Tisiphone. "She let out a little yelp, then started jerking around." Tisiphone's eyes met mine, and I saw something I'd never seen there before—not fear exactly, more its close cousin, worry. "She would have torn the athames out completely if I hadn't pinned her when I did. It was so fast, I barely made it. If I hadn't . . ." She swallowed hard. "If I hadn't, I'd have lost you without even a chance to say good-bye."

It was only in that instant that the full implications hit me. Ahllan was our connection to MimirNet, the link that allowed Melchior and me to project ourselves into the network. If she'd gone down while we were on the other side, it would have severed that link. We would both have died. That flicker of gray and indistinct armor was our lives flashing before our eyes, and I hadn't even realized it, though I certainly should have. If not in that instant, then moments later when Melchior had thrown me back into my body.

"We may have a problem," Loki said, coming up beside me.

I half turned so I could see both him and Ahllan. "Tell me about it, and I'll add it to the ever-growing list."

"RuneNet is locked up." He ran his hand through his hair. "No, that's not right. The system is still running; it's just not responding to any of our input."

"That's my fault," said Ahllan's voice through Melchior's lips. "Melchior has graciously agreed to let me talk through him." Mel nodded, pointed at Ahllan, and tapped the side of his jaw.

"I'm sorry." Ahllan's voice—so weak and spidery of late—sounded strong and confident coming from Mel's lips. "My seizure was caused by the chaos tap that powers my CPU. It's eroding away under the pressure of the more corrosive Primal Chaos in this MythOS. A pulse in the flow fused my connection to RuneNet. There are only three things that can sever or interfere with that link now: a full RuneNet system restore and reboot, physically breaking the connection between the two of us, or my death. Any of the three will effectively cause the other two at this point."

Melchior's eyes went wide, telling me he was getting Ahllan's words at the same time as the rest of us.

"Ugly," said Loki. "A full-system restore would put RuneNet out of commission for at least a day. That's time we can't easily afford."

"At a price we won't pay," I added firmly.

"The coin might as well be in the hands of the ferryman already," said Ahllan's voice. "I had to shut down most of my troll body's systems to prevent the surge from disabling or destroying RuneNet. I won't be able to reactivate them. I would guess that I have a day or two to live at most." She snorted. "Ironic that chaos ultimately does me in, as I was originally built to tame and channel chaos into the electronic web of Fate. Unfortunately, the flavor here is too foreign for this old palate. But let's leave the rest of the whys to answer themselves as it's the hows that matter now. How to use the time I have left. How to crack MimirNet. How you can protect yourselves in that effort if I happen to have overestimated my longevity."

I nodded inwardly, as she ticked off questions that had started tickling away at the back of my mind.

"Any suggestions?" I asked, forcing my grief for her into a little box for the moment. Before she could answer, I held up a hand. "Wait just a moment before you answer though. I should probably give a quick summary of what we found on our scouting run." I briefly outlined what we had learned and my thoughts on the subject, finishing with, "We'll need a distraction if we're going to get past Heimdall, and we'll need it soon. I hate to mention it, but once Ahllan goes, there's no telling how long it might take us to reaccess the network with Melchior acting as our conduit."

"To say nothing of the fact that it would probably kill him," said Ahllan, and again Melchior's eyes went wide. "The loop we inserted into the network takes enormous magical energy to run, energy *I've* been supplying since RuneNet can't perform magic itself. I've had to run my chaos tap flat out in order to supply the necessary power. I was designed for exactly such a task, and it is still killing me. I doubt Melchior would last an hour under the strain."

"Why didn't you tell us?" Melchior demanded, seizing control of his own mouth for a moment.

"Because I knew you'd try to stop me, to protect me," she answered simply. "What Loki wants to do here is too important for that. Unalloyed Fate is an evil I've fought my entire life. I will not allow an entire multiverse filled with humans and gods and all kinds of wondrous creatures to be destroyed because some foolish destiny says that is *the way things must be*. Nor to prove the power of persistence in the face of despair or whatever high-minded reason Odin might have for not fighting this to the bitter end. Ragnarok isn't just a war of good against evil. It is an evil itself, an evil of the highest order, and I will gladly die if that's what it takes to stop it."

"And we will stop it," I said, though a tight, hard throat made the words taste like broken glass. "Let's do this, people. As the lady said, we don't have a lot of time."

"I'll cover the distraction," said Loki with a grin. "I've the perfect idea. It'll even be a bit of a lark."

"What is it?" Tisiphone asked bluntly.

Loki looked taken aback for a moment at being questioned, then he shrugged. "Brisingamen."

"Bless you," Melchior said in his own voice.

"It's the necklace of Freya," Fenris said tolerantly. "A gaudy thing. All thick gold and oversized gems. It makes the wearer sexually irresistible to all who see them." He gave his father a curious look. "What are you going to do with it?"

"Steal it," said Loki, then his grin slipped. "Well, get caught attempting to steal it, actually. I had this marvelous idea for using it to . . . Well, maybe I'd better keep that to myself. Let's just pretend that as a purely intellectual exercise I cased Freya's palace a while back and figured a way to lift the thing right from her sleeping neck.

"I hate to throw away all that effort, and I hate even

more the fact that when I get caught, everyone will think I wasn't clever enough to pull off the theft. But I can't think of anything else that'll drag old Heimdall away from his post faster than a chance to ogle Freya in her nightgown up close and personal. He uses that long vision of his to do it from afar often enough that *Peeping Tom* might better be changed to *Peeping Heim*."

"Assuming that works, how will *we* know when to move?" I asked. "With Ahllan in her current state, we're not going to want to hang about in the net any longer than we absolutely have to. Even if we could, we wouldn't dare do it anywhere close to Heimdall. If we can see him, he can see us."

"Let me think about that for a moment," replied Loki. "I'll be too busy playing decoy to do much in the way of signaling, and any flare I sent up would likely make Heimdall suspicious. Hmm." His eyes went far away.

Melchior cleared his throat in a way that very much suggested Ahllan. "I've got another complication to add to the pile," he said in her voice. "I don't want you doing this remotely, not any more of it than you absolutely have to. As soon as you can make a gateway at the other end, I want you to bring your bodies through after you. That way if I die while you're working, I won't take you with me."

"No," said Melchior, "you'll just leave us physically trapped within Odin's sanctum sanctorum. All I can say to that is you'd better not die on us, old woman." His voice came out fierce and hard, but there were tears in his eyes.

"You've been in worse places," she answered back. "You'll be fine. But just to please you, I'll do my best not to die at an inconvenient moment."

"Jormungand," said Loki.

"What about him?" I asked.

"He wanted a piece of this if we could find one for him. Now I've got it. He can conceal his head under the waters below Bifrost. I'll scream bloody murder when Heimdall comes after me. That'll alert Jormungand, and he can pop up a coil back here. Hopefully, the noise I make will also draw the attention of the rest of the Aesir. Hmm, this will all take some setup, and I'd best be about it." With a snap of his fingers, he dissolved into flame and vanished into an air duct.

"I guess that's the plan, then." I pointed at Tisiphone, Fenris, and Laginn. "That leaves you three as backup if we need a rescue or another distraction."

Two voices cried, "No," in perfect synch with Laginn's silent gesture of refusal. *What a surprise.*

"Look," I said, "we really don't have time to argue about this. Fenris—"

"I know I can't come," he grumbled. "Not with this thing tied around my neck." He jerked on the silver cord. "It would probably decapitate me if I tried to project myself into the network, but I want Laginn to go in my place. We've a bond after all our years together, and he can act as my proxy."

"Fair enough," I said. "Now, Tisiphone . . "

"I'm going." There was no arguing with that tone, and I knew better than even to try.

It would have to be a combination of sweet talk and hard reason. I reached out and caught her by the elbow, trying to draw her toward the hall. I might as well have tried to move a mountain.

"Please," I said.

"Don't wheedle, Ravirn. I'm going."

"Pretty please," I said, and batted my eyelashes at her. "I just want a moment alone with you."

She rolled her own eyes but finally nodded. "All right, but don't think I'm changing my mind."

When we reached the hall, I stepped in very close to her. "Can you give us some real privacy?"

"You've got something nasty up your sleeve. I can just tell." She sighed, took me in her arms, then wrapped us both in her wings, hiding us in a cocoon of fire. "I don't know if this would shut out Loki since he's a power of fire," she whispered in my ear, "but it should close out the rest of the world. Now, why are we out here instead of in there preparing for our foray into MimirNet?"

"We *are* preparing a foray into MimirNet. This is part of it. I need you to stay here, Tisiphone." She didn't answer, so I continued. "It's not that I don't want you to come with us. In fact, given any choice in the matter, I'd much rather have you along as muscle. The problem is that if I bring you, that leaves no one here keeping an eye on Ahllan and the good people of Rune. Fenris I mostly trust, but the rest . . . Do you trust Loki? Or any of his surrogates here? After what happened to Ahllan and Melchior?"

"Not as far as Melchior could throw him," she said grudgingly. "We may be on Loki's side at the moment, but I don't believe he's on ours."

"Neither do I, and I really don't want to leave an ailing webtroll where his research staff can get their paws on her and claim her death was due to 'natural causes' if they need to. Especially not when she's our only ticket back out of MimirNet central once we've outlived our immediate usefulness by solving Loki's main problem for him."

She pulled her head back and met my eyes. Behind the fires there, I saw a darkness and loneliness she'd never exposed before.

"I don't want to let you go anywhere without me," she said, her voice much more sad and less angry than I expected. "It is such a rare thing for me to get to lay aside the mantle of the Fury, to spend time as Tisiphone and nothing more. I don't want to give you up even for a moment of it, but you're right, and parted we must be."

Something about the way she held her head made me wonder if she didn't want to say more. Instead, she leaned closer still and kissed me, squeezing me tight as she did so. A moment later, she let fall the curtain of her wings, gave me a second, lingering kiss, and released me.

"We've much to do and little time," she said, indicating the door of the computer room.

The next twenty minutes were spent scrambling to get ready, the twenty after that, impatiently waiting and checking and rechecking our gear. We had all the usual stuff including my pistol and sword. Though Occam was broken, I just couldn't bring myself to leave the blade behind—I'd really liked having a magic sword—and had affixed it to its usual place on the back of my jacket.

When the signal finally came, I opened my left hand on the table's edge, and Laginn climbed atop my palm and laid himself out like the second layer of a very strange cake. As soon as he settled, I plunged the athame through both hands and sent our souls into the net. Melchior was already there, waiting in the giant version of his winged-snake form.

Together, we hurried down the steps from Melchior's inner space to the margin of the network. There, he reared up—a serpent preparing to strike—and a cone of red light shot forth from his open mouth. It rendered a portion of the invisible wall both visible and permeable—a clear nod to our allies at Rune and the receptionist's version of a door buzzer. When I mentioned it, he smiled.

"I may not like Loki, but he does have style to burn. Now, if you'll just climb aboard, we need to be moving."

A saddle formed just forward of Melchior's wings, and I mounted, taking Laginn on my shoulder when he refused to ride inside my jacket. Melchior shot forward, and the rainbow blurred beneath us. Junctions zipped by so quickly that they flowed together visually, becoming a sort of rainbow fan that opened out on either side of the main path—a surreal echo of Melchior's own winged shape.

We paused at the entrance to the final trunkway that was the main body of Bifrost. A stop that lasted just long enough to check whether Heimdall had indeed left his post. He had, and we moved on to the far end of the rainbow. I'd like to say we found a pot of gold there, but that would make me a liar. There was no gold, only the gateway to MimirNet.

I'd also like to say it was guarded by spirits of fire and

water and air whom I had to defeat to win entrance; but that, too, would make a liar of me, though a lesser one. The spirits were actually those of encryption, authentication, and filtration. The first I cracked, the second spoofed, the third bypassed.

The details are too minor to recount. I had grown up hacking and cracking the systems of Fate, and the least child of my former family's three houses would have been embarrassed to claim triumph for beating a system as lightly defended as MimirNet's core.

You could mark the weakness of it down to Odin's faith in his iron rule over the end user, his trust in his equally rigid management of network access, his confidence in Heimdall, or simply the fact that in this universe the forces of chaos had chosen to build an alternate infrastructure rather than assault the existing one, thereby leaving Odin without a worthy opponent to keep him on his game. Whatever the cause, the effect was the same—a gate so flimsy it could barely hold back the wind.

Once inside, the absolute control invested in the admin became mine to use as I would. Temptation to explore the system from within, to own it completely, tugged at the cracker in me. I put it aside for the moment. I would wait to indulge myself until later, after we had finished our mission—if there was a later.

Before anything else, I had to ensure our short-term survival. That meant reuniting body and soul. Back home, it would have been a trivial matter to bring them hither. Simply open a locus-transfer-protocol link and whistle them up, but a traditional LTP—if such an application even existed here—would have required an actual authorized MimirSoft computer on both ends. While Ahllan, backed by the power of RuneNet, was a truly formidable device, she was most definitely not a MimirSoft box. That meant a certain amount of duct-tape-and-string-style hackwork.

So let it be written, so let it be run. The appropriate codespell, that is. Not too very many minutes after we'd left

Rune in electronic shape we stood within Yggdrasil, creatures of the flesh once again.

"Ever have a streak where everything goes right?" I said as I settled back into my body.

"No," said Melchior, suspiciously eyeing the long rows of beige boxes.

"Me neither." I sighed. "So, what do you suppose is going to go catastrophically wrong this time?"

"Besides Ahllan's dying?" he asked, his voice bitter. "I don't know, but if that's by way of the appetizer for our usual seven courses of disaster, I'd rather skip straight from here to dessert." He threw me a smile when he said it, but I could tell it reached no deeper than his lips.

Then he followed Laginn over to the nearest rack of servers and poked at one of the casings.

"This place looks like the end result of a fire sale at boringhardware.com," he said. "Does Odin really run all of existence from this room? If so, how does he stay awake?"

I shrugged. "Lots and lots of coffee?" The glare of the fluorescents and the endless rows of identical servers did make for an awfully dreary work environment, but we weren't there for a job interview. "Come on, let's find an access point and see what we can make this system do for us."

That proved easier said than done. Much. Oh, there were tons of PCs with monitors and keyboards to provide us entry to the system, and getting root-level access was pretty much a cakewalk. The problem was that MimirNet didn't seem to hook into Mimir-proper in any way we could actually use. The command structure all flowed in one direction—from Mimir to MimirNet and from there to the user. There were also no crosslinks to the abacuses or any part of the system aimed at the control of the universe. As far as MimirNet was concerned, the abacuses didn't exist, not even on the blueprints of the facility. Despite the fact that I could see the door from the machine I was using, MimirNet told me the room beyond didn't exist.

I could do anything I wanted to any MimirSoft computer from here. I could turn the personal machines of every single Asgardian into spam-sending zombies, but none of that would move us so much as a single step in the right direction.

"Now what?" asked Melchior from his cross-legged position on the desk beside the computer.

Laginn jerked his thumb at the door to the abacus room, and I had to nod.

"I think he's right, Mel. We need to try something different."

Mel sighed. "That's about where I was, too, but I hoped someone else would have a better suggestion. After our last experience with legacy hardware of the Bronze Age variety I'm a little hesitant about getting close to the stuff again."

"Believe me, little buddy, I'm none too thrilled by the idea myself."

That didn't stop me from getting up and heading for the door, or the other two from following me. The door had no handle or other means for opening it, and I didn't have the spear Odin had used as a knocker last time, so I started off by leaning in close and listening. Faint but clear came a continuous cascade of sharp metallic clicks—the copper beads doing whatever it was they did.

I touched my hand to the center of the door, about where Odin had knocked. A magical crackle rolled across my skin from that point of contact, and I shuddered but didn't pull away. I felt the feathers I didn't currently possess slowly rise and stand on end while every nerve in my body screamed about how this was a Very Bad Idea. I ignored the internal warnings and ever so gently pushed on the door. It moved soundlessly inward, and I followed it.

Once again, I faced rank after rank of giant bronze abacuses, every one ten feet tall and strung with hundreds of thick bronze wires. Everywhere I looked I saw motion, bright points zipping from left to right and back again as millions of copper beads slid back and forth under their

own power. I crossed to the nearest abacus and walked
around it. Odin had said this room held Mimir's soul, the
computer system that kept the Norse MythOS distinct and
separate from my own.

I circled the abacus again, and yet again. As far as I
could tell it was not connected to the others in any way.
I was reminded of the problem that had struck me when I
first saw Necessity's version of this place, and I repeated
what I'd said then. "How do you program a computer with
no interface, no visible inputs or outputs, and an unknown
programming language?"

"I don't know, Boss. I really don't."

I started around the abacus a fourth time but stopped
when Laginn poked at my ankle.

"What is it?" I asked.

The hand pointed back into the depths of the room, then
started off in that direction. After going a dozen feet, it
stopped and beckoned for us.

"How very Lassie," said Melchior.

"Have you got a better idea?"

Melchior shook his head, and once again we followed
the hand. It led us all the way to the back of the room,
where a deep, water-filled crack split the floor. The opening
was perhaps two feet by eight and the water within clearer
than the purest crystal. I could easily see the walls of the
crack as it slanted down and out, becoming a tunnel with
light at the far end. I squatted to get a better angle and . . .
just about screamed. Looking back at me from the far end
was a disembodied eye—a familiar disembodied eye.

The tunnel connected the room of the abacuses to the
deeps of Mimir's Well, and it was Odin's eye that met my
own. I discovered that its empty depths were every bit as
hard to look into as the darkness that filled the socket it had
once occupied. No, not empty; knowing, filled with a dark
and terrible understanding. I throttled a desire to run
screaming from the room in the face of that shadowed gaze.
I could sense there was something there, something I

needed to understand, though I didn't yet know what it might be.

A sharp, modulated buzz sounded from somewhere behind us, back toward the door.

"Alarm?" I asked as I spun to face in that direction.

"No," said Melchior. "Can't you hear it? That's home pantheoverse binary. Ahllan!" He ran back between the abacuses.

I wanted to join him, but instead found myself looking once again into the pool and Odin's eye. I could almost taste the thing I must learn there, knew that it wanted only a few more minutes of concentration to discern. I reached inward, searching for the shadow of the Raven. Found it, reached further, trying to touch the echoes of Odin's naming me Intuition. I had to find the way. Had to understand. Time passed.

Then, all in an instant, I had it. The eye *was* the answer, and a grim answer indeed.

"Boss!" Melchior cried from somewhere behind me, and I could hear his feet slapping on the wood as he hurried closer. "Boss!"

"What is it, Melchior?" I asked, when he skidded to a halt beside me.

"What are you planning?" he demanded. "Because I guarantee I'm not going to like it."

"How can you tell?"

"Because you never call me Melchior unless it's serious."

"You go first," I said. "What did Ahllan have to tell us?"

"She's dying . . . fast," he said, with deep pain hiding just beneath the surface of his voice. "She won't be able to hold on as long as she thought. Not more than another hour. Probably less. She said we had to crack this thing now and come home, or get out on our own. Your turn. What are you planning?"

"I'm not planning," I said. "I'm acting."

"Acting?" he asked, clearly alarmed. "On what?"

"Impulse," I said; then, as the shadow of the Raven enveloped me, I matched word with deed.

Reaching up, I plucked the eye from my left socket and dropped it into the Well of Mimir.

Pain rushed into my empty socket. Pain that brought a terrible empty darkness with it. I was drowning in the Void.

CHAPTER SEVENTEEN

Bad mistakes, I've made a ton. Tearing my left eye from its socket and throwing it into Mimir's Well would have to rank among my worst, and my best. The terrible, howling pain of it was only the least part of the blunder I'd just committed.

Had I known what Clotho was giving me when she named me Raven, I might have run screaming rather than accept the name. Or then again, I might not. I'm funny that way. At Necessity's behest, Clotho had wrapped me in the mantle of the Trickster. Now my own special divinity lived in the instant where good ideas became bad ones and vice versa.

See also, *Ow! Ow, ow, ow. Ooh!*

Long ago, Odin had sacrificed his eye to Mimir in exchange for all the knowledge in the universe. Now I'd made the same offering with the same stakes. But where Odin was a god, the greatest of his pantheon, I was only the most minor of powers. My mind could no more contain the torrent of information Mimir bestowed upon me than my open arms could encompass the sky. I knew everything, the position of every grain of sand on every beach on Earth, the smell of every flower, the taste of all the food that had ever been eaten, everything. It was too much. It should have broken my mind.

But I had once before merged my soul with that of a great power, the greatest in my pantheon, the goddess Necessity. Together we had destroyed the body occupied by her daughter Nemesis and returned the houseless Soul of Enmity to her eternal imprisonment in Tartarus. The contact between Necessity and me had lasted only a few brief seconds, but it had given me a taste of omniscience. It was that taste that saved me from madness now. The knowledge that it was possible to withstand such an onslaught and come out the other side gave me the strength to hang on through the first minutes of information overdose.

My salvation came not from what I remembered of that earlier event; it came from what I had forgotten. Almost everything. I knew that I had done those things, knew that I had briefly held an entire pantheoverse in my mind. I even knew how I had done those things, but the actual knowledge of the pantheoverse? Gone, and good riddance.

When we think of memory, we tend to focus on the power of remembering, of how we learn from our past and how that affects our future. But forgetting is just as powerful as remembering. It allows us to move beyond the pains of the past to live in the present. Mnemosyne, the Goddess of Memory, is the object of countless prayers and offerings, but in that moment I gave thanks to her sister, Lesmosyne, Goddess of Forgetting, for I knew that this, too, would pass.

That didn't give me control over the process, nor any hope of controlling it. It just allowed me to believe in my own survival long enough to stave off madness and thereby ensure that same survival. It also started me on the business of selectively forgetting.

I had been forgetting all along; my finite mind simply

couldn't hold all of the infinite knowledge Mimir fed me. A huge amount of data went in one synapse and straight out another. Unfortunately, it started pouring right back in again because my connection with Mimir was an ongoing thing.

As long as my eye remained in the well, we would be linked and the information glut would continue. How did I know that? See above, that bit about knowing everything. The trick was getting the right bits of knowing into the tiny focus point of my finite brain.

My earlier experience using the minds of the crows and the ravens in my search for Loki helped me now. It provided a model for the necessary winnowing process. *Not the only model, nor the most effective one,* informed the part of me that knew everything, but a model nonetheless. I used it to help forget that which I didn't need to remember and remember that which I dared not forget.

All that stuff about sand and flowers and food? Not important just then. I shoved it completely out of my mind.

How to force splits in the structure of the pantheoverse? *Ding! Ding! Bump that baby to the front of the line.*

I can't begin to describe the millions of fine details of the splitting process. I can say only that there and then I knew what I needed to do. The primary element was finding an important event that could go more than one way. The more important the event, the easier it was to create a fracture between the possible courses of the future.

In that moment, the most important event of all had to do with whether I *would* split the pantheoverse. I could sense that it might easily go either way. I reached out, homing in on the point of decision so that I could insert the crowbar provided by the power of Mimir and arrange for it to do both.

I found it in Ahllan, who hovered on the cusp between life and death. In that instant, she was Schroedinger's troll, both alive and dead, the ultimate example of quantum uncertainty. If she . . . No! Unfair! Unjust! Such a split point couldn't be, could it? But I could feel that it was, and I wept.

Because I *could* save her. But if I did, the Norse pantheoverse would remain whole and Ragnarok inevitable. By using the power of the abacuses, I could bring Ahllan back to our own pantheoverse. The return to home and hearth and the chaos she had been designed for would preserve her long enough for me to prepare a new troll body as I had once built a new goblin body for Melchior. The transfer would be successful, and she would live on as herself. That was one future.

In the other, I could use Mimir's control over MimirNet to send a great pulse of information through the network, the complete source code for the MimirNet OS. It would hit the loop we had installed like a data tsunami, swamping and tumbling the old troll I loved. Drowning her in information. She would reach for the chaos tap, try to draw enough power to manage the flood. She would fail. The raw chaos would ravage her soul, burning away much of what made her Ahllan. The MimirNet OS would rush in to fill the hole, merging with what remained of her soul and finishing the job her earlier seizure had begun, the fusing of her soul and the RuneNet supercluster. They would become one entity.

The hybrid would hold most of Ahllan's memories, but they would no longer make her Ahllan, not in the ways that truly mattered. At its core would be the soul that had once belonged to her, the part of her that made her a person and not a thing. But again, it would not be her. It couldn't be, because with the addition of Mimir's source code, it would have become the soul of a god. Ahllan/RuneNet would become a divine AI sharing dominion over the Norse universe/multiverse interface with Mimir and Odin.

She would become Mimir's Mirror.

Wars would be fought back and forth between her and

Mimir. Gods would die in them. But every battle and every death would go both ways. In some places, Ragnarok would come exactly as had been foretold. In others it would be averted. In a few it would be infinitely worse—with no rebirth following the great destruction.

And the responsibility for every one of those futures would be mine. I could give this universe the gift of uncertainty, of paths that avoided the ruin foretold, but only at the cost of the end of everything on other roads. Only at the cost of Ahllan's life.

It was a terrible decision to have to make for another. The most terrible decision. I knew what Ahllan would want me to do, knew that she had already offered her life if that was what it took to thwart a future of foregone conclusions, its people robbed of any real choice by the ultimate in cosmic determinism. Knowing what she would have told me to do didn't help. Knowing *everything* didn't help. I still had to make the choice.

Kill someone I loved to give freedom to an entire pantheoverse? Or save her and leave the place no worse off than it had been when I entered the scene? I had to decide in the instant, and I did.

The pain of my lost eye was nothing to the pain I felt when I killed Ahllan.

Oh, I could lie to myself and say that I merely chose to let her life end as it would have without my intervention. I could tell myself it was exactly what she would have wanted me to do. I could comfort myself with the truth that it was her or an entire pantheoverse's future, a myriad of them even. In fact, I told myself all those things and more.

None of it changed the fact that I had held Ahllan's life in my hands and had ended it. Nothing ever would. Her death was a stain on my soul, and I would carry it unto the end of my days. It was my decision and my burden.

I had saved the universe and killed a friend.

I am the Raven. I am Impulse. I am the Trickster.

My worst mistakes and my greatest triumphs are all too often one and the same.

When you know everything, sometimes it takes a while for you to whittle it down to knowing something. After I made my choice, I let myself get lost in the general to the exclusion of the specific for what felt like a very long time, though it wasn't—I knew that, too.

The specific thing that drew me back to myself was a rather important one. Odin. Leaning quietly on the wall beside the opening to Mimir's Well. He had been there for a while. Since the moment I'd entered the room, in fact. He was invisible. But I still knew he was there.

"Funny, isn't it?" he asked, flickering into visibility. "This knowing things."

"Does that mean you can see me now?" I asked.

"Only through the eye of my flesh, but you knew that."

I laughed, though not with amusement. He was right, though I hadn't known I'd known it until he pointed it out. I was really beginning to dislike omniscience. Mel wouldn't be thrilled about it either—once Odin released him and Laginn from the frozen state he'd put them in—he thought I was too much of a know-it-all as it was.

"You could have chosen to save her," said Odin with a sad smile.

Driving his spear into my heart would have hurt less.

"Thanks," I replied. "I really, really needed to hear that. I didn't save her. End of story."

"But it isn't. This is one fork of that first split. Not only could you have saved her; in another world you did."

"Great, the other me must be feeling pretty good about that right now. The me here in front of you? Not so much."

"I don't think that you is any happier than this one. That you has to live with the fact that he chose the life of a friend over everything he and that friend believed. That you has to bear the weight of an entire pantheoverse surrendered to

Fate. That you has to live with having made puppets of every living thing. I don't think he's any happier."

"So we're both depressed. Somehow, knowing that doesn't make it any better."

Odin snapped his fingers, and a handkerchief appeared between them. He blew on it, and it flew to me. As I snatched it from the air, I realized I was crying. Knew that I had been for some time. Tears from my right eye. Blood from my missing left.

"Nothing makes the hard choices any softer," said Odin. "Nothing ever will. Take my choice not to stop you just minutes ago. I could have prevented the rip you have torn in my nice, neat, clockwork universe. Never doubt it."

"Why didn't you stop me?" I asked.

"It would have made a waste of all the effort I went through to put you in a place where you could do what you have just done."

"I don't understand." But I did, because I knew the mind of Odin. "You couldn't do it. Couldn't make the choice that would lead to the split."

"No," he said. "I couldn't. Ragnarok is terrible enough. What you did opened the door to universes where things will go even worse. If I had done it, it would have been beyond all bearing."

"But it also created a path to one where the catastrophe is averted. Why didn't you . . . ? Oh."

I couldn't hold on to omniscience. It was beyond the capacity of my demidivinity. I had made my choice based on the limited knowledge I could focus on and the whisperings of my heart. I had done it knowing full well that the memories would fade, that over time Lesmosyne would draw the worst of the pain from my heart. Odin had no such release. Had he made the choice I made, he would never have been able to step beyond it.

"It's because you can't see me," I said. "You know neither my future nor my past. I am the closest thing you can do to forgetting."

"Yes. Did you honestly think that I love my children any less than Loki does his? That the deaths of my sons and daughters did not cut as deep? That I did not wish with all my heart that I might save them? I could not bear what was to come. But even less could I bear the worse things that now lurk on some paths to the future.

"When you came into this world, and I could not see you through my blind eye, I realized I had the rarest of opportunities, and I seized it. I made sure that you had freedom to move, and I learned what I could of you through as many sources as possible. I guessed that your nature would draw you and Loki together, and I thought that you might become friends. That or bitter enemies. Then you met Thor and told him of your fight with the Fate of your own multiverse, and I dared to hope that you would fight every bit as hard against the Fate of mine."

Odin smiled, and it was like the sun ripping storm clouds asunder. "Do you know what it means for me to have hope? To *not know* even for an instant, and so to dare to dream."

Then his gaze flickered to the water of Mimir's Well, and he laughed, rich and full and freer than he had in all the years since he traded his eye for knowledge. Knowledge he never would have wished for if he had known the cost beforehand. But such is the nature of knowledge and ignorance.

"Of course you know," he said. "For this one time in my life, I know less than the man I'm talking to. It's marvelous."

"It's also not true," I replied. "The knowledge leaks out my ears at ten thousand times the rate that it comes in via the void of my eye. I know but I don't *know*."

"True enough, but you'll forgive me the chance to wallow in ignorance. There is some truth in the saying that 'ignorance is bliss,' and it is a bliss I've not tasted in many, many long years. I must drink it deep while I have the chance."

That made me more than a little nervous. "You say that like you're not expecting to be ignorant for long. Since I am the very heart of your not-knowing, it suggests a certain expectation on your part that I won't be around to be un-known for much longer."

Odin's smile this time was grimmer. "Wisdom rides at the right hand of knowledge. You've just demonstrated both. No, you will not be staying. I need you to do me one more service."

"What's that?" I asked, my worry growing.

"Nothing too awful," he said. "I want you to go home, and I want you to take Fenris with you."

"Why . . . ? Oh." I looked into Odin's eye, and I knew the answer.

Fenris was Odin's fated slayer. By removing him from the here and now, I would ensure at least one of the futures where Odin would have a there and then. He would know beyond any shadow of a doubt that in one place and time he didn't end in the belly of the wolf. And the fact that I, who he could not *see*, had caused that particular split would make a hole in his foreseeing, a place where he could have hope, that most precious and rare of commodities.

I also knew how much it mattered to Odin. If I did not act as he wished in this, Odin the Hopeful would give way to Odin the Lord of Battles, and he would be most displeased with me. Though Odin could not *see* my future, in the present moment, I could. If I did not rid him of Fenris, I would die, and I would most definitely not be heading for Valhalla. Odin the Chooser of Souls would see to it that mine found its way back to home and Hades' overwarm hearth.

If I'd known less about the gods than I did, I might have resented such a banishment so soon after services rendered. But I do know gods. I had done Odin a favor, a favor of epic proportions, and he was duly grateful. He was also a god, and that meant he expected worship and obedience. To put it more succinctly, he was only as grateful as the *next* favor.

So, in a few moments I would leave there and return to Rune, where I would make every effort to convince Fenris to depart this world for my own. I would even lie and tell him that was what had to be if he wanted to create the split in the universe that his father had given so much to achieve.

"I'll just be off to take care of that, then, shall I?" I asked.

Odin nodded. "Yes, you shall."

Then he crossed his arms and leaned back against the wall, and I knew that our audience and accord were at an end. He was done with grateful. I turned away from Odin and the recent past and toward Melchior and the near future.

In that very instant Odin said, "Oh, and one more thing . . ."

"What now?" I grumbled, turning back toward him.

"This," he replied, and let loose a pitch that would have been the envy of any Major League pro.

Odin's fastball struck the left side of my face with tremendous force, knocking me half around. Blinding pain stole my breath and drove me to my knees. My whole head seemed ready to burst apart as I clutched at my thighs and tried to blink away the agony.

What had he just done? And why? I didn't understand. I didn't . . . know. I realized then what Odin must have thrown at me. Not *knew* it. Realized it. I climbed back to my feet and looked at Odin through both of my eyes.

"Why?" I asked, and it felt so good to be clueless once again.

"Do you remember what Skuld said that day beside Mimir's Well?"

I shook my head, and Odin summoned a ball of light to hover in the air between us. Within it I stood beside Odin and together we faced Fate.

"The head belongs to Mimir," said the Odin in the picture nodding toward the well, "onetime Lord of Memory and Information."

"The first Binary God," said Fate. "The first leg of the

triangle, just as Odin is the second, and the third is yet to come. Isn't that right, Mimir?"

With that, Odin banished the image. "You will not be that third leg. Not while I live and not after. I don't know what else your future holds, but that's not on the list. You are Zeus's responsibility, not mine, and I will not allow that to change. Go home."

Odin started quickly snapping the fingers of both hands, creating a wild, staccato wall of sound. Then he was gone. Or rather, we were.

"—you completely out of your mind?" yelled Melchior as we appeared in the computer room at Rune. "That was your eye! Your freaking eye! What do you . . . ? Uh, Boss?"

"Yes," I said, bending down so that my eyes met his and blinking innocently, though I could already feel my left one starting to swell shut. "Were you saying something?"

"I, uh . . . eye . . . you . . . your . . . What just happened?" he finally demanded suspiciously.

I had just started to frame my answer when Tisiphone caught me by the waist and lifted me high into the air.

"What happened? How did you get back? When Ahllan screamed and went limp I thought . . ." She pulled me in tight.

"Ahllan!" cried Melchior, running to the troll's side.

Simultaneously, Fenris yipped, "Chew toy!" I could hear nine kinds of worry in his tone as he asked, "What's going on? Did it work?"

The two-headed giant shouted something about Rune-Net then, but I couldn't make it out amidst the general bedlam that broke out. The next several minutes went by in a blur of shouted questions and evasive answers, while I desperately tried not to look at Ahllan.

Eventually people came to understand that, no, I wasn't going to give a detailed explanation, and, yes, we had won . . . sort of. At that, the madness died down enough that I could no longer hide myself within it, and I had to face the ultimate result of my actions.

"Let me see Ahllan," I said to Tisiphone, and she let me slip free of her grip.

"Ravirn," said Tisiphone, "she's gone. There was nothing I could do."

"I know," I replied over my shoulder. "It's my fault."

"You can't blame yourself," said Tisiphone as she trailed after me. "There was nothing you could have done. She said so herself, more than once."

"She was wrong."

Melchior stood beside Ahllan's chair, his forehead pressed against the side of her hand, his shoulders quaking ever so slightly. Silent tears ran down his cheeks and dropped to the surgically clean floor of the computer room. I took a moment to fix that picture of him in my mind. Here was one consequence of my actions, and it was important that I remember it.

The Raven is a Trickster, all intuition and impulse—clever triumphs over impossible odds equally distributed with ill-timed insults hurled into the teeth of the gods. My power is an irresponsible power that cares only about winning the game and damn the consequences. I am the Raven, and every fault of the Raven's is also mine. But I am also Ravirn, and where the Raven would forget the cost, I needed to remember. It was that or surrender myself wholly to my power. Death would be better.

Death. I had looked into the eyes of the power that wore that name and come away alive but forever changed. Now I lifted my gaze from Melchior to Ahllan's face and looked into the eyes of a friend's death and was likewise changed. Again, I fixed the moment in my memory, letting the pain wash over me, saving it up as a counterweight to the Raven's blithe disregard of consequences. Oh, I knew that Lesmosyne would dull the worst edge of my sorrow given time, but I would not let her rob me of all my grief. I owed Ahllan that and more.

"I am so sorry," I whispered, leaning forward to close her eyes.

"Don't be," said a bodiless voice that both was and was not Ahllan's. "She would not have wished it."

Melchior jerked like he'd been plugged into a 220 outlet when he was expecting 110. "Ahllan!" He whipped his head back and forth, searching for the source of the voice.

"I'm afraid the answer is both yes and no," it answered, and I noticed that the blinking lights of the RuneNet servers pulsed in time with the words. "There is a seed of her within me, but the Ahllan you knew is no more."

"RuneNet?" said Fenris, looking both worried and hopeful. "Is that you?"

"Physically," said the voice. "I occupy these machines"— the lights all blinked on, then off, then on once again— "but I am much more than RuneNet ever was. I am Mimir's Mirror. If you must have a name to call me, how about Reginkunnr? It means child of the gods, and I am that."

"I'm confused," Melchior said, giving me a hard look. "What really happened with Mimir? I feel like I'm missing some pieces. I saw you tear out your eye and throw it into the well. Now it's back. I might believe I'd hallucinated the whole thing if you weren't developing the world's nastiest black eye. I'm also wondering about the *way* you told Ahllan you were sorry and the way . . . Regin answered you back. That sounded guiltier than condolences."

"It was, Mel. I—"

Regin cut me off. "Let me answer that one, please. I am not Ahllan, but I have her memories, and I know all of her deepest wishes, including the last. Your Ahllan did not think much of gods and powers. She was not a praying troll, but she did offer up a few final words to one power before she died. That power was the Raven and the words were 'thank you.'"

I bowed my head to hide the tears that started in my eyes. "Thank *you*."

"The Raven broke Odin's hold on the reins of the future," said the voice. "He did it at great cost to himself and by making exactly the choice Ahllan would have urged upon him. I am the result of that choice, and I think she would call that a success worth the price."

"I still don't understand," said Melchior.

"Melchior," said the voice, sounding more like Ahllan than ever, "leave it there. Please."

"When you put it that way," said Melchior, "how can I refuse?"

I knew that later I would tell Melchior everything. I'm sure Regin knew it, too, but I silently thanked her for the mercy that would allow me to do it my own time and way.

"Thank you, Melchior," said Regin. "The part of me that was Ahllan appreciates it. Now, Ravirn, you have little time and much to do."

"What does that mean?" asked Tisiphone, and there was a note of worry in her voice. "What price did you pay?"

"I'll tell you about the price later," I said, "when it's a little less raw. Please don't give me that look; it's got nothing to do with the time issue. That's separate. While I was at MimirNet, I picked up our tickets home. Unfortunately, the bus leaves very shortly."

"I don't want to see you go," said Fenris.

"Funny you should say that," I replied.

"Funny why?" asked a hard, cold voice from the doorway.

Loki had returned, and he looked awful, covered in bruises and deep gashes like he'd lost a fight with a bear. He also looked suspicious and angry.

"Funny because I've a proposition to make." I smiled my best winning smile while swearing inwardly—I'd rather hoped he wouldn't get back so soon.

"I don't think I'm going to like this," said Loki.

"Probably not," I agreed. "But that's beside the point."

"What *is* the point?" Fenris asked, before Loki could speak again, and Loki looked none too happy about that.

"Making RuneNet into Mimir's Mirror is only the first

step on the road to averting Ragnarok," I said. "The next one is bigger and much more important."

"And that is?" Loki demanded of me.

"In order to make this universe into a multiverse and create the possibility of a future without Ragnarok, there has to be a first split in the fabric of reality." I mentally crossed my fingers and willed Regin to back me up on the next point. "Because Regin and Mimir are so closely balanced, the split has to be huge, or Mimir will be able to close it back up."

"Is that true?" Loki asked Regin.

"Substantially," replied the computer. "There is much more to it than that, but Ravirn is correct that the initial rift needs to be something that fundamentally changes the current trajectory of events."

"What does that have to do with my son?"

Fenris rolled his eyes. "You're not interviewing my date for the prom, Dad. I can speak for myself. "

I touched the bruising around my eye. "Do you know how I got this?"

"Do I care?" retorted Loki.

"You should. I got it when I took control of Mimir by the only possible means."

"You did tear your eye out and throw it into the well," Melchior said accusingly. "I knew I didn't hallucinate that."

"I did," I said. "Do you know what that means, Loki?"

"You're going to tell me. Why should I answer?"

"That sounds like a yes to me, Boss," said Melchior.

"Me, too. It means that for the time my eye was in the well, I knew everything. That includes knowing what it takes to create the future you claimed you wanted. The one in which you would know that somewhere, somehow, and in direct contravention of Odin's prophecy, your boys survived. I can give you that, but there's a cost."

"And it involves me," said Fenris, his voice filled with growling undertones. "So why the hell are you talking to

Loki instead of to me. If the price is mine to pay, then it's me you must convince."

"Fenris!" said Loki.

"Shut up," barked Fenris. "I'm tired of being told the equivalent of 'sit' and 'stay' whenever you want me to do something. I'm your son, not your hound, and I will make my own decisions. In this and in all things." He looked at me, his eyes hard, his ruff raised. "You will speak to me if you want something from me, not my father. Got it?"

"I do, and I'm sorry. That's what I should have been doing all along. Do you want to discuss this in private? Or would you rather I said it here?"

"Here."

I took a deep breath. If I wanted him to come with me, I had to get this exactly right.

"I want you to come with me back to my MythOS. If you remove yourself from this pantheoverse, it will irreparably break the chain of events that leads to Ragnarok."

"Is it the only way to do that?" asked Fenris.

I wanted to say yes. I really did. Odin had made it very clear that, if I didn't get Fenris out of the Norse MythOS, I was in for potentially eternal suffering. I tried to open my mouth to say yes. It was such a simple word. It should have been easy. It was impossible.

"No, it's not," I said. "It's a powerful way, but it's not the only one."

"I won't have it," said Loki, and I could see the chaos blazing high in his eyes. "Fenris, you are staying here, and that's final."

With hungry eyes, Fenris indicated the silver cord that bound him. "Will it break the chain around my neck?"

"I don't know," I said.

"It will," said Regin.

"I'm going."

EPILOGUE

■ ■ ■

If I lived in a fairy-tale world, that would have been the end of it. Fenris would have said, "I'm going," and we all could have departed to live happily ever after at Raven House. But Fenris was not the last to speak.

"I'm staying," Tisiphone said into the instant of silence that followed Fenris's declaration.

"What!" I yelled in the very same breath as Loki.

"You can't," we said together.

That was where the conversations diverged.

"I won't allow it," said Loki.

"I don't want to leave you," I said.

"Deal with it," said Fenris.

"I know," said Tisiphone.

Then she reached out and took me by the hand, leading me away from the computer room and the yelling match between Fenris and Loki. As we went out the door, I looked back at Melchior, reluctant to leave him at a time like this. He caught my eye and made a shooing motion. Out in the hall, Tisiphone wrapped me once again in her wings.

"I have to stay," she said, her voice barely above a whisper.

The words were soft, but I could hear the resolve beneath, and it was as hard as her claws.

"Why?" I asked.

"Would you believe it's for love?" She bit her lip.

"I might," I replied, "if you explain it to me."

"I'm more than half in love with you. You do know that, right?"

"Better to say that I suspected it. Just as I suspect that I'm more than half in love with you. That hardly seems a reason for you to stay behind when I have to leave."

"Do you really have to leave?" she asked.

"I do, and soon." I quickly told her about what had passed between me and Odin.

She nodded. "I suspected there was a deal involved, though I didn't know with whom or for what. Knowing you have to go and knowing the details makes it a little easier to say good-bye."

I was getting steadily more confused.

"Let's come back to that in a moment. You still haven't explained why we have to part at all," I pointed out. "Normally, when you proclaim you're half in love with someone, the next step is to spend more time with them, not send them off to an entirely different universe."

"It's because I won't be able to keep loving you if we go back. Here, I can remain Tisiphone and in love. At home, I will become the Fury once again, and Furies do not love. We can't. If I go home, I will have to give up what we have here. I have lived four thousand years and never felt as I do right now. I'd rather love you and be apart than not love you and be together. Do you understand?"

"I do, though I can't say it makes me happy, more like I've been punched in the gut."

"Would it help if we skipped straight from here to the part where we say our farewells with incredibly intense sex?" She winked at me, but there was a tear in her eye.

"Tempting . . . but first I still want to know why my deal with Odin makes saying good-bye easier."

"It's two things, really. First, I'm still bound to Necessity. She may have betrayed me, and I may not be a Fury here, but she is my mother, and I could not abandon her if I didn't know you were going back. I hate her but I also love her, and it's in my bones that she must be fixed. I know that you will find out why Necessity sent us here and if she is all right, and that you will fix her if she isn't."

I raised an eyebrow, but before I could reply, Tisiphone put a finger to my lips.

"You're about to tell me you're no hero," she said. "That's bullshit, and we both know it. A hero isn't a thing you are. It's what you do. If you look me in the eye and tell me you're not a hero, the only one who might believe the lie is you. Don't. Go and fix Necessity instead. Find out what happened. If you do that, I can stay here, stay Tisiphone, love you. Then, when you're done, you can come back to me."

"I see one tiny flaw in this plan," I said. Well, several, actually. Starting with the fact that anything that could mess with Necessity was likely to eat me for breakfast. But I decided to settle on the most immediate problem. "Its name is Odin. Tall fellow, one eye, two ravens, exceptionally grim disposition. I promised him I'd take Fenris away, and I rather think he frowns on those who break their promises."

Tisiphone grinned impishly. "Did you promise him you wouldn't come back?"

"I . . . uh . . . no."

Tisiphone's grin turned into a laugh. "Some Trickster you are. Can't even see a loophole when it practically crawls into your pants and bites you in the ass."

"Speaking of getting into my pants," I said, "you mentioned something a couple of moments ago about the part where we say our farewells with incredibly intense sex."

"I did."

"Why don't we skip to that part now."

* * *

Sometime later, Tisiphone and I lay side by side on the giant bed.

"Do you think we should go back to the others now?" she asked.

"I suppose we'll have to. I've a promise to keep."

"How will you get back?" she asked.

"I don't know. I didn't ask about the details. I probably should have—"

"Click."

"Did you hear that?" I asked.

"What?" asked Tisiphone.

"I'm not sure. It sounded metallic, kind of like an . . . abacus."

"Click. Click."

Oh.

I caught Tisiphone's hand in mine and drew it to my lips. "I'll be back," I said, brushing her knuckles with a kiss. "I promise." Then I dived for my clothes.

"Click. Click. Click."

Blackness darker than any night caught me in an invisible hand and moved me through space. For a brief instant the lights flickered back on, and I found myself standing naked in the computer room, my leathers clutched in front of me along with Occam and my pistol. Fenris and Loki were still arguing. Melchior was sitting at Ahllan's feet, less than a yard from where I'd appeared.

"What the—" he began.

"Time to go," I said.

"Click. Click."

Fenris let out a howl that made the walls shake, and Loki stopped speaking, looking stunned.

"Good-bye, Father," said Fenris. With a great leap he joined me.

"Click."

"Good-bye," cried Loki, "and . . . good luck!" Then he smiled like the first breath of spring after a thousand-year winter, and whispered, "Somewhere. Somehow."

I waved back, then looked around for Laginn—I owed him a farewell. Something grabbed my bare ankle.

"Clash."

In a huge room carved from the living wood of the World Tree, Yggdrasil, a million copper beads all moved in the same direction at once.

The world ended. And, as so often happens in such moments, a new one began.

KELLY McCULLOUGH has sold short fiction to publications including *Weird Tales*, *Absolute Magnitude*, and *Cosmic SF*. An illustrated collection of Kelly's short science fiction, called *Chronicles of the Wandering Star*, is part of InterActions in Physical Science, an NSF-funded middle school science curriculum. He lives in western Wisconsin. Visit his website at www.kellymccullough.com.